ALSO BY GISH JEN

*Typical American*

# Mona in the Promised Land

# Mona in the Promised Land

## GISH JEN

Alfred A. Knopf   New York   1996

THIS IS A BORZOI BOOK
PUBLISHED BY ALFRED A. KNOPF, INC.

Copyright © 1996 by Gish Jen

All rights reserved under International and Pan-American
Copyright Conventions. Published in the United States by
Alfred A. Knopf, Inc., New York, and simultaneously in
Canada by Random House of Canada Limited, Toronto.
Distributed by Random House, Inc., New York.

A portion of this work was published in somewhat
different form in *The Atlantic Monthly.*

Library of Congress Cataloging-in-Publication Data
Jen, Gish.
Mona in the promised land / by Gish Jen. — 1st ed.
p.    cm.
ISBN 0-679-44589-7
1. Chinese-American families—New York (State)—Westchester
County—Fiction.    2. Chinese Americans—New York (State)—
Westchester County—Fiction.    3. Girls—New York (State)—
Westchester County—Fiction.    4. Westchester County
(N.Y.)—Fiction.    I.    Title.
PS3560.E474M66    1996
813'.54—dc20              95-44447
CIP

Manufactured in the United States of America

First Edition

*For my mother,*
*who sat on her father's lap and read scrolls—*
*and for my father,*
*who tucked Tai Shan under his arm, and jumped over the*
*North Sea*

I'm becoming Chinese, I know it.        —Richard Rodriguez

And having grown up next door to Skokie, Illinois—the land
of perpetual spring, a Rosenbloom on every corner—I knew
more Yiddish than Japanese.                —David Mura

. . . all things change. The cosmos itself is flux and motion.
                                                    —Ovid

He dissolves his bond with his group.
Supreme good fortune.
Dispersion leads in turn to accumulation.
This is something that ordinary men do not think of.
                                            —the *I Ching*

# I

# Mona Gets Flipped

There they are, nice Chinese family—father, mother, two born-here girls. Where should they live next? The parents slide the question back and forth like a cup of ginseng neither one wants to drink. Until finally it comes to them: what they really want is a milk shake (chocolate), and to go with it a house in Scarshill. What else? The broker hints patiently, in a big round voice; she could have modeled her elocution on the cannonball. "The neighborhood!" she says, appreciating herself in the visor mirror. Her enunciation is something for someone doing her lips while she talks. Now she smooths her French twist. In smell she is cultivated, this realtor, a real Chanel No. 5; however, she is married to a conspicuously hairy husband, as the minor Changs know via spying skills and nosiness. She powders her nose. "Moneyed! Many delis!" In other words, rich and Jewish, she! for one! would rather live elsewhere!

This is such a nice thing to say, even the Changs know to be offended, they think, on behalf of all three Jewish people they know, even if one of them they're not sure about. Still, someone has sent the parents a list of the top ten schools nationwide, and so *many-deli* or not, they settle into a Dutch colonial on the Bronx River Parkway. For they're the New Jews, after all, a model minority and Great American Success. They know they belong in the promised land.

Or do they? In fact, it's only 1968; the blushing dawn of ethnic awareness has yet to pink up their inky suburban night. They have an idea about the blacks because of poor Martin Luther King. More distantly perceived is that the Jews have become The Jews, on account of the Six Day War; much less that they, the Changs, are The New Jews. They are just smitten with the educational opportunity before them—that golden student-teacher ratio—and also with the dumb majesty of the landscaping. Three giant azaleas they have now, not to say a rhododendron the size of their old bathroom, and in addition a topographical feature of forsythia. Two foothills of the forsythia they are moved to address immediately with hedge clippers (feeling quite hardy and pioneering, Westward ho! and all that), only to discover that to render your forsythia into little can shapes is in this town considered gauche. And so they desist. Leaving an effect, as their nice new neighbor, Mr. 20-20, helpfully points out. Older sister Callie dubs it *Two Small Cans with Wild Mountain Range.*

Still they figure there's much to admire about their house, what with its large brick chimney and considerable wood door, and not to forget its stucco-clad walls. Never mind that when younger sister Mona asks, she discovers stucco to be designer cement. They've never lived in a place *clad* in anything before. Their house is still of the upstanding-citizen type. *Remember the Mayflower!* it seems to whisper, in dulcet tones. They could almost be living on Tory Lane, that's how fetching their road is, how winding. So what if drivers miss their turns, plow up their flower beds, then want to use their telephone? *Of course,* Helen tells them, like it's no big deal, they can replant. They're the type to adjust. The lady drivers weep, Helen gets out the Kleenex for them.

The Changs are a bit down the hill from the private-plane set, in other words. Only in their dreams do their jacket zippers jam, what with all the lift tickets they have stapled to them, Killington on top of Sugarbush on top of Stowe; and they don't even know where the Virgin Islands are—although certain of them do know that virgins are like priests and nuns, which there were more of in the town they just moved from, than here. This is Mona's first understanding of class. In the old neighborhood, everybody knew everything about virgins and nonvirgins, not to say the technicalities of staying in between. Or almost everybody. In their old town, Mona was the laugh-along type. Here, she's an expert.

"You mean the man . . . ?" Pigtailed Barbara Gugelstein spits a mouthful of Tab back into her pop-top can. At this age she has chin-to-chest disease, but even so you can see how riveting are her dewy green eyes. These are not set in regular sockets like your everyday cup and ball, but rather in most exquisite deep hollows, big and thought-provoking as TV dish antennae. Naturally, she does not see this. Naturally, she is obsessed with hair frizz, and what's more is convinced that her nose resembles a half-open sleep sofa. To everyone else she looks like Cleopatra. Ostrich fans, she brings to mind. Languid nights on the Nile.

"That is *so* gross," she says.

Pretty soon Mona's getting popular for a new girl. The only hold-out is Danielle Meyers, who, what with her blue mascara and contact lenses, not to say other attributes, has gone steady with two boys. "How do *you* know?" she starts to ask. Proceeding to edify the eighth grade at large with how she French-kissed one boyfriend and just regular-kissed the other. ("Because, you know, he had braces.") They hear about his rubber bands, how once one popped right into her mouth. Mona begins to realize she needs to find somebody to kiss too. But how? She can't do mascara, her eyelashes stick together. Plus as Danielle the Great Educator points out—Mona's *Chinese*.

Luckily, she just about then happens to tell Barbara Gugelstein she knows karate. She doesn't know why she tells Barbara this. Her sister Callie's the liar in the family, ask anybody; it's a result of looking exactly like their mother, only with granny glasses instead of regular. Callie's got the kind of beauty that makes you consider where you stand in life, whereas Mona doesn't see why they should have to hold their heads up. But for some reason, Mona tells Barbara she can make her hands like steel by thinking hard. "I'm not supposed to tell anyone," she says.

The way Barbara backs off blinking, Mona could be the burning bush.

"I can't do bricks," Mona says, just to set things straight. "But I can do your arm if you want." She sets her hand in chop position.

"Uh, it's okay," Barbara says. "I know you can—I saw it on TV last night."

That's when Mona recalls that she too saw it on TV last night, in fact at Barbara's house. She rushes on to tell Barbara she knows how to get pregnant with tea.

"With *tea*?"

"That's how they do it in China."

Barbara agrees that China is an ancient and great civilization that ought to be known for more than spaghetti and gunpowder. Mona tells her she knows Chinese. *"Byeh fa-foon,"* she says. *"Shee-veh. Ji-nu."* This is Shanghai dialect, meaning, "Stop acting crazy. Rice gruel. Soy sauce." Barbara's impressed. At lunch the next day, Danielle Meyers and Amy Weinstein and Barbara's crush, Andy Kaplan, are all impressed too. Scarshill is a liberal place, not like their old town, where the Whitman Road Gang used to throw crab-apple mash at Callie and Mona, and tell them it would make their eyes stick shut. Here they're like permanent exchange students. In another ten years, there'll be so many Orientals they'll turn into Asians; a Japanese grocery will buy out that one deli too many.

But for now, the late sixties, what with civil rights on TV, they're not so much accepted as embraced. Especially by the Jewish part of town—which it turns out is not all of town at all, that's just an idea people have, Callie says, and lots of Jews could take them or leave them same as the Christians, who are nice too; Mona shouldn't generalize. So let her not generalize, except to say that pretty soon she's been to so many bar and bas mitzvahs, she can almost say herself whether the kid chants like an angel or like a train conductor. At seder, Mona knows to forget the bricks, get a good pile of that mortar. Also she knows what is schmaltz. Mona knows that she is, no offense, a goy. This is not why people like her, though. People like her because she does not need to use deodorant, as she demonstrates in the locker room, before and after gym. Not to say she can explain to them, for example, what is tofu (der-voo, they say at home). Her friends' mothers invite her to taste-test their Chinese cooking.

"Very authentic." She tries to be reassuring. After all, they're nice people, she likes them. "De-lish." She has seconds. On the question of what her family eats, though, Mona has to admit, "Well, no, it's different than that." She has thirds. "What my mom makes is home style, it's not in the cookbooks."

Not in the cookbooks! Everyone's jealous. Meanwhile, the big deal at home is when they have turkey pot pie. Her sister Callie's the one who introduced them—Mrs. Wilder's, they come in this green and brown box—and when the Changs have them, the girls get suddenly interested in helping out in the kitchen. Meaning, they stand in front of the oven, watching the cuckoo clock. Twenty-five minutes. Callie and Mona have a deal, though, to keep this activity secret from school, as everybody else thinks frozen food is gross. The girls consider it a big improvement over authentic Chinese home cooking. Oxtail soup—now, that's gross. Stir-fried beef with tomatoes. One day Mona says, "You know, Ma, I have never seen a stir-fried tomato in any Chinese restaurant we have ever been in, ever."

"In China, we consider tomatoes as delicacy." (With the sun behind her head, Helen looks to be a cross between a saint and an eclipse.)

"Ma," Mona says. "Tomatoes are *Italian*."

"No respect for elders." Helen wags her finger. Having been a reluctant beauty in her youth, Helen could now graduate to the dignified kind if her greater desire were not to try and shame Mona into believing her. She turns, abandoning her halo; sunlight washes with corny radiance her brow, her eyes, her mouth, all beautiful, as she scoots her glasses down and makes a gorilla face. "I'm telling you, tomatoes *invented* in China."

*"Ma."*

"It's true. Like noodles. Invented in China."

"That's not what they said *in school*."

"In China," Helen says, resorting to facts, "we eat tomatoes like fruit. Just like we eat apples here. Of course, first we drop them in hot water to take the skin off. Because, you know, Chinese people don't like to eat anything with the skin on."

And at this show of authority, Mona reluctantly makes a gorilla face too. For if she ever had to say what means Chinese, it would have to include a predilection for peeling grapes in your mouth without moving your jaw—also for emitting the peels without opening your lips. On the other hand, her mother once admitted that China was such a long time ago, a lot of things she can hardly remember. She said sometimes she has trouble remembering her characters, that sometimes she'll be writing along, and all of a sudden she won't be sure how the strokes go.

"So what do you do then?"

"Oh, I just make a little sloppy."

"You mean you *fudge*?"

Helen laughed then, but another time, when she was showing Mona how to write her name, and Mona said, just kidding, "Are you sure you're not fudging now," she was hurt.

"I mean, of course you're not," Mona said. "I mean, *oy.*"

Meanwhile, what Mona knows is that in the eighth grade, people do not want to hear about how Chinese people eat tomatoes without the skin on. For a gross fact, it isn't gross enough. On the other hand, the fact that somewhere in China somebody eats or has eaten or once ate living monkey brains—now, that's conversation.

"They have these special tables," Mona says, "kind of like a giant collar. With, you know, a hole in the middle, for the monkey's neck. They put the monkey in the collar, and then they cut off the top of its head."

"Whaddathey use for cutting?"

Mona thinks. "Scalpels."

"*Scalpels?*" Andy Kaplan is going to turn out the sort of spatial brilliant that can rotate irregular objects in his head, but for now he's just a pale sprout of a guy with spittle on his braces.

"Kaplan, don't be dense." Barbara Gugelstein straightens as if to lock into firing position her twin early maturities. "The Chinese *invented* scalpels."

Once a friend said to Mona, that everybody is valued for something. This friend explained how some people resented being valued for their looks, others resented being valued for their money. Wasn't it still better to be beautiful and rich than ugly and poor, though? *You should be just glad,* she said, *that you have something people value.* She said it was like having a special talent, like being good at ice-skating, or opera-singing. She said, *You could probably make a career out of it.*

Here's the irony: Mona is.


But to return: Mona is ad-libbing her way through eighth grade, as described. Then comes one bloomy spring day. Scarshill is everywhere azaleas and other understory plants offering year-round interest; even Mona is looking spriggy, what with the bluebell she has tucked behind her ear in the manner of a Honolulu tour bus hostess. This is not so easy on account of her glasses being in the way, and also on account of her having her father's ears—i.e., the fold-out kind that if life were fair would also fold in. These go, somehow, with her blue-ribbon cowlick, and best-of-class freckles; it's no wonder (not to boast) that she has developed some aplomb to go with all these looks. How much aplomb, however, remains to be seen on said bloomy spring day, as she saunters in late to homeroom, only to experience a personal seasonal shock—a new kid in class.

Chinese.

So what should she do—pretend to have to go to the girls' room like Barbara Gugelstein the day Andy Kaplan took his ID bracelet back? She sits down. She is so cool she reminds herself of Paul Newman. First thing she realizes, though, is that no one looking at her is thinking of Paul Newman. The notes fly:

"*I* think he's cute."

"Who?" Mona writes back.

"I don't think he talks English too good. Writes it, either."

"Who?"

"They might have to put him behind a grade, so don't worry."

"He has a crush on you already, you could tell as soon as you walked in—he turned kind of orangish."

Mona hopes she's not turning orangish as she deals with her mail, she could use a secretary. The second round starts:

"What do you mean, who? Don't be weird. Didn't you *see* him??? Straight back over your right shoulder!!!!"

She has to look, what else can she do? She thinks of certain tips she learned in Girl Scouts about poise. She crosses her ankles. She holds a pen in her hand. She sits up as though she has a crown on her head. She swivels her head slowly, repeating to herself, *I* could be Miss America.

"Miss Mona Chang."

Her bluebell falls to the floor. Barbara rescues it for her, but still the blackboard ahead seems to swim with yesterday's homework equations.

"Notes, please."

Mrs. Mandeville's policy is to read all notes aloud.

Mona tries to consider what Miss America would do. She envisions herself, back straight, knees together, crying. Some inspiration. Cool Hand Luke, on the other hand, would quick, eat the evidence. And why not? She should yawn as she stands up, and boom, the notes are gone. All that's left is to explain that it's an old Chinese reflex.

She shuffles up to the front of the room.

"One minute, please," says Mrs. Mandeville.

Doom looms.

Mrs. Mandeville loudly uncrinkles a piece of paper.

And Miss Mona Chang, who got almost straight A's her whole life except for in Math and Conduct, is about to start bawling in front of everyone.


She is delivered out of hot Egypt by the bell. Mrs. Mandeville still has her hand clamped on Mona's shoulder, though, and the next thing Mona knows, she's holding the new boy's schedule. He's standing next to her like a big blank piece of paper.

"This is Sherman," says Mrs. Mandeville.

"Hello," Mona says.

"Non how a," Mona says.

She's glad Barbara Gugelstein isn't there to see her Chinese in action. "Ji-nu," she says. "Shee-veh."

Later Mona finds out that Sherman's mother asked if there were any other Orientals in his grade. She had him put in Mona's class on purpose. For now, though, he looks at her as though she's much stranger than anything else he's seen so far. Is this because he understands she's saying soy sauce rice gruel to him, or because he doesn't?

"Shah-man," he says finally.

Mona looks at his schedule card. Sherman Matsumoto. What kind of name is that for a nice Chinese boy?

(Later on, people ask her how she can tell Chinese from Japanese. She shrugs. It's the kind of thing you just kind of know, she says. Oy!)


Sherman's got the sort of looks Mona thinks of as pretty boy. Monsignor-black hair (not monk-brown like hers), kind of bouncy—not the kind that lies down slick and flat, his is almost bushy. Crayola eyebrows, one with a round bald spot in the middle of it, like a golf hole. She doesn't know how anybody can think of him as orangish. His skin looks white to her, with pink triangles hanging down the front of his cheeks like flags. Kind of delicate-looking, but the only really uncool thing about him is that his spiral notebook has a picture of a kitty cat on it. A big white fluffy one, with blue ribbons above each perky ear. Mona's opportunities to view this are legion, as all the poor kid understands about life in junior high school is that he should follow her everywhere. This is slightly mortifying. On the other hand, he's obviously even more miserable than she is, so she tries not to say anything. Give him a chance to adjust. They communicate by sign language, and by drawing pictures, which he's much more proficient at than she is, although not as fast. He puts in every last detail, even if it takes forever. She calls on her patience.

A week of this. Finally she explains, "You should get a new notebook."

He turns the sort of pink you associate with bubble gum and hyacinths.

"Notebook." She points to his. She shows him hers, which is psychedelic, with big purple and yellow stick-on flowers. She tries to explain he should have one like this, only without the flowers. He nods enigmatically, and the next day brings her a notebook just like his, except that her cat sports pink bows instead of blue.

"Pureety," he says. And, after a moment, "You."

He speaks English! Has he spoken it all this time? *Pretty,* she thinks. *You.* What does that mean? If that's what he said at all. She's assuming he means pretty, but maybe he means pity. *Pity. You.*

"Jeez," Mona says finally.

"You ahh wer-u-come," he says.

She decorates the back of the notebook with stick-on flowers, and holds it so that these show when she walks through the halls. In class, she mostly keeps her book open. After all, the kid's so new, Mona thinks she really ought to have a heart. And for a livelong day, nobody notices.

Then Barbara Gugelstein sidles up. "Matching notebooks, huh?"

Mona's speechless.

"First comes love. Then comes marriage, and then come Chappies in a baby carriage."

"Barbara!"

"Get it?" she says. "Chinese Japs."

"Bar-*bra*," Mona says to get even.

"Just make sure he doesn't give you any *tea,*" she says.

Are Sherman and Mona in love? Three days later, Mona hazards that they are. Her thinking proceeds this way: She thinks he's cute, and she thinks he thinks she's cute. On the other hand, they don't kiss and they don't exactly have fantastic conversations. Their talks are improving, though. They started out, "This is a book." "Book-u." "This is a chair." "Chai-a." Advancing to: "What is this?" "Dis is a book-u." Now, for fun, he tests her. "What is dis?" Already he speaks more slowly than he used to, and with less staccato. He throws in fewer extra syllables; he gets his accents in the right place. For actually, his English teacher at home taught him all this before, he just needed to get his mouth to listen. As for Mona, she dutifully answers, "This is a book" when he asks, as if she's the one who has to learn how to talk. He claps. "Good!"

Meanwhile, people ask her all about him, Mona could be his press agent.

"No, he doesn't eat raw fish."

"No, his father wasn't a kamikaze pilot."

"No, he can't do karate."

"Are you sure?" somebody asks.


It turns out he doesn't know karate, but judo he does. She is hurt she's not the one to find this out; the guys know from gym class. They line up to be flipped, he flips them all onto the floor, and after that he quits eating lunch at the girls' table with her. She's pretty much glad. Meaning, when he was there, Mona never knew what to say. Now that he's gone, though, she's still stuck at the *This is a chair* level of conversation. Nobody's interested in China anymore; it's just more and more questions about her and Sherman. "Got me," she's saying all the time. *Are* they going out? They do stuff, it's true. For example, Mona takes him to her family's restaurant, where they spray whipped cream in their mouths and eat fudge sauce straight from the vat. Also she takes him to the department stores. She explains to him who shops in Alexander's, who shops in Saks. She tells him her family's the type that shops in Alexander's. He says he's sorry. In Saks, he gets lost; either that, or else she's the lost one. (It's true Mona finds him calmly waiting at the front door, hands behind his back, like a guard.) She takes him to the candy store. She takes him to the bagel store. Sherman is crazy about bagels. She explains to him Lender's is gross, he should get his bagels from the bagel store. He says thank you.

"Are you going steady?" people want to know.

How can they go steady, when he doesn't have an ID bracelet? On the other hand, he brings her more presents than Mona thinks any girl's ever gotten before. Oranges. Flowers. A little bag of bagels. But what do they mean? Do they mean *thank you, I enjoyed the trip,* do they mean *I like you,* do they mean *I decided I liked the Lender's better even if they are gross, you can have these?* Mona knows at least a couple of items were supposed to go to their teachers; Sherman told her that once and turned red. She figures it still might mean something that he didn't throw them out.

More and more now, they joke. For example, he often mixes up *thinking* with *sinking*—which they both think is so funny that all either one of them has to do is pretend to be drowning, and the other one cracks up. And he tells her things. For example, that there are electric lights everywhere in Tokyo now.

"You mean you didn't have them before?"

"Everywhere now!" He's amazed too. "Since Orympics-u!"

"Olympics?"

Nineteen sixty-four, he reminds her, humming the Olympic theme song. "You know?"

"Sure," Mona says, and hums with him happily, they could be a picture on a Unicef Halloween can. The only problem is that Mona doesn't really get what the Olympics have to do with the modernization of Japan, any more than she gets this other story he tells her, about that hole in his left eyebrow. This is from some time his father accidentally hit him with a lit cigarette—when Sherman was a baby. His father was drunk, having been out carousing, and his mother was very mad, but didn't say anything, just cleaned the whole house. Then his father was so ashamed he bowed to ask her forgiveness.

"Your mother cleaned the house?"

Sherman nods solemnly.

"And your father *bowed*?" Mona finds this more astounding than anything she ever thought to make up. "That is so weird."

"Weird," he agrees. "*Fader* bow to *moder!*"

They shake and shake and shake their heads.

MONA IN THE PROMISED LAND

As for the things he asks her, they're not topics Mona ever talked about before. Does she like it here? "Of course I like it here, I was born here," Mona says. Is Mona Jewish? "Jewish!" She laughs. "Oy!" Is she American? "Sure I'm American," Mona says. "Everybody who's born here is American, and also some people who convert from what they were before. You could become American." But he says no, he could never. "Sure you could," Mona says. "You only have to learn some rules and speeches."

"But I Japanese."

"You could become American anyway," Mona says. "Like I *could* become Jewish, if I wanted to. I'd just have to switch, that's all."

He looks at her in alarm.

She thinks maybe he doesn't get what means switch.

She introduces him to turkey pot pies. "Gross-u?" he asks. She says they are, but that she likes them anyway. "Don't tell anybody." He promises. They bake them, eat them, agreeing turkey is just like chicken, only spelt differently. While they're eating, he's drawing her pictures with a pencil stub.

"Dis American," he says, and on a napkin he draws something that looks like John Wayne. "Dis Jewish." He draws something that looks like the Wicked Witch of the West, only male.

"I don't think so," Mona says.

He's undeterred. Partly this is because there is next to no lead in the pencil stub; difficulty seems to bring out in him resolution. "Dis Japanese," he says, and draws a fair rendition of himself. "Dis Chinese," he says, and draws what looks to be another fair rendition of himself.

"How can you tell them apart?"

"Dis way," he says, and puts the napkin of the Chinese so that it is looking at the napkins of the American and the Jew. The Japanese is looking at the wall until Mona finds him a replacement pencil, a red one. Then he draws a color picture of a Japanese flag, so that the Japanese is looking at his flag. "Chinese lost in depart-o-ment-o store," he says. "Japanese know how to go."

"What do you mean?" says Mona.

"Atomic bomb dropped on only one people," Sherman says. "The Japanese do not forget." On the back of an old mimeograph sheet, he draws another Japanese flag, a bigger one, which he puts on the icebox door with daisy magnets. "In school, in ceremony, we dis way," he explains, and bows to the picture.

When Helen comes in, her face is so red that with the white wall behind her, she looks a bit like the Japanese flag herself. Yet Mona gets the feeling she'd better not say so. First her mother doesn't move. Then she snatches the flag off the icebox, so fast the daisy magnets go flying. Two of them land on the stove. She crumples up the paper. She hisses at Sherman, *"This is the U.S. of A., do you hear me!"*

Sherman hears her.

"You call your mother, tell her come pick you up."

He understands perfectly. Mona, on the other hand, is stymied. And how can two people who don't really speak English understand each other better than she can understand them? "But, Ma," Mona says.

"Don't *Ma* me." Helen hands Sherman the telephone. (This she accompanies with Kleenex, out of habit.)

Later on, she explains that World War II was in China too. "Hitler," Mona says. "Nazis. Volkswagens." She knows the Japanese were on the wrong side, because they bombed Pearl Harbor. Helen explains about before that.

"What Napkin Massacre?" says Mona.

"*Nan*-king."

"Are you sure? In school, they said the War was about putting the Jews in ovens."

"Also about ovens."

"About both?"

"Both."

"That's not what they said in school."

*"Just forget about school."*

Forget about school? "I thought we moved here for the schools."

"We moved here," says Helen, "for your education."

Sometimes Mona has no idea what her mother is talking about.

"I like Sherman," Mona says, after a while.

"Nice boy." Helen gives the icebox door a quiet slam.

Meaning what? Mona would ask, except that her dad's just come home from the restaurant, which means it's time to start talking about whether they should build a brick wall across the front of the lawn. Recently a car made it almost into their living room, which was so scary that the driver fainted and an ambulance had to come. "We should discuss this problem," Ralph said after that. "Find solution." In appearance, Ralph could be an archetype of himself—his ears still stick out, his hair still sticks up. He is as padded as ever. Also his elbows still tend to rise and float in the air when he talks, as if he is standing in his own private water tank. But internally he is given to abrupt resolutions and real changes of outlook, for example about solving this problem. And so, for about a week, every night they'll be discussing how.

"Are you just friends, or more than just friends?" Barbara Gugelstein is giving Mona the big cross-ex.

"Maybe," Mona says.

"Come on. I told you *everything* about me and Andy."

Mona actually is trying to tell Barbara everything about Sherman, but everything turns out to be nothing. Meaning, she can't locate the conversation in what she has to say. Sherman and she go places, they talk, one time her mom threw him out of the house because of World War II.

"I think we're just friends," Mona says.

"You think"—Barbara pulls up her fishnet stockings—"or you're sure?"

Now that Mona does less of the talking at lunch, she notices more what other people talk about. Who likes who, whether to wear pants to rec night, this place in White Plains to get earrings. On none of these topics is Mona an expert. Of course, she's still friends with Barbara Gugelstein, but Mona notices that Danielle Meyers has spun away to other groups.

Barbara's analysis goes this way: To be popular, you have to have big boobs, a note from your mother that lets you use her Lord & Taylor charge card, and a boyfriend. On the other hand, what's so wrong with being unpopular? "We'll get them in the end," she says. It's what her dad tells her. "Like they'll turn out too dumb to do their own investing," she says. "And then they'll get killed in brokers' fees and have to move to towns where the schools stink."

"I guess," Mona says, shifting her weight a little.

But the next thing Mona knows, she has a true crush on Sherman Matsumoto. *Mister* Judo, the guys call him now, with real respect; and the more they call him that, the more Mona doesn't care that he carries a notebook with a cat on it.

Mona sighs. "Sherman."

"I thought you were just friends." Barbara Gugelstein lifts an eyebrow, something she learned to do last week.

"We were." Mona employs her own new air of mystery. For this, she's noticed, is how Danielle Meyers talks. Everything's secret, she only lets out so much; it's obvious she didn't grow up with everybody telling her she had to share.

And here's the funny thing: The more Mona tells people that she and Sherman are more than just friends, the more it seems to be true. It's the old imagination giving reality a prod. When Mona starts to blush, he starts to blush. They get to a point where they can hardly talk at all.

"Well, there's first base with tongue, and first base without," Mona tells Barbara Gugelstein.

In fact, Sherman and Mona have brushed shoulders, which was equivalent to first base, Mona was sure, maybe even second. She felt as though she'd turned into one huge shoulder. That's all she was, one huge shoulder. They not only didn't talk, they didn't breathe. But how can Mona tell Barbara Gugelstein that? So instead she says, "Well, there's second base and second base."

Danielle Meyers is her friend again. She says, blinking bluely, "I know exactly what you mean," just to make Barbara Gugelstein feel bad.

"Like *what* do I mean?" Mona says.

Danielle Meyers blinks bluely some more.

"You know what I think?" Mona tells Barbara the next day. "I think Danielle's giving us a line."

Barbara picks thoughtfully at her split ends.


If Sherman Matsumoto is never going to give Mona an ID to wear, he should at least get up the nerve to hold her hand. Mona doesn't think he sees this. She thinks of the story he told her about his parents, and in a synaptical firestorm realizes they don't see the same things at all.

So one day, when they happen to brush shoulders again, Mona doesn't move away. He doesn't move away either. There they are. Like a pair of bleachers, pushed together but not quite matched up.

After a while, Mona has to breathe, she can't help it. She breathes in such a way that their elbows start to touch too. This is in a crowd, waiting for a bus. They are both wearing short sleeves. She cranes her neck to look at the sign that says where the bus is going. Now their wrists are adjoining. Then it happens: He links his pinky around hers.

Is that holding hands? Later, in bed, Mona wonders all night. One finger, and not even the biggest one.

Sherman is leaving in a month. Already! Mona supposes he will leave and they'll never even kiss. She guesses that's all right. Just when she's resigned herself to it, though, they hold hands all five fingers. Once, when they are at the bagel shop; then once more, in her parents' kitchen. Then one day, when they are at the playground, he kisses the back of her hand. He does it again not long after that, in White Plains. She begins to use mouthwash.

Instead of moving on, though, he kisses the back of her hand again. And again. She tries raising her hand, hoping he'll make the jump from her hand to her cheek. It's like trying to wheedle an inchworm out the window. You know, *This way, this way.*

*All over the world, people have their own cultures.* That's what they learned in social studies.

If they never kiss, she's not going to take it personally.


It is the end of the school year. There've been parties. Kids've turned in their textbooks. *Hooray!* Outside, the asphalt steams if you spit on it. Sherman isn't leaving for another couple of days, though, and he comes to visit every morning, staying until Callie comes home from her big-deal job as a grocery checkout clerk. Mona and Sherman drink Kool-Aid in the backyard, holding hands until they are sweaty and make smacking noises coming apart. He tells her how busy his parents are, getting ready for the move; his mother in particular is very tired. Mostly he is mournful.

The very last day, he holds Mona's hand and does not let go even when their palms fill up with water like a blister. They talk more than usual. How complicated is his address, whether the Japanese have aerograms too. Then suddenly he asks, looking straight into his Kool-Aid, will she marry him?

*I'm only thirteen.*

*But when old? Sixteen?*

*If you come back to get me.*

*I come. Or you come to Japan, be Japanese.*

*How can I be Japanese?*

*Like you become American. Switch.*

He kisses her on the cheek, again and again and again.

His mother calls to say she's coming to get him. Mona cries. She tells him how she's saved every present he's ever given her—the ruler, the pencils, the bags from the bagels, all the flower petals. She even has the peels from the oranges.

*All?*

*I put them in a jar.*

She'd show him, except that they're not allowed to go upstairs to her room. Anyway, something about the orange peels seems to choke him up too. *Mi*ster Judo, but she's gotten him in a soft spot. They are going together to the bathroom to get some toilet paper to wipe their eyes, when poor tired Mrs. Matsumoto skids up onto the lawn.

"Very sorry!"

They race outside.

"Very sorry!"

Mrs. Matsumoto is so short that about all they can see of her is a green cotton sun hat, with a big brim. It's tied on. The brim is trembling.

Mona hopes her mom's not going to start yelling about World War II.

"It's all right, no trouble," Helen says, suddenly on the steps, behind Mona and Sherman. She's holding the screen door open; when Mona turns, she can see her mother waving. Helen is wearing a dress you would never guess she's mended twice, and she is practically standing on her toes, as if trying to hail a taxi. "No trouble, no trouble!"

"No trouble, no trouble!" Mona twirls a few times with relief. Sherman is blushing; the air smells of summer, which is to say of Mr. 20-20's roses next door.

Mrs. Matsumoto keeps apologizing; Helen keeps insisting she shouldn't feel bad, it was only some grass and a small tree. Crossing the lawn, she insists Mrs. Matsumoto get out of the car, even though it means mushing some lilies of the valley. She insists Mrs. Matsumoto come in for a cup of tea. Then she will not talk about anything unless Mrs. Matsumoto sits down, and unless she lets Helen prepare for her a small snack. The coming in and the tea and the sitting down are settled pretty quickly, but there is more negotiation over the small snack, which Mrs. Matsumoto will not eat unless she can call Mr. Matsumoto. She makes the mistake of linking Mr. Matsumoto with a reparation of some sort. This Helen will not hear of. "Please!" "No no no no." Back and forth it goes. "No no no no." "No no no no." "No no no no." What kind of conversation is that? Mona looks at Sherman, who shrugs. Finally Mr. Matsumoto calls on his own, wondering where his wife is. He comes over in a taxi. A strong-jawed businessman, friendly but brisk, he is not at all a type you could imagine bowing to a lady with a taste for tie-on sun hats. Helen invites him in, as if it's an idea she just that moment thought of. And would he maybe have some tea and a small snack?

Sherman and Mona sneak back outside for another final good-bye, next to the house, behind the forsythia bushes. They hold hands. He kisses her on the cheek again, and then—just when Mona thinks he's finally going to kiss her on the lips—he kisses her on the neck.

Is this first base?

He does it more. Up and down, up and down. First it tickles, and then it doesn't. He has his eyes closed. Mona closes her eyes too. He's hugging her. Up and down. Then down.

He's at her collarbone.

Still at her collarbone. Now his hand is on her ribs. So much for first base. More ribs. The idea of second base would probably make her nervous if he weren't on his way back to Japan, and if Mona really thought they were actually going to get there. As it is, though, Mona isn't in much danger of wrecking her life on the shoals of passion. His unmoving hand feels more like a growth than a boyfriend. He has his whole face pressed to her neck skin so she can't tell his mouth from his nose. She thinks he may be licking her.

From indoors, a burst of far-off laughter. Her eyelids flutter, she can't help it. She starts to try and wiggle such that his hand will maybe budge upward. Does she mean for her top blouse button to come accidentally undone?

He clenches his jaw; and when he opens his eyes, they're fixed on that button like it's a gnat that's been bothering him for more than long enough. He mutters in Japanese. If later in life he were to describe this as a pivotal moment in his youth, Mona would not be surprised. Holding the material as far from her body as possible, he buttons the button. Somehow they've ended up too close to the bushes.

What to tell Barbara Gugelstein? She says, "Tell me what were his last words. He must have said something last."

"I don't want to talk about it."

"Maybe he said good-bye? Sayonara?" She means well.

"I don't want to talk about it."

"Aw, come on. I told you everything about . . ."

Mona says, "Because it's private. Excuse me."

Barbara squints at Mona with her dewy green eyes as though Mona is a distant horizon she's trying to make out. She straightens her back maturely. Then she nods and very lightly places her fingertips on Mona's forearm.

The forsythia seemed to be stabbing them in the eyes. Sherman said, more or less, *You will need to study how to switch.*

And Mona said, *I think you should switch. The way you do everything is weird.*

And he said, turning pink, *You just want to tell everything to your friends. You just want to have boyfriend to become popular.*

Then he flipped her. Two swift moves, and she went sprawling through the late afternoon, a flailing confusion of soft human parts such as had no idea where the ground was.

It is fall, and Mona is in high school, and still he hasn't written. So finally she writes him on her new electric typewriter.

*I still have all your gifts. I don't talk so much as I used to. Although I am not exactly a mouse either. I don't care about being popular anymore, I swear. Are you happy to be back in Japan? Jackie Kennedy married a Greek, but neither one of them switched—that's what Barbara says. What do you think about that? I know I ruined everything. I was just trying to be entertaining. I miss you with all my heart, and hope I didn't ruin everything.*

He writes back in fountain pen: *You will never be Japanese.*

She throws all the orange peels out that day. Some of them, it turns out, were moldy anyway. She burns the letter with the help of Barbara Gugelstein. She tells her mother she wants to move to Chinatown.

"Chinatown!" Helen says.

Mona doesn't know why she asked.

"What's the matter? Still boy-crazy?"

"No."

"Forget about school."

Later she tells Mona that if she doesn't like school, she doesn't have to go every day. Some days Mona can stay home, like Callie.

"Stay home?" says Mona. In their old town, Callie and Mona used to stay home all the time, but that was because the schools there were *waste of time.*

"No good for a girl be too smart anyway," says Helen.


For a long time, Mona thinks about Sherman. But after a while, she doesn't think about him so much as she just keeps seeing herself flipped onto the ground. Lying there shocked, as the Matsumotos get ready to leave. Her head has hit a rock. Her brains ache as though they've been relocated in her skull. Otherwise, she's okay. She sees the forsythia, all those whippy branches, and can't believe how many leaves there are on a bush, every one green and paniculate and durably itself. And past them, real sky. She tries to remember what makes the sky blue, even though this one's gone the kind of gray you associate with words that end with *nk. Dank. Sunk. Stink.* She smells their neighbor's roses, but also she smells grass. Probably she has grass stains all over her back. She hears Helen calling through the back door, *Mon-a! Everyone leaving now* and *Not coming to say good-bye?* She hears Mr. and Mrs. Matsumoto bowing as they leave—or at least she hears the embarrassment in her mother's voice as they bow. She hears their car start. She hears Mrs. Matsumoto directing Mr. Matsumoto how to back off the lawn so as not to rip any more of it up. She feels the back of her head for blood. Just a little. She hears their *chug-chug* grow fainter and fainter, until it has faded into the *whuzz-whuzz* of all the other cars. She hears her mother singing, *Mon-a! Mon-a!* until her father comes home. Doors open and shut. She sees herself standing up, brushing her shirt off so she'll have less explaining to do if someone comes out to look for her. Grass stains, just like she thought. She sees herself walking around the house, going over to have a look at their churned-up yard. It looks pretty sad—two big brown tracks right through the irises and the lilies of the valley, and that was a new dogwood they'd just planted. Lying there like that. She hears herself thinking about her father, and how he had always considered gardening a waste of time to begin with. *That's for rich guys,* he used to say; sometimes he just wanted to cut everything down with the lawn mower. It was only when he saw her mother out there digging the hole herself that he agreed to help with the dogwood. And now he was going to have to go planting the thing all over again. Adjusting. She thinks how they probably ought to put up that brick wall.

And sure enough, when she goes inside, no one's thinking about her, or that little bit of blood at the back of her head, or the grass stains. That's what they're talking about—that wall. Again. Helen doesn't think it'll do any good, but all these accidents are giving Ralph stomach gas. Should they or shouldn't they? How high? How thick? What will the neighbors say? They have to check about the zoning, Helen claims, but Ralph, eating a danish, seems suddenly to have never heard of such a thing. *Soning? Ah, zoning! Begins with "z."* Mona plops herself down on a hard chair. And all she can think is, they are the complete only family that has to worry about this. If she could, she'd switch everything to be different. But since she can't, she might as well sit here at the table for a while, discussing what she knows how to discuss. She listens and nods to the rest.

CHAPTER 2

# Her Life
# More Generally

When is a pickle dish more than just a pickle dish? Two years later, Mona ponders this in tenth-grade English class; also pickles in general. She used to love pickles, but now hesitates to bring them to school (even if they are satisfyingly crunchy and low-calorie to boot), for fear of setting off a sublimation lunch—i.e., the kind of lunch where everyone discusses which people are sublimating and, in particular, whether she is. Also if all of life, in reality, is sublimation. If it is, Mona would rather not know about it.

By now, Mona would love to have forgotten about Sherman—to have proven disloyal, impulsive, fickle, a regular *femme fatale*. But though she is in the sweet bloom of her youth, she hasn't exactly had to worry about catching mono like Danielle Meyers. There was that fling with DeWitt Traub freshman year—all forty-eight hours of it before he went back to Farah Liason, the ham radio queen. And it did also transpire once, after a Dead concert, that Mona somehow found herself slow-dancing with one of the roadies—a musician in his own right, it turned out, who used just one name for his first name and last name both. Jupiter. Of course, even he seemed to feel that something was missing, for when he introduced himself, he never said just Jupiter, period, but generally added *like the planet* in such a way that that almost seemed to be his last name. And after the nice warm dance, Mona told him that she had noticed this; which she later thought must have impressed him. For though, like his namesake, he proved to have many moons in orbit, he sent her a postcard a week for a good two and three-quarters months, and almost half of them

were addressed to her, Mona Chang, and not to Pee-pee Vulva, whoever she was.

All the same, her chief hangout is still Barbara Gugelstein, and one
of their chief activities is a game called Wonder What Sherman Is
Doing Right Now. It seems that this is how they have always wiled
away their afternoons—imagining what Sherman is wearing, imagining what Sherman is eating, imagining whether Sherman is thinking
about Mona. Of course, in all their imaginings, he is pining so desperately that his mother keeps having his blood drawn, thinking that
something is the matter. He has decided to return to the U.S. He is
obsessed with student exchange programs. He plays a game with his
friends called Wonder What Mona Is Doing Right Now—only, of
course, in Japanese. Does he, in his wildest imaginings, imagine that
right at that moment, his Mona is actually imagining him, imagining
her? "It kind of like blows your mind," says Barbara Gugelstein.

Other interests: fashion. Mona and Barbara both wear ponchos,
peasant blouses, leotards, bikini underwear. Hip-hugger bell-bottoms.
Water-buffalo sandals. Barbara favors elephant-hair earrings and love
beads; Mona has a necklace with a tear-shaped peace symbol she got
in Greenwich Village. (This, she maintains, looks nothing at all like
a declawed chicken foot.) She wears her hair long and straight and
parted in the middle, as do Barbara and Cybill Shepherd, among other
fashion leaders. At night, Barbara has to roll hers all up on an orange juice can; Mona has her cowlick to contend with. Sometimes
she Dippity-Dos it down, but mostly she leaves it to do its anti-
gravity thing.

A subinterest: fashion design. Mona uses scissors to get the bottom
edge of her hip-hugger bell-bottoms to fray. Also she washes them
a hundred times with bleach. She debates whether under her knee
patches there ought to be real holes. She would cut some, except that
Barbara Gugelstein told her she did that once, and then her jeans really ripped—not only across the front completely, but around the back
too. Mona wonders about this. Didn't the rip get stopped by the side
seams? Still, she doesn't exactly want to risk pedal pushers, given all
the time she spent arguing about her pants with her mom.

"Waste water, waste electricity, waste soap, I don't know what
is the matter with you," Helen kept saying. "You want to wear old

clothes, you can borrow some from your parents. Everything we wear is washed soft already. Save you a lot of work."

"You know, Ma," Mona said, "I'd be happy to pay for the electricity if you want."

To which Helen answered, huffily, "You want to pay for something, you can go stay in hotel."

This, for the record, is not what Barbara Gugelstein's mom would have said. At Barbara's house, the kids get fined if they're incurring costs over and beyond the reasonable. For example, with a bird phase: Somebody gave Barbara a pair of Australian zebra finches, which she decided to try and breed. And this, it turned out, was just like they learned in sex ed. You got the boy bird in the vicinity of a girl bird who hadn't gotten the big talk-to, and before you could say, *Think of your future* there were some hundred birds at least. They took up a whole wall. And these birds were not going to any four-year college, that was obvious. They were just flying around their cages, and kicking their seed out the bars, and generally making such a big delinquent mess that the maid insisted on being paid extra to clean it up.

It was just lucky Barbara could finance this. She got forty-five dollars for helping paint their backyard fence alone (that was fifty cents a picket for two coats plus cleanup). Also she gets paid for things like bringing in the paper and setting the sports section by her dad's cereal. For Barbara is her own separate accounting unit, unlike Mona and Callie.

Mona and Callie, that's to say, are slave labor. Never mind their handy on-call restaurant service. They mow the lawn and don't get paid. They vacuum the living room and don't get paid. They wash the storm windows and don't get paid, Callie especially—Callie's always been the power scrub of the family. But even Mona the mother's favorite helps dry and is not paid, not that it really matters. For even if they did get paid, they couldn't exactly spend the money on hot pants just because it was their money and they'd earned it. After all, this is what it means to be a family member: There is nothing so small but that you've got to ask the parents' permission. Once, Callie and Mona tried to unionize and go on strike, but instead of becoming folk heroes, they turned into Disappointments. "Mom's tired," Helen said, and they could see that she was. Who wouldn't be, working all the time the way she did? Some days she went straight from the restaurant to bed, instead of going grocery shopping and doing the cooking; these were the days she was likely to start brooding about her family in China, wondering whether everyone was dead by now or still being tortured. The Disappointments came home to find their mother in her bathrobe; and then they felt about ready to put on their bathrobes too. For her mood had turned into their mood, it was like a forest fire jumping a ditch.

And so the girls toil on. Helen is always talking about who really suffered, as in "Your aunt Theresa, she really suffered"; from which the girls deduce that women distinguish themselves in life by their misery. Ergo, they strive to be as miserable as possible, Callie especially. For Callie used to want to be a martyr anyway, back when they were in Catholic school; she had that head start. Now she makes people feel sullied by the world, and in need of confession, and this is great, since she's on the school newspaper. "Scoop," everyone calls her, nobody gets the story like she does, she was even asked to be editor in chief. Naturally enough, though, she declined.

For this is the difference between Mona and Callie: Mona would probably have said sure, which is exactly why nobody is asking. Who needs to draw her out? After years of everyone emphasizing the Importance of Class Participation, Mona can finally be counted on to volunteer. With the result that at least one of her teachers, Miss Feeble, has begun to ignore her hand up in the air. *Now, Mona, you have to give someone else a chance to talk.* This she is not supposed to have to say to nice Chinese girls. So what does it mean that she has to say it to Mona?

Miss Feeble has apparently been pondering this question, because one day she asks Mona if she is really Chinese. This is while Miss Feeble pushes desks around, arranging them in a horseshoe.

"Of course I'm Chinese," Mona says, helping out. "I'm Chinese American."

"And your parents?" continues Miss Feeble, pushing. "They're Chinese too?"

"Of course," Mona says. "They're *immigrants*." She knows as she says this, naturally, that her parents would never use that word on themselves. They think it means people who try to bring live chickens on buses and don't own real suitcases.

All the same, it works on Miss Feeble.

"Ah." She repeats the holy word. "Immigrants." It is as if Mona has cut a little window into the fence of a construction site. Sure enough, there it is, the big crane.

The restaurant: This is not the first restaurant Mona's family's owned. The first was a fried chicken palace, to talk about which is now verboten, on account of it all but brought about the untimely demise of Aunt Theresa. How this came to pass is the complicated subject of another whole book. Suffice it to say here that since Theresa was the one who lay on death's doorstep, staring down that old house cat, she is the only one who can crack jokes about it now. Calling the chicken palace the Forbidden Palace, for example. Wondering wherefore the imperial freeze on the subject. It's not as if we staffed it with eunuchs, she'll say.

In response to which, everyone is supposed to laugh politely and not ask what a eunuch is, especially since she's sure to explain. For apparently this is what being plucked from the jaws of eternity will do to you; a certain derangement has to be expected. Now she's up and moved to California, where she strolls around on the beach with Uncle Henry all day—rumor has it, in a two-piece bathing suit and sometimes less, and without having gotten married, either. Leaving this narrator here to report that the one good thing about the chicken palace fiasco was that it forced Ralph and Helen to sell their house. Because that's how it was that they had the cash to go in on the new franchise Uncle Henry's old wife was buying. *One countertop,* Ralph and Helen joked then. But even that was a help to poor Aunt Janis; and with time, they could call more and more of the Formica their own—poor Aunt Janis having moved on to shopping centers.

So that the next thing they knew, they were moving too, out of their old town and into this Dutch colonial with landscape problems, as you've heard. For this is what pançakes can do. It's true the magic's been patchy at times, for example, the day dear old Fernando socked Cedric the new cook in the nose on account of some missing minute steaks. Cedric lifted an eyebrow at an inopportune time; and then it didn't matter who had really been stealing and who had not, Fernando had to be fired for punching.

Which was why he put a curse on the restaurant—sort of like the curse on the house of Atreus, Callie said, except that theirs was a house of pancakes; and hopefully nobody was going to get murdered in the bathroom like poor Agamemnon, who worked so much harder than that Aegisthus ever did. Still everyone was upset for a good long time. There was something in Fernando's voice, hoarse and crazed and serious, that made them wish they still believed in Buddha, or God, or Guan Yin—someone. They would have liked to have burned some money, left some fruit, lit some candles.

Instead they took refuge in the register. *Wha—inng!* They never completely forgot Fernando, or the unnatural strength of the outraged. But in time, it made them appreciate all the more what came quietly together for them. For ever since Helen started helping, the fact has remained: On those light-as-air stacks, the Changs did rebuild their lives.

Nowadays: They don't really have much to complain about, the girls. Except, well, that the pancake house isn't the greatest place for the lovelorn, especially on Saturday nights, when people you know are always coming in with other people you know. Mona dishes them up some extra-big scoops of ice cream, then goes to find herself some side work—unlike Callie, who won't come out of the back at all. She says she doesn't see why they should be working in the family restaurant when everybody else is out going to concerts to begin with. She says it isn't normal, and that she's sick of being Chinese. And with that, she plops herself on their father's red recliner and puts her feet up, as if officially taking a break from it—for which Mona can't blame her. She knows what Callie means, after all, even though neither one of them would ever say so to anybody but themselves.

It's not just the restaurant. It's not just the fact that they have a real brick wall blocking off their lawn. It's everything. For example, if one of them gets their father a bowl of rice before he asks for it, everyone approves. *She knows her father's mind,* say the parents. But if they know their own minds instead, watch out. And no one in their family is allowed to prefer not to eat something. If someone makes a face at, say, the fish, she has to eat the whole thing while everyone else watches.

Plus their father pushed their mother out the window once, and their bathroom doors don't close all the way, and the parents never wash the car. In fact, Mona had never even noticed that other cars got washed until someone wrote in big letters on the side of the Rambler: WASH ME! Now the girls do the car every single week.

Callie would sooner die than have anybody catch her in the dining room. But Mona figures everyone already knows the part about their being abnormal; waiting table isn't going to make any difference. However, Valentine's Day is hard, it's true. It makes Mona weepy to do the doilies and cherubim for the window. Do they have Cupid in Japan? And what about heart-shaped boxes, and funny little rhymes involving thees and thines; and what about long-stem red roses? Something about the long stems seems particularly un-Japanese to her, even though she realizes that to imagine everything in Japan to be short, like the people, is a type of thinking likely to result in low SATs.

Autumn: By this time, Mona has turned sixteen and gotten her learner's permit. This enables her to crash the car into the garage door the very same day that Barbara Gugelstein marches into the pancake house and announces that she's Jewish.

"Oh, really," Mona says, sharp-minded and quick. "Now, this is news. And what were you before?"

Barbara does not answer. Instead she takes out something from her pocket and begins to blow. This is not a harmonica, which would be bad enough. This is something more like a pipe crossed with a fire alarm—operating, it seems, on the principle of naked harassment. Customers spring up. Manny the salad boy glides forth from the kitchen like the priest he almost was; ever so effortlessly, he emanates a composure that spells crisis. Cooks Cedric and Alfred crane their necks behind him.

Mona, a bit sprung herself, says, "Barbara! Whaddayadoing?"

"Ancient Jewish music custom." Barbara starts to let loose another blast.

"Bar-*bra*," Mona pleads. "Most honorable friend."

"Please to give up on old jokes."

"So sorry," Mona says. "I just would fain see so good a personage start forsooth to toot her own horn."

Barbara laughs, tossing her hair.

"Nu?"

"A ram's horn," Barbara says. "It's for making new beginnings." She honks one more time. "Which I am now doing and which you should do too."

"Okay," Mona says. "Uncle. From today on, you are going to be Jewish. So, fine. But what do you want—that I should be Jewish too?"

Barbara laughs and tosses her hair again; it's the sort of instant replay that makes you realize something important must be happening.

And sure enough, next thing you know, they have embarked on a new chapter of their lives.

# CHAPTER 3

# The New Chapter

Religion? Confirmation? In this anti-establishment age? Mona got confirmed in the Catholic Church, but she did it the way you were supposed to, which is to say with a certain big roll of the eyeballs. How can the classmates be discussing whether G-d is good or just neutral, and whether Judaism is a religion or a culture? Yet they are. Also they talk about what it means to be Jewish, which so far as they've been able to tell mostly seems to be about remembering that you are. Naturally, if you asked a rabbi, there's a lot more to it. But asking Barbara Gugelstein, the message comes back, *Don't forget, don't forget.* Mona tries to imagine what it would be like to forget she's Chinese, which is easy and hard. It is easy because by her lonesome she in fact often does. Out in the world of other people, though, Mona has people like Miss Feeble to keep the subject shiny. So here's the question: Does the fact that Mona remembers all too well who she is make her more Jewish than, say, Barbara Gugelstein?

A most interesting inquiry, especially since before you can say matzoh ball, Mona too is turning Jewish. It happens this way: Barbara gets her driver's license. Her parents buy her a VW van, despite their opinion of the Germans. And pretty soon Mona's tagged along to so many temple car washes and food drives, not to say weekend conclavettes, that she's been named official mascot of the Temple Youth Group. There she is, helping build the sukkah for Sukkoth—knotting up the corners, arranging the roof boughs so as to avoid overt danger to human life and limb. She's even helped give tours to some of the Youth Group members' parents, who have never seen a sukkah before, and want to know what it means. They poke at the shaky walls from the outside. Mona explains edifyingly how the gaps in the roof appear due to faulty construction, but in fact afford a view of the sky symbolic of the desire to live spitting distance from G-d.

"Come Yom Kippur, those kids are going to be swinging chickens around their heads," mutters one, but Mona reassures him.

"How orthodox can they be?" she says. "After all, here I am."

The man works his sinuses as if he is in an Excedrin ad. He slides thumb and forefinger down his nose; he raises his bleary gaze. "Don't you have a home?"

"I do."

"Then what are you doing here?"

Trusty Barbara Gugelstein, rising to Mona's defense, says, "This is her home, you turkey."

"That's right!" chime in some other kids. "You tell him!"

"What?" says the man. "You live here?"

"I guess you could call it my home away from home," Mona says.

"I get it. It's your vacation place. Some people go to Palm Beach, you come here."

Mona shrugs. "Why spend the airfare?"

The man laughs and leaves. But two days later, Mona's still chewing the cud of this conversation. A stranger in a strange land, that's her, she concludes after two more days of rumination. Finally she approaches Rabbi Horowitz, who turns out to be less easygoing than he seems. He looks like a Hasid turned rock star, what with his long black hair and his untrimmed beard, and he doesn't mind being called Rabbi H., or the Big R.H., or even Rabbit H. He is young enough to sit cross-legged; he listens to Crosby, Stills and Nash; he plays the harmonica. He doesn't insist that anyone learn Hebrew, much as he'd like to encourage it. But when it comes to a sixteen-year-old choosing her own faith, what he professes to hear is mainly the reaction of other people. That of her parents, for example. Is she sure she doesn't want to see a school counselor? Rabbi Horowitz connects up his thick flat brows, so that they look just like the road by which one thing leads to another. He worries about her parish priest, who happens to play shortstop in their Batters of Conscience League (their cheer: *Holy Homers!*), and also about the temple board of directors. With the board it seems he is not so popular already, being anti-Vietnam, and also pro things like letting the kids wear what they want at confirmation, including bare feet.

"To tell you the truth, I'm not so sure I'll even be here next year," he finishes, cracking his knuckles.

Isn't that all the less to keep him from helping her?

"Also," he says—and by the way he clears his throat, Mona can tell that he is coming up on his real point—"I have to wonder, excuse me, how serious is this wish."

"You mean, whether this isn't my just wanting to be like my friends?"

"Like your friends, and also, an important factor at your time of life, unlike your parents."

Behind the rabbi's shoulder hangs a full-size human skeleton, with a fedora hat and necktie—something of which his parents would undoubtably approve. Mona does not point this out. Instead she says, "You mean, is this adolescent rebellion? Maybe. But also I like it here at the temple. I like it that you tell everyone to ask, ask, instead of just obey, obey. I like it that people are supposed to be their own rabbi, and do their business directly with G-d. I like it that they're supposed to take charge of their own religion, and that they even get to be general-rabbi-for-a-day when they get bar and bas mitzvahed. In the Catholic church, you know, you're always keeping to your place and talking to God through helpers. I like it that you tell people to make a pain in the neck of themselves."

"Who told you to make a pain in the neck of yourself?"

"Brian Levi." This is the TYG adviser. "And I don't mean to sound conceited, but I figure I'm a natural at that."

"At making a pain in the neck of yourself?"

Mona smiles sweetly.

Rabbi Horowitz's eyebrows come far enough apart for Mona to see what nice laugh lines he has. He wheels back in his chair, rattling Mr. Bones. "Brian is speaking for some Jews," he says. "Other Jews think you should study your whole life before you should dare to make a challenge. Sure you can talk to G-d yourself, and how can you learn if you don't ask questions? But without study, what are you? An ignoramus."

"I am!" agrees Mona. "Although I practically celebrate the High Holy Days already, and know that hamantaschen are supposed to represent the hat of that What's-his-name, may he roast in hell, Haman." As is proper, Mona stamps her feet to drown out the name of the infidel.

Rabbi Horowitz laughs aloud. "There's more to Judaism than that," he says, and the studying begins. Mona finds out for starters that God revealed the Torah in seventy languages (including Chinese), so that everybody could understand it; it just so happened that only the Jews read it through. Also that in Roman times, the Jews did lots of proselytizing. If she'd lived then, she could've probably just signed right up to be a fellow sufferer. But sign 'n' pray went out with the toga. Now the idea seems to be to discourage prospectives three times in theory—in practice, as much as is practical. Rabbi Horowitz assigns so many books that Mona feels like she started on a mud bath, only to end up on a mud swim.

Still she slogs through. A lot she knows already. All about the holidays, for example, and what is a mitzvah—namely a good deed. Also what is rachmones, namely a type of mercy every human should extend to others but sometimes doesn't. That part is easy and fun. It's like watching a home movie, you get that little shiver of recognition. Aha! So that's why they light eight lights at Hanukkah, and not seven or nine. Then there are new parts Mona likes—all the big ancient stories of blood and gore and guile. Rabbi Horowitz makes her glad she never had to put up with those stiffs the Egyptians—what do you expect from people who wore so much eye makeup—or wander around the desert for forty years. She feels concerned for those ten lost tribes of Israel. She wishes she'd been around for the liberation by the Persians and the era of the Great Prophets. She likes debating like a Pharisee faced with a stick-in-the-mud Sadducee. She likes looking at maps, especially now that she's finally getting her real driver's license. What a down-to-earth religion this is! It's not like Catholicism, with people electing to get crucified upside down, as if right side up wasn't bad enough. The whole purpose of Judaism seems to be to avoid these things when possible. And why should rabbis be celibate? It does seem more natural to let them dutifully procreate, that instead of manning their seminal gates, they might sprinkle the earth with useful ideas. Things they can do about the world, for example. How they can help, how they can fix, how they can contribute and illuminate; and how they can stay, forever and ever, Jews.

The last subject is one on which Mona could use a *Guide to the Perplexed*—it's okay to turn into a Jew, but not to turn out of one?—and even harder to take in is not only the Holocaust, but the whole endless history that spirals up to it like a staircase in a nightmare. It winds on and on, a torchlit, hellish thing, bristling with caesars and czars; there's a lot to contemplate about the nature of this sweet world and most noble humanity. Do her happy friends in Scarshill with their patios and lounge chairs really live at the mouth of a stone age tunnel? It was hard to make out at first, but now she can see it plain, their own express lane down the centuries.

It makes her want to dig in her heels and extend them a steadying hand, though in fact, they're more likely to steady her. For while Callie and Mona know what it's like to have rocks thrown at them, this kind of welcome is for their family a novelty. Their group hasn't always been the oppressed. They used to be the oppressors; and that makes them, as a minority, rank amateurs. The Changs don't have their friends' instincts, or reflexes. They don't have their ready alert. They don't have their friends' institutions, or their ways of reminding themselves who they are, that they might not be lulled by a day in the sun. Prescriptions and rituals, holidays and recipes, songs. The Jews have books, they have games, they have tchotchkes. They have catalogs. And soon, G-d willing, so will Mona.

In the meantime, she is not the only one starting anew. Callie is being allowed to go to college, even though Helen found out over the summer that Callie's roommate was named Naomi, which she thought might be a black name. Not, of course, that Helen and Ralph had anything against blacks. In fact, they had a lot of blacks working for them at the restaurant. For example, Alfred the number-two cook. But seeing as how they happened to know someone who had a friend who had a daughter also going to Harvard, they couldn't help but wonder why this nice Chinese girl and Callie couldn't room together. This nice Chinese girl had a roommate too, Helen pointed out. Why couldn't this nice Chinese girl's roommate room with this Naomi? Helen said that she also knew somebody who knew somebody who worked in the financial aid office; maybe she could arrange something. And there was someone who knew someone who knew someone who worked at the Faculty Club. That's where all the professors have lunch, said Helen. Even the president himself eats there.

"Mom, those people can't do anything," argued weary Callie, sewing on name tags. "Especially since there's nothing the matter with a roommate turning out to be black. And anyway, the last thing I want to do is room with some nice Chinese wonk who's going to study all the time."

To which Helen managed to answer both "Not everyone Chinese studies all the time, that's *stereotype*" and "It would be good for you to study all the time with your roommate. Study together is nice."

Now it turns out that Naomi is indeed brownish black as the most serious-looking spines of her considerable personal library. Naomi works on her shelving system; the parents leave Callie to assist. How diligent this Naomi! And how well she speaks English!

The parents appear relaxed. On the way home, though, Mona notices that the car seems unexpectedly empty, a regular rattletrap, even though it is loaded full of Callie's boxes (which she personally collected from dumpsters all over the county). And when they get home, Mona discovers another unexpected thing: that she has her parents all to herself. This is not something she had counted on. In fact, Mona had rather expected they would think of nothing but Callie, their daughter at Harvard. Instead it is as if Mona is suddenly famous, the most interesting person in the room, every day, all day, even when she's asleep. If she goes out, it's only to be replaced by her palpable absence. *Where's Mona? How long has she been gone for? What time is she coming back home?*

Once, when Mona's ballet class was doing *Swan Lake*, her teacher gathered all the young cygnets around her. She described how Anna Pavlova beat her arms, and elongated her neck, just exactly like a real swan, though of course Pavlova never hissed, or bit anyone. And then this teacher described the effect all this beating and elongating had on the audience: *It stirred them,* she said, pulling up her leg warmers. (She knit these herself, with a pattern she copied out for her students for free.) It stirred them so much that the day Pavlova died, nobody could bear the thought of an understudy. Of course, this class would still have understudies, in case somebody got the hiccups, or the mumps, or something. But when Anna Pavlova died, the show went on without anyone. The light was moved around just as if she were there, and the audience pictured her in its mind's eye—pictured her beating her arms and elongating her neck.

And now, as with Anna, so with Mona. Truly: she could up and expire, and her parents would still be moving the beam around. Imagining where she would be if she were there, and in what fine fashion she would flap. This makes it hard to work on turning Jewish. If only Callie would come home! So Mona wishes, most ardently.

Until, all too soon, Callie does.

Thanksgiving already. At temple, Mona has begun to consider with Rabbit H. the holidays, and how very much she unfortunately likes the family Christmas tree. Not that they have always had the tasteful real Scotch pine they have now, with the fresh woodsy scent and the tendency to drip real pitch on the living room carpet. Before they moved, they used to unpack their tree out of a box, and sort out the silvery limbs by size, and poke them into little coded holes in the tree trunk. They had a revolving colored light to shine on it, so that it would turn blue, then red, then yellow, then green, and there was a Styrofoam tree skirt too, all sprinkled with glitter that used to fall off. New Year's Day meant having to vacuum that glitter up. But the Changs liked that tree and its rituals, or at least Mona did—even the vacuuming. If you asked her, she'd have to say that she's only just gotten used to the idea that they now have a new kind of tree, with a fabric skirt—the kind of skirt that matches the kind of people who say, as they do now, "fridge" for "icebox," and "wastebasket" for "garbage." That's to say that it's hard to contemplate moving on—already!—from a basic change of tree to no tree at all.

Yet that seems a distinct possibility, not just because of her conversations with Rabbi Horowitz, but also because of Callie. Is this what it means to be sisters, to come up with the exact same idea, only for opposite reasons?

When Callie first comes home, all's simple hilarity. Callie has changed her hair; she hadn't meant to go so short, but her roommate Naomi was doing the cutting, and though she started at Callie's waist, she ended up above her shoulders. This makes Callie, by the standards of the day, practically bald. But Callie doesn't care. She says at least all her split ends are gone. (Plus it makes her cheekbones stick out, and her lips look swollen up as if they maybe got bit by a bug.) She and Mona and Helen stay up past their bedtimes, way later than they ever have before, giggling on Callie's bed. Helen has her slippers on the wrong feet, and is sitting cross-legged with one of her pajama buttons undone; Mona tells dirty jokes and even Helen laughs, covering her mouth with her hand. They discover that all three of them know what is a diaphragm, even though each of them thought the others couldn't possibly, and only Callie knows how to spell it. With a *g*, she says; they can look it up in a dictionary if they don't believe her. And so they do. A silent *g*! It's almost enough to make Mona want to go to Harvard too, to learn such things. Never mind that Callie insists she didn't learn this at Harvard and wishes Mona would stop saying that. Especially since she isn't even going to Harvard, she's going to Harvard-Radcliffe, and anyway she learned how to spell *diaphragm* from reading *Goodbye, Columbus*. A serious book, she maintains, although under questioning she admits that she originally only read it because the movie version was being filmed over at the high school. And because it had a diaphragm in it.

It is ascertained that for all concerned, a knowledge of reproductive technology is theoretical. The topic swerves to Ping-Pong diplomacy, and how mainland China can join the U.N. when it is not even a proper country but a bunch of leather-eating peasants. "You mean like belts?" Mona asks. "You mean like shoes?" Helen nods. Mona wants to know if they cook them first, and how. With soy sauce? With ginger? "That was only on the Long March," says Callie. "Those Communists eat rats too," says Helen, "and what do you call—you know, on the head? Lice." The night goes on. Did So-and-so really hitchhike all the way to Chicago, just to find So-and-so had completely given up baking? Does So-and-so really bleach her underarms?

The next day, turkey. As a surprise, Ralph has arranged for the head waitress to come serve the meal. Magdalena has had a fight with her family and has nowhere to go, he says. He offered for her to just come and eat, but she insisted she'd rather help out. So what could he say? Of course, he knew from the beginning that she would offer something like this. He claims the real reason he made the offer was so that Helen wouldn't have to run around like crazy the way she usually does.

But Helen knows a gift horse when it kicks her. "Your father just like to act like big shot. He thinks this is China."

A familiar complaint. In fact, one of the lilting refrains of their melodious lives. Sometimes it seems like no one even has to sing;

everyone can hear how annoying it is that Ralph should treat the help like far-flung family—buying them glasses and dentures and shoes, but also expecting them to run errands, or help fix the furnace at home. In general, he is getting better. He is learning to say, *That's your problem.* Also to expect people to say it to him. But from time to time he suffers relapses, and now what to do? Send Magdalena home?

"I always thought you like to sit there, doing nothing, instead of run around, do this, do that," Ralph says, cleaning out his ears. (Though they stick out, he still has to pull at them to get a good angle.) "Act like lady. Join some country club. I thought you sick and tired of work in the restaurant all day, then come home and work again."

"What did you say?" Helen is so stunned by this acknowledgment of her efforts that it seems she needs to clean her ears out too. "You hear that?" She addresses Mona and Callie. "Your father actually noticed that someone works at the restaurant and then comes home and works some more. All these years he acts like the food we eat comes from heaven, but actually he has his big eyes open all the time."

"Of course, I see everything," says Ralph, bugging his eyes first at Mona and then at Callie. They laugh. "And that's why this Thanksgiving, our nice waitress Magdalena coming here to help." He winks and grins, triumphant, only to have Helen set aside her hurt with breathtaking speed.

*"This is the U.S. of A.!"* she says. "Who has a waitress come to serve at Thanksgiving? Who?" She appeals again to the girls. They shrug obligingly.

But in the end, she doesn't want to fight in front of Magdalena, or to spoil Callie's first visit home, or even to show Ralph up. (It's bad enough the pancake house only started running in the black with her help.) Plus she feels sorry for Magdalena.

And so Magdalena swoops around. She sets Ralph's and Helen's plates down gently in front of them. However, Mona's and Callie's she sends skating down the wood-tone table, the way she would at the restaurant. What a champion she would be at horseshoes! The plates stop just in front of the girls; everyone claps.

She murmurs modestly, in her husky staccato, "I practice every day." She rolls some more *r*'s on request. Then she sits down with the family to eat. Troubles or no, she is sweetly flamboyant, thick-scented as a gardenia farm. Her long hair coils like a black and white snake on her head; she applies makeup with the feathery restraint of a diva. Still, in small things she attends to nicety. For instance, she expresses polite amazement that they stuff the turkey with stir-fried rice stuffing; also that Ralph carves the turkey with a knife and chopsticks.

"Is that your Chinese tradition?" she asks.

Ralph nods gravely. "This is the Chinese tradition when we cannot find the big fork."

No sooner have they sent Magdalena home, though, than the subject of Christmas shopping comes up. This spurs Callie to announce that she doesn't think they should have a tree anymore.

"Naomi says it's a symbol of oppression."

Helen nods amiably. "Did Naomi go home see her family too?"

"Naomi says Christmas trees aren't indigenous to China." Callie says this with an insistence that is rare for her; she is not exactly the type to steer the conversation like a grocery cart. Even Helen has remarked how, though Mona and Callie have identical voices on the phone, you can easily tell who's who once the conversation gets going. If it twists and turns, it's Mona. Callie does not exactly hold forth.

Or at least she didn't use to. Now that she's at practically Harvard, though, she seems to have points to make, ideas to advance, albeit with more doggedness than bravura.

"Indigenous means what?" says Helen.

Callie thinks. "Natural."

"Native," Mona supplies. "I had that on the PSATs, and *natural* wasn't even one of the choices."

"Native." Helen mulls it over.

"Native means what?" asks Ralph, cutting the crust off his second piece of pie.

"Guess," Mona says.

"A kind of Indian people?"

While Helen translates for Ralph, Callie whispers to Mona, annoyed, "I was just trying to define it in a way they would get." Ralph nods; Callie goes on. "Naomi says we should hate them just as much as you hate Panasonic radios. She says you probably didn't have Christmas trees, growing up, why should you have one now? She says we should stick to our guns, like the Jews."

Mona pretends to be choking on her whipped cream.

"But we did have Christmas tree, growing up," says Helen evenly, one hand in her lap. "Every year. Not so a big tree as we have here, but still, we had it. Shanghai, you know, is a big city, we have everything. You know what we eat every morning in Shanghai? Bagels."

"Bagels!" Mona says.

Helen says the bakery used to string them together by the holes the way that people once used to string money. That was a long time ago, she says, when coins had little square holes in the middle.

"It was just because you went to a convent school that you had a tree." Callie is so busy talking that she hasn't eaten one bite of dessert. "The question is why you were going to a convent school to begin with."

"It was run by missionaries," says Helen. "French missionaries. Oh! We played a lot of tricks on them. I remember one nun especially, we used to call her Boat Feet, and when she came down the hall—"

"They were imperialists," says Callie, still not eating. "That's what Naomi says. They were bent on taking over China and saving the heathen. But you weren't heathen. You were civilized."

"Of course we were civilized," says Helen. "Chinese people invented paper. Chinese people invented ink, and gunpowder. We were wearing silk gowns with embroidery before the barbarians even thought maybe they should take a bath, get rid of their smell."

"But is that what the missionaries thought?"

"Oh, the missionaries just wanted to teach us some nice songs in French, and to tell us what nice food they eat in France. Especially they have nice pastries. The Chinese, you know, don't think so much about dessert." Helen looks at Callie, as if to reinforce her point.

"And to convert you, right?"

"Of course," says Helen. "But we don't mind."

"You didn't mind?" So nonplussed is Callie that she picks up her fork by accident. "But didn't you use to be Buddhist?"

"Oh, well, we are still Buddhist after we are baptized," explains Helen. "We are Buddhist, and Taoist, and Catholic. We do however we want." She maintains that her family liked having a Christmas tree, and that it was fun, and that it had nothing to do with oppression. Callie finally eats. Still she insists later that she will have nothing to do with the tree this year. Also she says that in the spring she's going to drop French so that she can take Chinese instead.

Everyone laughs.


Mona expects that when Rabbi Horowitz hears she is in charge of the family Christmas tree, he will tell her that her days as a prospective convert are up. Instead he gives her the kind of nod you associate with deeply significant moments in the movies—column A but column B moments, Mona calls these. In this case, disappointed but understanding.

"It's like an election. Some votes you win, some votes you lose. You're all right so long as you've got more on your side than the other," he says, straightening a pile of books. "Also you must realize that these days a lot of Jews have trees. It's not kosher, but that's the way it is. If they don't have a tree, they have a bush, and at the top they put the Star of David. And for you, please understand there's a lesson in this."

"What kind of lesson?" says Mona.

"The lesson of a lifetime." He gestures at his book-lined study. "What you're discovering is that it's not so easy to become Jewish. As, excuse me, I believe I tried to tell you. You can read and study, study and read, but still it will probably take you your whole life."

"My whole life?" Mona gulps.

And all over Christmas break, while everyone else is eating and opening and trying on and exchanging for credit or cash (including Callie the anti-imperialist), this is what Mona is pondering. Does she want to be converting for the rest of her life, Amen? New Year's Day, she drags around with such a heavy heart that when it comes time to take down the tree, Callie offers to help—also taking this opportunity to comment on how bushy the tree was this year. And why did Mona insist on getting a new star for the top when the old one worked fine?

For a resolution, Mona considers giving up converting. It seems against the spirit of New Year's—who resolves to strive less?—but so what. Rabbi Horowitz is right. Kosher is great, but nonkosher is the way things sometimes happen to be.

Just when she is ready to break the news to him, though, he naturally enough decides he's impressed enough; it's time to order her to her optional mikvah. And so it is that on a melty January morning, Barbara and Mona drive over to the bath. This happens right after Mona's real license arrives in the mail, so that Mona is for her inaugural celebratory spin able to drive herself and Barbara through the fresh-fallen slush to the ceremony—which, it turns out, is not unlike getting baptized by John the Baptist, except with chlorine. It's not so easy to get her hair to submerge; Mona is called upon to employ her best sinking skills. But finally, success. Through a sheet, three witnesses listen solemnly to the dunk. She chants her Shema Israel. She burns her special four-stranded candle. Her three witnesses sign neatly her nice framable certificate. And in this way, she becomes Mona-also-known-as-Ruth, a more or less genuine Catholic Chinese Jew.

Maybe there are people who do not accept her, as Rabbi Horowitz has warned. Also it is tricky to be a solo Jew with no family. Still, it is a promotion to be no longer a mascot. The TYG throws a shindig in her honor; Mona attends happily a host of seminars, slide shows, art exhibits. For orphans she makes caterpillars out of knee socks; for the elderly she makes draft dodgers, also out of knee socks.

The only problem is that she has been unable to break the news to her family. And so it is that when Helen finds out, it is from Saint Callie at Practically Harvard, who you'd think would have better things to talk about. Like what she thinks about the coed bathrooms now that the novelty's worn off, and whether there really is a pool where everybody swims naked. Or what about a recap of how Harvard plays football against Yale every year? Callie told them that already, but Mona knows there were details she left out—for example, how everybody has to sit on concrete to watch, except people who are smart and bring pads. This might not be conversation for everybody. However, her parents, Mona knows, would be captivated.

Instead Callie has to go passing on some high school gossip she heard from somebody who knows somebody who knows somebody.

"Callie told us some surprise." So neatly does Helen fold up her Chinese newspaper, you would think she was planning to return it to the newsstand for credit. "She said you weren't going to tell us. She said you were going to keep it a secret. She said you did it behind our back."

"I guess I forgot to mention it," Mona says.

"Don't tell me that. That's . . . that's . . ." On the wall, the cuckoo clock ticks louder than normal. "That's *crap*."

"Ma! That's no way to talk." Mona wags her finger, expecting her mom to smile.

But Helen looks as though she's about to start crying. Her eyes redden; her face whitens. If she put a carrot on her nose, she would look just like the snowman that happens to adorn her at-home sweater. "A lot of crap!" She takes a drink of her tea. "Who do you think you are, you can lie to your mother like that?"

Mona looks down, penitent.

Helen goes on with a delicate bang of her cup. "You are daughter. *Daughter.* Do you remember what is a daughter?"

"I remember."

"Who are you?"

"I'm your daughter."

It's like being in church, right down to the moment of silence— which Mona takes to be a chance for Helen to turn misty-eyed again, that Mona might feel what a Disappointment she is. Helen swishes around some tea in her mouth, a good sign. Mona makes a gorilla face, and out of habit, her mother almost makes a face back. But in the midst of furrowing her brow, she suddenly starts talking.

"We agree, except what kind of daughter lies to her mother?"

"No kind."

"I have no daughter."

"What about Callie?" Mona means to be comforting.

Helen claps the lid on her teacup. "You know, you bring shame on our family, you act this way. What do you think people think of us?"

Mona contemplates the kitchen table.

"People talk, how do you think I feel? You have no consideration for others. You have no consideration for how other people feel."

Above Helen, the hour is struck. The clock door swings open, but what you see in place of the long-broken cuckoo bird is (courtesy of Callie) a glued-on Statue of Liberty pencil sharpener. *Cuckoo!* this cries. *Cuckoo! Cuckoo!*

Mona shrugs.

"Wiggle your shoulders is not a way to talk. How can you be Jewish? Chinese people don't do such things."

"They don't?" Mona asks this in her smallest, meekest voice—just wanting by this point to say the right thing, the thing that will make Helen look hurt again. Then Mona can feel ashamed, and they can make up, and Mona will be her mother's favorite once more. But what is that thing? Mona thinks and thinks. Still the right thing will not come to her—which must be why she abruptly gives up and says the opposite of what she should. As the Statue of Liberty pencil sharpener retreats, Mona says in her school voice, as if she's talking to Miss Feeble, "I guess I must not be Chinese, then."

"What do you mean, not Chinese?"

And from there on in, they are stuck in the land of words, until they are no longer speaking to each other and are forced onward to the land of deeds.

There was a time when Helen made this trip quietly, if at all. How demure she was! It was Ralph who barreled through life, crackerjack active. But since then they've switched positions, one fading back right when the other came forward, the way the day bird replaced the night bird, back when there were birds in the cuckoo clock. For Helen was so mad when she realized Ralph couldn't take care of her—wasn't that what a husband was for?—that she had what amounted to a personality transformation. She'd gotten used to the idea of helping, of working hard, even of going out of the house to work. But she'd never adjusted to the idea of becoming a main pillar of the family, standing there all by herself like the kind of ruin people went to Greece to see. In a way, she was proud of what she'd learned to do. But in another way, this so wasn't what she'd counted on, growing up in China, that if you pointed out how energizing was her fury, she'd probably give you a nice maternal whack such as would excuse you from gym for a month. Mona knows this because Helen's done it to Callie from time to time—not meaning to, of course. And of course, it's not as if she hasn't been whacked herself. In fact, Ralph can be credited with pioneering the whole tradition.

But whereas he has given up that sort of thing in practice, Helen has given it up in principle. So that in a way, Mona is getting off easy when Helen confiscates her Hebrew dictionary, and her menorah, as well as the mezuzah Barbara made for her out of some parchment and an avocado-green toothbrush holder. She says something about having Ralph take her door down.

Ralph, though, first wants to get the facts straight. He sits Mona down at the kitchen table when he comes home; he turns on all the lights, as if to help him see better. His face is soft with worry, and he has mysteriously equipped himself with a pad of paper, a mechanical pencil, and a slide rule. Also the soles of his feet are planted on the floor, in position to lever him forward. *How do you get this idea? When is the first time you go with your friend? Who is the driver?* She tells him everything—what the traffic was like, what the weather report was, how they had trouble parking. He listens as if he is hoping to discover a clue to her—as if he hopes to find out that one morning Mona ate something fishy, only to come down with this idea in the afternoon.

Of course, he hasn't always been like this, so methodical. It is how he learned to be as a result of his impulsive youth. *Things are not always how they look,* he likes to say now, and *Watch out before you leap.* Has somebody tricked her into turning Jewish? He himself has been tricked, he says, with a slight averting of his face; and Mona knows, naturally, that here he is referring to the disaster that was the chicken palace. Still Mona says, "You? Really?" as if there was no one in the world she could imagine less trickable—which is true in a way. These days he turns every stone, he thinks of all the angles. *In back every wise man is fool,* he likes to say, although he is also quick to point out that not every fool becomes a wise man, and also that it is not easy to tell the fools from the wise men. *For the really wise men, they like to look as if they are fools.* He nods to himself, and with this chestnut, switches the lights back off.

Only to have another light turn on, illuminating the slight crevasse between him and Helen. Is there an icy split between every two people in the world? Anyway, this one is blue and wide and deep, and cold enough, Mona's sure, to freeze a child or two to death, though thankfully there are ways of skipping right over it. It's just a matter of watching where you put your feet, and keeping a certain spring to your step, and figuring a crack's a crack. Helen has to care extra about everything, for example, because he doesn't keep up his end. To wit: He does not even care who really suffered and who didn't. To him, everyone's suffered. To talk about it is just a matter of sitting one person on a little higher branch than another, and what are people doing up in a tree to begin with? He says this with his Ancient Wisdom voice, which to Helen is the voice of someone who isn't even trying anymore. In her opinion, all he does is philosophize—he might as well be a hippie. She thinks that if it weren't for her, who knows, he would probably stop taking baths, which of course matters, seeing as it separates people from rhinoceroses and hippopotamuses and other low-standard animals who consider mud wallowing a proper way of life.

What surprise then that according to Ralph, this whole affair with Mona's converting is nothing to flip your lid over; whereas to Helen it takes absolute top place in an entire escalating series of incomprehensible and distinctly menacing developments, such as Mona's buying a down jacket, and her wanting not only her own car, which she can forget about, but her own telephone line. (Which she can forget about as well.) There is no use in talking to Helen about rachmones, or about her converting too, never mind the act of remembering, which Rabbi Horowitz calls the doorway to wisdom. There is no use in reminding her that Mona is her favorite child, and that she, Helen Chang, likes a lot of American things herself.

For if you asked her, she would say that she signed up for her own house and garage, but not for her children to become big-mouthed separate accounting units, and what is the matter with a regular coat with a nice interlining such as she has worn her whole life? "There's nothing warmer than down," Mona tries to tell her, but all Helen hears is what she wants to ask next—namely, why should Mona need her own telephone line? "So you won't eavesdrop," Mona says. To this Barbara Gugelstein's mother certainly would have said, "I don't eavesdrop," even if Barbara could hear her munching potato chips as she listened in. Once she even broke into the conversation to give some advice; she couldn't resist. Helen, on the other hand, said, "If I like to know what my daughter is up to, I don't see what's wrong about it." It all has to do with the Chinese way versus everyone else's way, as Mona sees it, but Helen doesn't even agree with her on that. "I think I'm very Westernized. I brought you children up without you even speak Chinese." Helen points out that some of her friends make their children all sit together around a big table at night, and study. They work out problems together, and none of them puts the stereo on loud; in fact, they don't even own records. Mark and Carole Louie's kids, for example, have no idea who is Jimi Hendrix. Which sounds like a path to a National Merit Scholarship, except that one of the boys set the curtains on fire, and another one got in trouble for climbing the water tower and throwing rocks from the top. It wasn't a lot of rocks—after all, he had to carry them up in his pockets. But he got a JD card for it just the same. "The way they live is too difficult for the children," Helen said when she heard. "The parents should be like bamboo, bend in the wind. Not stand there stiff, like a telephone pole."

"That's right," Mona says now, during yet another discussion of her religious freedom. "You are the one who brought us up to speak English. You said you would bend like bamboo instead of acting like you were planted by Bell Telephone. You said we weren't pure Chinese anymore, the parents had to accept we would be something else."

"American, not Jewish." Helen assigns Mona a piece of pork to slice while she herself cleans the fish, and it calms them both down to see what a nice job Mona can still do—thin, and across the grain. (Lucky for them, Mona is the reformed kind of Jew that does not observe the many rules regarding fins and hoofs, mollusks and ruminants.)

"Jewish is American," Mona says. "American means being whatever you want, and I happened to pick being Jewish."

"Since when do children pick this, pick that? You tell me. Children are supposed to listen to their parents. Otherwise, the world becomes crazy. Who knows? Tomorrow you'll come home and tell me you want to be black."

"How can I turn black? That's a race, not a religion." (Mona says this even though she knows some kids studying to be Bobby Seale. They call each other brother, and eat soul food instead of subs, and wear their hair in the baddest Afros they can manage.)

"And after that you are going to come home and tell me you want to be a boy instead of a girl."

"Blood, Mom," points out Mona.

Helen glances up at the cuckoo clock as she crooks a knife-nicked finger; she runs it under the faucet while starting to stir-fry the pork with her other hand. After the pork, there is still the fish and also some spinach to do, and then it's time to get back to the pancake house. Behind her, the space heater flares up in ominous fashion. The kitchen used to be the warmest room in the house, but recently they had to turn the radiator off because of a leaking valve. "And after that you are going to come home and tell me you want to be a tree."

"Whoever heard of someone turning into a tree?" Mona tactfully refrains from bringing up this poet Ovid her English class is reading, never mind that he didn't write in English. Instead, she gets her mom a Band-Aid. She goes to sleep thinking that they have had a heart-to-heart communication such as leads to true intergenerational understanding and tolerance.

The next morning, however, Mona discovers her new down jacket outside on the milk box. This is after some searching that Mona finds it, and with some surprise. Did Helen really put it out there to freeze all night? Mad as Helen's been of late, Mona still can't imagine her doing such a thing; and later she finds out that it was in a way her father's idea. If Helen was so upset, he said, why didn't she just throw the jacket out? (That's Ralph for you, always a proponent of the concrete solution.) Except it wasn't so simple, in the end. Outside was dark and cold, and Helen didn't feel like going all the way to the garbage cans.

Now Mona has unmasked her treachery. "How can I wear this? It's freezing."

"Nothing warmer than down," Helen quotes her.

"How could you do this?"

Mona must look really forlorn, because Helen softens. "Oh, not that big a deal, you don't have to cry," she says, and taking the jacket from her daughter, she drapes it on top of the space heater to warm. "There." She says this in a leave-it-to-mommy voice she seems to have learned from TV, even though the Changs don't have a TV. (*The idiot box,* Ralph calls it.)

"Ma," Mona says, "I don't think that's such a good idea."

But Helen is the mother, and Mona is the daughter, which means that Helen knows what is a good idea and what isn't. And so it is that they take the jacket back off the heater really at the first whiff of trouble, before too large a hole has been burnt. Still down goes exploding through the kitchen. Who could believe a couple of jacket baffles could produce such a veritable snowstorm? But it just goes to show what a good value Mona got on her jacket, that so much went into it. There are goose feathers flying everywhere. Mona and Helen have to wave their hands in front of their faces to keep from breathing them; Helen very sensibly closes the door to the dining room while Mona opens the regular window, and the storm window too. Cold air rushes in as she tries to shoo the feathers out. "A broom!" Helen cries, and so they try that. Sweeping at the air with long swings, short swings— they could be the sorcerer's apprentice, it's that effective.

Still they keep on, so that this is what they're doing when Mickey the milkman appears on the other side of the sill.

"Having a problem?" Mickey is a trim man with an ever-moist mustache they have ascribed to nasal drip; Mona stops shooing feathers in his face, for fear one might stick.

"Oh, no," Helen says, nonchalant. "Just helping my daughter with her homework."

"It's a science project," Mona says. "There's a contest at school."

"Well, good luck with it," says Mickey. "God knows, if I had any money I'd put it on you two." He walks away whistling; they hear the gate bang shut then bounce open, an old problem. They sneeze.

CHAPTER 4

# Hot Times at the Hot Line

This is Mona's theory about her parents: that Ralph thought they should live in their own little world, whereas Helen thought they should belong to society. Even she never intended that they should be a minority, though, and especially an outspoken one. Mona explains this to Rabbi Horowitz as he gravely cracks his knuckles.

"First of all, they don't like the word *minority*," Mona says. "They say they were never a minority when they were in China, why should they be a minority here."

"But there are few of them, and many of everyone else."

"That's what I said. They said they're just as good as anybody, why should they ask for help? Also they do not want to have to riot. I told them they don't have to riot if they don't want to. I told them they can just march in parades and protest. Or else, if they don't want to go outside, they can write letters, like the Jews. I told them that was one of the reasons I turned Jewish, because I thought writing letters was smarter than standing out in the freezing cold, which I knew was not for them, being from Shanghai and everything. I said I knew how much they worried about catching cold, and that I had recently discovered that they were absolutely right when they said people caught cold through their feet. For instance, when they stood on street corners for hours on that cold concrete. I told them writing letters was much warmer, and also that the kind of letters that worked best were the ones that got sent off to big shots. I thought they would like that, writing letters to big shots and not having to get their feet cold."

"But they didn't like it?"

"No. They said they grew up arranging things. Their friends arranged things for them, they arranged things for their friends."

"And what about the poor people? Who did the arranging for them?"

"Got me." Mona shrugs. "I think that's why they had to have a revolution. But my mom said before that nobody yelled. Yelling just meant you had no self-control. She said in fact people knew what other people meant without their hardly saying anything. They understood each other perfectly by what it was that wasn't said."

Rabbi Horowitz clears his throat. "Well, of course, nobody likes to yell," he says. "But your parents want to be Wasps. They are the only ones who do not have to make themselves heard. That is because they do the hearing. And how is that possible?"

"That's what I said. But my mom said it's possible. She said it's all a matter of manners. You have to know how to stand, how to sit. She said people in Shanghai knew who you were right away, you didn't have to open your mouth."

"And is that true?"

"I think you also had to wear a lot of jewelry. Anyway, I said, we are a minority, like it or not, and if you want to know how to be a minority, there's nobody better at it than the Jews. I said it's our job to ask questions now. We can't just accept everything the way they did in China. We can't just go along."

"And what did she say then?"

"She said that as soon as the Communists leave she is going to take me back to Shanghai, where I won't have so much to say."


Naturally, Helen cannot take Mona back to Shanghai; that is the good news. And so Mona continues to be Jewish. Also she takes up the guitar, which involves growing out the nails of her right hand while keeping the left ones short. Helen points out that there are many instruments that do not require asymmetrical nail-growing—for example, how about going back to the piano? Such a nice instrument after all, and you don't have to tune it yourself, a convenience. But in the fashion of the day, Mona is more interested in symbols of wayfaring than in things associated with living rooms and arm protectors and miracle-fiber carpet. How about the harmonica, Mona says, or the mandolin? She has never actually seen a mandolin, but she knows it is anti-orchestra. Helen knows this too. They move diplomatically on to sports, which Helen considers unladylike except for ice-skating and tennis. Does this explain why Mona takes up rock climbing, which she might have otherwise recognized to be, past the rope and carabiners, a form of crawling?

Over Callie's spring break, she journeys out to watch Mona at the Gunks, even though Mona is officially not speaking to her. Callie attempts to patch things up with sisterly concern.

"It just looks so dangerous," she says.

They are perched on a rocky ledge, becoming acquainted with the brevity of life. Callie puts her arm around a tree; she got her ears pierced at college and is wearing large multipart earrings that do not help her balance. Otherwise, she looks more outdoorsy than you'd expect, on account of her also having gotten herself contact lenses. These mean she can now hold her head at funny angles, not to say let her hair swing around as if she's in a hair conditioner ad. "Mom and Dad would have a canary if they knew."

"But of course they're not going to know." Mona surveys the stratosphere.

Callie answers, "Of course not."

The right answer. But then she goes on, by way of changing the topic, to sweetly wonder if that jittering Mona was doing out there on the rock face is what people call sewing-machine knee. Naturally, she is just making conversation. Mona realizes that Callie would just as soon say nothing, except that to say nothing in this case would be to emphasize how big a fight they are having. The silence might fill up with anger and explode, for instance if Mona had a chance to demand whether Callie realized what she was doing when she decided to squeal to the parents like a low-phylum invertebrate; why doesn't she just admit that she has been lusting her whole life to knock Mona off her throne? Instead Callie elects to bravely forge on in a conversational manner, never mind if it means saying the exact wrong thing. For example, How did such a crazy sport become so fashionable? And is it truly intrinsically enjoyable to clutch at nothing for hours, worrying about gravity? Her tone is full of intellectual inquiry. Mona's has the sweet sibilance of a sibling who has learned to use words but atavistically prefers teeth. She insists her interest in climbing is far more than a matter of fashion, and that she finds it spiritually satisfying to pit herself against unyielding nature. She informs Callie that she expects to be climbing as long as her skeletal and muscle groups allow, and that it is a matter of passion she would not expect a milquetoast to quite comprehend.

This is before Mona is treated to a demonstration of the pulley. One day at the Gunks, she sees a climber fall and fall until, just at the point where he's supposed to arrest and dangle, he keeps falling. His partner, meanwhile, is also in good-paced motion—going up, you might say, like there's no tomorrow.

A hunch comes to her about then that her G-d-given sport talents are better exercised at the temple than at the cliffs. She accordingly trades in her trusty climbing rope for the Youth Group hot line, thanking G-d Callie will not be home to make Ivy League observations until June. Also Mona thanks G-d that the swap has become possible—an offshoot result of confirmation class. For Rabbi Horowitz has talked so much about I-and-Thou and so on, that many people have been elevated, if not up to his level, then at least a rung or two out of the subbasement. Hitherto sacred distinctions between cool and uncool have thus lost their sanctity. They are all the chosen, or at least the as-good-as-chosen-let-us-not-split-hairs.

Barbara Gugelstein and Mona are thus, through the rigor of the special training course (with its extra-heavy rap sessions, and stress interviews, and mock emergency drills), suddenly friends with all manner of people. Some of these are eminently regular types like Rennie Klingenstein, and Hilary Rothschild, and Aaron Apfelbaum, and Eddie Levine—kids who've gone skinny-dipping once or twice and are not strangers to the agony of blackheads. But included too are the distinctly higher likes of Danielle Meyers and Chip Weinstein, not to say exquisite Eloise Ingle with the Rapunzel hair, who everyone thought was Wasp, seeing as how she thought so herself until just recently. That was when she discovered the truth about her dead mother's extraction.

Said extraction being a fact her stepmother had been purposefully hiding in the name of sensitivity—said sensitive stepmother having wanted Eloise to feel on a par with her stepsibs. (It was bad enough that they sat so killingly well on their horses and played such cunning games of tennis and got snapped up by Phillips Andover, which she didn't despite alumni pull.) One day in a temple rap session, she reveals how she discovered her identity from a long-lost cousin; and though Rabbi Horowitz is quick to point out that the stepmother meant well, still the group sympathy flows. Indeed, the class stands with Eloise in a solidarity such as bards will someday sing of, and in the meantime, is happy to fill her in on various points she missed as a child—such as the use and meaning of the dreidel, and who is Elijah, and what to make of his drinking habits. Rabbi Horowitz likes to call on Mona most of all for these details; and if Eloise is taken aback by the breadth and depth of Mona's knowledge, she is too well bred to let it show, except to ask whether Mona also plays tennis and skis.

"Not really," Mona says.

Her stepbrothers sail, Eloise informs her, and of course they all ride, and they summer on an island in Maine. "Mid-coast," she says.

"You mean you have a summer place?" Mona says.

"A cottage," says Eloise. And this seems to be the match point, because Eloise then graciously affords Mona a glimpse of her orthodontic work, and in conclusion says how splendid to see a Chinese girl turn Jewish. Here they are, two newcomers. She just hopes that Mona feels welcome.

Eloise feels less pressed to extend her welcome to anyone else in the class; and after a few weeks, she has no need at all—having decided to go back to being Wasp. This, even though she is actually still a Jew, according to some people (staunch adherents of the what-the-mother-is-the-child-is rule). Others, though, think how she was brought up determines at least as much who she is, if not more. "Think about what she grew up eating," they say. "That's who she is, you can't deny it." "Like an Eskimo who prefers hamburgers to walrus meat is American," says somebody. "That's assuming walrus is what Eskimos eat," says someone else. "And why can't a person be both?" People nod. Yet another person thinks Eloise can be what she wants. Who are they to say what she is actually, because of her blood or her diet, either? Like the Changowitz, says this person, meaning Mona. People nod again. Should Mona take offense, though, that with this the conversation ends?

Eloise remains friends with a few of the temple crowd—especially Danielle Meyers, but also Barbara Gugelstein, whose father, it turns out, works in the same Wall Street house as Eloise's. That's to say, her ghost lingers hauntingly. For example, Mona notices Barbara start to look down, as if putting away some more pressing matter, before turn-

ing her head to answer someone; she does this the exact slow way
Eloise Ingle does. In fact, once she takes so long that Mona worries
Barbara is not going to respond at all. Not that it is necessarily Mona's
business. Mona knows herself to be fatally afflicted with excessive concern, it's because of the parents from China. Still Mona taps her friend
on the elbow to remind her to say something. *Oh, he just caught me
daydreaming.* So says Barbara later. But another time, she accuses Mona
of being too nice. She says that if there's one thing she learned from
Eloise Ingle, it's that she doesn't owe it to people to listen just because
they want to talk.

"But it's rude," Mona argues weakly. "What happened to honor-
ing other people as you would have them honor you?"

Barbara replies that she doesn't expect that people should listen just
because she wants to talk, either. But she doesn't look too sure of
this, and when Mona doesn't answer, she goes on to say, nonplussed,
"Oh, Mona, you really need to think more like an American. You're
too polite."

"Doesn't Eloise have manners? And she's American."

Barbara concedes that Mona's right in a way, but she's wrong in a
way too. According to El, Barbara says, manners are not about being
nice to everybody. In fact, the whole key to manners is to be aware
what set you're talking to.

"Very nice," Mona says. "And what set, pray tell, is she?"

She stomps off in self-righteous fashion, feeling the might of the
moral—even though, to be honest, Eloise Ingle's way of thinking is
not so different from that of Mona's parents. This Mona admits to
Rabbi Horowitz.

"So your parents are snobs. That makes you a snob too?" he says.

"It's more like they'd like to be snobs," Mona clarifies. "The trouble is that here in America, they often can't tell what set they're talking to. And they're not sure what set we are, either."

Rabbi Horowitz listens, working his knuckles as usual, only more
sporadically. To appease the temple board of directors, he has recently
trimmed his beard, so that his Adam's apple shows; as a result, he from
time to time leaves off what he calls his wisecracking, in order to cup
his hand over this—his naked compromise.

"With their Chinese friends, it's different. There they can, say,
make allowances for So-and-so who's Cantonese but has made some-

thing of himself here in America. Which of course they need to do partly because they themselves are from Shanghai, which is sort of like being from New York. People in Peking think they're uncultured and slick." Mona stops. "I've always thought that was so Chinese. I mean, to think like that, everyone looking down on everyone else all the time. I've always thought that was so undemocratic, and un-American, and I've always been glad they at least had redeeming character traits, such as being hardworking. I thought they were the only ones."

"But now you discover what." Rabbi Horowitz, uncharacteristically gloomy, tilts back in his chair. The skeleton rattles behind him.

Barbara is teaching Mona to be cool. The first lesson: When in doubt, act like you couldn't care less.

"But what if you do care?" Mona says.

Barbara doesn't answer. Sometimes when Mona calls these days she finds Barbara's line tied up for hours. Also Barbara now attends concerts without warning. ("El called me up on a whim.") There's a new privacy zone around her; she seems always to be burning incense. Indeed the air is thick enough, that by the time Barbara announces where she is going to sit for the PSATs—namely, next to Eloise—Mona has already lumpenly begun to prepare a defense. Barbara maintains that she would sit next to Mona if their last names were alphabetically closer. But as it happens, Mona is glad enough to be conjoined instead with sweet Rachel Cohen.

Sweet Rachel! Such a true heart she is, sincere and gentle, not to say of a composure you might not predict for a dentist's daughter. She does not sweat. She does not swear. She glides where others lumber, blinks feelingly where others moan. In fact, with her large oval face and sweet limpid eyes, she could almost be the heroine of a long Victorian novel—you would just have to add a little salt—and just as she is, she could no kidding be the heroine's dear sister. Which would make her an ace companion for Mona, except that Rachel is ever-so-gently heavy into making jewelry, and truth to tell (though Mona knows it churlish to say so), she stretches the limits of Mona's interest in solder.

"I notice you didn't like the tiger's eye," says Rachel. "What about these?"

Over Helen's objection, Mona gets her ears pierced like Callie's,

and soon they hang noisy with creativity. She sounds like Mr. Bojan-
gles, complete with tambourine. During a math exam, the teacher has
to ask her to please stop tinkling, so that other people can think.

"Far out," Rachel says when she hears. "Now for some rings."

After the rings come necklaces, and after the necklaces, bracelets.
Rachel is not interested in rap sessions. She takes after her grandfather
and great-grandfather—scholars who kept to their small world, and
found everything there. They were dreamy people, like her father, a
dentist whose life goal is to produce a quartet. (Rachel is the viola.)
He will stop in the middle of drilling a tooth to hear how a passage of
music develops; also he has been trying to make sense of the new
music, though this irritates his clientele. Mutiny! they've threatened
(being music lovers themselves). At least one patient has climbed out
of the chair, bib and all, to change the tape.

Mona laughs to hear this. How wonderful! She too would like to
spend her life among the grace notes—and eventually, maybe she will.
For now, though, a callow youth, she's not ready to retire. In truth,
she deplores but adores the bloody fray. What would life be without
developments?

For example, a cool front happens to blow into Eloise just as the
Gugelsteins move to a new house—leaving Mona to help Barbara
with the adjustment. Not that the Gugelsteins haven't always lived in
something nice. But this house is French provincial to begin with,
meaning turrets to house the AC ducts in the Norman style. Also there
is a pool, and a tennis court, and a greenhouse with automatic vent
flaps; there is a circular driveway, and a two-story, four-bay garage,
with servants' quarters up above. There is a screening room for showing movies; there is a library with chestnut paneling; there are six bedrooms, each with its own bathroom. There is a plug-in vacuum
system, and an intercom; and instead of regular wallpaper with stripes
or birds or flocking, there are in the hallways hand-tinted murals of
country scenes in France. Barbara points out the milkmaids for Mona.
The scenes begin in the fields and end with wheels of cheese, though
there also seem to be a number of rafter-hung hams. Barbara and
Mona debate whether hams get dried or smoked, and how many hams
a regular rafter can support. Also how many hams one nets per dead
pig. They agree that when it comes to production, those milkmaids
are an inspiration, Henry Ford himself could probably have picked up

a tip. They agree too that the house is some house, and that's not even counting its humanitarian side: Barbara claims that in the basement is a real-life entrance for the Underground Railroad.

"The Underground Railroad was a big deal around here," she says. "That's what the realtor said. It's because this area used to be crawling with Quakers."

"I thought the Underground Railroad wasn't really underground," says Mona.

"Some of it had to be. Otherwise, they'd have called it something else, right?" Barbara retwists her French twist, clamping it into position with a leather-and-stick affair decorated with runes, then goes on to say that according to the realtor, the original house was a colonial. The present house was built on the old foundation plus some, who knows why.

The girls descend the basement stairs. Barbara's head is almost on a level with Mona's, even though she's a step lower; Mona keeps slightly back, so as to avoid being poked by the stick of Barbara's hair affair. More steps. And then, sure enough, in a far corner, behold! A wooden panel the size of a short door, soft with rot. The basement walls are dungeonlike, all ancient rock and hairy mortar, you wouldn't be surprised to find a skeleton built into them. And when Mona and Barbara remove the wooden panel, the rough hole is of a similarly creepy feel. It exhales a cool musty air, though its dirt walls are dry; Mona thinks this must be what catacombs are like, the ones where the early Christians hid to get away from the Romans. Or was it the Jews who hid there to get away from the Christians? Anyway, the hole is just high enough for Mona to stand in; when she steps forward, her hair is teased by the gravel-encrusted ceiling.

"It probably doesn't go very far," Barbara says. "The realtor said the tunnels are mostly blocked off."

"I dare you to go in," says Mona.

But Barbara is chicken; Mona bravely ventures into the tremendous dark alone. One step, two. She's not planning on going far. Hard-packed walls to either side of her; she braces her hands against them. More gravel. "See you later!" she calls. "I'm going to Alabama for to see my Susanna!" Her voice seems sluggishly amplified, as if she is singing in a large padded shower.

"Singing Polly Wolly-doodle all the day?" answers Barbara. Her voice is reassuringly close—right at Mona's back. Two steps more. Now this is the heart of darkness, thinks Mona. But before she can remember who wrote that story, much less what *The horror! The horror!* in it was, she bangs into some kind of metal rack. There is more air beyond this; smooth objects stuck into it. She reemerges, heart thudding, with a pair of bottles.

"Bordeaux!" says Barbara. "Wait until my dad sees these! Are there more?"

"Underground Railroad, wine cellar," mutters Mona. "Very easy to get them mixed up."

Better lit is the last stop of the tour, Barbara's new bedroom, which is so enormous that she's positioned her bed center stage, to take up some of the space. It's the sort of thing you associate with bed-and-bath stores. She's placed a night table next to the bed, and there's a blanket chest at its foot, but all around this island, instead of alluring merchandise, there's just space. For wallpaper she's picked a blue and white sprigged print exactly like the one she had before, in her old room; and her hi-fi too is set up just the way it used to be, with the speakers on either side of the turntable. This, even though she now has the space to separate them for realistic stereophonic sound.

"Where are your records?" Mona asks her.

"Under the bed." This is where she always used to keep them in her old room, in her old house.

"Maybe you should keep them standing up now," says Mona.

But Barbara simply shrugs, digging out her Simon and Garfunkel, her Carole King, her Laura Nyro. "They're warped already anyway," she says. And when she puts them on, you can see that indeed the needle surfs most alarmingly up and down, just the same as ever.

Although the hot line begins as a temple activity, in time Gentile classmates are also encouraged to join, provided that they pass the screening and get trained. And some do, such as Jim Magruder, and Jill Spence, and Georgina Elliott. Also Eloise Ingle. And why shouldn't they be allowed to, after all? The Jews are the Chosen People, but they have always invited outsiders to their Sabbath meals. *You shall love strangers, for strangers you were in Egypt.* Plus they are, Jew and Gentile alike, against suicide—although without an attempt every so often, what will staffers do while on duty but eat fruit leather and gossip? And make out, Barbara says—which Mona would not believe herself, except that Jim Magruder and Aaron Apfelbaum have signed up for every night shift available with Danielle Meyers and Eloise Ingle (who Barbara wishes would sign up with her and Mona, but never does). Also Mona discovers a rubber in the bathroom. Unused, it's true, but as Barbara points out, it could have been used, and why was it there unless someone had ideas?

"You mean as in a Big Idea?" Mona says; and this becomes a joke between them. "What an Idea," they say, and "He was keeping his Idea to himself," and "Now, that's an Idea." Still Mona wonders if Barbara's right. Is there hidden within the circle to which they've been admitted, another, smaller circle? It seems like something out of Nancy Drew: *The Secret of the Temple Hot Line.* Until one day, sure enough, Seth Mandel starts signing up as senior counselor for their shift.

Seth Mandel is a shortish, bright-eyed, pony-tailed guy, with big broad shoulders and the surprise domestic side you associate with primates like the silverback gorilla. Not only is he the type to offer people back rubs of surprising penetration, but he'll pick a piece of lint off your sleeve if he sees it, saying, *Excuse me, I can't help it; I'm driven by early training and the force of neurosis.* And then his eyes will crinkle, and a crack will open in his red-brown beard, and you'll know he's smiling his wide crooked smile. He doesn't laugh much—the enigmatic smile is more his style. But once in a while, he'll let out a guffaw, shocking people, and then he will smile to see their reaction. For this is what he likes more than anything, to conduct little experiments— or as he puts it, to send up balloons. *This is how you see the wind. That is, if you are interested in seeing the wind.* He smiles again.

Seth is the youngest of the senior counselors, meaning that he has graduated from high school, but hasn't from college on account of never having gone. Instead he is taking time off to decide whether college is a socializing force to which he can submit. How this came to pass has been a topic of town debate for some time. To some parents, this is obviously related to the war. Humans are generalizing animals, goes this line of reasoning. Once the kids get the idea they can resist the draft, they start to resist whatever they want. Other parents, though, blame the high school social studies curriculum, and especially advanced placement American history. This everyone knows is taught by a radical extremist in half-glasses. He starts the year by explaining how the Constitution had as much to do with economics as with noble ideals; pretty soon the kids think they know everything, it's only just lucky that this doesn't stop them from going to Ivy League schools if they get in. Seth is the exception, probably because he was the star student, and also because he got in everywhere he applied. That gave him an attitude, say some people. Needless to say too, he'd have gone if he had drawn a lower draft number.

But as it is, Mr. Above-It-All is now more or less educating himself. This is easy enough, since he is the kind of guy who compares translations of Dante for the hell of it, and who goes almost only to foreign films. The exception being *Romeo and Juliet* with Olivia Hussey, which he saw thrice in order to ascertain that (*a*) he doesn't think she is so beautiful, and (*b*) he is personally against girls parting their hair in the middle as if to suggest purity when in fact all they have on their minds is popularity. In other words, he's deep.

Is he interested in Barbara or in Mona? In the beginning it is not so clear, and then it is. He is interested in Mona, partly because of her superlative grade point average, but mostly because she is a phenomenon. A Chinese Jew! He says he sees her sometimes in the pancake house, and that he can't believe she is the same person he sees at temple. What a world-spanner!—a regular Yoko Ono. He takes her, in other words, for a high-wire freethinker, perhaps of his own school— no small compliment since he has, at age nineteen, all but broken away from the small-minded bourgeois thinking of his father, a paper-products mogul and in-the-flesh subscriber to *Pulp* magazine. He does not even live in his father's house anymore, but in a teepee in the backyard, except for when it is really cold. (And of course he helps himself to whatever from the fridge, and leaves his laundry for the maid.) *What do you like to read?* he wants to know. Which inquiry, in truth, Mona finds something of a thrill, seeing it as a level up from *Do you speak Chinese?* and *What do you eat at home?* Her mind, her mind! Someone cares about her mind!

A delicious thought for a closet reader—Mona has never admitted how much she reads, figuring, Why act brainier? It was one thing for JFK to speed-read; it's another for people in the sweet bloom of their youth. As it is, people say things like, *Don't you just hate her?* Meaning her. Last year somebody switched out of Mona's math class, saying he didn't want to be on the same curve as she was, even though Mona wasn't the one pulling down the perfect scores, it was Andy Kaplan. Mona always managed to make some little mistake.

Moreover, as Mona tells Seth, she immediately changed her part from the side to the middle after seeing *Romeo and Juliet;* and she is not interested in being a phenomenon (this being a Feeble excuse for a love affair, it seems to her). In addition, she fails to be charmed when he attempts to woo her with a synopsis of *A Critique of Pure Reason,* even if he did distill it himself from a most hefty original with only a small amount of help from a lecture series he's been listening to on tape. *The Great Thoughts Condensed for the Modern Mind,* this is called; and yes, the reel-to-reel tape machine is indeed installed in his teepee. Likewise, a telephone.

Says Mona, "Why didn't Kant just say, 'Thou shalt not use other people'?"

"Because only G-d can issue commandments," says Seth, gesturing with his hands. (He likes to make a kind of cage with them as he listens, each fingertip lightly touching its comrade on the other hand. When he talks, the cage opens, as if to let the truth flap out.) "And Kant wasn't G-d."

"So why didn't he say it was just his suggestion? Why didn't he say it was just his Big Idea?" This is for Barbara's sake. Mona can tell Barbara feels left out by the fact that she's even checked that Kant book out of the library and looked to see how it ends.

Barbara laughs appreciatively.

"Because," sputters Seth.

Another fact, not to be ignored: When Seth is too nonplussed to hold forth any further, Mona feels for him. Is he really so terrible for a pseudointellectual? Plus how can he help but leave Barbara out? After all, he's so in love with Mona, poor fellow.

Still she staunchly defends the status quo that is Barbara and her 4-ever—thereby officially forgiving her friend her E.I.L. (Eloise Ingle lapse). Until after a while, he begins to get the hint. He begins to share with Barbara his synopses and hypotheses and analyses, his assumptions and suppositions. Whereupon, to Mona's confoundment, Barbara goes intellectual. There is suddenly no question like a higher question, and wherefore are there depths to existence, except for to be plumbed?

Creepingly, creepingly, things begin to change. At the outset they all make a show of taking their turn at the phone; and after the calls, they review them as usual. Somehow, though, it begins to transpire that Barbara and Seth happen to have cases requiring extraordinary attention. And so elaborate are the discussions they happen to get involved in while Mona is on the phone, that they are still engrossed in them when the phone rings again; so that it seems only courteous for Mona to answer it. Then it begins to seem only courteous for them to remove themselves and their discussion to the next room, so that they are not disturbing Mona's concentration. And then it seems only courteous that they shut the door.

There being no door between the rooms, they are obliged to move into a large utility closet. This is not such a hospitable place, being full of cleaning supplies and other objects of large utility. Still Mona's friends repair there uncomplainingly, turning out the light so as better to explore the hitherto hidden complexities of this case or that. Every now and then, Mona hears a pail get knocked over, or a mop. And one day, there is a giant crash, which can only be the wet-dry industrial vac. The vac, Mona happens to know, is loaded up with a temple art class project (somebody's still-wet, life-size, papier-mâché armadillo having been sabotaged by felons wielding granola and Gatorade). Is this why the crash is followed by muffled yelling that sounds like "Help! Help!" but could also be "Pulp! Pulp!"? (The latter being a favorite cry in the Mandel household, apparently.)

Mona approaches the closet door but does not knock. "Barbara? Seth? You okay?" The closet door seems to her amazingly wooden.

Silence.

Mona explores with her toe the nub of the indoor-outdoor carpeting. It feels the way it looks, bluish green. "Hey, Kugel Noodle. You vant I should call an ambulance?"

Says Barbara, "I'm fine. But what's that ringing?" Then she says, "Please to go answer it, Polly Wolly," and makes a giggle-like noise.

Was it a giggle? That night, Mona considers this question closely and with tears. "Barbara," Mona says the next time she sees her friend. This is in AP English class. "Barbara."

"That's my name, don't wear it out," she says.

Mona gets up her courage. "What am I, chopped liver, you should do this to me?"

"Wait. What? I'm doing something?"

Mrs. Thompson has left the room. Everyone knows this is because she has a collapsed uterus and needs a bathroom break—during which time, they are supposed to be writing an in-class essay defining irony.

"To you?" Barbara looks honestly puzzled. In fact, so sincerely does she look at Mona with her dewy green eyes, that it is Mona who looks away. Outside the classroom window, the lawn slopes steeply up the road; Mona wonders suddenly who mows that lawn, and whether the person ever feels discouraged. "I thought you didn't want him."

"I didn't, I don't think."

"You were so clear about it, you hurt his feelings. A lot."

"Oh," Mona says, feeling as though she has more to say. But as she doesn't know what it is, she turns her eyes to her page and begins to write.


Mona is waiting, once again, for the hot-line phone to ring. Confirmation class seems for now a light-year away; also Rabbi Horowitz. Mona sees him there at the temple, not preoccupied with his beard length, as he has been of late, but cheerfully snapping one after another of his joints in place. She should shrug too. Instead she thinks about calling him just to say hi, or maybe to ask why it is that now that she's Jewish, she feels like more of a Chinese than ever. Is there some grand explanation—Hegelian perhaps? (Ah, Seth, how you've expanded her wardrobe of trenchant and other thoughts.) All this would tie up the line irresponsibly, though; and so it remains an idle eddying notion, one of life's spin-off ideas that curl to the sides of your mainly rushing existence. It's like wishing that she could call herself up. Or like wishing, when callers are done with themselves, that she could then call them back and tell them how it feels to behold her best friend and erstwhile suitor closeted up with the cleaning appliances. Is this what it means to be your own accounting unit? Mona would ask. And then maybe she would tell them how she's not sure what she thinks about that. In a way she understands that this is how life operates in America, that it's just like the classroom. You have to raise your own hand—no one is going to raise it for you—and then you have to get ready to stand up and give the right answer so that you may gulp down your whole half-cup of approval. But how tempting to stay hunkered down with everyone else, in the comfortable camaraderie of the hungry! After all, you are so tall when you stand up. People look at you with their stomachs rumbling, and you can't help but notice how around you there is so much air.

Of course, this is a foolish way to think. Mona understands that according to the rules, if you don't eat up, someone else will. None of this *nali, nali* Chinese self-effacement. *You've got to look out for number one.* No one sits lumpenly when opportunity knocks—except her, every now and then, and of course Callie, a self-cleaning oven if ever you met one. Is this a matter of their genotypes? Or is it just that other people grew up eating their individual portions from their individual plates; whereas the Changs help themselves from bowls in the middle of the table, and no one can leave until everyone else is done.

A true story: A friend of Helen's comes to visit, some years later, from China. The friend is going to a university, where she will share a room with two other Chinese students. Unfortunately, due to travel and other miseries, she is the last one to arrive. The result: she gets the best bed. No one else would take it! The first to arrive took the worst bed, the second to arrive, the second-worst. And so for an entire year, she is closest to the bathroom and the radiator, farthest from the window opening out onto the fire station. Of course, she tries to make it up to her roommates bit by bit. She brings them fruit, and folding umbrellas, and tickets to the movies. Still she feels the difficulty of her position.

Is this a way to live? Mona ponders the question. Meanwhile, the phone rings—someone calling about her boyfriend. Since he started doing speed, all he will eat is baby food; everything else he suspects. *Trace minerals,* she says he says. *Did you ever think about what they mean by trace minerals?*

The phone rings again. This caller is shook up because in the middle of her parents' divorce, their giant cactus became possessed.

"So I said, Mom, it's moving, I swear, just like in *Rosemary's Baby*. And she said she knew I needed attention, but that she didn't appreciate my trying to get it in this manner, and also that I just wouldn't believe what my papa was putting her through. Even her lawyer had never seen anything like it, and he'd been in the divorce business as long as anybody. Way, way, way before it got popular. So I called up my papa and said, It's moving, I swear. And he said he loved me, but did I have any idea how many times his phone rang an hour? And so the next day, guess what. The whole plant exploded. It turned out it was full of tarantulas hatching, and then there were baby tarantulas everywhere, and they attacked my dog, her name was Sheepie, even though she was a beagle, because that was what I wanted originally, a sheep dog. The vet thought that she would live, but she died, and now they want to bury her, but I won't let them. I told them I didn't want my dog buried by her own murderers, especially since all they care about is who's going to pay for the exterminator, and how long my mom and me are going to have to stay in a hundred-dollar-a-night hotel."

The caller is remarkably poised until she describes how in order to bury the dog someplace her parents don't even know exists, she somehow has to first get Sheepie's body back from the veterinarian. Unfortunately, he won't let her have it because she's a minor. "But she's my dog, I told him. I had her since she was a puppy. I raised her up. I taught her tricks. She slept in my bed." She sobs and sobs. Mona tries to say what Rabbi Horowitz would say. She tries to bear in mind what they were taught in training, which is that everyone is calling out of loneliness, and that their job, on some spiritual level, is to take the caller's side. Is it working, though? Suddenly the caller whispers, "Uh oh, it's my ma," and hangs up. Mona waits, hoping she'll call back, but when the phone rings again, it's someone else.

Luckily, none of the day's callers is code red—meaning that none of them is calling from the train tracks, or from the nether reaches of a hallucinogen. Though Mona has been specially trained to deal with drug overdoses, she is first supposed to try to hand such calls over to the capable senior counselor. As for what is the protocol if the capable senior counselor happens to have his hands full, who knows.

Mona tries, between calls, to ignore the loud quiet emanating from the utility closet. Mona tries, between calls, to read an Irish book called *Dubliners*. This is an assignment for English class, meaning that Mona is supposed to be on the lookout for epiphanies. It turns out there is one at the end of each story. The phone rings again. This is no divorce; neither is it a drug-related, or a parent-related, or a school-related call. And it doesn't seem to be Andy Kaplan, either. The boy identifies himself as Japanese, the son of a businessman, and though his English pronunciation is now textbook clear, there is something familiar about his voice.

If he weren't supposed to be in Japan, Mona would almost believe this to be Sherman Matsumoto.

Or is it? Anyway, if this person is in trouble, he won't say what kind. They exchange pleasantries about the weather, and also about how beautiful an area is Westchester, what with the landscaping and lawns. Mona explains about lime, and turf-builder, and preemergent crabgrass control. He replies that he lived in Scarshill some years ago. Now he is living in a neighboring town, near a duck pond with a willow tree. Is he happy to be back? He is enigmatic about this, and about what moved him to call. All he will say is that he is upset because someone trimmed the willow. He had liked the way the branches reached almost all the way down to the water; in the slightest breeze they would touch the pond, and then it would be as if it had been raining just there, right under the tree. The water would be all shivery where it had been touched—as the caller puts it, *full of spirit*—and the bits of light that reflected back up into the undersides of the leaves would toss and dance wildly.

"Crazy in the leaves," he says. "Everywhere else, it is a nice day, sunny. But in just this one tree—monsoon."

"It sounds beautiful." Mona is amazed at how clearly she can picture this private storm, especially the light-in-the leaves part. It's one of those things you've seen a hundred times without noticing it—how magically the water splatters the sun, like nature's own mirror ball.

"They should not have cut the tree," he says.

"No, they shouldn't have," Mona agrees. "Although did they cut the tree or did they cut the branches?"

"The branches."

"Ah, well. Maybe they'll grow back."

He is suddenly quiet.

"Trees do grow back quickly." Mona tries to take the long view like Rabbi Horowitz, to put things in the comforting context of universal natural principles. "Did they cut a lot or a little?"

Still he says nothing.

"If they cut a lot, it might take a while. If they cut a little, it might be pretty quick."

"It can never grow back," he says with vehemence.

"Are you sure?"

No answer.

"Is there something else you'd like to say?"

The caller hangs up.

Her note in the call log reads this way: *Japanese (?) male calling for (is this prejudiced?) somewhat inscrutable but probably profound reasons. Although who knows, maybe also/just for language practice (English). Good vibes established despite long silences and short sentences. More attention should probably have been paid to drug education. Given caller's depressed state of mind, probably ought also to have explored caller attitude toward hari-kari, even if that's a stereotype. Instead discussed lawn care (fertilizer) and duck pond with tree (willow). Caller disturbed by the pruning of aforementioned tree, which he characterized as full of lights like a monsoon and incapable of ever growing back. All this before suddenly hanging up. A hidden message here? Cultural considerations certainly a factor, perhaps major or minor. Still questions remain.*

For instance: Is this Sherman? Sherman! The idea seems at once impossible and preordained. Are they sixteen already? Here he is, as promised. It's kind of young to get married. All the same, Mona studies up on Japan.

*An elongated isle,* says one book. *Crowded.*

Mona would not have thought she could become Japanese, but here she is, Jewish, right?

She wonders if she is not getting ahead of herself. Why would she want to be Japanese? What if this caller has nothing to do with her at all? The next week, as soon as she comes in, she checks the log to see if he's called, which he hasn't. She waits to see if he calls while she's there. It's amazing how little it matters to her what goes on in the utility closet now. How reoriented she is! So to speak.

The Japanese caller calls again, with about as much to say as last time. They talk about how he's gone down to visit Monticello, in Virginia, with his parents. She's never been there, but he says it's very beautiful, except with too many sides, and he can't understand why Thomas Jefferson had a slave as his mistress.

"Maybe he loved her," Mona says.

"But he is President of whole United States," he says. "Of course, at that time, the United States is only half the size we see now."

"Love is unpredictable."

"That way he makes everyone unhappy."

"But what if he loved her?"

"If he loved her he should leave her alone. When a nail sticks up, people hammer it down."

"But is that right?"

Silence. "That way brings peace and harmony."

"What about right and wrong? Don't you think that's important too?"

No answer at first. Then, "It can't be helped."

"You know," says Mona, "in America, we don't care so much about peace and harmony."

"Oh, really."

"That's right."

"Then why all the time those peace marches?"

"That's different."

He starts to sing: " 'All they are say-ing / is give peace a chance.' "

"Where'd you learn that?"

He hangs up.


The next times he calls, it's about how he walked right under Niagara Falls, which he thought was worth getting soaked—the first thing he's said that they've agreed on. He says this even though as a result of getting wet, he got so sick he ran a fever. Then he calls about Kentucky, and the horse farms there. He does not think these are fundamentally undemocratic. He thinks they are beautiful. Also he says he wouldn't mind being a horse, even if he had to be shot for breaking a leg, and that he wouldn't mind being bred, either.

In short, a pattern has emerged. He calls, always on her shift, offers two or three comments about scenic spots he has visited, then hangs up so abruptly Mona can't help but wonder if there isn't something he doesn't want to go into. For instance, how it is he travels so much. Doesn't his father work? Doesn't he go to school? Is he making it all up about these adventures of his? The last seems unlikely. If she's being read to from *The Scenic Wonders of America*, it must be some special haiku edition. So much is unspoken that when they get to the end of an entry, she doesn't feel nearly so much like saying *Aah* as *Huh?*

What he's holding back may not be trouble—that occurs to her too. Mona wonders if she shouldn't try on some of those wooden platform shoes, see if she can walk in them. She recalls that once she tried stilts and did okay. Also she's a whiz on a pogo stick. And what about the weather in Japan, and do they have mosquitoes? She can almost believe that they don't. For mosquitoes go with cut-offs and camp shirts, who has ever seen a lady in a kimono swat at her pulse points?

She dreams about Sherman, and about what his life is like in Japan, and she finds that in her dreams it is a lot like her life at home, except that her family is like everyone else's. People read each other's minds. They share their food. Everything is simpler. Of course, the Changs also have to eat their fish raw, and sleep on the floor, and wear socks with their sandals; and what with her cowlick, it is not so easy for Mona to get her hair up into that big breakfast-bun style you see the geishas wear. But life is serene. Her family is an interlocking piece of a vast and complex puzzle. There is no Eloise Ingle, and no Seth Mandel; and it is not like China, either, taken over by leather-eating Communists.

Here is the odd thing, though: In her vision, Mona is always fifteen, and never old enough to drive. In fact, she doesn't even have a learner's permit. This is an unreasonable conception, she knows. She knows that people do drive in Japan, although in smaller cars. Still the next time the caller calls, Mona asks, "Do you mind if I ask you a question about driving?"

"Driving?"

"Driving cars," Mona says. "I was just wondering how old you have to be to drive a car in Japan."

He hesitates in a way that makes her wonder if she is being too personal. But how can the driving age in Japan be too personal? "I don't know," he says finally.

She tries to speak more clearly. "I mean, do you have learner's permits there? Here they have learner's permits, and then you have to do the three-point turn, and then you can take the driving test and get your license."

"I see."

"I've been wondering, that's all."

A long silence. So long, Mona wonders if he's hung up. Then he says, "Are you going to Japan?"

"I'd like to. Someday."

"Why?"

"Oh," Mona says. "I guess I've never been there. Why did you go to Monticello?"

"To see the cherry trees. Of course, they are not so nice as the trees in Japan."

"I see."

"Do you like Japan?"

"Oh," Mona says. "I hear it's very interesting."

"I see."

"Very crowded, and with small cars and earthquake trouble," says Mona. "An elongated island. I've never been in an earthquake. Also with volcanoes, I think."

"Mount Fuji," he says politely.

"That's right," Mona says. "Isn't that the one with snow on it?"

"In the wintertime," he says, "snow falls on many mountains. All over. Just like here."

"I see," Mona says. And then, not knowing what else to do, she pretends to knock the phone over. "Whoops." She hangs up. He does not call back.


Seth and Barbara are having a fight. This is because Seth is interested in free love, whereas Barbara is interested in ownership.

"I can't help it," she says. "I do want to be able to say *my* boyfriend, and I just don't see what capitalism and serfs and the Russian Revolution have to do with it." Seth wants her to read *Das Kapital*. She wants him to read Ann Landers. "He has no idea what real love is about," she says. "Him and his Big Idea." She stops.

"Oh, Barbara," Mona says. "You didn't."

Barbara begins to sob.

"You let him give you his tea?"

"We were stoned. And it's just like everyone says—it ruined everything."

Mona takes her friend's backpack for her. She helps her friend sit down on the grass, well away from a pile of dog doo.

"I thought it meant we were definitely going out with each other. But he said we contributed to the social good by reducing world horniness; he doesn't see why that's not enough. He said that all that mattered was if I liked it too, and if I was acting out of my own free will."

"Were you?"

"I was. That's the worst part, except for what he said. Why should he be just my boyfriend, he said."

"What a shithead!"

"It's just what my mother always warned me. What does he really want, a guy like Seth? A guy like Seth, what he really wants is a shiksa."

Nineteen. Eighteen. They count down the days until Barbara's next period while, outside, the dogwood blooms virginal yet again. May! Most merry month. Seventeen. They discuss abortion. First of all, how lucky that it's legal in New York; second of all, what exactly it is. For this information, Mona calls Callie at college. Who else to ask about the special vacuum cleaner, and whether there are nowadays special coat hangers too? Callie looks up the info in *Our Bodies, Ourselves*, which she seems to have sitting right next to the phone; apparently you need it more in college than a dictionary. She does not lecture unduly, except to suggest that Barbara tell her mom. Barbara would sooner throw herself in front of a commuter train.

Sixteen. Seth wonders why the snap freeze. Even pleads, professing concern. Barbara refuses to address His Ignoramus. "Let him use his higher intellect and figure it out himself," she says. "He who reads Nietzsche and can spell it too," agrees Mona. Fifteen. As if Barbara and Mona don't have enough to worry about, they have to take the SATs. They sharpen their number-two pencils together; they try to avoid Eloise Ingle. Mona still sits with Rachel Cohen, though, and so far is this from the G–R section that Mona does not even witness how Barbara breaks down crying in the middle of the test and has to leave the room. Barbara is bravely philosophical about this later. She says she'll try again in the fall, assuming the special vacuum cleaner works.

Fourteen. They try to gain perspective. They discuss whether entertaining a Big Idea was at least fun. Barbara says it wasn't, although it was exciting. Meaning what? Also she says that it was messy and smelly and sticky, and that she dripped for a whole day afterward and had to take about eighty showers to get rid of the smell of him. "Eighty showers?" says Mona. Barbara concedes this to be a manner of speaking. Still the words haunt Mona, rekindling themselves like trick birthday candles. *Eighty showers. Eighty showers.*

Thirteen. Mona lies in bed and wonders: Will Sherman Matsumoto ever make her need to take eighty showers? She feels guilty wondering this. She thinks she should have thoughts only for Kugel Noodle, her friend in need. At the same time, she figures it can't be that bad to wonder, seeing as how there is so little to wonder about. For how should Sherman make her take anything when she hasn't seen him in years? Also the Japanese in general don't seem as if they smell. Maybe this is a stereotype. Maybe if she saw the statistics for deodorant sales in Japan she would be shocked. But what matter, when there is a yet greater misstep in the analytic march of her thinking? For while Mona is antisublimation and can see herself as almost old enough to get married, she finds that she does not see herself as old enough for sex.

How can this be? Mona was the first one in her entire grade to get her period. Plus she surmises by the population problems of the Far East that she is appropriately equipped. But she doesn't look like, say, Barbara. If her friend is a developed nation, Mona is, sure enough, the third world. Barbara's is the body Mona is still waiting to grow into: Her breasts, for example, are veritable colonies of herself, with a distinct tendency toward independence. Whereas Mona's, in contrast, are anything but wayward. A scant handful each, hers are smooth and innocent—the result, you might think, of eating too much ice cream. They meld into the fat under her arms. Even her nipples seem somehow dietary, smallish brownish nubs—areolaless, perhaps, due to inadequate consumption of true adult drinks such as beer and tonic water. Later Mona will realize how in the popular conception Orientals are supposed to be exotically erotic, and all she'll want to say is, But what about my areolaless nubs? Not to say my sturdy short legs—have you ever seen a calf so hammy? And no billowy, Brillo-y bush, alas. How should she have one when she does not even need to shave her legs? This last a convenience of sorts. Although how can she let her legs go natural when they already are natural? Her underarms too—actually she boasts a few wisps there. If only she didn't have to put her hands on her head for anyone to notice! Hair, hair, hair, she thinks. And especially facial hair, body hair. It's different for the sexes, of course. But in general, these are the dead cells that spell wild-side bohemian. She feels condemned to the straight and narrow.

Of course, this whole train of thought will one day prove not her own train at all, but a train set on track by racist sexist imperialists. She will one day discover that it is great to be nonhairy, and what's more that not all Asians are areolaless, just her and some others. Plus that she is yellow and beautiful—baby boobs, hammy calves, and all. She will ask for an extra print when people take her picture. She will come to recognize, with a little squinting, her goddess within.

But for now all Mona can think is, Oh, that subcutaneous fat! So young she looks; so rounded; so unavoidably, irrevocably cute. Oh, to be angular and gaunt! Oh, to be tall! (How she hates the word *petite*.) Oh, to be leggy and buxom like Barbara Gugelstein, and Oh, to have a crisis with Seth Mandel! It seems so awfully glamorous, except when Mona tries to put herself in Barbara's shoes. Then Mona recalls that she would not be in Barbara's shoes. Because if Mona got pregnant, the baby would be mixed. Meaning what? She's not sure, but something complicated, that's certain, and also something for which she's too young.

Twelve. "Ma," Mona says. "Have you ever seen a mixed baby?"

Helen says that she has, yes, two, and that one was beautiful, but the other looked completely Caucasian. That baby had blue eyes and brown hair, and when she grew up she was as big as a horse.

"And what about her legs?"

"Why do you want to know about her legs?" asks Helen, chopping scallions. But then she answers that the girl's legs looked as though there was something the matter with them. "She was still a nice girl. Very smart, and never give her parents any trouble."

"Like me, you mean."

"You!"

"What do you mean, something the matter with them?" Mona asks, after a moment. "What was the matter with her legs?"

"Too long."

"Hmm. I wish my legs were longer."

"Your trouble is not your legs." Helen adds the scallions to the chicken, which is steaming.

"What if I had a mixed baby?" Mona says. "What if I had a mixed baby, and it looked completely Caucasian?"

"Are you having a baby?"

"No. But what if I did, and it looked completely Caucasian? With a big nose and blue eyes and everything."

"Oh, then I would throw it in the garbage," says Helen, turning the heat down.

That night Mona dreams Helen is having a new baby, a boy, which is also the baby that Mona is having, except that Helen doesn't realize it until she notices how long the baby's legs are. Then she shouts, "This baby is Jewish! Throw it in the garbage!" and will not be appeased until Mona throws herself in the garbage instead. The garbage looks to be mostly paper, but turns out to have eggplant at the bottom, which Mona thinks is Italian. Helen insists it's Chinese, though; and when Mona looks again, she sees that her mother is right. There's no mozzarella. She wakes up sweating and feeling like she needs eighty showers.

Eleven. Barbara is friends with Eloise Ingle again, but things so aren't what they were that Barbara doesn't even tell Eloise she might be pregnant. As for Barbara and Mona, they are able to continue working on the hot line as a result of Seth's diplomacy: Knowing an awkward situation when he's engendered one, he graciously cedes his place to an out-of-work comptroller named Mathilde. "You need any help, why, speak right on up," she says, knitting. Her sweater pattern involves chipmunks in a tree full of letters that are going to spell LUV YA.

Barbara wants to quit. Mona, though, explains about the phone calls from Sherman. "Why didn't you tell me?!" says Barbara then. And she's right, Mona should have told her. First of all, because Barbara is telling Mona everything, but also because she knows something Mona doesn't.

"Oh!" she says. "That Andy Kaplan!"

*"Andy Kaplan?"*

They review the evidence. Now that they are discussing it, Mona can recall certain weird moments in her conversations with the Japanese caller. Barbara analyzes these incisively; Mona is suddenly the one who wants to quit the hot line, post-haste. In fact, Mona wouldn't mind quitting town, quitting New York, quitting North America. She wishes she were old enough and had good enough eyes for the space program. Barbara, however, absolutely wants to stay. "Aren't you curious, Watson?" Holding up a pretend monocle, Barbara proposes that Mona let her listen in on the next call. After all, aren't they telling each other everything?

Ten. They wait. Nine.

The mystery caller does not call.

Eight. Barbara Gugelstein's theory (advanced as she taste-tests a can of Diet Dr Pepper) is that Andy Kaplan is afraid to call now because he knows she will catch him out. But how can Andy Kaplan know what Barbara is planning? "He doesn't have ESP," says Mona. Whereupon Barbara, opening a second can for Mona, introduces her to the Theory of Blood Knowledge. Barbara says she believes some people are linked by ancestral memory. She believes that there are genes for ways of thinking, and that if you come from the same gene pool, you are likely to have the same genes.

"I even asked Mr. Ed about it," she says. Mr. Ed is their biology teacher—a horse lover who people say is starting to resemble his favorite ride. "And he said it's possible."

"Possible is only possible."

"Andy Kaplan and I have always been on the same wavelength. Even if he did turn cool before I did."

She says this last because ever since Andy grew his hair and took up the electric guitar, he's been considered the cutest guy in their grade. Not that he rose to this summit without hormones; for a long time he was just like anybody else, only shorter. People noticed that he was golden of aspect and had been to a crack orthodontist, also that he was coordinated and musical, not to say the sort of class-A mimic you would definitely want on your side for charades. But after he suddenly grew eleven inches, he became the sort of guy with whom people liked to claim some connection. His mom worked with their mom on the library committee. They used to be on his paper route. Even Seth claims to play chess with Andy now and then; and Mona sometimes imagines a strange vibe between them, on account of his mom staking her prize chrysanthemums with chopsticks. Also the Kaplans have been to Taiwan and Japan; his father is a professor of East Asian civilization. Around their house, people say, are *belly many Buddhas.*

But of everyone, Barbara feels that she knows Andy best. Not only did they get the same thing for their mothers for Mother's Day, they also have the same hiking boots, the same camping stove, the same Kelty backpack.

"Maybe you should get married," Mona says, sipping away, but Barbara says it would be like marrying her brother. Even going out with him would be like going out with her brother. However, every so often they do smoke pot together, and then it's amazing what they share with each other, the depths of their souls; it's only too bad that the next day she can never remember what they found way down there.

"It's kind of like the tie between you and Sherman Matsumoto," she says. "Now, if you guys end up married, I won't be surprised."

But wouldn't that be like Mona marrying her brother? And what kind of tie is it between her and Sherman Matsumoto if Sherman is not Sherman at all, but actually Andy Kaplan?

Seven. Six. Five. Barbara reports feeling fat. Then, finally—a day early!—her period comes. Hooray! She and Mona celebrate with a ritual egg smash. *O ovum, dear ovum,* they intone. *Be thou ever chary!*

"Chary, or wary?" says Barbara. Mona isn't sure. Still they spend their hot-line shift composing an ode with the rhyme scheme *chary/ scary/marry.* They are finagling a way to work in *hari-kari* when, lo and behold, guess who calls?

"Long time no speak," Mona says.

Barbara Gugelstein picks up the other handset. Sherman is talking about a weekend trip to Boston. "Many bricks," he says. "Some of the sidewalks are very hard to walk, and some of the streets have rocks."

*No hiking boots?* writes Barbara, and passes the note to Mona.

"Those cobblestones," Mona says.

"That's right, cobblestones," he answers, sounding delighted. "All over. Very rough. So hard to drive in Boston! Even we look at the map, we are lost all the time." Still he had fun. He liked the gas lamps, and the swan boats, and the Freedom Trail, although he couldn't understand the Boston Tea Party. Why did the colonists dress up to dump the tea overboard?

"And why they like tea? To drink with their hot dogs?"

Mona explains that in the colonies, there were no hot dogs.

"No hot dogs?" he says, with what seems like real surprise. But then he goes on. "How about hamburgers?"

*Ha ha,* writes Barbara Gugelstein. *Very funny.*

The caller is generally glad not to have lived through the Revolution. The absence of hot dogs is one reason, but the main reason is that he prefers peace to big fights. On the other hand, he says that he went to Walden Pond and that the man who lived there seemed to him a nut.

*He went to Walden Pond too? All in how long?*

Mona tries to explain what is a nonconformist.

"Different drummer," Mona explains. "Like in a band."

"If he is in band," the caller says, "the drummer must drum like everyone else."

*Get off it!* writes Barbara.

The caller goes on to describe how he visited Harvard while he was in Boston, and MIT. (*All in ONE weekend?!*) Both of these he thought very nice, although a little dirty. Also he says the students looked sloppy, and even some of the professors.

"They're just anti-establishment," Mona says.

"What is anti-establishment?"

Mona hesitates. How can he not know what means anti-establishment, when he knows about protest songs?

*Ask him what professors wear in Japan,* writes Barbara.

"What do professors wear in Japan?"

"What?"

*Ask him what he's wearing right now.*

"What are you wearing?" Mona asks. "Right now."

"Me? What am I wearing?"

*Ask him if he's wearing blue jeans.*

"Are you wearing blue jeans?"

*How could he not know what he is wearing?*

"I am wearing blue jeans," he says finally.

*Tell him you are too, with no underwear underneath.*

"I'm wearing blue jeans too," Mona says. "Mine have pretty big bells."

More silence. Has he hung up?

"I am so busy these days," he says.

"Schoolwork?" Mona says.

"Sure," he says. "Schoolwork, and sports also."

"Sports!" Mona says. "What sports?"

"Oh," he says. "Some judo, and baseball."

*Some judo!!!*

"Some judo?" Mona says.

"Judo is very popular sport in Japan."

*Did he do it when he lived in America?*

"Did you do it when you lived in America?"

"Sure," he says.

*Tell him you used to know someone who did judo.*

"I used to know someone who did judo," Mona says.

*Tell him you were completely in love with him.*

"Really," he says.

*Tell him you have been saving yourself for him.*

"He flipped me on the ground once," Mona says.

"Oh," he says. "You must have done something very bad, that he was so mad at you."

Mona says, "I don't know if it was really that bad."

*Now's your chance! Just ask, Do you mind if I ask you a question? Is this Sherman M.?*

"Do you mind if I ask you a question?" Mona says.

"Sure," he says.

"I used to know someone named Sherman Matsumoto," Mona says. "Many years ago. Do you know anyone by that name?"

"Sure," he says.

*Ask him!*

"Are you Sherman?"

Silence.

*Or is this Andy Kaplan?*

"Or is this Andy Kaplan?"

"Andy?" he says.

"Andy Kaplan," Mona says. "K-A-P-L-A-N."

"Who?" he says. "Kaplan?"

"You heard her," Barbara chimes in. "Give it up!"

"Who's this?" he asks.

"Your friend Barbara," says Barbara.

"Barbara? Not Mona?"

"Also Mona," Mona says.

"Barbara and Mona? What do you mean?"

"Kaplan . . . ," starts Barbara.

"Oh, God. I'm sorry, Sherman," Mona says. "This is Mona. I'm really sorry. It's just that—"

"You will never be Japanese." He hangs up.

# CHAPTER 5

# A Turn in the Car

Barbara buries her head in her hands. Her hair is not at all frizzy, and so what about the curly commas that most adorably punctuate her forehead? She would be pleased if she could see how well does work her orange juice can. Instead she is upset. "You'll never forgive me."

"You're right," Mona says.

"I'm turning into my mother. It's already happening."

"Seems like you should at least get to go to college first, huh?"

"I hate it when she jumps right into the conversation like that. She's so rude. She just has this urge to fix everything all the time. The other day she started to scrape the dirt out from between the floor and the baseboard with a toothpick. And now I go and do the exact same thing."

"With a toothpick?"

"No, jumping into conversations. I mean, I'm sorry I jumped into yours."

They are sitting on a curb. Mona shrugs; and though Barbara can't see her, she must sense something, because she tosses her hair behind her shoulders, bites a cuticle, and tucks her two hands between her knees as if praying for a bathroom. "Tell me how I can make it up to you." She appeals to Mona with her dewy green eyes.

"It's all right."

"Aren't you mad? Aren't you upset? You know, sometimes I can hardly even tell whether you're upset or not."

Across the street, the trees buzz loudly with assorted winged bugs; Mona has never noticed before how loudly.

"Why don't you just go ahead and yell. I'll tell you what my mom would say if she were in your shoes. If she were in your shoes, my mom would look me right in the eye—"

"Kugel Noodle," Mona says. "I'm not your mother."

Barbara looks back down. "I know how I'll make it up to you," she announces finally. She speaks from behind her hairy curtain like a cross between Cousin It and the Wizard of Oz. "I'll give you my van."

"Okay."

"Or how about you can borrow it for a month? It's the end of the year anyway; I'll only have to walk to school for a bit. Plus I do have a ten-speed."

"Don't worry, I'll give you a ride."

"Thanks," says Barbara. And then to Mona's surprise, she actually hands over the keys. These are still warm from their home in Barbara's pocket; the key fob is a roach clip.

"Don't you need your house key?" says Mona.

"Forsooth! I did forget." Barbara accepts back the key to her house, also the key for the burglar alarm, and the roach clip. Mona puts the keys to the van on her own ring, which is boringly fobless.

"What am I going to tell the 'rents?" says Mona.

"Tell them this is America; anything is possible. And if they don't believe you, tell them the truth."

"Which is?"

Barbara smiles. "This isn't America. You among others are simply confused."

Haight-Ashbury, watch out! In the spirit of the day, they decide to go driving off into madness and anarchy as soon as their shift at the hot line is over. Why the simple fact of Mona driving should put them in mind of the Merry Pranksters is not clear even to them as they tumble reasonless outside, happy for an excuse to fix dandelions in their hair. Never mind that milk leaks from the stems, trickles down behind their ears. The road, the road, the open road! Will they pick up hitchhikers? They decide yes, of course, in fact they'll hunt for them; Barbara knows the streets with the best selection. First, though, they head prankishly for Mona's old hometown, where there is a great new burger place. What a day! Neither one of them has ever noticed before how musty the hot-line office is, though they do notice how twinkly bright and leafy is the rest of the world. They wind their windows all the way down. At stoplights, they lean out of the car and close their eyes, turn their faces to the sun so that their eyelids go red. They count floaters. The light turns, people honk. Barbara laughs and turns and blows kisses while Mona pulls slowly, slowly, maddeningly slowly, into the intersection. Hope they're in a hurry! Barbara giggles. They turn up the radio, they pretend they are Joni Mitchell. At the burger place, the girls prankishly ditch their diets, and down a whole thinga-majig of french fries each. And from there—since it's sort of far to Big Sur—they drive to a certain neighboring town, in search of a pond with a willow.

This town looks a lot like Scarshill, only infinitely more exciting. Old, green, lots of houses, landscaping. Ponds. Mona and Barbara circle these, making their inspection. Are there too many ponds? Too few? What about the willows? They try to look as though they are doing a school project. *Can you believe it?* they're going to say if they actually run into Sherman. *This biology teacher . . .* Et cetera.

Their actual goal is not to talk to Sherman. Their actual goal, what with Barbara in the car, is to spot him and run; they don't want to remind him of the phone call. In fact, Barbara has promised to duck if they see anyone remotely Japanese. She practices squashing herself down into the footwell, though she is hardly a handy fold-up size. But they do not see any Japanese people at all, only many white denizens, engaged in their sundry activities.

"Try the phone book," Barbara suggests finally. They stop at a phone booth. No luck. When they call up directory assistance, though, they find that a Matsumoto is indeed tantalizingly listed, under new listings. If only the operator would give out the address! Mona begs shamelessly. Barbara calls information again, and then again. But the stalwart operators prove dishearteningly true to their operating procedures.

"Call," Barbara urges Mona, holding out a dime.

Mona accepts the coin. In sad truth, though, being sixteen, she believes the boy should call the girl. Moreover, she believes Sherman believes this firmly and without exception—recalling as she does, for example, the button incident of long ago. Of course, that was eighth grade. Still she pockets the coin, climbs back into the van, and heads to the pancake house.

Cedric the cook waves his spatula. "Welcome, welcome to the two human beans."

An old joke; all the same, Mona and Barbara laugh. Being not-so-long-ago-from-China, Cedric has even more *pronounce-trouble* (as he puts it) than Ralph, and mostly it's legitimate. He's been known to ham his problems up, though, as if he considered his job description to include making Ralph's English look good. No one could exactly prove this. However, his pronunciation got noticeably better after he got his green card: He stopped saying "meck" for "make" and "tlaks" for "tracks." Now he yells at the busboys the same as everybody else. "Make tracks!" he says. "Don't give me no jive!"

"What kind beans we have today?" he continues, flipping flapjacks. He turns the hood fan down so he can hear them. "Green beans? Black beans? Soy beans?"

"Dried beans," they say. "Dried up and died beans. Tired of bein' beans."

"Oh," he says, still smiling. "Too bad." He is a round and genial man with a serene shiny face; in his chef's hat, he looks like a Taoist immortal trying to pass for a short-order cook. Today his smile tightens ever so slightly as he turns the fan back up, and Mona wonders if he's thinking about his family in China. Two children he's left behind, and a wife, and his parents, all of whom agreed he should grab his chance to get out. He promised in return that he would get them out when he could. But how is he going to do that, and when, and are they surviving the Cultural Revolution in the meantime? Listening to him has made Helen and Ralph worry anew about their long-lost families—about who is dead and who is alive, and who is being tarred, or stoned, or peed on. Cedric knows things they don't; he knows what to imagine—namely, anything. This Helen and Ralph can't quite do anymore. However, Mona can. When Cedric first arrived, she would regularly describe to him the goriest, grossest things, and ask him if the Red Guards would do that.

But seeing as how he hasn't had a letter in months, she has shut up. Also she knows the answer by now—always yes. There is nothing too gory or gross for the Red Guards. When it comes to torture, they appear to have a gift. And this is why Cedric has gone on sending his family money, even if he doesn't know if they'll get it. Ralph and Helen sent money for a long time too. They had no way of helping Helen's family, but they did know someone in Hong Kong to whom they could send money in the hope it would be sent on to someone else, who they hoped would in turn send the money to Ralph's family. Then one day something happened to the friend in Hong Kong, they never knew what—only that the special bank in Chinatown couldn't wire the money through. The first explanation was that the account was too full. There was no second explanation.

How lucky Cedric seems, to have someplace to send money! And to be able to write to his family! Never mind that they could very well be dead. He says he tells them everything except about his American girlfriend: Wendy, her name is, Mona sees her almost every day. A divorced social worker, white, not young, with a jalopy, and no snow tires in the winter, and three alarming kids. Rats her hair. Cedric says he will never marry this Wendy, and that this Wendy knows that. Still she waits for him to get off work, her motor idling. The kids hang out the windows, yelling, "Uncle Cedric! Uncle Cedric!" What kind of problems can Mona have, compared to what he's seen? Now Cedric rubs his feet together as though he has an itch in his left heel—a private gesture that goes with an even broader, tighter smile. An instant later, though, he seems returned to himself, a genuine friend again.

"Drag my cigarette?" he offers, winking. He nudges an ashtray toward them with his spatula. Barbara takes him up on his offer, and after checking on her dad's whereabouts, Mona does too. Cedric's not supposed to smoke while he cooks—it's against code—but he seems to have a butt going all the time anyway, he doesn't care what kind. When he's a real American, he says, he'll pick a favorite. For now he smokes anything that doesn't explode, which today means unfiltered cigarettes so strong Mona can feel the rush in her fingertips. Her head reels.

"Sit down, have seat," Cedric offers, as if they're guests. They wander out into the busy dining room and settle themselves in a booth. The table is sticky; Mona cannot help but think how she really should talk to the new busboy. First here comes Magdalena, though, with two banana splits so overpiled and goopy that one whole slope of whipped cream avalanches onto the tray.

"And what kind of behavior is this?" demands Magdalena of the ice cream, in her most rapid-fire voice. The ice cream doesn't answer. "Back to the kitchen!"

But Mona will not hear of the sundae going back anywhere, especially since the maraschino cherries have survived—bulwarked, luckily, by the banana halves. There are five cherries on each sundae, their stems sticking more or less into the air; their color bleeds into the whipped cream in a pleasantly psychedelic way. Capturing this effect, though, is no easy matter. Mona has to quick, snatch the sundaes off the tray herself before Magdalena can assert her standards. Magdalena retires in seeming defeat, only to reappear with a whipped-cream gun. "Ready or not," she chortles, exuberantly adding a whole new range of peaks to Mona's mountainside. Barbara's sundae likewise sustains some unexpected geologic activity. The girls agree to restart their diets tomorrow—a life ritual so agreeable that their real aim does not seem to be to lose weight, but rather to sighingly start and gleefully abandon their regimen with a friend.

Barbara leans forward like a school psychologist. "So what's the next step?"

"Nu?"

"*Sherman: The Search Goes On.* Will young Mona Chang ever get the man she deserves?" Barbara searches the ceiling as if the answer might be written on the acoustic tiles.

"*Seth Mandel: Fiend or Friend?*" answers Mona. "Sweet Barbara Gugelstein says that they're through, but can she just kiss him good-bye?"

"That's a book with just one chapter. I was in love; he was having an experience." Barbara's eyes fill with tears—not from the bottom up gradually, but instantly to the point of overflow, as if they have this routine down. Her handkerchief likewise leaps readily to hand. She mops up impatiently, heartily sick of being heartsick, as they review the possibilities in their grade.

"How come there's no one like *him*?" says Barbara, when Alfred the number-two cook comes in for his shift. For besides being a spatula whiz, Alfred is movie-star handsome from the neck up. From the neck down, he is trim, athletic, tall—more than he resembles Tarzan, though, he resembles a two-by-four. No, his fortune is in his head shot. Not only has he got the mysteriously sullen aspect occasionally broken up by the boyish big grin; he has the piercing gaze and steely jaw that put you in mind of dinner jackets and diplomats, maybe even Mount Rushmore, if you can imagine those chalk cliffs, brick brown.

What college does he go to? Mona says he doesn't, meaning that he did, but only for a month. "He said he couldn't see the point of it. He asked this professor what kind of car he drove, and it turned out the professor didn't drive any kind of car at all, he couldn't afford it. So Alfred up and dropped out. He said even he had a two-year-old Chevy with whitewalls, he thought the professor should be studying from him."

"How old is he?" asks Barbara.

"Twenty, twenty-two?" Mona further reports that he wasn't drafted because of something about his hearing. "You'd have to shout your sweet nothings."

Still Barbara moons.

" 'Lady-killer like him don't need to go to war, he notch his belt right here.' That's what they say in the kitchen."

Barbara continues to moon.

"And of course Andy Kaplan is out?"

"I told you before, we have the same backpack. Plus we got our moms the same present for Mother's Day." So Barbara says. But then she looks up, takes two shanks of her long hair, ties them under her chin, and makes a face.

"I see." Mona smiles tactfully.

For her part, Barbara points out that there are many people in whom Mona could be interested if she put her mind to it. "Even if you do end up marrying Sherman Matsumoto, there's no harm in enjoying yourself while he's Sherman Incommunicado, is there?"

Mona concedes that there are other fish in the sea. Benny Meyers, for example, who has a girlfriend, and Alvin Nickelhoff, who might as well have a girlfriend, being so in love with his model T Ford. "What about Chris Allefart?" Barbara says. Mona tries to have an open mind about him even though he's six-foot-four and descended from John Jacob Astor. They are still discussing how many inches true love can surmount when Andy Kaplan saunters in, hand in hand with Eloise Ingle.

Barbara looks to be doing brave battle with her tear ducts. But then Mona whispers, "Can you believe it? You've even been seeing the same person!" and Barbara has to laugh. She, quick, unties her hair before anyone sees.

To go with his height, Andy has developed a lumberjack's stride, and to extend the woodsman theme, he is wearing a red bandana on his head. (A lot of guys do this when they're hiking, to keep out black-flies—never mind that their moms did the same getup for them when they were pirates for Halloween.) Beside him, Eloise scurries. She is pre-Raphaelite as always, and takes what look to be three tripping steps to his one, so that for once her breathlessness seems a matter of breath. When they stop to say hello, though, it is Andy who flushes, as if from her exertion. Eloise coolly turns her front foot out, sits back on her hip, and with a little shake of her mane, lifts and angles her chin. She could be a Degas if the background weren't a franchise dining room.

"Well, if it isn't the Gugelsteiner and her better half." Andy bows. "Most honorable Miss Changowitz."

"Andy! El!" Consciously or unconsciously, Barbara is brandishing a fork in a manner that predates table manners.

"Have a cherry?" Mona says, filling in.

Andy Kaplan gives her a cuff. "Very funny. Where'd you get that wit of yours from anyway?"

"I'm afraid I'm a self-made mouth," Mona says.

Andy laughs.

"How long has this been going on?" Barbara asks finally.

"Oh, maybe a week. Would you say?" Eloise looks to Andy. "Three weeks, at most. I've been meaning to tell you."

"Really," says Barbara.

"But the moment was never quite, oh, how shall I say . . . ?"

"Right to break it to me?" Barbara's eyelashes begin to clump up with tears.

"What's this?" says Andy.

"How could you not have told me?" says Barbara.

"But it was quite impossible," says Eloise. "You . . ."

Andy Kaplan looks off into the air as if to make clear to some important observer that he, the male of the species, is in no way involved in this squabbling.

"I what?" says Barbara. "And what do you mean, impossible?"

"Nothing's impossible," Mona puts in.

Everyone looks at her.

"You just have to put your mind to it," Mona says. "Like the Little Engine That Could. Just repeat to yourself, I think I Chang, I think I Chang."

Andy laughs, Barbara smiles, Eloise is not amused.

"I was brought up to understand that it's rude to interrupt," she observes.

"That's for conversations. The rules are different for catfights."

Eloise glares.

"Uh oh," says Andy Kaplan, astutely observant. "Time to exit left?"

"I wish you would," says Mona, his accomplice. "You're bad for business."

Andy and Eloise turn to leave. Then Eloise pivots. "Will you join us?" she asks Barbara.

Barbara hesitates.

"It was not a catfight," says Eloise. "It was a tiff."

Barbara looks to Mona, who says, "You've got matters to investigate, I know."

And so it is that Barbara leaves Mona at the booth by herself, with more melting glop than one person could possibly get up an appetite for.


Mona is glad to see Barbara's van out in the parking lot, though the sight of it makes her feel even lonelier in a way. It's a good-time car, the kind of car that would talk to everybody at a party instead of standing under a spider plant all night, getting stoned and counting the spiders. She drives over to the temple to see what's up. Rabbi Horowitz is out. Brian Levi is out. Mona methodically reads all the cartoons on Brian's oak-wood door. She takes in the blinking, buzzing death throes of the overhead fluorescent light. Everywhere there are branches: She examines the menorahs in the glass case; the big brass tree full of generous-donor leaves; the mitzvah bush for the kiddies. The halls smell of fresh paint. There's a sign up for an afternoon drop-in rap. She's never gone to any of the drop-ins but figures why not try it.

When people show up, though, there doesn't seem to be anybody she knows very well. Confirmation isn't until next week, but already there's a new crowd, it seems. Has Brian been recruiting? Or maybe these are kids from the next town; the temple sits right on the border. Somebody says to her, "You sure you got the right kind of temple, now?" and though someone else rejoins, "Shut up, jerkface, if you had half a brain your head would tilt," Mona still finds herself examining the finer architectural details of the room. For instance, the all-metal radiator covers, now beaded up with air-conditioning condensation. The talk today centers around things like nose jobs—how the doctor starts with a hammer and breaks the bone, moving on to what he restructures, and where the scars are. It hurts, someone testifies, a lot. They go around the circle talking about why they would want to do such a thing to themselves, a serious subject until they get to her.

"Do Chinese have operations to make their noses bigger?" someone asks.

Mona laughs with everyone else before explaining that actually, yes, there are operations like that. She too envies the aquiline line, she tells them. In fact, she envies even their preoperative noses.

"You can't mean like this schnozz here?" somebody says, exhibiting his profile.

*We-l-l,* thinks Mona. Still she politely nods.

"Now, that's bad," says someone.

"And your eyes too," Mona explains, scrambling for firmer ground. This much she can say about herself: She knows her good material. She starts to explain how there are also operations to make single-fold eyelids into double-fold lids, then backs up to explain what that means—about how her eyes look the way they do because of subcutaneous fat, and how that's what the Eskimos have. Also how some people think the Chinese evolved for the cold, although Mona herself wonders, seeing as how most of China is hot. She leaves aside the related topic of the shallowness of her eye sockets, along with how tricky it is to wear eye shadow as a result, and how you have to use an eyelash curler to wear mascara. Her turn is going on too long. She fast-forwards to how lids can also be made to look double with Scotch tape (not that she's ever tried this herself); and she ends with a demonstration of her sidelong look. She shows them how, when she looks all the way to the side, one of her eyes appears to be in the corner of her eye, but the other appears to be in the middle.

"Wow," says somebody. "You look like straight out of the Twilight Zone."

"Jesus H. Christ," says somebody else. "How insensitive can you get?"

"I'm just sharing with you my honest reaction," says the first person. "I think you should thank me for contributing in an up-front way instead of—"

Brian Levi intercedes. "Anything else you would like to share with us, Mona?"

She considers a demonstration of how she can hang a spoon on the end of her nose, that's how flat it is. But on further consideration, she decides to save it for the temple talent show.


Barbara's white van shines in the late-June dusk like a truth made manifest. Mona's parked it away from the other cars, to be sure nobody backs into it or opens a door against it; Barbara would sooner die than the Big V should know touch-up paint. And in its solitude it appears even more possessed of some strange coherence—*Mingle not with me.* Of course, this is romantic projection on Mona's part. In fact, the van is only a van. What does it carry besides full replacement insurance?

Mona cranks down the window, and cracks the vent window too. She starts the engine; the radio comes on by itself. Some love song she's never heard before, but she finds that after a couple of bars she can hum along just the same. New song. Then comes the refrain—she could be Janis Joplin reincarnated with straight hair—when suddenly there's a bass accompaniment in the back seat.

She shrieks and stalls out in the crosswalk.

"You sing better than Barbara," says Seth Mandel. "But you let the clutch up too fast."

"What are you doing here?"

"Did Barbara give you her keys?"

"She did." Mona quickly restarts the engine. "She lent me the van. For a month."

"Well, she lent it to me too."

"Are you kidding?"

"I used to surprise her like this all the time."

"She never told me that." Mona glances up to the rearview mirror.

A smile-like opening appears in his beard. "Didn't she ask for the keys back when you broke up?"

"She did. But when I tried to give them to her, she was too mad to take them."

"And you are here today . . . ?"

"To try to give them back again, even though the whole concept of keys is totally bourgeois." He leans forward and gathers Mona's hair into his competent hands, lifting and draping the mass of it over the back of the seat. His forefingers brushing her neck are warm and dry and slightly rough, as though he is too much of a man to use hand lotion.

She shakes her head. "Excuse me."

He slides into the other front seat. "You smell nice."

"I do not smell," she informs him. "If you smell anything, it's yourself."

"Really." He lifts one of his arms as if to sniff his armpit.

"You are grossing me out."

"Just playing my part of the love scene." He winks. "We're into improv now."

"Let me set you straight. I'm not into communal property, and I'm not into free love. I'm into keys. Private property. Private enterprise. Banks. Safe-deposit boxes."

"Being a nice Chinese girl, you mean."

"Exactly."

"What happened to the big rebellion?"

"I had it, and now I'm a nice Jewish girl such as knows kosher from kosher."

"And I'm not?"

"Treif is your middle name."

"Such a nice Jewish girl, but already you are talking about eating me," he observes.

"Seth!" Mona is so embarrassed that she takes a bend wide, bumping the curb. Seth gets thrown against the door.

"We don't have to do this James Bond style," he says. "If you want me to get out, you can just stop and say so."

"Okay."

"We should probably take a look at the tire anyway."

What with the streetlight above them on the blink, it's hard to tell for sure, but the tire looks leakless. Seth feels one suspicious section, then rubs his hands on his thighs. In the poor light his blue jeans look gritty, as if they are some sort of denim-and-newspaper blend.

"I hear you are practically engaged," Seth says.

"Who says that?" Mona is thankful for the dark.

"Barbara."

"And what business is it of yours?"

"None, of course, but if you want to know what I think . . ." Does he leave off midsentence because he realizes she's about to start crying of embarrassment?

"Pray tell."

"I think you're a little young to be entering a bourgeois and bankrupt institution designed for the stultification of life-giving impulses." (At least he says this gently.)

"Thank you for the free advice." Mona takes a breath. "And now may I ask how you are going to get home?"

"It appears that I'm going to run."

He says this with an air of expecting to surprise her, when in fact Mona already knows not only that he runs, but that running is not Seth Mandel's only sport. He is also a cyclist, which according to Barbara does not mean puttering about with your chain falling off every time you try to switch your big gear. No, Seth Mandel will pedal the sort of distances that a Seth Mandel must—id est, eighty or ninety miles a day. He carries his own tool kit, and no one has ever seen him stand on his pedals going uphill. Is this what Nietzsche on tape will do to you? He says he believes that people are enslaved by their cars. In Turtle Wax he foresees the demise of the Holy American Empire. There is no article he holds in greater disdain than a chamois cloth.

So why then does he insist on giving Barbara's keys back in person? Why doesn't he just leave them for her—unless at some level he does not really want to return them? Mona broaches these delicate subjects as he tightens his sneaker laces.

"By introducing a random element to her car use, I help her maintain a level of consciousness about it," he claims. "I keep her from developing at least one of the sorts of habits people use to avoid living their lives."

"How interesting," Mona says. "Though it must also be convenient to have keys to other people's cars."

"That is a competing truth," he admits cheerfully. Then he strides away, ponytail bobbing up and down behind him. This is not a jog he is doing. He opens his legs so that they seem twice their normal length, and there's real gallop to his feet. His white T-shirt floats above his legs; his arms appear the arms of a soloist in *Swan Lake*. How Mona's ballet teacher would approve! Except he's no swan, of course. No— of course, he is Prince Siegfried, all he needs besides a jerkin and tights is to stop rushing the beat. (*Why do we race the music?* her teacher used to say. *Can we beat it and win?*) Mona watches him in the rearview mirror: He disappears into the dark, only to reappear in the next pool of streetlight. Disappear, reappear. Disappear, reappear. Really the sight would be just the thing for a one-year-old. Still Mona backs the van up slowly, watching, keeping pace, until in her absorption she smacks one of the side mirrors on a telephone pole. *Oy!* The mirror looks okay—only jolted enough to remind her that the vehicle she is driving is not her own. She switches gears from backward to forward, and heads home.

Mona means to tell Barbara about Seth. But at the last minute Barbara's parents decide to take a June vacation, and so, though it means doing two research papers without a library, not to say missing confirmation, Barbara is suddenly gone. Probably Mona could have interrupted her friend in her flurry to get ready. However, Mona hesitated, and just like that, her hesitation erupted like a spotty mildew all over her. For what was she thinking at that moment, but of how Barbara and Eloise could possibly be buddy-buddy again, and with Andy Kaplan too?

For the first few days of her van proprietorship, Mona parks her wheels out on the street, around the corner from her house. For the van, it's not that secure a situation, being just too close to the parkway exit ramp. All manner of Homo sapiens pass through—some of whom, Mona knows, have got to have the big eyes for a shiny new mobile. In fact, there have been articles in the Scarshill *Inquirer* all spring about this very subject. MAKE WAY FOR THUGS, read the headlines. PARKWAY

BECOMES LARKWAY. Mona knows she'll be doing some praying on the van's behalf. But what else can she do?

And as it turns out, the only real problem is that Mona sometimes gets it in mind to avail herself of her freedom and mobility, only to discover the van gone—borrowed, it seems, by Seth Mandel to sweat in.

She surmises this because on one occasion, he left a well-used gym towel on the passenger seat. On another, he very generously left his bicycle parked where the van had been; and how did it get there unless under the perspiring tush of philosophic enlightenment? Mona could not help but wonder, as she beheld Seth's black ten-speed, leaned against a tree, what Sherman Matsumoto would think of the sight. Seth had considerately lowered the seat so that Mona could use the bike if she needed to; it was just too bad that what she wanted was the van. Which he did eventually return. She found it at the mercy of the world—unlocked, windows down, all but out of gas.

Granted there were on the driver's seat five dollar bills, also a note explaining how he didn't notice the tank was low until it was too late to fill it up. Still Mona pictures Sherman shaking his head. *Boy, but that schmuck has got you in the bath,* says he. Says she, *Who asked you, and since when did you start with the Yiddish expressions?* Says he, *Bubbela, about the same time as did you.* He shakes his head some more. *Talk about no manners. Talk about no shame. Talk about no consideration for others. What do you see in that Seth that you've forgotten me entirely?* Says she, *I have not forgotten you entirely.* But he continues as if he hasn't heard her. *And what if Seth shows up again? Will you make him run home the way you did before? Or will you give him a ride to wherever he likes?*

With the car, several more incidents of the aforementioned ilk. Then it begins to transpire that Seth does not even return the car sometimes. Sometimes he leaves it wherever he happens to be going—in Scarshill Village, for example, or at temple. One day Mona leaves a note for him. It reads: *This is my car, seeing as how Barbara lent it expressly to me. Would you please knock it off?* He responds: *If you want to discuss it, why don't you call?* He includes the phone number for the teepee.

This is when, against her better judgment, Mona moves the car onto her family's driveway.

Helen notices.

"Barbara lent you her car? How could be?" Helen these days is not so much shocked as irritated—the general trend of their relationship, it seems. "Her parents said okay?"

"I guess they must have."

"How about insurance?"

Mona can tell this is not Helen's real concern. Helen is just stalling for time, trying to figure out what her concern should be. In a world where kids want new clothes to look old, not to say turn suddenly Jewish, it is no easy matter to sort strange out from strange. Still she tries.

Mona makes something up about the insurance.

"Just no more trouble," says Helen.

"Okay."

"Just send the car back to Barbara, say thank you very much. Tell her our family has our own car, practically brand-new. Only break down once in a great while."

"I can't. Barbara's out of town."

Helen helpfully suggests Mona should leave the van on Barbara's driveway until she comes back.

"I can't." How to explain about Seth? "It's not safe."

"What do you mean, not safe?"

Mona tells her there's something the matter with the locks—a calculated risk. Unfortunately, Mona calculates wrong. Helen encourages Mona to show her what's the matter; and sure enough, when Mona tries to demonstrate how the ignition key fails to open the door lock, Helen inquires as to the purpose of the other key on the ring.

"How do you like that," Mona says. The door opens wide, revealing the driver's seat.

Helen says nothing.

"So much for that problem."

Helen says nothing again, only to go on to a related matter—namely, how Mona thought she could get away with such murder. What is she becoming these days? What kind of daughter? Helen does not yell at first. She doesn't have to, in order to make herself clear, for what she means is already clear. And yet the more she articulates, the madder she gets. Pretty soon her eyes flash, and she does not close her mouth right on the last syllable of her last word, but a moment later, as an afterthought. For a moment her jaw hangs open, her lips open and relaxed, though the *er* of *daughter* has already left them; and whatever type of daughter Mona is, this makes an impression—how in her anger her mother has so forgotten herself as to assume the look of a largemouth bass. (*Close your mouth,* Helen always used to say. *Leave your mouth open, the fisherman catch you for supper.* It was one of the reasons she hated gum-chewing, that people not only chomped away, but more often than not did it with their mouth guts showing.)

But here she is, momentarily slack-jawed herself, a lapse. Indoors, her anger is a force of nature, inexorable; but out here in the open, it seems part of the afternoon—an interesting moment such as makes time seem not a forced march after all, but a regular change of scenery designed for one's improved mental health. Mona could be a tour guide: *Today we have the garage and the wall and the house and a mother, mad as all get-out. See how she has closed her mouth finally, though her body still seems to fill; she seems more fleshy than normal, as if her specific gravity is going up. She has of late been bothered by a tic near her eye, but for now it has stopped, and look again as she swallows. She sighs with a little gasp, as if surprised that her magnificence should require so much air. She turns and strides back to the house, leaving footprints in the grass. These are the light green of glowworms and produce a similar feeling of squirmy fascination.*

End of tour. Mona resigns herself to putting the van back out around the corner. In the meantime, though, it does stay for just this one evening on the driveway—Helen thinks it too late to bring the van to Barbara's. Ralph comes home; Helen is duly reminded of the events of the day; Mona has an astoundingly miserable supper in which the driveway is revisited and hostilities are resumed until Mona gets tangled up in the idea that she is indeed an etcetera, not like Callie who got into every college she applied to and then some.

It is the sort of evening when Mona learns for the first time how an unspecified number of colleges actually wrote to Callie and all but begged her to apply. Hinting broadly about what a strong candidate she was. Who is going to write Mona a letter like that? Ralph and Helen want to know. Who? And when a list does not readily spring to mind, they make it clear not only that even they, Mona's very own parents, wouldn't write her a letter like that, but that even they, her very own parents, wouldn't so much as send out an application on request if they knew just what kind of daughter she was. And so on in this tenor, it's the song of songs, you'd have to be deaf not to catch the refrain: *Not like Callie, not like Callie.*

Of course, of the two of them, Mona has always been the mouth. That's because Helen used to laugh at Mona where she would have frowned at Callie and said, *You don't know how to talk.* So that Callie turned long-suffering, as has been described—so well-behaved that people used to remark on the extraordinary way with which she did things like ride her bicycle. Now she rides rounded over à la Gumby like everybody else; those dropped handlebars don't leave you much choice. But she used to ride with the posture of someone who had just come back from ballet class, and was still pretending a string came out of her head. Even her faults were model faults, such as reading in bed with a flashlight, and secretly wanting to be normal instead of perfect. She has never gotten thrown out of class for talking, or otherwise made trouble; and all this because she was never her mother's favorite. Some people might think the exemplary behavior will make her the favorite eventually, and indeed it might. Other people might think it not right to have favorites to begin with.

But the Changs understand the basic structure in life to be the hierarchy. Better and worse, number one and number two, more loved and less. Even now, when they come home, Helen will prepare a dish and say, *For you I cooked shrimp and peas, your favorite,* whether it is your favorite or not. Indeed, whether you have a favorite or not. For you must have a favorite; if you do not, she will simply pick one for you, because this is the sort of fact they live by. And to understand how Callie got into all those colleges, you would have to understand how this sort of fact has kept her running the steeplechase all her life. *I earn my keep,* she said to Mona once. The unmouthed part of the sentence being, *Unlike you.* And these days, Mona can see better how Callie felt. For now Mona's been signed up for the family project too. After all, one generation is supposed to build on the last, ascending and ascending like the steps of a baby bamboo shoot; and how nice indeed for the parents to be able to say, "The girls go to Harvard"! Mona realizes this herself, the misty elegance of the sound—it lingers in the air like something out of a perfume spritzer.

· · ·

Later, she gazes out her open window at the Trouble itself, white and innocent as a bathtub, as Sherman Matsumoto complains. *You've forgotten all about me.* Mona says, *I haven't.* He says, *You could care less about, say, Hershey, Pennsylvania, or wherever it is I've been recently. You don't care how big the chocolate factory is there, or whether chocolate can sweat. You have other adventures in mind.* Mona says, *Like what?* He naturally cannot answer.

Actually, she does wonder about Sherman in a long-distance kind of way. Will he ever call the hot line again? She wonders how he would feel if she were to call him to apologize. Would he say, *Thank you very much, I accept your abject efforts, let me tell you about my trip to the Grand Canyon . . . ?* Or would he say, *Please to go to hell, if I saw you in person I would flip you on the ground all over again . . . ?* In truth, he'd probably hang up. But what if Mona called and called? Wouldn't he finally have to talk to her, if only to keep his mother from asking nosy questions?

Mona sighs. The dark seems like heat to her tonight, a mysterious energy such as can turn one thing into another. Objects seem to be losing their edges and, slowly, their innards too. The van on the driveway begins to seem a hollow affair, more shell than motor, while around it, weird shadows wax energetic. Mona watches these sway with the trees. She listens as they jiggle with the lock.

She sits up. Lock?

A distinctive metallic sound that can only be Seth Mandel.

She has made her stealthy way down the stairs and out the house before she's had a thought. Whatever she's doing, she starts by putting her hands over his eyes.

"Hold it right there," she says.

He twists both her arms behind her back, so hard he's practically dislocated her shoulders.

"Ow," Mona says. "Seth." There's a large hand over her mouth, its fingers smelling of cigarettes; and then there's a patch of moonlight as a cloud blows by. The light is wavery but clear blue and bright enough for her to tell even through a stocking cap that this person is not Seth Mandel.

"Help," she tries to call. She tries to scream, but his hand is clamped tight. She tries to kick, but only manages to jab his kneecap with her heel. She can feel bone meet bone—also the brush of the hair on his legs. He's wearing shorts; Mona wishes she weren't barefoot. She wishes she were wearing shoes, or at least sandals. Her glasses have slipped down her nose; she can feel them slip more as he twists her arms up higher, tighter, forcing her body toward the ground. Her hair is everywhere, she can feel it caught in the crooks of her elbows; the front of her shoulders scream, also her wrists. Mona can feel her hands high against her back—an oddly placed warmth, like the squashy heat of his gut against her side, and now the twin hairy warmths of his legs, straddling one of hers. His thighs sweat, there should be an antiperspirant for legs. He smells of cigarettes, and something else—something thickly personal. Mona fights to crane her neck. She wiggles her nose, trying to work her glasses up closer to her eyes. Everything is a blur, but she thinks she can see her parents turn their light out for the night. She thinks she can see that their window is open. Mona tries to yell, and manages a small noise. She tries to bump her hip against the car, hoping that that will make more. She tries to scrabble her bare feet against the loose gravel on the asphalt.

And sure enough, the bedroom light turns back on. The bathroom light. Mona continues to struggle. Is that someone closing the window? Most anyone else would think it too hot to sleep with the windows closed. But Helen has never liked to sleep in a draft; she says it makes you sick to have something blowing on you. The bathroom light goes out again, and the bedroom light; and the dark that then drapes itself close over the driveway seems like no night Mona has known before. Even the brick wall disappears into it, gone. The man maneuvers her against the car. He rubs himself against her hip in a way she strangely recognizes. It is as though she knows this, what is this sweating thrusting rubbing; she remembers later that she'd seen something like this at the zoo—it was gorillas—and that her classmates all giggled when their teacher tried to explain what was a female in heat. *Oh, she's in heat,* they joked for weeks afterward, dismissing the teary prickliness of certain simple girls. They never considered what state the males were in, what name there was for this. *This is the forest primeval,* Mona thinks—not the right thought, not even quite a thought. She is locked stiff with fear, even as she struggles harder, using her legs. She can feel the warm asphalt crazing her feet. *I still have my clothes on,* Mona thinks, *I still have my clothes.* Even though a nightshirt is not exactly clothes. *I still have my glasses.* Grunting, gasping, then suddenly he lets go. Released, Mona shrieks; she pushes up her glasses and begins to run when she realizes that the man is headed for the brick wall, and that she can stop. For standing over her is who else?—but Seth Mandel, her avenging angel, bicycle pump in hand.

II

CHAPTER 6

# Into the Teepee

She doesn't tell the parents. Instead she squirrels the incident away as if she were once again in second grade, drying a doll's dress over the kitchen stove. Back then she held the dress over the flame with a pair of chopsticks; and so satisfying was it to see how the skirt lightened and stiffened, that she almost didn't notice that the hem had caught fire. She threw the dress quick into the sink as it shrank to a one-armed blouse, and from there to a white puff sleeve with still-stretchy elastic; it had glued-on Swiss dots, like the flocking on wallpaper. The flames reached up to the sink faucet, but looked to be shooting out of the faucet instead—not like regular water, but like rust water after a repair's been made and the pipes have been finally turned back on. Which is to say that the flames seemed to start, then stop, then sputter and start again, in a way that seemed to promise better service with time.

This more recent event, of course, is of a whole different order. Still, her reasoning in keeping it to herself is the same. She thinks the parents will punish more than comfort her. She thinks they will prick her all over with questions, that the truth, when they heat her up, may steamily escape. For small example, why did she sneak up to that man? And suppose it had indeed been her crazy friend Seth and not a real live attacker. What was she intending? With no lights on, and the two of them alone but for the bugs. What is she becoming? She does not think they will ask how she saw their lights go on by a miracle but then turn off, or about the ensuing dark—about how strange a night it was, how violet and grainy. Mona thinks they will see instead what they would've seen if they'd known about her little doll's dress, swallowed up by flames—namely, their house burning down.

This, then, becomes a bond between Seth and her, that he knows something nobody else does. She might have told Barbara, if Barbara were around. She might have told Callie, if Callie weren't an automatic door with a big black mat, mouth-wise. She might have told Auntie Theresa in California, if Auntie Theresa were in New York instead. And she might have told Rabbi Horowitz, had he not been fired, it so happened, the very day of the incident. Unfortunately, he was. Fired! The exact same day! Also he disappeared, no one knows where, Seth says. Maybe he went backpacking. Or maybe he moved to Boston, where rumor has it he has been seeing someone with something the matter with her. Not a woman but practically a girl, goes the hearsay. Possibly a shiksa.

Is that why he was fired? Mona is outraged, even as the coincidence of timing between his firing and her attack snags her imagination; she cannot believe it to mean nothing in particular. She believes that out there, somewhere, in the machine rooms of the universe, there exists a small crossed wire. Once there was a short in her parents' car, she says, and guess what? When you turned on the blinker, all the idiot lights blinked too—idiot lights that they were. Everything is connected, weirdly connected. Hasn't Seth ever heard someone else talking on his telephone? A far-off voice, but definitely talking, and not to you?

Seth nods and smiles. *Yes indeedy*. But he goes on with his accounting of the firing, insisting that crossed wires or no, the possibly shiksa girl was only part one of the problem. Part two being the fact of confirmation coming up. The temple board wants a seemly affair, he says. Meaning no bare feet. Also, yes, an end to things like Chinese people turning Jewish, since she asks, but if there is a part three to the problem, it is probably the marriage service Rabbi H. did for a Christian couple. Nobody could exactly divine why two Christians would elect to get married by a rabbi; it had to do with transcending worldly allegiances, and really, everyone thought the ceremony just beautiful/ in the interests of world peace, except for the temple board of directors. Says Seth, arms packed up in front of him like camp-table legs, *You want to know what happened, that's what happened*. He says he's going to write a letter of protest.

"How is it that you know everything," says Mona, hating him for his details. There is nothing more annoying than being contradicted in detail. At the same time, he is not hateful at all. He is gentle, he is patient, she tells him everything. About the hands up her back, the wrenching. "Here?" He kneads her shoulders. He explains about her trapezius, her scapula, her deltoids. He has the warmest hands of any human being Mona has ever known; they could be the broad-palmed touch of the sun itself, except that they reach her in the dark. He says everything will be tender for days, and it is. He says that she'll ache, and she does.

It's the first time anyone's touched her so intently. It's the first time anyone's held her, stroked her, kissed her. She's surprised by the details. How much stretching and shifting of weight and arms, how much limb arranging, how much neck discomfort. Not to say unintended bumping, and mingling of body fluids otherwise thought gross. And how inconveniently placed is the nose! A chaperon to be worked around. Seth sucks and nibbles; he circles her face; he removes her glasses and knows to put them someplace safe. She has never taken her glasses off with someone before. His beard tickles and scratches. He kisses her eyelids, her brow, a pimple she tried to steam out. He returns aimlessly to her mouth, holding her head in his hands. The rest of her attends, attends, even as she wonders about the etiquette of teeth—of teeth clinking in particular, and of teeth exploring also—and is it proper to keep your mouth as wide open as possible, as at the dentist?

She had not known that the hairs on her arms could stand on end. She had not known her mouth to be so engrossing, much less wired to her breasts. Indeed, she had not even known herself to be possessed of erectile tissue. With Seth, lesser play leads quickly to greater. Too quickly to be proper. Her glasses are one thing, her clothes she keeps on. She allows and disallows. A nice girl, recalling all her mother told her—namely, *Don't let anyone touch you down there.*

Still she finds that she owns a whole self inside the self that she knows, someone sharing her skin. It is as if she's discovered that when she gets up each day, another self comes to sleep in her bed, except that her second self does not sleep. Her second self carries on in ways that threaten to bring the police. How common she is! For how else can it be that on early acquaintance, someone can know her so much better than she knows herself? She did not realize how wholly she fit the word *female*, just as she did not realize how partly she fit other words. How she's had to take them up, like the clothes in department stores. *Those are way long.* But everything is, all that matters is how they'll fit after she fixes them. Is she a proper best friend? A proper sister, a proper daughter, a proper student? None of those things. Between her and other people there has always been a moat of explaining, work and explaining, until now.

Some days she doesn't want him to touch her, and he doesn't. Other days they talk about what the man felt like, and what he did, and what she did, and how she felt, and it's like a temple rap session. At first she is shy. But later she boggles herself with the things she can say and do. Seth helps her by reenacting the whole scene. Sometimes they do it over and over, and in the dark, and it's like what happened, except that she can say stop when she wants, and cry. Seth gets shorts like the burglar's; he rubs cigarettes on his fingers; and sometimes the terror comes back. But other times, Mona wants him to go on. Other times, they kiss at the end, or more. She keeps her legs together; they roll together on grass, on carpet; she always knows where her glasses are. She keeps her clothes on, keeps her clothes on. He proves less shy about his. His largeness. She pets him the way she would a gerbil—marshaling up enthusiasm. Poor pinkish-blue thing, so veiny, and with only one eye. She is astounded by his hair. His hair gets caught in his fly zipper, she thinks he really ought to wear underwear. *I'm just talking sanitary.* A word she'd never thought she would need in an intimate situation. She is surprised when it comes out *se-an-i-tree,* she sounds exactly like her sixth-grade gym teacher, only without the bouncing of basketballs in the background.

But this is her prerogative, to use whatever words she wants, just as she can always say stop. She can always say, *Seth, you're becoming the attacker.* The attacker seems more and more to be becoming Seth; she can't remember things so clearly. He ran away, she remembers. She wishes now Seth had run after him, and caught him.

But Seth didn't run. He says he didn't care about vengeance; his care was for her. Anyway, the attacker was bigger than he was. Plus he could have been armed. The real mistake, says Seth, was in not calling the police, they ought to have informed the police. Although the parents would then know about her being out on the driveway, et cetera. They agree it's not great for the attacker to be at large. Should they file a report now? Would she know the attacker if she saw him? At first she isn't sure. Then she is. By the end of the week, she would have to say no. That stocking cap, after all. She could not point him out, no.

Between kissing with tongue their variety of body parts, Mona and Seth go to see movies. These are not the kind of movies Mona is used to. These are movies Seth considers *fine*—movies like *Women in Love*, and *A Clockwork Orange*, and *Claire's Knee*—movies where the people have highly unusual ideas. Some movies Seth likes, you have to go into the city to see. They are not even in color. He explains to her about sadism and voyeurism and onanism and other isms unlikely to be found in the vocabulary section of the SATs. She tells him she knows how to spell *diaphragm*. With a *g*, she says. She says she read a book about it, sort of. Not about how to spell *diaphragm*. A book with a diaphragm in it. He explains about conceptual art and why he hated *Fiddler on the Roof*. She does not tell him that she has the original-cast album and knows every song by heart. He gives her a book, *Notes from Underground*. This, it turns out, is not exactly *Love Story*.

Should she say so to someone who not only went to Woodstock but knows it wasn't in Woodstock at all, and who in addition marched on the Pentagon (never mind it was with his stepmother)? Seth can tell you why Bill Graham closed Fillmore East, not to say what is in napalm, and what they speak in Cambodia, and what you should call people who live in Laos. She thinks about how he got to the end of *Finnegans Wake* and sure enough started reading at the beginning again. She decides, Probably not.

But in the end she does anyway, figuring he'd most likely see through her if she didn't. For he's the type to see through things. Not only does he live in a teepee, for example, he soaps his hair once when he washes it, instead of the twice recommended by your average sham-poo label. He claims once is plenty, the wily manufacturers just want you to consume more of their nice capital-producing product. Also he doesn't use regular soap bars, but a kind of peppermint liquid that comes in a squeeze bottle. And he uses just that one kind for every-thing—hair, underarms, clothes, dishes. (When he does his own clothes and dishes, that is, for example on camping trips.) Soap is soap, he says, the rest is just mind games. He says that if he had a job he wouldn't pay income tax, just like Thoreau. Why support the war machine and a capitalist system that requires ever-expanding markets and control of world resources? He says he doesn't believe the Russians are evil; in fact, sometimes he wonders if they're even Communist. That's just what the newspapers say, he says. Who knows what the truth is, or if Communist even means what we think.

"What else could it mean?" says Mona.

"I'm not sure. That's the point."

"Hmm," says she, admiringly. Only Seth could be so brilliantly ignorant.

As for things he believes in, these are for the most part sweat related. Running, biking. Sex and its warm-ups. Student strikes. Tutoring in Harlem, even right through the summer without air-conditioning. (That wasn't the hard part, he says. The hard part was deciding whether to agree to play Santa at the project Christmas party.) (He did.) Also he believed in Rabbi Horowitz, before the Big R.H. got fired; and though it's heavy on retribution, Seth's liked Judaism so far, what with its radical implications.

"What do you mean, so far?" Mona says. "What kind of way is that for a nice Jewish boy to talk?"

He grins his big crack-in-the-beard grin. "I am afraid I am an authentic inauthentic Jew," he says. "More ethnic than religious. However, in the process of becoming an inauthentic inauthentic Jew."

"Not to be confused with an authentic Jew?" says Mona.

"Exactly." Seth grins.

He says this foray into Judaism is one part of finding out who he is, and that this is why he didn't go to college—because he needs time to see what takes hold in him, what he does with himself. When he looks back on this period of his life, he says, he'll know more. As for his immediate future: He says he once met somebody who was hiking the whole Appalachian Trail, and that he thinks he might try the same thing, as a first step. So to speak.

"By himself?" Mona says. "The person hiked the whole Appalachian Trail by himself?"

"Herself."

"Alone?" A question close to what Mona means. A question she happens to have at hand, that shows interest, and not dismay.

But a few minutes later, when he is talking about the Northern Cascades, and how you can see caribou up there, and spawning salmon, and a starry sky worthy to be called the heavens, he says she should come with him sometime to witness these wonders. And this, she realizes, is as good an answer to her question as any she's likely to get. For Seth, no surprise, does not believe in love, but only in a kind of long-term mutual survival-related imprinting, not unlike what Konrad Lorenz described in geese.

Personal matters: She tells him all about the calls from Sherman Matsumoto, which it turns out he knew about but didn't know about. He listens. They pore over the log so carefully, it could be the Talmud in ballpoint.

"So he flipped you," says Seth finally. "So what? I can flip you too, if you'd like." And he goes on to conjecture what manner of ism that would be.

"That's not the point."

"The guy's not a person, he's an idea. Everyone's first love is an idea."

"Oh, really. And how would you know?"

"It just so happens I do know," he claims vaguely—talking, Mona guesses, about poor Barbara.

The teepee: Seth has a tent too, of course, with a rain flap and a window and a built-in floor, and that's what they would take with them if they went to witness prolific nature in the Northern Cascades. But here in the backyard he prefers the roomy ambience of his authentic canvas teepee, which he inherited from a brother he met at a peace rally. An *Übermensch*, this guy was; he gave a speech so powerful people were hugging total strangers by the end. And yet he was broke. He wanted to go on messing up the establishment, but all he had left in the way of worldly goods was this teepee in Tennessee. Hearing which, Seth gave the Joe—his name really was Joe—all the money he had. He even gave away his emergency traveler's checks, signing the whole wad of them with a fluorescent Magic Marker. Joe, in turn, wrote Seth's address on the inside of his forearm; and lo and behold, a month later, what should arrive in the U.S. mail but most of the teepee, everything but the poles. These the post office apparently refused to accept for shipping, as they were not properly packaged in a sealed and labeled box.

Death to the ornamental birches! Seth hacked down with an ax a clump of innocent paperbarks; the thunder of his efforts echoed through the yard, so loud the neighbors called. Which is how his stepmother Bea found out. (It occurred then even to Seth that maybe he should have consulted her first.) Still he went on to design his own lashings, using his ingenuity. And, voilà, the result: a living, breathing edifice that huffs and luffs like an asthmatic, but has yet to collapse entirely. In cold weather Seth keeps a fire going in the middle, and sleeps in a down mummy bag rated to minus ten; in warmer weather he sleeps right smack on some sheepskins, with nothing whatsoever between him and high heaven. He's talking about upgrading to a heated water bed. Mona, though, likes the sheepskins; she likes their smoky smell and their splat-flat shape, never mind if they're scratchy and reminiscent of roadkill. Also she likes hanging out in a room with a hole at the top. It's like the sukkah, except that in the sukkah there were chairs and other furnishings conducive to normal social conduct. Here there are only books, and a reading lamp, and a tape recorder, and a sky-blue princess telephone, push-button— leaving much room for mingling and commingling, and resultant strange tinglings.

Inner probings: He shows her his amalgam tattoo. *See it? All the way in there?* It's exactly the kind of oddity you can leave it to Seth to know about—that your fillings can leave tattoos in your mouth. Mona wonders if even daughter-of-a-dentist Rachel Cohen knows this. His is from the first filling he ever had, on a way-back molar. Flashlight in hand, Mona beholds with suitable wonder an iron-gray butterfly on his pink pulpy cheek innard.

"You probably have one too," he says. "They're common."

And sure enough, eureka! Hers is not so much a butterfly, though, as a most ghostly leaden egg.

· · ·

More sensitive issues: Seth shares with Mona how the family stocks are doing, which is not at all well. Also how his stepmother has the money in the family—his father is not a mogul, actually, but a middle manager with more realizations that prospects. He's learning to keep his mouth shut, reports Seth with disgust. Seth tells her what percentage of the money is liquid, what percentage not, and what liquid means. *For example, stocks. Stocks are liquid.* He explains how his stepmother has gone short where she ought to have gone long, long where she ought to have gone short, and how she took a beating in the stock market crash.

"Crash?" says Mona.

Seth is dumbfounded. "A year, year and a half ago." The Dow-Jones, the price of gold, the devaluation of the dollar. "We almost had to move to Edgewood, where the Catholics live." He winks. "Then the market rebounded."

"Is that what Barbara's dad says isn't going to last? The rebound? Maybe your stepmother should talk to him."

But Seth says he personally wouldn't mind if his stepmother lost everything. It would only go to show that there was some justice in the world.

"Wait, what?" Seth's stepmother Bea seems like a nice lady to Mona, if you can call a lady a lady who does things like march down South for civil rights. To be honest, Mona admires her. Mona thinks it's nice she marched, especially since it's hard to imagine how much fun it could've been, what with the general lack of air-conditioning or even cold drinks out on those roads and bridges.

"At least she didn't have to wear riot gear like the police," Seth says.

"That's what she said."

"That's what she always says. She tells everybody that."

Does that matter?

A scene in Seth's backyard: Seth retires to his teepee for some peace pipe. Meanwhile, Mona (abstaining) chats with the stepmother at the other end of the yard. Said stepmother appears to know the whereabouts of her postadolescent but does not appear to mind. Neither does she appear to mind that this teepee business is sure to leave a big dead spot in the chem-green grass. For her three real sons have had rebellions of their own, and one of her friends has a daughter who moved to Germany—of all places, Germany! for a Jew!—so that to move to a genuine canvas teepee seems tame by comparison. So what about the birches? A tree is just a tree. Never mind that Bea planted those trees herself, and arranged the rocks around them in a ledgy look; this is the official line. "That all kids should leave home by staying home." She shrugs.

Now she swings back and forth on the old swing set. "At least we didn't have to wear riot gear," she says. A skinny-legged woman with a certain mid-body loft, she is soupy-eyed and pouffy-haired, and easily pushed by her ragamuffin granddaughter. "Would we have killed for a glass of ice tea? You bet. But you just don't think about those things." The wrinkled back flap of her sailor shirt balloons.

"You don't?" Mona says.

"Not if your heart is in what you're doing." Bea pumps a little, but her granddaughter protests, *No, Grandma, I push*. Bea relaxes. "What's the difference between a chicken and a pig at breakfast?"

Mona thinks. "One's a big sausage and the other's a yolk?"

"Very good." Bea laughs. "In fact, that's better than what we used to say."

"What did you used to say?"

"That the chicken's involved, but the pig is committed." She starts to pump again, then stops. "It took me a long time to learn that lesson. People think it's brains that makes a pig smart, but that's only part of it. Commitment counts too."

"Commitment counts too," Mona echoes, hanging on to the swing set herself.

What's not to like? It's true that Bea sometimes orders people around. On the one hand, she tells you to help yourself to whatever; on the other, she expects you to put your own dishes in the dishwasher, and while you're at it to give the counter a wipe. But that's just the flip side of her general disregard for what Helen would call the proper way to do things—easy enough to forgive when you think of her out marching. And to think of how she's allergic even to dust up here! Can you imagine the roads down there? Says Mona to Seth, "She must have been living on her inhaler."

Seth answers, "That's a different kind of dust, and in reality she's still a capitalist oppressor, committed to the principle of her own private property."

"Oh, really," says Mona.

"You're just seeing her guilty conscience," he goes on. He's re-lashing his teepee as he talks, using an idea that he got while stuffing kneesock dachshunds at temple. "You've got to understand that every woman like Bea has a cause. They all volunteer. It's part of their life-style, not to say a way of keeping clear of socialism. The great Re-publican way."

"But isn't Bea a Democrat? And I don't see how marching for civil rights is doing away with any government agency."

Seth thinks. "Touché." He smiles. "You got me there. Still, aren't we talking about housewives who just have to let the world know they don't work? Isn't it a status symbol?" He saws off the twine with his Swiss Army knife.

"They could spend all their time playing mah-jongg."

"It would be more honest."

"But not as useful for society, and maybe Bea is doing her best, given that she's no rebel. I think you should be proud of your stepmother that she doesn't mind getting dirty and thinks about higher things. Even if she does have a big house and a stock portfolio. Can't normal people do good, maybe even despite themselves? It's like what Rabbi Horowitz used to talk about, only the opposite. The banality of goodness. I think it's nice of your stepmother. I mean, my parents would never even go marching for themselves, much less for a bunch of blacks."

As soon as Mona says this, she knows she has on her hands a big wet fish.

"They wouldn't?" Seth is so shocked he leaves off his lashing.

"It's hard to explain," says Mona. "You've got to understand. I mean, people they've never even met."

"You mean your parents are *racist*?"

"No," Mona says. "That's not what I mean at all."

That night, though, Mona is party to a discussion about who could replace Cedric, if necessary. For sale in the next town is another fran-chise, a great buy; Auntie Janis is pushing Ralph and Helen to think about how to afford it, instead of how they can't. Price, however, isn't the only problem. There's also been trouble in the other staff, and Mona's parents are wondering—if they can get rid of the trouble-makers—where they're going to find proper replacements.

"Can't Alfred do Cedric's job at the old restaurant while Cedric does Cedric's job at the new?" Mona asks. Alfred Knickerbocker being, after all, the next-best cook.

But her parents dismiss the suggestion. "Cedric, we know who he is." They say this because it so happens Cedric's hometown in China was not far from Ralph's; they speak the same dialect. Moreover, by dint of some highly creative sleuthing, it has been determined that Cedric's uncle went to school with Ralph's second cousin's best friend's youngest brother. "Alfred, who is he?"

"Do you mean you can only trust other Chinese?"

"Not only Chinese. But other Chinese, you talk to them, you get a kind of feeling. More sure."

*Make sure, more sure*—the endless refrain of her parents' lives. Sometimes Mona wants to say to them, You know, the Chinese revolution was a long time ago; you can get over it now. Okay, you had to hide in the garden and listen to bombs fall out of the sky, also you lost everything you had. And it's true you don't even know what happened to your sisters and brothers and parents, and only wish you could send them some money. But didn't you make it? Aren't you here in America, watching the sale ads, collecting your rain checks? You know what you are now? she wants to say. Now you're smart shoppers. You can forget about *make sure*. But in another way she understands it's like asking the Jews to get over the Holocaust, or like asking the blacks to get over slavery. Once you've lost your house and your family and your country, your devil-may-care is pretty much gone too.

Anyway, there's another reason her parents don't want to have too much to do with blacks—namely, that they don't want to turn into blacks. *Come on, guys,* Mona wants to say. *Really! How can we turn black? Jewish is one thing, that's a religion.* Even her Bobby Seale-nik friends are finding the color row tough hoeing. But Helen's been testier than ever on this count, and all because one day some lady came into the restaurant with a petition. A clinic she wanted to establish. Birth control, prenatal care, treatment for venereal disease—the works, she said, and all for free or just about. A sliding scale depending. *And of course you people would be welcome.*

"Excuse me," said Helen then. She grabbed two menus and showed a party to their table, only to discover there were four of them.

*You people,* said the lady again, as Helen came back for two menus more. *Common cause.*

"We own this restaurant," Helen said in reply. "We live in Scarshill. You should see our tax bracket." And she very nicely showed the lady out. She didn't slam the door, that would have been rude. However, she let it clap shut by itself on its nice stiff spring, and later, at home, she said, "Can you believe that woman? What is she talking about? Venereal disease! Birth control! She want to lump us with black people!"

"Are you sure?" Mona said.

" 'You people! You people!' What people is she talking about, that's what I want to know. Is she talk like that to her friends?"

"But Mom, she didn't say one thing about blacks."

"You think you know everything," said Helen. "But let me tell you something. She is talk that way, you know who she is talking to? She is talking to us as if we are black! She is talking to us as if we are Negroes! She is talking to us as if we are—"

"Mom!"

"I can talk however I want," Helen said. But she didn't say what Mona thought she was going to say next. "If that lady can talk how she wants, I can talk how I want too. And make no mistake. We are not Negroes. You hear me? Why should we work so hard—so people can talk to us about birth control for free?"

And after that, she makes more observations about general character than Mona has ever heard her make before.

"Those black people, they just want to make trouble," she says. "Those black people, you never know what they are going to do next." And how similar the Chinese are to the Jews, all of a sudden! What with their cultures so ancient, and so much value placed on education. How are classes at the temple? she asks Mona for a change. What is she studying there? Mona explains about how the classes have stopped; it's a boycott on behalf of Rabbi Horowitz. *He was fired,* says Mona. *It wasn't fair.* Ah, Helen says, and is it true that Jewish mothers are just like Chinese mothers, they know how to make their children eat?

Mona, meanwhile, is interested in this clinic. Birth control for free! When will it open? Not that she is planning on sleeping with Seth, however well acquainted she is becoming with his very nice teepee. Other questions: Has Seth lit for her more dark chambers of his heart, explored with her more misty haunts of his soul than he has for/with Barbara Gugelstein? Should Mona care? What will be Barbara's surprised reaction when she comes home? And are Seth's true druthers for free love and an antibourgeois experiment in living?

Mona suspects this last because ever since the incident with the attacker, Seth has been only too glad to keep the van in running order. "You are really selfish," Mona tells him one day in a pizza shop. This is part of an argument about whether Nietzsche would order anchovies if they totally nauseated his companion. And this is early enough in their relationship that she expects him to flinch to hear himself so characterized. She expects this because if someone had called her selfish, instead of enumerating with feeling all the well-meaning ways in which she made life easier for other people at her own considerable and barely mentioned expense, she would have made herself write, *I shall be nice if it kills me,* until the pen ran out of ink.

Instead he wholeheartedly agrees. "I am," he says, and grins with approving satisfaction to see her freethinking.

Is this the same person who used to quote Kant? And is he ever going to move on from Nietzsche?

Once, Mona went with Seth and another couple to a concert, during which he spotted some other friends down in better seats. (This was the kind of concert where a few people were dancing in the aisles but most were dancing in their own paid-for spots.) The friends down below were waving and gesturing: There were two empty seats next to them. So what to do? Mona thought they should stay up in the rafters with the couple they had come with; or, if one couple were going to move down, she thought they should at least draw straws to decide which one. But before she could say so, Seth was asking if it was all right for he and Mona to leave. She could see his reasoning—he was friends with the people down below, whereas the couple they were sitting with were not. And that couple agreed. Still, Mona felt bad, and when she looked up, it seemed to her that the friends they had left felt abandoned. Seth said later that they had increased the social good by moving down, and that to be selfish was to be human. He had simply acknowledged his will to power rather than become a sick animal.

"That's two different arguments," said Mona. Adding that she thought he should try reading Jane Austen, or George Eliot. "Those were people who knew what was right."

"Those were Christian sops who didn't realize that they were enticed with social approval to give themselves away. Plus there is no good and evil, and G-d is dead."

"Why do you go to temple if G-d is dead?" Mona said. "And anyway, this has nothing to do with your philosophic enlightenment. This has to do with the fact that you grew up with a stepmother who assigns her guests chores like cleaning up their own bathroom. As a result of which, you have no manners."

"Manners!"

This is the kind of thing Mona has always believed: that you should never open a present in front of the giver, for example, since the giving is what matters. If someone presents her with a wrapped box, Mona says thank you. Never mind if she is dying to know what's inside. She acts as if she could care less, with the result that she does care less than she otherwise might. For how you act influences how you feel; she believed that completely even before she became a Jew.

Meanwhile, if someone presents Mr. Authentic Self with a box, he says, "What is it?" Then he opens it, and if he likes it, he says, "Oh, wow." Otherwise, he might say, "Oh, man, this is just like the one I got from So-and-so." Which he says is just an honest response, in keeping with what he believes—that between the inside person and the outside person there should be no difference. He does say thanks if he feels thanks, and he says please when making a request—or, more accurately, he says *if you please*, like his father, the most solicitous human being ever to walk a golf green. But whereas Mona worries about the gift-giver's feelings—don't those matter?—he worries that he remain true to himself. *How self-centered*, Mona says. She says what her mother always says—*You have no consideration for others!* But he is simple as a sack of potatoes. There should be no front stage and backstage; to have a private face and a public face is to be two-faced.

"You mean everyone should be up-front," Mona says. "Like Thoreau. Everyone should have one set of clothes."

"If they wear clothes at all."

This is what she will say to him, years later: that that was a nice experiment Thoreau had in the woods. However, in the present-day world there aren't enough ponds to go around. There isn't room enough in this country for everyone to be authentic all day long. We need to have *consideration for others*. Or else what will we have but what we have? Fisticuffs without cease.

For now, though, she just shakes her head, enjoying their anchovy-free pizza.

"People should say what they mean and mean what they say," he says.

"They should let it all hang out, right? This is the age of Wood-stock. We are the stars; we don't believe in shoeshines."

"Very funny." Seth reminds her of how Rabbi Horowitz used to say that the inside of a person should fit the outside like a hand in a glove.

"Rabbi Horowitz was talking about moral action," Mona says. "Remember? All that stuff about the first letter of the Bible, and how *bet* was shaped like a horseshoe laid on its side, and how if you were standing in it, there was nothing to do but go forward." *Do not ask what's above,* he said, *or below, or behind; just go.* "He meant we should act on our beliefs. It had nothing to do with manners."

"Hmm," says Seth.

If only they could ask Rabbi Horowitz himself! (They've written him a letter, care of the board of directors, but who knows if it will be forwarded.) "Where do you think he went?" Mona asks later. "And are we going to picket confirmation?"

"Of course we'll picket," promises Seth.

"Let's have a sit-in too." She drapes herself over his back like a sweatshirt with legs.

"We can organize it together." He knots her arms around his neck.

And so, in a few days, they do.


Another true story: Mona once went to an exhibit on Chinese portraiture, in which only the faces of monks were depicted in all their idiosyncratic detail. Members of society were depicted in terms of their activities and their clothes, which was to say their rank. For these clothes were not about self-expression; these were closer to uniforms. And that was what mattered—not these people's inner selves, but their place in society. At least to the artists who drew them. But what about to the subjects? Mona was with a friend that day, who thought that if the people portrayed had drawn the pictures, they would have presented themselves very differently. Mona wasn't so sure, though. Mona thought they would have liked to be seen in those beautiful gowns and high-status silks. For she understood what mattered most to the people in the pictures as if it still mattered most to her: not that the world would know them for themselves—they would never dare to dream of any such thing—but only that they might know that they belonged, and where.

# CHAPTER 7

# Social Action Comes to the Pancake House

Barbara Gugelstein is sporting a fine new nose. Straight, this is, and most diminutive, not to say painstakingly fashioned as a baby-grand tchotchke, if a little blue and green. Mona does not gasp with immediate shock, though for support she does lean a bit against the warm and stable van. "Barbara!" she says, in so many words. Mona returns to her friend the van keys, saying, "Thanks so much for the vehicle, which I enjoyed and didn't scratch and just had hot waxed at that place on Central Avenue." In short, she does not immediately say, Barbara, don't you realize you will be excommunicated from the Temple Youth Group just for starters? That is, if Jews do excommunication. Instead she says, "What a surprise. And here I thought you were going to the beach for a suntan." She says, "How nice, and so little swelling." Barbara's face is in places colored to match her nose; Mona admires her friend's nostrils, which are a triumph of judiciousness and taste. Really, it's a shame to think about them used just for breathing. Also Mona notes how much more attractive are small oval nostrils than their large round counterparts—small oval nostrils conveying a certain hairlessness that large round nostrils can never quite attain.

"Don't you think that's true?" Mona presses Barbara to agree or disagree, in any case to talk. In the spirit of friendship, Mona figures she'll back into the truth later and with tact.

Seth arrives on his black bicycle. *How vain,* he says, in not so many words. *How shallow.* His hands sit square on his handlebars, his fingers lined up like a most knuckleheaded jury.

Barbara flees into the garage. This is through a side door, since she does not have handy her remote control opener. Her new nose she cups in her hands.

"It was my mother's idea," she sobs. "She said I should have the tip sculpted, it would be so nice. She said she knew the surgeon, nobody would even notice. Especially with the summer to forget what I looked like. It was only because of a cancel that we could even get in with this guy."

"Oh, Barbara. I almost didn't notice, I swear."

"She duped me!" Barbara's eyes are so puffy, she could be a blowfish with hives. "My own mother! And now everyone will say how vain I am, and how shallow, just like Seth said."

It turns out that this is all related to her mother not wanting to talk Yiddish, or to vacation on the east coast of Florida, where she claims there are too many Jews. "She said they spent their whole lives getting out of the ghetto, why should they go back for vacation? She's anti-Semitic," Barbara cries. "My own mother!"

Mona locates some Kleenex in one of the cars. These are the boutique kind that come in a cubelike box—a kind Helen would never consider buying even for their best drop-in guests.

"What about bangs?" Mona is thinking *distraction*: Let people sensing something ascribe it to a change of hair. Is this not a helpful idea?

Barbara, though, is not ready for a helpful idea until after lunch. She polishes off some yogurt with granola. Then, with the slightly shiny look of someone new-basted by the brush of divine inspiration, she says, "Bangs."

To the hairdresser! It turns out Barbara has always wanted bangs. She just never had them before because they put too much emphasis on what she calls her proboscis.

"Bangs are feature-enlarging," agrees the hairdresser. A baby doll in a beehive, she sports white lips and go-go boots. "See the new emphasis? How they bring out those baby greens?"

Mona and Barbara drive home singing songs. They discuss how Barbara is going to keep her new bangs from frizzing up. They part two happy friends.

But in the teepee that evening, by the light of a pillar candle with a painted-on peace dove, Mona says, "You were cruel and unfeeling. Barbara will probably never speak to you again, and I can't blame her."

She and Seth rehash their argument about manners. Says he: If you had any respect for Barbara, you'd have told her the truth. Says she: If you'd had any respect for her feelings, you'd have thought twice about hurting them. He calls her liar. She calls him jerk. The head of the peace dove caves in, olive branch and all. Mona slaps at herself, noting how even the mosquitoes choose her over Seth, that is how truly thick of skin and skull he is. For once the lovers do not make up with feeling and fond fondling.

And what happens? A jolt. Three days later, Barbara announces in the privacy of her kitchen that she is once again in love, unfortunately with who else? This is over twin dishes of crunchy peanut butter with vanilla ice cream. Barbara's nose by this time approximates its normal color.

"After what he said to you?" Mona says. "And what about Andy Kaplan?"

"Andy Kaplan," Barbara says vehemently, "is the brother I thankfully never had."

"Really," says Mona.

"He and Eloise broke up."

"Such terrible news."

"Now he's going out with Danielle Meyers."

"Danielle Meyers?" Mona, like Barbara, has always assumed Barbara to be Andy's very close second choice. "But I thought he went to Colorado to do Outward Bound."

"She went too. On purpose, I swear. And you know what all that singing around the campfire leads to. They're going to start a band— get that. She can't even sing on tune, or at least she never did in Concert Choir."

"Maybe she's not going to sing. Maybe she's going to play guitar."

"I hadn't thought of that." Barbara looks even more despondent. In fact, Danielle is such a great guitar player, she's gone on to twelve strings; six weren't enough for her. Mona wishes she'd made some crack about Danielle eating the mike instead. That is, at least, until Barbara says, "I hope you don't mind."

"Mind?" Mona's mouth gloms up with peanut butter. "Mind what?"

"About Seth." Barbara puts her hand behind her waist to feel the ends of her hair.

"He's not my property."

"I don't mean that I should go out with him too."

"You don't?"

"Oh, no," she says, tilting her head back some more, so that her hair falls to her hips. "I wouldn't do that to you. Plus I don't think he's interested in me anymore. He even gave me my car keys back. That's how little he wants to have to do with me, ever since . . ." She straightens, pointing to her nose.

For this is how she talks all the time these days: "ever since . . ." and "before . . ." More than ever too, she seems to be considering who she is, picking out her personality. When they repair upstairs, for example, Mona sees that Barbara has not only moved her records and gotten rid of her bedframe, so that her mattress rests straight on the floor, but also that she's changed the wallpaper. In a hostile manner, her mother has said, and indeed the style does seem antiparent—a Day-Glo-yellow op pattern swirls around so vividly that the walls seem to be pulsing, rolling, heaving in waves. It's a phosphorescent ocean such as you just hope doesn't glow by black light. Mona and Barbara discuss in detail how Barbara had this all hung without her mother knowing; and over the next few days, it becomes apparent that the fluorescent ocean is only one part of a much greater sea change: For every morning now, Barbara looks in the bathroom mirror and just wants her old nose back.

On account of Harvard-Radcliffe getting out so much later than other schools, Callie's had to go straight from exams to her summer job in Rhode Island. As for why she needs to go to Rhode Island to waitress, who knows? Ralph and Helen inquire politely. Why doesn't she waitress at home? But Callie makes so much of how everybody working at this resort is either from Harvard or Yale that they begin to feel she is practically getting a joint degree. And while lots of their friends have kids in Ivy League schools, who has a daughter going to Harvard and Yale both? In truth, there are a lot of waitresses from nearby Brown too; but Callie knows better than to dwell on a hippie school where everything is pass-fail so you can't even tell the A students from the rest. Also not dwelt upon, except literally, is the golden crescent beach with its sparkly azure wavelets. These Mona has heard about from Barbara Gugelstein, who it turns out has stayed at this resort before.

(Not that the Gugelsteins ever went back; Barbara says her dad didn't like it because of the beach towels, which in more generous moods he said appeared to be genuine Yankee heirlooms, passed down through generations and fashioned in the Puritan manner—i.e., without undue use of cotton. In less generous moods he called them Greenwich dishrags—for instance, to the attendant at the bathhouse, from whom he always demanded three of them: one for his overused head, one for his much-abused tush, and one for his foot-to-shin area, which after all were with him on vacation too.) All the same, by the rays of the no doubt mind-improving sun, Mona hopes, perhaps toward the end of the summer, to be illuminated. In the meanwhile, Callie the sophist has been working on her schedule, until finally she has traded enough breakfasts and dinners and buffet luncheons so as to be able to come home and practice her Mandarin for a few days. Of course, she's been speaking it all semester. But she hadn't wanted to unveil her new skills until she felt more confident. She says she still doesn't feel very confident.

However, by day two back in the house, she feels confident enough to tell Chinese from Chinese; it turns out English isn't the only language the parents speak with an accent. "I can hardly understand them," she sighs when they've left the room. "It's because they're from Shanghai. They say *san* for *shan*, *si* for *shi*. Plus I swear they're talking too fast on purpose." And in fact, they are; Mona has noticed this too. In the beginning they seemed just to be having trouble talking as slowly as they needed to. Habit, they said. But now it seems as if they don't exactly mind demonstrating how fluently they still do speak after all, accent or no accent. This is unconscious. They don't intend to put phrases by Callie in the manner of the Harlem Globetrotters. All the same, it's pick 'n' roll and around the back and plain through the legs sometimes, and all because, though Callie's trying not to make a big point of it, they sense that the language she's learning to speak is not their language at all.

"Harvard Chinese," Ralph jokes. "Not like how we speak, right?" He winks. "What Callie learns, every word is standard Chinese. As if she is come from Peking, not some low-class Shanghai guy, all he understands is money. She is speak some real Chinese. Classical stuff."

To which Helen replies, "What do you mean, our Chinese is not real Chinese? Shanghai people are just as good as Peking people."

"That's not how they thinking at Harvard," says Ralph. "You are so-called native speaker, but do they ask you go teach there? The answer is no. Because how we speak, that way is not so standard. You want to know how the correct way sound? You can ask Callie. She can give us lessons." He laughs. "Come on, Callie, you teach us. What means this character here, huh? Can you tell us, please?"

They all laugh, but not too much later, Callie is complaining that instead of speaking too fast, they are now saying a few words and then losing interest. They don't have the patience, she frets. Plus Ralph thinks learning Chinese is basically a waste of time.

"Has no use," he says.

Of course, in good time, even Ralph will be affirming his heritage; in good time, even he will be celebrating diversity in this, our country the melting pot—no, mosaic—no, salad bowl. Mostly this will mean writing checks. He'll be too old for going to unity dinners, and he won't be too sure what everyone is talking about, anyway. Community? What community?

For now, though, he would rather see Callie study engineering. Or accounting: "Even people lose money, they still need make report," he says. "Somebody need to figure out where is the trouble, how much the trouble cost."

Callie tries to explain to him about how Harvard doesn't offer accounting, or engineering either.

"I thought Harvard is supposed to be the number-one school," says Ralph.

Helen explains "what is so-called liberal arts education," and he nods at the end of the explanation. But the fact remains that Callie's best conversational opportunity is still Naomi, who thinks it's great for Callie to be in touch with her ancestry. *Forget your parents,* she says.

"But aren't my parents my ancestors?" says Callie.

"Only if you so choose." Naomi herself claims for her ancestors a number of people not related to her—for example, Harriet Tubman and Sojourner Truth. These are famous people of whom Callie is just now hearing. Luckily, another ancestor is Roberta Flack. Callie and Naomi attempt to discuss in Chinese what a moment it was for Naomi, seeing a natural on an album cover.

"*Zemme shuo* powerful?" says Naomi.

Callie has no idea, either.

"Do you think my fourth tone still sounds wishy-washy?" she asks, and when Naomi answers, she sighs. "I'm never going to speak as well as you," she says. "Let's face it."


For work, Mona is likewise working in a restaurant, only hostessing. And *naturellement* at the pancake house, where to keep herself company, she gets Seth a job waiting table. This is after he gets into a fight with his boss at the gas station—the problem being, according to Seth, that his boss was a fascist. Benito did breath checks on his employees every day; also he inspected their pupil size and kept track of their bathroom breaks. They had to sign in and out, says Seth, and though they were not required to write down what they did in that interval, Seth liked to note a little 1 or 2 next to his times. This baffled Benito at first.

Then Seth was called into the office. "I just thought you'd want a complete record of my activities," he said.

What next? Mona agrees to talk to Ralph about Seth waiting table. In principle they have only waitresses at the restaurant, no waiters, but no sooner does Seth get wind of that than he naturally absolutely has to work out front. Mona tries to talk him into salads, but he claims he has never held an iceberg lettuce without feeling an urge to bounce it off the wall; and such is the power of suggestion that Mona soon finds that she too is having trouble taking iceberg lettuce seriously as a food item. More and more it looks to her like someone's failed agricultural experiment, or like the inside of something else, the zip-out lining of a raincoat trying to pass on its own.

Mona makes Seth's case to Ralph. How useful to have someone with extra-long arms, he'll be able to balance more dishes than anybody, she says. He can specialize in large parties. And when the ice cream barrels run out, he can change them himself instead of complaining until the cooks go nuts. This last, Mona knows, is a particularly potent argument, as sometimes the front freezer ends up all but empty. *Pistachio or nothing,* the waitresses tell the customers. *Take it or leave it.*

But Ralph, though hardly insensible to this problem, is not fooled by its prospective solution. "Is he so-called boyfriend?" he asks suspiciously, feeding a large sheaf of paper into the jaws of his clipboard.

Mona answers, "Sort of"—how to explain?—and braces herself.

The first time Callie brought a guy home, Helen locked the screen door after he left, and then all three door locks, and this just because he asked how old was the bottle of warm beer they offered him. (Also, when they told him ten years, he asked for water.) *Typical American no manners!* said Helen when he left. And Ralph agreed, saying it was a good thing the kid didn't stay for supper; you could tell he was the type who put soy sauce on everything.

But Ralph is, as ever, given to changes of outlook. "In that case, he can work however he wants," he says with a wink. "Just remember: no kiss in front of the customers."

Helen is less sanguine. "That boy good for nothing!" She tells him to cut his hair, he looks like a girl from the back. She tells him to shave his beard off, he looks like a gorilla from the front. And what college is he going to in the fall? Seth says that he's not going to college, he's taking a thirteenth year at Eton instead. This is a joke. He says this expecting Helen to say, "Eton?"

As she does. "Eton?"

But when he starts to explain what is Eton, an explanation that involves a punch line, she says, "That's the place where the gunboats come from." And from then on, she glares at him as if to say she knows an old empire type when she sees one, and cannot be fooled by any amount of hair.

Seth is not the only person Mona gets hired at the pancake house. No sooner is he stomping up and down the aisles in his hair net (complete with bobby pins, this is, a victory for Helen) than Mona manages to get Barbara a real job too. Over this, Barbara is beside herself. Originally slated to spend the summer chez 'rents, she decided on account of the nose incident to stay home by herself. *Think of the beach,* her parents pleaded desperately. *Think of the new outdoor shower.* But when Barbara's cousin Evie volunteered to come live with her, they sighed and gave up. Evie the Responsible, after all; they'd always hoped for a little Evie to rub off on their Barbara. It was just lucky that Evie was coming East for some photography course. Who knew but that they just might return to new wallpaper?

And so it is that Barbara comes to hang out at the pancake house all day. When a waitress quits, Barbara hardly even needs any training to sub in. She already knows a German pancake from a French; she knows how to jiggle open the walk-in door; she knows only a rookie checks the bottoms of the syrup jars by looking, you have to feel them to be sure they are clean. Plus she knows the lingo—who the wheel is, and that she should call him sir. She knows that to order a Denver omelet she should say, *Mile-high city, and make it pretty.*

No sooner does she settle into the official job, though, than it turns out someone is desperately needed on salads: Saint Manny of the holy demeanor has unfortunately decided to move to the city, where his girlfriend lives. (He's going to put her through music school or die, people say, apparently she's some type of genius.) And so Barbara good-naturedly just switches, even though white people generally work out front. Other staff members point out how she isn't going to make as much money in back, but Barbara of the new nose shrugs.

"This is fun too," she says.

"Fun?" says Alfred the number-two cook. "You can't have no fun, girl. This here is your *job.*"

But having any kind of job is fun for her—never mind that she gets to work with Alfred the Handsome. To watch, you would never believe her once under the spell of Eloise Ingle. For Barbara positively thrives on the cutting up of carrots and cucumbers, and yes, even iceberg lettuce; and pretty soon she's thriving on the company too. *Alfred! Cedric! Darryl! Seymour!* Before you know it, she's greeting them like the oldest of friends, even the dishwashers. *Rhumba Rick! Jack of Hearts! Why, if it isn't the Moriarty!* She's lending them records; she's sharing her dope; she knows names for the busboys Mona's never heard before. *Darryl-darryl-do!* for example, and *El Commandante!* She's even making up names, names to which the people addressed duly respond. Can this be old Kugel Noodle, lately of the nose job? The staff calls her Miss B.—not for Miss Barbara, but for Miss Blanco, which sounds like an insult but isn't actually. Mona shakes her head, flabbergasted; Barbara might as well be giving her van away for good this time.

The staff is an assorted bunch, prone in general to changes in life status. They end up in and out of jail; they move out of state without notice; they break their limbs and facial extremities, or have them broken for them. Always there are losses to contend with. They lose their cars, their licenses, their leases, their kids, their welfare, their watches. They lose their willpower, and go back to drugs; they lose their minds, and knock up their girlfriends. They lose their temper. Once, a cook and a busboy cut off another busboy's ear, it was even in the newspaper. (*Those guys rough, that's I can tell you,* said Ralph.) Yet none of this much ruffles Cedric and Magdalena, the unofficial overseers, who expect from their previous life experience to always be pinch-hitting. Whereas Magdalena is an ever-faithful reporter of events, though, Cedric doesn't necessarily tell Ralph about so-called *everyday crazy*— things like Seymour's friends taking up all the parking spots while they wait for him to get off work. For Cedric, these things are like the details of the franchise magic mix. He says Ralph doesn't care what's inside, just so long as when you add water, it works.

Or so Barbara reports from the kitchen. She brings new kinds of cigarettes to the waitresses to try. She explains to the busboys just how rich she is, describing all about her house, and the four-bay garage. She counts up how many gardeners her dad's gone through this year.

Meanwhile, Seth and Mona make out in the pantry. This may well be a step up from the hot-line utility closet, who knows. It most definitely is not the teepee, however, what with all the cans and boxes— *Peaches in Syrup. U.S. Grade A Kidney Beans. Steak Sauce.* There is also the time-to-time threat of getting busted by Helen or Ralph—which prospect, of course, Seth pretty much adores. For him, confrontation is *confrontation!*—while Mona is just glad that the parents are these days engaged, once again, in considering that second restaurant. They had recently definitely decided they absolutely couldn't swing it. But then Auntie Janis found out about a new road going in, practically right up to the welcome mat. Now they're definitely deciding again. This has entailed investigations. Exit ramps, gas stations, preexisting HoJos. Average number of storms a year, and do storms really make people pull off for coffee?

There are all the same a number of false alarms in the pantry, including an avalanche.

"O brave new world, that has so much Jell-O in it," sighs Mona, from under a pile of boxes.

The love doves finally give up, and on their breaks retire to the attic storeroom instead—a spacious if warmish hangout, sumptuously outfitted with a table fan, a netless Ping-Pong table, and crates such as leave your tush most decoratively indented. It reeks so charmingly of cigarette smoke that Mona wonders why anybody bothers to light up. There are no windows; the ceiling slopes. When it rains, the metal roof sounds as if it is being pelted with gum balls.

And yet hanging out there is fun, if only because Barbara's new nose has indeed brought her to life, just as her mother planned, only as a Jew above all. She has decided to go work on a kibbutz with Rachel Cohen next summer; she's saving up to pay for her own airfare. In the meantime, a mitzvah: She is thinking civil rights right here in the restaurant.

Why would she want to go plant trees in a desert? She makes a most careful explanation to her new friends, especially Alfred, who speaks more freely to her than he ever did to Mona. For example, on the subject of how he cannot understand this desert-tree thing, even if the land did look different back at the time of the Bible. That was a long time ago, he points out, and he hasn't heard of nobody getting rid of no cars just because there weren't none at the time of the Bible. However, Alfred can certainly understand Barbara's wanting to get right out of this, our sweet land of liberty.

Seth says, "You mean, like you yourself would like to make like a hockey player and get the puck out of here."

Alfred's laugh seems to come from deep in his chest. "You motherfucking got it, man, how do you like that."

People discuss Israel with more curiosity than animosity, even though they are vaguely pro-Arab. Meaning that what they mainly want to know is, Why do Jews live in the United States, if they already have a homeland? Barbara endeavors to explain among other things how there's a war going on in the homeland, it's not all apple pie. Also she's not sure she'd want to actually move to the homeland, the Law of Return notwithstanding.

"It's like you could probably go back to Africa if you wanted," she says, poised on one corner of her crate. "But what about your friends and everything? Just because a place is your homeland doesn't mean you would feel at home there."

"I know a cat who says we ought to go anyway," observes Alfred. He's stacked two crates together so that they form a kind of stool.

"Hang out with our black brothers and sisters. Because there ain't no way whitey is ever going allow us no elbow room here. That's what my brother Luther says. He says there is only one reason to stay in this here country, and that is to bring down whitey's government. Black power!" He raises his fist.

Some of the other staff raise their fists too, in laid-back solidarity.

"But say you really had to move to Africa," says Barbara. "What then?"

Alfred shrugs. "They speak English there?"

"That's what I mean," Barbara says, tipping her crate so that the back edge leaves the floor. "I don't speak Hebrew. And there's no Holocaust going on now, and I'm not on that ship the *St. Louis*, and this is not the attic Anne Frank got stuck in. I think every Jew should visit Israel, and try a kibbutz, and make a donation. But does that mean everyone should live there?"

She backs up to explain who was Anne Frank, and what was the *St. Louis*, and what is a kibbutz. Alfred breaks out a cigarette, but waits until the fan rotates by him to light up. For an ashtray he is using a banana split boat.

"You've got to be shitting me," he says.

"I shit you not," says Barbara. Also she explains that America is a great country if you forget about Vietnam and maybe some other details. Or at least it's been great for the Jews. For once the Promised Land has turned out more or less as promised.

"So why don't you turn plain American, if this country's so great?" asks Alfred. "Why do you still call yourself an American Jew?" He says this expecting that he has cagily trapped her, and that the truth of her opinion will shortly emerge.

But instead she maintains that there's something special about being Jewish she wouldn't want to give up. Look at all the great people who are—Einstein. Freud. Woody Allen. Sandy Koufax. Einstein rings a bell with her audience, but Freud and Woody Allen do not, even after Barbara explains how they both have to do with sex. Sandy Koufax they recall as that crazy cat who refused to pitch in the opening game of the World Series. Barbara explains about Yom Kippur. Barbara says being Jewish is also great because it's about fighting for freedom. "We're the original Freedom Riders. Just think if everyone in the world were Jewish, how much better off we would be."

"What you talking about, girl?" says Alfred. "How can everybody in the fucking world be Jewish?"

Barbara says she only meant to say what if. But that's not to say that everyone couldn't indeed become Jewish, theoretically. "For instance"—and she points to Exhibit A, namely Mona, who is sitting cross-legged on the soft wooden floor.

"Jewish?" says Alfred, peering down. "You expect me to believe that? Uh uh. Not until you grow your nose, baby. Then you come see old Stepin and see what he say."

"Stepin?" says Mona. "Who's that?"

Alfred smiles mysteriously and winks. "That's me," he says. "Yeah, man. Stepin Fetchit. That's me."

Other staff members laugh. "Now, now. No *making mockery*," says Darryl the busboy, in a vaguely British voice.

Alfred winks again; his dimples lengthen. "Never you mind the riffraff here. Alfred, you can call me, man. Alfred the cook. Once you grow your nose, you come see Alfred the cook, all right? Maybe that day he'll say, All right, now you are a nice Jew-girl indeed, you can have some nice Jew-babies. But you've got to have that nose grown out *big* now, you hear?" He wags his finger at her. "See, I don't want to hear how you got your nose grown out like your friend Barbara here and then stopped. Her nose is some aberration of nature, man, her mama must've kept it in a little nose mold when she was a baby so it would never get to regular size. But now, you hear cook Alfred. A nose like that don't convince nobody of nothing. No, ma'am. See, that there's one unconvincing nose. That nose of yours has got to grow out so big you've got to sneeze in a dish towel. That nose of yours has got to grow out so big you've got to cut your nose hair with hedge clippers."

"Grow your nose," chants Darryl. Jack and Seymour, the dishwashers, chime in. "Grow your nose. Grow your nose."

"Tell them," urges Barbara. "Tell them how it's changed your life, turning Jewish."

"I think you guys are stereotyping," Mona says instead.

"Typing? Stereo? I've never heard of no stereo that could type," says Alfred. "No hi-fi, neither, man. But back at my place, now, I've got me a stereo that can cook." He winks. "That stereo can cook!"

"You tell 'em, Alfred!" Darryl and Jack and Seymour laugh; also Seth.

"Come on, guys," he says to Mona and Barbara. "You're not really offended, are you?"

Barbara looks as though she is going to cry. Still she manages some facsimile of a smile. "Grow your nose," she tells Mona.

"You grow *your* nose," says Mona, gently.

General laughter.

"Seriously, though," starts Barbara.

"Hey, man, we're serious," insists Alfred, winking. "We're most seriously serious."

"Mona is Jewish now, and it's made a big difference in her life."

"You trying to convert us, sister?"

"She's trying to educate you," says Mona. "So you can have a big house and a four-bay garage and a gardener too."

"We're never going to have no big house or no big garage, either," explains Alfred. "We're never going to be Jewish, see, even if we grow our nose like Miss Mona here is planning to do. *We be black motherfuckers.*"

"You can be Jewish too," Barbara says.

"Even Stokely Carmichael originally wanted to go to Brandeis," Seth says. "He learned a lot from the Jews."

"The whole key to Judaism is to ask, ask, instead of just obey, obey," Mona says. "That's what I learned. Also you've got to know your holidays. You've got to know all the ritual, so you know who you are and don't spend your time trying to be Wasp and acting like you don't have anything to complain about. You've got to realize you're a minority."

"Man, but we're asking, all right," says Alfred. "We're asking and asking, but there ain't nobody answering. And nobody is calling us Wasp, man, and nobody is forgetting we're a minority, and if we don't mind our manners, we're like as not to end up doing time in a concrete hotel. We're black, see. We're *Negroes.*" He says this emphatically, but rotates his head as if to judge the reaction, scanning the room like a second table fan. He is wearing a red shirt that glows in the dim light; everyone watches as he stubs out his cigarette. Cedric runs up the stairs.

"Chow time!" Cedric calls, spatula in hand—meaning not that it's time for the staff to eat but that there are hungry customers out in the dining room, waiting to be fed. This is the latest in a series of time-to-get-going orders, all of which have been, usage-wise, slightly odd.

"Crack the whip!" for example, and before that, "Feed the masses!"
At one point, he did try a straight-ahead "Back to work," but somehow he didn't realize he'd hit the right phrase, and went on trying
others—which so amused the rest of the crew that they allowed him
to continue fumbling. Of course, beneath the amusement ran a sneaky
current of lower-motive calculation. At least some staffers figured
Cedric to be on a path to owning his own place someday; why should
they help him? But that wasn't to say there wasn't pillow-time figuring on his side too. Callie once said she thought Cedric softened his
position as sub-in boss by getting people to laugh as they stood up.
*Otherwise, what?* she said. *Otherwise, wouldn't they grumble about how a
Chink happened to choose for a right-hand man another Chink?*

*Correctly perceiving the truth,* Mona tells Barbara and Seth that evening,
in Barbara's kitchen. It's not something Mona planned on telling them,
just as she had not planned on smoking so much dope. She's generally
a social toker, a real two-puff type, as a result of the Opium War.
(Which of course happened a long time ago, you wouldn't necessarily
predict that those British gunboats in the Shanghai harbor would have
much to do with Mona now. Except that so violent are Helen's feelings about narcotics that they do; who knows if Mona ever even got
to properly enjoy her baby bottle.)

Still, here she is, sharing a water pipe in the almost dark. Barbara's
turned off the lights, so that all they can see is what they can make out
by the moonlight through the window, and words seem to bubble up
with the smoke.

*Wow,* says Barbara, taking a toke.

*Wow,* says Seth.

Mona feels as though they are engaged in a primitive rite, in a bear-
clawed cave, at the dawn of civilization. She relates what her parents
said about trusting Alfred.

*Wow.*

She explains to them too about things that have happened in the
past—for example, how Fernando got fired for stealing minute steaks.
Which may or may not have had to do with her parents preferring to
hire Chinese.

"It was a big deal," says Mona. "He punched Cedric in the mouth.
He put a curse on the restaurant."

*Wow.*

On the other hand, who else was going to hire Cedric? And is Ralph such a bad guy for wanting to keep some China around him, for wanting to *make sure*?

"You're defending him," says Seth, rummaging for munchies.

But Mona says that her father's been through a war and a revolution and an uprooting they can probably never understand. And Mona does think that's relevant. Plus think how hard he works, she says. They all acknowledge this, a fact. For they've seen themselves how he is always there before they are, and is still there when they leave; it's as if he is under some special court order, pancake house arrest. Is it so terrible for him to want as a helper somebody who speaks his first language? Especially since, if he himself were to look for a job, somebody might just prefer not to hire him. His English being what it is.

They talk on (through four bags of Fritos and a six-pack of Tab) about how with the Chinese it's just like with the Jews: Some people get to Scarshill, but a lot get stuck on the Lower East Side, namely Chinatown. And is Cedric really on a path to owning his own place?

"Where's he going to come up with the capital?" says Mona. "He's got some management experience, but he probably doesn't even know that on every street there's a good side and a bad; we wouldn't have known that either if Auntie Janis hadn't told us." Also she bets he has no idea how important it is to have a parking lot you can see. "He probably thinks it's the same thing to have your parking behind the store," Mona says. "Or to have no parking at all."

*Wow.* Barbara and Seth shake their ponderous heads, taking a few more tokes. Poor Cedric. On the other hand, what about Alfred? They debate which is worse—not speaking English and having no visa and leaving your family behind to be forced to drink their own piss, or having a black face and living in a project and having a great-grandmother who was a slave? Not that all blacks live in projects; they realize they shouldn't generalize. "But not to forget the white great-great-grandfather who was fifteen years old and just trying out his prick," says Seth. He betakes himself to a bean-bag chair, that he may better contemplate the tragedy.

*Wow.*

On the subject of tragedy, they find that crowding in next—after the auction blocks and the Ku Klux Klan and the fuss over getting even a library card—is, of course, the Holocaust: the hiding and the trains and the ovens and the dentistry. Seth explains about how his mother survived. She luckily fled east from Cracow during the war, he says, so that she ended up in a part of Poland taken by Russians instead of Germans.

"Your mother was almost in the Holocaust?" says Mona. "She spent time in a Siberian refugee camp?"

Seth nods dully. "She was only eight at the time."

"And then what happened?"

"Then she came here and got married and got hit by a drunk in a German car."

*Wow.* Nobody knows what to say. This is the most Mona has heard of Seth's real mother—besides, of course, that she was nothing like Bea.

"We need a point system," says Barbara finally, getting back to the comparative-tragedy project. And they do indeed start to devise one. But in the end they go to the vote instead, figuring it's as American a way as any to arrive at the shining truth.

Which is how it is that, though it's a tough decision, they finally, generously agree: The Chinese revolution and the Holocaust notwithstanding, by and large, in present-day America, even if there was a black *Hello, Dolly!* on Broadway, it's generally an advantage to look more like Archie Bunker than like Malcolm X.

What to do with this terrible realization? *"Teshuvah,"* says Seth. "We need to think how to undo the harm done." Yet how?

"Let's ask the kitchen gang what to do," suggests Barbara. "Maybe they have a favorite charity. I'm going to give them all of my paycheck."

They agree that this would be most generous of her, since her *tzedakah* would only be ten percent of her net income after taxes. They consider starting a *pushke*—a donation can—for emergency funds.

"That's not enough," Barbara argues. "That's the kind of philanthropy my parents do."

"The stay-out-of-it kind," says Mona.

"Exactly!" says Barbara.

"That's like my parents," says Mona. "Only without the money part."

"My mom says she learned something from the fifties," says Barbara. "She says that Rabbi Horowitz could blab on about how Jews should do this and Jews should do that because he was busy pottytraining when other people were finding out what trouble is."

"But what about Seth's stepmother, Bea?" says Mona. "How come she's still doing this, doing that?"

# 141

"Her number didn't come up," says Seth.

Is it that simple? Anyway, Barbara goes on. *Gemilut hassadim,* she says, meaning acts of loving-kindness. She says they must think how to promote black independence, an idea astonishing to Mona. For while Ralph will jump off a bridge for *his boys,* his object is to keep them *his boys.* Why would you want them to simply up and leave? *Waste of time,* he'd have to say if they did, shaking his head mournfully. *Today we have no relationship.*

Meanwhile, Seth couldn't see things more differently. Of course the goal should be independence; let the workers throw off their chains! Wherefore, after all, is there Sabbath rest for everyone, if not to make plain that the proletariat and his oppressors live under the same sky, one as human as the other? The true condition of man being one of equality! He holds forth about Poland, land of his forebears, and how his mother's father refused to learn Hebrew. Yiddish was the language of the workers, said this grandfather, who by the way was not in favor of Israel, either. For why should Israeli workers stand separate from Polish workers? There should be no nations whatsoever, that was his opinion. The oppressed should stand together.

"You mean like us," Mona says, and Barbara and Seth agree. *Like us!* They agree that they are one nation—no, nationless. However, pro-Israel.

Where to go from here? Mona doesn't at first see why they should have to go anywhere, but then she recalls that she is Jewish. So that when Barbara says, "There must be something we can do," Mona does not say, as Helen would, *To do nothing is better than to overdo.* Instead Mona agrees, "There must be something."

But what? They think and think. So solid is their mutual resolve, however, that they cannot seem to get past it. A duet: "What action can we take?" says Barbara. And Seth: "What action is possible?"

"Action," Mona echoes. *Action. Action.* It's like trying to hum along at the opera. Most of the notes are too high for her, but still she can make out the nobility of the enterprise. *Action! What action? They need to take action!*

Two days later, an opportunity. Alfred arrives for his shift in mourning, having lost his apartment. Turns out he'd been fooling around on the side and his wife found out, but that was just the precipitating incident. The real problem being that she couldn't stand his friends, especially one black power type who always had to be out protesting and organizing to prove how much blacker he was than you. A field nigger, he called himself, even though he was one of the lightest Negroes Charlene ever did lay eyes on; almost as light as Charlene herself, who could pass for white easy. People sometimes took her and Alfred for salt-and-pepper, no kidding. Charlene said this troublemaker just didn't know how to appreciate what he had. And she couldn't understand how Alfred could be friends with this cat—his name was Luther the Race Man.

But they hung with the same brothers, and so far as Alfred was concerned, a bro' could wear a dashiki if he wanted, he could wear an Afro if he wanted, he could have a little something on the side if he wanted. See, these sisters have no motherfucking sense of humor, he says, especially when they come home from the night shift at the emergency room. They don't realize it's a free motherfucking country. She said his friends were a bad influence, wanting everything the way they did; that was because her mama and papa were from Jamaica, where Negroes didn't always realize they were Negroes, according to Luther. Some of them got pretty airy; that's what happened when you gave a Negro a lawn and a pool. In fact, Luther said, she wasn't hardly black at all. He used to point out to everybody how you could see the veins in her arms right through her skin. Made her so self-conscious she wore a high-neck long-sleeve shirt even in the summertime around him. And then he had a game he liked to play called Make a Request of Nurse Char-lene. He'd ask her something like, *Hey, Nurse Char-lene, might we have some of your de-licious ribs here? This boy's dying for one of your ribs.* And if she said *I would fix you a bone except that I am saving it for my dog to chew on,* he would wink and mention how on such and such a subject, the white folk had such and such an opinion. And then he would turn to Charlene and ask, *Ain't that right now? Ain't that what the white folk say?* Charlene thought Alfred's friends were a bad influence, but here Alfred had a steady gig and everything, and if he finally got to having a little on the side, why, see, that Charlene drove him to it, man, what with her house nigger ways. And so what if Charlene's doctor daddy was going to be proclaiming how right he was about these American blacks? Charlene shouldn't have had the locks changed, and hidden the car away somewhere, and taken all the money out of their bank account, man. She could've at least left his clothes out on the steps, and how's he going to get back and forth now to keep his steady job? That was a brand-fucking-new Buick he was driving too.

"What am I going to do, man?" he finishes. "I've been shut out like a fucking hound dog."

And just like that, Barbara offers him a room in her house.

"Aw, no," says Alfred, flipping pancakes. "That's right nice of you, Miss B. But see, poor Alfred here can find himself his own house." He grins after a fashion, itching with his forearm his unshaved chin.

Barbara continues to insist, poor Alfred continues to refuse. And later on, Mona tries to point out to Barbara that this is just as well.

"You have to consider how long he might stay," Mona says. "Plus you don't want to get into trouble."

"I'm not in love with him, if that's what you mean."

"And what about your cousin?"

Evie, Barbara claims, has been working so hard on her photography that they barely even see each other. "She's living in a complete other part of the house," Barbara says. "She's got this bathroom she's set up as a darkroom."

"In any case," Mona says, "he's got another place."

"Good," Barbara says, a clear look to her dewy eyes. "He was welcome at mine."


Mona thinks of her friend's words a number of times over the next week or so. In fact, Mona thinks so admiringly of Barbara's spontaneous generosity of spirit, that everything about her own life begins to seem small and self-centered and shrunken up. She feels like a discount troll doll, one that doesn't even come with colored hair.

This is exacerbated by an encounter with Bea in the supermarket, where Bea is stocking up on pineapple rings. A luau, she explains, the proceeds to benefit a halfway house. She is friendly and flatteringly open to advice on several matters Polynesian. Would coconuts make good bowling balls, for example. Bea is thinking of having a bowling competition with coconuts for balls and wooden palm trees for pins.

Mona reassures her that this is very much in the Polynesian spirit. Bea thanks Mona for her contribution to the cause.

"It's nothing," says Mona, and means it. How disappointed Bea would be to know the true her! Mona resolves to be more Jewish, to do Rabbi H. proud.

"You are right," Mona tells Barbara one day. "We should've done what we could have for Alfred."

"We spend so much time protecting our bourgeois interests," Barbara says, standing tall. Her hair falls straight as a plumb line down her back.

Meanwhile, Seth beams; more and more, he has been regarding Barbara with warm approval. True, there was that ice age after her nose. But the thaw that began with Barbara's dialogues with the help has continued steadily, especially since Seth moved his stereo to the teepee. Now he puts "Lay Lady Lay" on every time he and Mona make out. Which Mona wishes he wouldn't. She says she already knows he wants to sleep with her, it's a hard fact to miss. So to speak. He doesn't deny it. Is this why he starts engaging Barbara in higher talk again? One day he even brings in a book for her to read— *Siddhartha* this is, all about how the noble spirit wars with the most ardent body. Barbara accepts this loan with her two hands and two eyes, you would think he was handing her the Torah to kiss.

How can Mona yell at Seth for lending a book to Barbara? What's a little intellectual exchange between friends, and who's to say higher ideas turn lower? Barbara jets up to visit her parents for a week, giving them all time to consider what means friendship.

And so it is that when Alfred falls out with his new girlfriend, Mona is the one who comes to his rescue. Her nose is no bigger than it ever was, she jokes; but she would like to offer him, out of the Jewishness of her heart, refuge in Barbara's garage.

# CHAPTER 8

# Further Changes of Occupation

Barbara, when she comes home, is as shocked as she is sunburned. However, she quickly says, "How can he stay in the garage?"—and in the process of saying the right thing, is transformed. She is a balm for the weary, a veritable aloe vera rub, especially compared to Mona, who meanly reports how Alfred has a mattress, and a cube fridge, and a Sterno camp stove with little fold-up legs. These are basics she had thought would keep him comfortable. But Barbara, her new nose pinkly peeling, insists he move to the house like a proper indoor guest.

A generous idea, a magnificent idea. Unfortunately, however, he refuses. This is on account of his hoping this Whole Trouble with Charlene is almost over; he's hoping that pretty soon the lights will come up and the credits will roll. Or at least so goes Seth's analysis of the situation. For Seth has read about these things, it turns out—how a person who hopes to return to his old digs might just refuse to get comfortable in his new.

"This is called denial," says Seth.

"A psychological thing," says Barbara.

"Like sublimation," says Mona.

All nod knowingly.

Seth goes on to say that he thinks he knows Alfred's second-choice accommodation, and that is not at Barbara's house, either. Alfred's second-choice accommodation, thinks Seth, is with one of the brothers. But how can he stay with them, when they are the very cats Charlene can't abide?

Mona and Barbara ponder this quandary. "Poor Alfred," they say. They note how these matters psychological seem to bulk up mysteriously, like yeast breads. Still, on Alfred's behalf, they begin to hope what they think he hopes.

But Charlene doesn't call and doesn't call, and then even Alfred starts to see how a hardworking babe like her might not have time for his brand of shit. That's why he finally calls her, only to find out she's changed their phone number to something unlisted. He discovers she's signed up her coworkers to run interference at the hospital. He starts to realize he's never going to get her on the line there, or anywhere. And that's when it comes to him, finally, a subrealization: that she means to take her own sweet time softening up, maybe it wouldn't be such a bad thing to wait out the duration in the house.

Especially since there's also been a discovery regarding the new girlfriend—namely, that the whole time Trixie was seeing Alfred, she was also wrinkling up the sheets with somebody else. Some white dude, no less, who is now claiming he's going to move her into a real house, with real furniture.

"Appliances too," complains Alfred. "A dishwasher. A washing machine. A dryer, and not the bottom of the line, either. No, sir. See, he's going to get her the permanent-press cycle. He's going to get her the stackable if she wants. Of course, first he's got to slip-slide his rich ass out of his correctional institution." Alfred smiles gamely as he shakes his head, but the motion's got no swing; it puddles down like ink into his fine steel chin. "And that's the fucking story, man. My baby done traded me in for a washer-dryer combination."

"How do you know?" Seth asks, cracking his knuckles like Rabbi Horowitz.

"The bitch told me herself, live and in English. I called her up and told her, Trixie, baby, your Alfred's coming on back, and that's when she told me. She said, Alfred Knickerbocker, don't you do nothing of the kind. She said she's got her a dude who's going to do her right for a change. They're going to get married in a motherfucking church. They're going to ride up in a motherfucking limousine. She said she's got the ring already, it's flashing like the roof light on a motherfucking goonmobile. She said this dude, man, he's not like some regular motherfucker. Uh uh. She said he's something else." He laughs loudly. "Yessiree. Sounds like he is something else indeed. And that makes old Alfred the something on the side, except he ain't even on the side no more, man. See, now he's just plain something." He winks a wink reminiscent of a wince.

Practicalities: How to get food to Alfred, and what route would be the best for him to take in and out, and how to be sure Barbara's cousin Evie won't notice. And what about the neighbors? Will they assume he's a much-needed manservant, worth his weight in gold? Or will they turn into sleuthy private eyes, discuss him between rubbers of bridge?

"We don't want them to phone the police or anything," says Barbara, at a meeting around her kitchen countertop. To this everyone agrees. They are perched on their padded stools, with a bowl full of bridge mix, discussing the Problem Most Serious—namely, that Barbara's house so convincingly commands its little knoll. The major sport facilities are hidden behind a hedge, but on account of a Y in the road, the house itself sits in intermittent view of two streets. One side of the property does fetchingly undulate down to a patch of town woods. But even if Alfred comes and goes from that side, how will he manage the fetching undulation? Alfred volunteers to plain hoof it, a time-honored solution. However, Barbara points out that smack across the street lives a boy with a telescope.

Mona spins around on her stool. "How about the Underground Railroad? If it really is a railroad, and not just a wine cellar. Can Alfred go back and forth that way?"

"What a genius idea!" exclaims Barbara. "Except, is there more tunnel back behind the wine rack?"

"And does it go in the right direction?" Mona says this modestly, not wanting to seem as though she too thinks this is a genius idea. "Anyway, it's worth checking out."

"What you talking about, girl?" says Alfred.

"What railroad?" says Seth.

Barbara explains. Seth leaps barefoot from his stool to investigate.

Alfred pushes back more slowly. "Those tunnels are short, man. My grandpa used to say they're something smelly besides. He said his pa came up from Dixie for a stretch that way. Mostly he came up the rivers, see, on account of the dogs. But every now and then he came up a tunnel, and he said they are something noxious, man. He said a body can't hardly breathe down there."

But in the end Alfred too is overtaken by the spirit of exploration. In the basement with Seth, he pries out the wine rack, complete with four more bottles of wine; they could be Lewis and Clark, except that beyond them stretches, not an unsullied continent, begging to be ravished, but instead a long hole, as low as Alfred predicted, and reinforced with bits: bits of brick, bits of stone, bits of wood. Also something that looks to be the tip of a buried bone, but which turns out upon excavation to be a doorknob.

Says Barbara, "That's got to be antique."

They pass it around like a talisman of their tribe. How cool, how smooth, how round. They conclude it to be ceramic. They cradle its heft; they turn it in the air as though it still might unlatch some door, who knows—as if it still might open to them some room, some mystery. Seth tosses it playfully into the air.

"Hey! Don't do that! You're going to break it," says Mona. And for safekeeping she presents it to Alfred.

Seth and Mona repair home to round up proper orienteering equipment; when they reconvene at Barbara's, it is with ropes and shovels, flashlights, water bottles, a first-aid kit. Gorp. A compass. Carabiners. It's clear they all know their way to Eastern Mountain Sports. As for who's going to go in the tunnel, they agree it makes more sense for Seth to go than Alfred, Seth being so much shorter. Mona, for the same reason, is a definite go too. But should Barbara go or stay? It seems to make sense for her to stay, but she wants to go, so that no one can say she chickened out.

"No one's saying anything," says Seth.

Still Barbara insists that she's going, and whatever her intention, Seth is suitably impressed. She ties up her hair to get it out of the way; Mona ties up her hair too. Then they link themselves, expedition style. For this purpose they pick the orange and blue climbing rope that is Mona's old favorite; they argue over the knots, which no one quite remembers, except to be able to tell that they're tied wrong. Alfred shouts into the tunnel, trying to get a sense of the acoustics. If he hears anything that sounds like trouble, he's going to get help, he says. Also if they haven't come back in a half hour. They synchronize their watches.

Equipped with six flashlights—they each have a spare—Mona and Barbara and Seth set off. The tunnel is cool enough that Mona's glasses fog, and so low on headroom that only she can stand up straight. Barbara (behind her) and Seth (in front) have to crouch. For Seth in particular this is not so easy, since he has to walk holding their one big shovel out in front of him; he shuffles like a camper on latrine duty. Twice he stops. He squats all the way down on his heels so that he can at least rest his back, but pretty soon his arms ache too, it's a relief when at one spot he has to stop and shovel. Behind him, Mona and Barbara wait encouragingly; they can feel his efforts via the tug of the rope around their waists. They check the compass. Northwest, they're headed—toward the woods! They whoop it up quietly, not wanting to alarm Alfred. Still they hear him shout to them.

"Everything okay?"

"Yes," they shout back, as clearly as they can.

They note that the tunnel is sloped gently downhill, a good sign. Seth finishes shoveling; they move on bravely, forging the considerable muddy spots. These are caused by the hoses for the in-ground lawn sprinkler system, which cross the tunnel in a number of places, and leak primordially; for sure they'll be growing stalactites in another thousand years. Or is it stalagmites?

Quietly they discuss their worst fears. Mona's is of coming upon a porcupine. She says she is afraid that when it realizes they are coming at it, it will shoot. However, Seth says this fear has nothing to do with porcupines at all; he says it has to do with the war and just goes to show that the nation has been traumatized right down to its deepest subconscious. Is that true? Anyway, Barbara's worst fear is of skunks. She says tomato juice doesn't work; if they get sprayed, they'll have to cut all their hair off. Seth's fear is snakes; he trains his flashlights with disproportionate interest on the floor until Mona points out that snakes could just as well be coming out of the walls. At this, Seth jumps slightly out of his skin, occasioning a head thump. They go on to other fears, agreeing that for all of them, the first-place nonanimal nightmare is a cave-in.

"We could be buried alive!" observes Mona helpfully. "Like in 'The Cask of Amontillado' or something."

" 'The Cask of Amontillado,' " muses Barbara. "Is that a song?"

"It could be," says Mona. And to the tune of "If you're going to

San Francisco," she sings, "If you're going to Amon-till-ado . . ." No one else sings. "Be sure to inter me in an oaken casket there . . ."

The tunnel is very quiet; none of them has ever been in a place so quiet. If Alfred has yelled again to them, they haven't heard him.

"Get it?" says Mona finally. "Oaken casket, open casket?"

"Very punny," says Seth. "Just what we need, a little black humor."

"Jewish humor," says Mona.

"But of course," says Seth. "It's your Jewish heritage speaking."

"Singing," says Mona. "It's my Jewish heritage singing." She clears her throat. "And for my next number, 'Singing in the Grave.' "

Seth laughs and joins in; Barbara checks her compass again—still headed for the woods. They cross another hose line. Another. More mud. They agree that should Alfred truly come to use the tunnel on a regular basis, he will have to wear hiking boots. If he has any, that is.

Finally Seth says, "How are we going to know when we've come far enough?"

"One more hose, and that'll be the edge of the woods," says Barbara. "There are eight sprinklers between the house and the edge of the lawn. I think."

"Plus won't there be tree roots?" says Mona. "If there are trees?"

They soldier on. Until there it is, finally, the eighth hose, bright green and, sure enough, leaking like the others. And just beyond it, an underground forest of tree roots. These are as enormous and ropy as anything in *Babes in Toyland*, you half expect them to start talking.

"Now what?" says Seth.


Later it will turn out that this is not exactly the Underground Railroad. Later it will turn out that this is the Underground Railroad remade into a passageway for a bomb shelter. But for now the explorers explore as explorers will, which is to say with their feet firmly planted on what they think they know. Back up on the open lawn, by the brilliant light of the sun, they count the water sprinklers. The eighth one to the northwest of the house does indeed skirt the woods; they dig a little here, a little there, starting from the sprinkler, making their way on out along the feeder hose. The ground begins to look like the acorn pantry of a large forgetful squirrel. Until just when they are about to give up, a piece of ground collapses under Barbara's foot. Hooray! They do a little dance, until they realize that the tunnel too has collapsed some, and they are collapsing it more by celebrating.

They stabilize the tunnel with two-by-fours. This takes some enterprise. Also they fashion an entrance, with a stepladder down; the door is a metal garbage can lid laden with mossy camouflage. Worried as they are about the dirt needs of the moss, Mona can hardly lift the lid. However, Alfred can, which is what matters. The moisture in the tunnel they soak up with kitty litter; Alfred they equip with a heavy-duty flashlight. And the next thing they know, it seems the most natural thing in the world for Alfred to be popping in and out of Barbara's basement.

As for his room: Barbara's house having an annex, there is a series of tiny rooms right upstairs from the garage. These were servants' quarters at one point, and now are mostly empty, only the last two still house objects once useful to their occupants. It's as if someone had meant to clean out the whole shebang but for some reason quit three quarters of the way down the hall. With the result that in one room there are lamps and tables; an old phonograph turned into a potter's wheel; some old dresses with perspiration stains; and a beasty mink stole complete with a beady-eyed head and businesslike claws. Also a girdle. Barbara holds this up.

"I came, I held in my stomach, I conquered," says Mona.

Alfred occupies himself with the closet door. "This door's not hung straight," he says. "I bet it doesn't close right, either." He seems pleased when, sure enough, it doesn't. He sits down on a bare gray mattress, bounces a little, trying it out. There's no bounce. "It's all right, I guess," he says.

"You sure?" Barbara sits down too.

Alfred strokes his smooth-shaved jaw, contemplative. They move on to the next room, expecting more of the same. But, surprise: This room is completely furnished, and splendidly. There is a moth-eaten blue velvet chair; also lace curtains. And children's toys—the owner before Barbara's dad had some six or seven kids. But these are small distraction from the lion's head door knocker on the door, and the full two thirds of a fancy-stitch throw on the bed. There is even a mural on the cracked walls (hand drawn in imitation of the ones downstairs), along with a painted fireplace. The fireplace sports a roaring red fire. Who could have lived here? And why did the person leave everything behind? There is a definite atmosphere, as Seth observes, of unplanned departure. As for what could have precipitated this unplanned departure, there are clues. For instance, whereas there are only milkmaids in the mural downstairs, in this one there is a master wielding a whip in one hand while fondling his private parts with the other. The milkmaids by and large pull at their pigtails and cower behind the cows. However, one vengeful lass seems to be taking aim with an udder.

Perfect! Stroking his smooth chin some more, Alfred agrees: This should be his new place of residence.

"Make yourself at home." Barbara proffers Alfred keys to the house and alarm, and when he hesitates, tosses the ring into the air. He catches it, of course—this being reflexive in men, not to let things get by them. "I mean it," she says.

"She really does," offers Mona. "She lent me her van for a month, I swear."

"She's like that," echoes Seth. "Born to give things away."

Barbara flushes. "Anyway, you mostly won't even be using the door. And we haven't been using the alarm, either. You just should have the keys in case."

"Well, now," says Alfred, contemplatively. "I guess a body can't help how they're born, now, can they?" He throws the keys up underhand, then he catches them overhand, easily.


Alfred seems happy enough at first. Living at Barbara's is like camping out for him, not that he's ever gone camping or even considered going camping as a voluntary activity. "That's for white folk," he says. His idea of fun would be closer to the fanciest hotel you could imagine, with push buttons everywhere, and revolving beds and bars, and everything polished up to a bright mirror shine. But if he can't see the fun in the stripped-down life, he can at least see the peace and quiet of it, that's true. Nobody busting in or calling him on the carpet, and no cars or windows or brothers getting smashed up either, the big activity here being the crickets. "Listen," say Barbara and Seth. "They do that by rubbing their legs together." *Chirp, chirp.* And here he'd thought he needed to pop his ears or clean out his wax or blow his nose or something, he says. Being a mite hard of hearing. He explains about how he had so many ear infections as a child that he plain wore the clinic out. So that now he wasn't sure if that noise was inside his head or something automatic about the house, maybe the driveway warmer gone and fried itself up. Barbara laughs when Alfred tells her that, but he says he's being seriously serious. He's heard that before, that there are houses with driveway warmers to melt the snow off in the winter; you can tell which ones in a storm because the flakes die as soon as they hit the asphalt. The little shits be white, he says, but they might as well be black, they never stand a chance.

And let Charlene wonder how come he's not howling like an alley cat at her door—little does she know he's living in a big house on a hill with a free ride to work and all he can eat and no rent to make! This life has its considerable satisfactions. Plus he's never seen so many TVs outside of a department store, or so much furniture either, and he can't believe all the silver; nothing is plain old metal. And all that carpet, wall-to-wall everywhere. He's never lived so fat. Forget high heaven, he says, it's like living in a fucking movie.

On the other hand, it's right quiet. Of course, he understands why he shouldn't play no music, and why he can't turn no lights on at night, and why he can't have no telephone or no television. He understands that he's lucky. He's lucky to be hiding out here like a fugitive. He's lucky to be going back and forth in a tunnel. He's lucky to have a servant's room to live in. Barbara has stuck her neck out for him, and as likely as not will get her head chopped off like a turkey tom if he does not abide by the rules. But the truth is that after a week it begins to feel like prison, the house, except that there are no other inmates. It begins to feel like solitary confinement, only with crickets instead of roaches the size of cigarette lighters and other pet-size vermin. Not that he can't hang out with Mona and Seth and Barbara, getting high and shooting the shit. But what's he going to do the rest of the time—lie in the dark and play with himself? And the more he looks around, the poorer he feels; and the more he looks at Mona and Seth and Barbara, the older he feels too. "Twenty-one, man," he says. That's almost as old as his father was when he croaked. He was getting along fine, had himself a steady job, just like Alfred. But then he croaked.

"Did he get shot?" Mona wants to know.

"Naw, nothing like that." Alfred says he knows people who've gotten shot up, naturally, but that his dad got a pneumonia in his heart. Turned his heart into a bag of worms, and according to the doctor, that's why he died. A bag of worms can't pump. That's when Alfred's mother came down from Hartford. She was headed back to Georgia, to where her people come from: Racist or not, Georgia still was a whole lot friendlier than the North, that was her opinion. *I don't think so*, she liked to say. *I know so.* Also kids didn't go getting ideas down there; they didn't go getting uppity. But she got stuck in New York and had her a stroke, and here's Alfred now, alone; all he had was Charlene.

"You know the difference between you white folk and me?" he says one day in the kitchen. He's talking to Mona and Barbara and Seth, only two of whom are white; Mona thinks she should point this out.

But instead she says, "What?"

"See," he says, "you white folk look at the calendar, and at the end of the year comes Christmastime, and at the beginning of the year comes a whole new year, maybe the year you pack your white ass off to college, maybe the year you go off traveling somewhere nice. Me, I look at that calendar, and at the end of the year there's flapjacks, and at the beginning of the year there's flapjacks, and when I die, man, they're going to cover me with flapjacks, and put the butter and the syrup on top, and they're going to write on the tombstone, He done burnt only a couple of jacks his whole life, and that's when the stove was broke and burning like a hellhole."

He laughs. Mona and Barbara and Seth laugh too.

"So why don't you go back to college?" Mona reaches for a barbecue potato chip.

But if Alfred does anything, he's going to start himself a restaurant. They discuss what kind of restaurant. They discuss social justice. There is nothing about which they do not totally agree.

A few days later, though, Alfred's restless. For one thing, something's disagreeing with his stomach. Maybe it's all that deli Jew-food, he says, he ain't used to it.

"I don't think you should call it Jew-food," Mona says.

"Pastrami is Jew-food, don't tell me no different," he says. (And later on, it turns out Seth and Barbara are unoffended—making Mona, she supposes, too sensitive.) Or maybe it's the fucking crickets that's bothering him, continues Alfred; he wants to go out and kill them. He wants to know if you can just stamp on them or have to do something special.

"Probably you can just stamp," says Mona. "But it's kind of a big lawn."

Alfred gazes out at the acreage. He adjusts the pads of his lounge chair.

"Maybe you can mention it to the gardener." Mona moves into the adjustable shade of the patio umbrella. "His name is Willie."

"The gardener." He lowers his chin. "You got a gardener too?"

"Sure," Mona says.

"He black?"

"She," Mona says.

"She! You got yourself a lady gardener?"

"Sure."

"What for, man, what for? You tell Alfred why you got a lady gardener."

"It just so happens."

"She black or white?"

"I'm not sure."

"In that case, she's black."

"What do you mean?"

"White is white, man. Everything else is black. Half and half is black."

"Are you telling me I'm black?" Mona says.

He looks at her, puzzled, then grins. "Are you pulling poor Alfred's chain again?"

Mona grins back, offering him a beer. "Couldn't help it," she says. "It was hanging right there." For herself she has a diet soda with a loopy straw.

The sun shines.

"How come your daddy don't drive no Caddy-lack yet, all those flapjacks we send singing all day?" asks Alfred. "Why are you the gardener?"

"Ancient Chinese tradition, I guess. No rice paddies to tend, so I mow the lawn instead. Have you ever seen a rice paddy?"

"No, ma'am."

"It looks like a golf course, except actually it's the putting green and water trap all rolled up in one. I've seen pictures."

"How about that," says Alfred. Then he says, "That bitch landed me in prison, man. She got everything."

"You mean Charlene?"

"Who else?"

"Oh, whew. I thought maybe you meant me," says Barbara, sneaking up behind them.

"What? You? Oh, no, I don't mean *you*, Miss B.," says Alfred. "You're one good shit, all right, helping me out." He glances at the sliding door through which Barbara appeared, as if making a mental note. *Keep an eye on that sucker.* "Alfred's just lucky," he goes on, getting up some steam. "The day he dies, he's going to leave everything he ever owned to you. The day he dies, they're going to read his will, and it's going to say, To my main savior, Barbara G., otherwise known as the Blanco, I do leave all my clothes, and my hi-fi if she can get it back from my bitch wife, and maybe even the toaster. If she can fix it, it's hers to burn up her bagels in before she lays on that cream cheese and five-dollar-a-pound lox."

They laugh. The sun shines some more.

Barbara says, "You feel like you're in prison?"

"Oh, no," says Alfred. "It's beautiful here. Like a movie or something."

"Except that he feels like killing the crickets," Mona says.

"Why'd you say that, girl?" says Alfred.

"Because it's true," Mona says. "It's okay, you can tell Barbara. It's too quiet for you here, right?"

He hesitates. "It's on the quiet side."

"And maybe a bit on the lonesome side too?"

"That bitch Charlene," he says. "She got everything, man. How can anybody even call me? After she went and changed the fucking phone number."

"You miss your buddies?" Mona asks.

Alfred takes an elaborately casual swig of his beer.

"Or are you trying to steer clear of them?"

"Ain't steered clear of nobody in my life, man." The veins in his neck stick out.

"So why don't you call them up, then? I know my dad's pretty strict about making calls from work, but maybe he'll make an exception."

"The day the Rice Man makes an exception," snorts Alfred, sitting forward, "is the day the clouds come down from the sky and lay on the ground so as we've got to shovel 'em up." He swings his bare feet down to the hot flagstone, but then quickly returns them to the chair pad.

Meanwhile, Mona's flinching too. "How about the pay phone?" She says this even though the pay phone is right between the bathrooms, everybody can hear every word you say. "Or some other pay phone."

"How're the brothers going to call me back?"

"Do they need to call you back?"

Alfred downs some more beer.

"Is something bothering you?"

He laughs sharply. "What're you talking about, is something bothering Alfred?" He suddenly recalls something he needs to get from his room.

Mona watches him hop across the patio, and when he's out of sight, she discusses this conversation with Barbara. Mona half expects that her generous friend will offer Alfred use of the phone at the house. But what if Evie answers? And what if the phone bill comes and there are all these calls to who knows where? Barbara presents him instead with an AM-FM radio.

"You got to keep it down low," she tells Alfred. "I don't want my cousin to hear."

"Low," he says. "Alfred's going to play this baby so low anybody would think it's just one more little cricket got born—it can hardly make no noise, it's so small."

But a week later, the cricket is getting louder.

"It's growing up," says Barbara, taping her bangs down to dry. She uses special pink tape, and Dippity-Do besides. "What should I do?"

"Did you try talking to him?" says Mona.

"I did. But he has that problem with his ears."

"He can hear crickets."

"I guess that's different."

Back and forth, until finally Mona has another genius idea. They leave a radio on in the kitchen; also they plant a number of other radios and lights around the house, on timers. These slavishly switch themselves on, switch themselves off, and naturally Evie complains in this squeaky voice, you'd swear she cleans her vocal cords with vinegar. But Barbara holds her ground. She insists that the house is giving her the heebie-jeebies. *It's too empty. It's too quiet.* The lights and radios help her relax. Plus they'll scare away burglars.

Evie concedes that she can always shut her door if the commotion bothers her; Barbara and Mona congratulate themselves on their creative social management. They tell Alfred that they want him to feel at home. *We are willing to go the extra yard for you.* He allows that this seems to be true.

Barbara offers him additional proof of their goodwill. She tells him he can use the den TV if he is really, really careful and sure to get out of there by six-thirty at the latest. That's when Evie comes back from her course for dinner. Not every day, but enough days, she says. To which Alfred nods, delighted. He expresses gratitude, he expresses comprehension, and without further ado heads for the set.


Seth, meanwhile, has been arriving late at the restaurant. Ralph has had to yell at him twice; and now here it is, day three, and Seth is late again. Not to say stoned, which means he will do things like serve up the Salisbury steak with a series of forks stuck in it.

"Mysteries of the universe," he told a customer last week, as he set it down. "Stonehenge." The customer was so absorbed in the sports section that he didn't even react until one of the forks fell over with a clink.

"There are forks in my meat!" he exclaimed then, indignant. "Forks!" He put down his paper to express his moral outrage. "Waiter! There are forks! In my meat!"

Seth swooped in. "Oh, my! We'll send this back right away!" And bearing the plate aloft on his fingertips, he disappeared through the swinging kitchen doors. The staff roared and clapped.

"Sett," says Ralph now, sitting at his desk. His feet are planted on the ground, his face is serious. However, he is peeling an orange with a letter opener as he talks. "You late third day in a row now, what's happen?"

Says Seth, blinking, "I guess I got lost or something."

"Lost? How could be?" Ralph continues his peeling. "Every day you coming to the restaurant, suddenly today you are lost? I don't know what you talking these days. Cedric tell me last week you put fork in customer's food. Are you crazy?"

"It was a joke."

"That's how you make joke? Seems like very strange. And you talking some kind funny today. Are you maybe drink some beer before you come?"

"Beer?" Seth starts laughing.

"What you laughing now? Some more joke?"

"Oh, no, man. I mean, I've been known to kill some soldiers every now and then, but—"

"Kill somebody!" says Ralph, jumping up. The naked orange rolls off the desk; Seth catches it, and when Cedric steps in, lobs it to him. Cedric fumbles but recovers. And soon enough, Ralph is eating his orange, everyone is back to work. But Seth isn't satisfied.

"Your old man," he says to Mona at break time, then launches into his worshipful opinion.

"Actually, he has a great sense of humor," Mona says.

Seth goes on. "What does he do besides milk his workers like a capitalist oppressor? Doesn't he have any hobbies?"

Mona tries to explain that while no, Ralph doesn't have any hobbies, this is only because he was an oppressed proletariat not so long ago. Or if not a proletariat, at least oppressed. Or if not oppressed, at least not an oppressor. Ralph might seem like Seth's parents to Seth, she says, but he isn't. She says her family's seen some rough times.

"This pancake house is everything for us." She is lying on her back, squinting up at the attic rafters. "We're not like you. We don't have investments. We don't read the *Wall Street Journal*. I've never even seen a stock certificate." For argument's sake, she omits from mention the new franchise her parents have finally decided to try and finagle a way to afford.

"You've never seen a stock certificate?"

Mona shakes her head.

"Have you ever seen a coupon?"

"You mean, like for cereal?" In fact, Mona knows what kind of coupon he means; she only says this to impress upon him the messy essential truth.

It works. "Excuse me for confusing your class status." Seth emits a quick whistle through his beard before planting on her lips a nice scratchy kiss. Mona kisses back, fondling his ear as she adjusts for him his hair net.

That same evening, seven-thirty. Barbara and Mona saunter into the house, only to behold Alfred watching baseball on the color TV. It's a red-socked team versus a white-socked team, the eighth inning, a tight game, and Alfred's excitement is apparent from the kitchen. They can hear him shouting at the screen. He jumps up. He cheers.

"Is Evie here?" Barbara checks quickly for her cousin. Luckily, Evie's out. Barbara goes to talk to Alfred, but doesn't step all the way into the room. Instead she stalls in the doorway, one hand on the jamb. Mona lines up behind her like someone waiting to use the ladies' room.

"Alfred," Barbara says. "It's seven thirty-three."

He swivels in his BarcaLounger. Mona and Barbara perceive that he is holding a beer.

"I see you are looking at my beverage here," observes Alfred.

"I am not," says Barbara.

"You know who you remind me of, looking at my beverage? My bitch wife Char-lene."

"It's seven thirty-three," Barbara says again. Her voice rises slightly; her fingers curl around the doorjamb so that her fingernails whiten. Mona peeks around her. "You know, I wish you could just stay here, but Evie is going to come home any minute. In fact, she could've come home an hour ago."

"*E*-vie," he says, letting the name roll on his tongue like something delicious. He stretches out the "Eee" and lets it drop down into the "vie" with the spilling acceleration of a ball into a golf hole. He says it like it is all sound and no meaning; and from this, Mona and Barbara can see that he is, as he claims, not drunk. However, he is more than usually relaxed. He grins a Cheshire cat grin as he enunciates again—"Eee-vie." He might as well be tossing an antique soup tureen in the air—catching it with sure hands, but setting everyone on edge all the same.

The red-socks steal a base, the crowd goes wild, but now Alfred doesn't seem to care. He hovers between the world of the TV set and some other world that is not quite the world inhabited by Mona and Barbara.

"Who gives a shit about Evie, man?" He says this, smiling. "Why don't you just tell her to shut her clam?"

"Because I know she won't," says Barbara. "If she doesn't tell my parents, she'll tell my aunt. Evie's always been a tattletale."

"So what," says Alfred. "What's it going to matter, man? What's your Jew-daddy going to do to you? Take away your shiny new au-to-mo-bile?"

Barbara, shocked, backs up a step.

"Her dad," says Mona, bravely, straight into her friend's shoulder blade, "is not a Jew-daddy."

"What you know back there? You're not Jewish, don't give me that shit." Alfred addresses Barbara again. "You know what Luther says about you? He says you're willing to be giving us all those pennies and nickels that be stretching out your pants pockets. He says you're willing to be giving away those nickels and dimes that be hanging down and banging your leg when you walk. But you ain't going to be giving out no quarters without going on about how you be sufferers just like we be sufferers; and how you be our Moses, that is going to lead us out of the desert, so long as we turn off the TV before E-vie come home so's nobody don't get in no trouble and lose any au-to-mo-bile." He smirks, glancing back at the TV. "That's what Luther says, man."

"Jesus Christ," Mona says, as Barbara stalks away. "When'd you see your friend Luther?"

"Called-him-on-the-tel-e-phone," chants Alfred. He laughs a heh-heh laugh. "You hear me? I-done-used-the-tel-e-phone."

"But why, Alfred? Why?"

"I-done-picked-on-up-the-tel-e-phone. I-done-dialed-on-up-the-tel-e-phone, and when the phone stopped ringing, you know what I said? I said, Hey, Luther. This is Alfred. I'm-call-ing-on-the-tel-e-phone."

"But Alfred, why? What are you going to do now? Have you got some other place to stay?"

"I'm moving, all right. I'm moving today, man. See, I'm moving right this minute." He puts his feet up on the BarcaLounger footrest.

"Oh, Alfred," Mona says. "Don't be like this."

"Like what, sugar?"

"Don't be angry."

"Who's angry?" he says. "What for?"

*How could he talk to me that way? How could he? I didn't have to let him stay here. I didn't have to stick my neck out for him. I didn't have to do shit for him.* This is what Mona expects Barbara to say. And Mona expects to console her: *You've been a mensch. I can't tell you how sorry I am that I invited him to stay at your place to begin with, and without even asking.*

But by the time Mona joins her friend on the hall stairs, she finds to her amazement that Barbara's calmed down.

"Of course he's angry," she says. "He's angry about his whole life. And he's right. Here we are so rich, and we're willing to help him up to a point. But not to the point where we're going to lose some of our own privilege, right?"

So astonished is Mona to hear this that for a moment her voice volume doesn't work. "Barbara," she whispers. "Barbara Heloise Gugelstein!"

Barbara makes a modest wave with her hand, as if trying to tell a hairdresser no hair spray. "I don't think he even really believes I have a cousin. I mean, he hasn't seen her, he hasn't heard her. So far as he's concerned, she's just a phantom. I think he thinks I'm making it up about her."

"So what are you going to do?" says Mona, hanging on the banister. "Introduce them?"

"Such a helpful idea," says Barbara.

But the next evening, Seth too proposes they drop the secrecy. "What are we, the CIA? I think we should just call the elder Gugelsteiner and let him in on the news. Why not be up front? Why not stand up for what we believe?"

"Are you kidding?" Mona says. "If you call Mr. Gugelstein, it's going to be lawyers and police and forcible removal. We'll probably all get JD cards. Our pictures will be on the front page of the paper."

"Let's do it!"

"And what about Alfred?" continues Mona. "What if he ends up in jail? Have you thought about that?"

Could Alfred end up in jail? Anyway, not even Barbara has the stomach for the kind of confrontation Seth has in mind; and so Mona's original idea is resurrected with some seriousness. Why not tell Evie, indeed? For even if Evie blows their cover, there'll be time for Alfred to move out if he has to; and then what can the parents do? Of course, Barbara stands to lose her car and allowance. But she's making her own money now anyway.

"Think of what's to be gained if Evie does keep her mouth shut," she goes on. "No more sneaking around, no more worrying . . ."

And so it is that Barbara and Mona and Seth and Alfred are soon making like hovercraft outside Evie's darkroom door.

"Evie?" says Barbara.

"Just a sec, okay?" says Evie Squeaky Voice. "I'm right in the middle of printing some stuff."

"Okay." They wait outside the darkroom for another five minutes. They watch the red light at the bottom of the door until everywhere else they look, there's a green stripe. "Are you ready yet?" says Barbara.

"Are you still waiting?" says Evie. The phone rings; there's a vertical flash of red as Barbara hands the phone in to her cousin. Evie talks without leaving the darkroom. Barbara and Mona and Seth and Alfred wait.

"When you get a moment, I have something to tell you," says Barbara finally. "It's a big surprise. Why don't you come downstairs when you're ready."

But Evie never does come downstairs, and eventually the gang just calls it a night.


More and more, Alfred does as he likes around the house; and somehow he manages to avoid Evie in a way that begins after a while to feel magical. Then it feels mysterious; and then fraught with higher significance, like Easter Island, or the Bermuda Triangle. *It's a sign,* Seth says, and who could disagree? It's hard to look at the way Alfred and Evie pass without meeting and not say it was ordained. Alfred was meant to live here, unencumbered, and they were meant to relax about it. Indeed, Alfred-and-Evie-watching begins to become a sport. *Sighted, 5:45: Alfred entering via the tunnel. Sighted, 5:49: Evie entering via the front door.* Evie is elfin, and light of foot, and easy to miss as she leafs through the mail in the front hall; she sashays away kitchen bound, just as Alfred heads for the john. Probably he should be more careful. But his hearing, after all; anyway, Evie fails to look up at the sound of the toilet flushing, becomes immersed in a letter as Alfred makes for the den, crossing her line of vision. He, of course, is not exactly elfin, or light of foot either. The gang wonders, *Is she blind?* and it's hard not to laugh at the idea. A blind photographer! Whoever could imagine such a thing? But Barbara says Evie's not blind, she's just not using her eyes because she's concentrating on other things. For example, her photography, and also some love affair she's conducting long-distance. Evie spends a lot of time imagining the Philippines, says Barbara, and of course this immediately becomes a joke. *What's the matter?* says person A. *Are you imagining the Philippines?* To which person B is supposed to answer with suitable intonation, *Yes, behold yon volcano, it explodes, I am full of wonder.* Or, *Yes, there are rice paddies everywhere, oh my dearest, my feet are wet with love.* Or, *No, I ain't imagining no nothing. See, I'm just as deaf and blind as I look.*

This last is Alfred's contribution, which he makes without prompting. For as they relax, he seems to relax too, a true member of the gang. His anger seems to have dissipated; he seems finally to trust that Mona and Barbara and Seth, his friends, are the exception to some general rule. He finally seems, in fact, to feel gratitude. One day he runs smack into Evie outside. He tells her he works for the gardener. She accepts this explanation without apparent surprise.

Mona and Barbara and Seth relax some more, and being relaxed, begin to belatedly realize that it is summer. They begin to notice the way the heat hangs in the air, as if too lazy to move up or down; they notice the thin-stretched sky, and the blunt muzzy glare of certain avenues. Also the way that the trees, which in autumn seem to stand so high and mighty, now seem to have inexplicably lost their dignity. Everything melds together. Everything needs water. How nice it would be to go to the beach, Mona thinks; and Seth, as if reading her mind, agrees.

"Why don't you go visit Callie," he says, massaging her neck. "I'll still be here when you come back."

"What an interesting prediction," says Mona.

Still she is on the fence until she runs into Bea.

"Mona!" trills Bea from her Thunderbird. "Stay right there, I'm pulling over." And pull over she does, in a dazzling U-turn such as blows her sun hat right off.

Mona asks how was the luau; Bea reports how much the guests enjoyed the bowling, not to say how they raced pineapple boats across the country club pool. Only the grass skirts flopped; her theory was that certain women were afraid they would look fat in them.

"So no hula dancing," she says, rescuing her hat from the front passenger seat. "And nobody swam. Maybe it's just as well, after all those piña coladas. Still, can you imagine that? In this weather. You'd think everyone would be dying to get in the water."

"I'm dying to get in the water," says Mona.

"So then why don't you go visit your sister with the resort job?"

"How did you know where my sister is?"

"Anything that doesn't matter, Seth tells me," says Bea.

"Maybe I will go visit Callie at the beach."

"A terrific idea. Need a ride somewhere?"

Mona shakes her head; a car honks; Bea waves. "Aloha!" she cries. "Have a good time!" And with another traffic-stopping U-turn, this time with one hand on her head, she is gone.

# CHAPTER 9

# The Expressers in Rhode Island

"What are you doing?" Mona finds Callie on the golden crescent beach. It is early morning, so early even the sun's still all zipped up in its nice warm sleeping bag, just as Mona would like to be. Instead she is feeling astonished to have discovered Callie not only up but already into what appears to be her regimen—an enthralling aspect of Callie's grown-up life that Mona might have missed altogether, had she not happened to waken to go to the bathroom, and on the return trip stumbled upon Callie's absence. Now she beholds her sister in what is in their family considered a most compromising state—namely, one in which she's bound to catch a cold. For despite the chill, Callie is barely dressed in an orange swirly-print kimono-like gown, with a fringe at the bottom. Attached to the fringe at random intervals are beads and what look to be rabbit feet, although they could also be some other manner of rodent extremity. Mona holds out the limp hope they may prove synthetic. As for Callie's own feet, they are bare, like her hands, which appear nonetheless objects of intense interest. They drift slowly around her; she scrutinizes them as if for signs of dishpan damage. For this activity, she has put in her contact lenses. Also she has put her hair up—the better to swivel her neck, it seems. She bends and straightens her legs in slow motion, all the while rotating and stretching her back and shoulders as if to demonstrate for a science fair how very remarkable are her many functioning joints. Indeed, Mona has never before appreciated how jointed her sister is, a regular praying mantis.

Callie answers, "Exercises."

"What kind of exercises?" says Mona.

"Chinese exercises."

"But I always thought the Chinese don't believe in exercise." Mona says this because one of Helen's greatest points of life pride has been not only that she has never sweated, but that she has only rarely perspired, and that in times of record high temperature and humidity both. Of course, she owed much in this accomplishment to the aid of talcum powder.

"Well," says Callie, looking at her hands. "That's wrong."

"Don't tell me," guesses Mona. "The Chinese invented exercise."

Callie doesn't answer.

"Table tennis, for example, a game played for thousands of years. Witness the fossil balls unearthed by that world-famous archaeological team, who were they? Ah, yes—Ping and Pong."

"Oh, Mona," says Callie. "The morning was so peaceful without you."

"Just tell me what you're doing, and I'll go back to sleep."

"*Tai qi,*" says Callie.

"Is it for your flab?"

"Please be serious."

"I am. I'm being seriously serious."

"It is not for my flab. It's for my *qi*—my breath. My spirit."

"It's probably good for your flab too. I mean, it can't be bad."

Callie stops.

"I never heard of anybody doing exercises for their spirit, but it sounds like a good idea. I'm surprised, though, that you can't do them in bed. I mean, if they're for your spirit."

Callie puts her hands on her hips—a forbidden gesture their mother has deemed low-class. "Have you thought about going back to sleep?"

"Okay, okay," Mona says. "Just one more question and I'll go, okay? Just one more question?"

"One more question."

"How come you're turning Chinese? I thought you were sick of being Chinese."

It isn't until breakfast that Mona is finally tendered this explanatory sweetmeat: Callie is indeed sick of being Chinese, but there is being Chinese and being Chinese.

"I see," Mona says. "How true."

Instead of Wheaties or an English muffin, Callie is eating *shee-veh*, with assorted pickled and deep-fried condiments, something like what their parents used to eat in China. Of course, Helen and Ralph now prefer raisin bran—less work, they say, and good for your performance. (This last being a delicate reference to their alimentary output.) Still Callie eats on, saying she didn't understand what it meant to be Chinese until she met Naomi.

"Really," Mona says. "And can Naomi teach me to be Chinese too?"

"If you ask her, I'll kill you," says Callie pleasantly.

And so it is that when Naomi and Mona are introduced—really, reintroduced—Mona prepares to ask her immediately. This being, after all, Mona's pesky nature. Her pesky nature is for once checked, though, by her dumbfounded fascination. For Naomi is a formidable presence and certainty such as puts you in mind of somebody like Oliver Wendell Holmes; you just know one day she'll be using three names too. Also her voice does not scrape along like a regular old voice, but somehow seems to resonate with delight and sorrow at the same time. Hers is an outsized, magnificent instrument: the voice of a woman, thinks Mona, and an older woman at that—a woman of amplitude, and bosom.

Naomi, though, looks more the way you might expect, which is to say that she is tall, and loose-limbed, almost hipless, and of completely average shelf size. Her facial addenda have a kind of mythic circularity—round glasses, hoop earrings, basketball Afro; if she were an archaeological ruin, you would surmise circles to be of central significance to her culture. *Large round eyes too!* you might note, the opening lines of your thesis typing themselves before your eyes. But a few paragraphs down, you'd be stumped, for her face is square as a chessboard, and below her fetching dimples and ever-so-pouty mouth juts a jaw of the no-truck type, sweet as the prow of an Arctic icebreaker. No one would dare call her pretty.

And yet you wouldn't call her not beautiful, for she conducts herself like a beauty. She has a beauty's bearing—her circumspection, her poise. She has a beauty's air of restraint. You get the distinct feeling she does not go home from parties feeling like a jerk.

Is this what happens when you take a pom-pom girl from Chicago and set her to reading Lao-tzu in a fancy New England prep school? Mona gathers over the next few days that Naomi grew up on powdered milk, just like her and Callie; but also that Naomi sewed her own clothes and darned her own socks, and had a biggish hand in raising up her brother and sister. Her mom was a car-rental agent, her dad a mechanic. Before she went and got herself that scholarship to prep school, her most daring dream was of a job that did not involve arch supports.

Now she requires a lot of time by herself. She is flattered to hear tell of her most impressive self-possession. However, this surface, she claims, is a mere product of preparation. The way other people get dressed in the morning, she puts herself together—meaning that in the past she has donned like a lift-and-firm foundation a kind of dignity that almost seemed an argument. But now she has *tai qi*, she says; it's all about grounding. "I thought it was about the spirit," Mona says. Naomi, though, just keeps on with her explaining. She's not rufflable, like Callie. She's something closer to Buddhist—meaning that she does meditation, and yoga. She chants, and drinks tea, and makes kites—that's to keep lively her spirit of play. For this has been her experience, she says. The outside world presses in on you, and you have to maintain an equal pressure, in the opposite direction, so as not to implode.

"You make kites? You implode?"

"Spiritually," she says.

Callie nods, basking in reflected wisdom.

"What about jazz?" Mona says. "What about sweet potato pie?"

She blurts this out in stupid fashion; luckily, Naomi likes *all that* too. And later she will discourse a bit about Duke, Monk, Bird, Train. She will tease cool jazz from free jazz, bebop from hard bop. Jazz is definitely one of her interests, and she scarfs down her collard greens with as much gusto as anybody, maybe more. For she also likes Chinese dumplings and diet soda, not to say Scrabble, film noir, star gazing, soccer. She is, in short, a statistical outlier and overcompensator, a Renaissance woman such as Mona would have envied mightily had she not been black.

But as it happens, pretty soon Mona worships her, just like Callie. She does everything Naomi says. She strives to think the way Naomi thinks. In terms of *white folk,* for example. Naomi never says they're out to get your ass, the way Alfred does. She talks about them in a gentler way that makes them seem involuntarily stuck to one another by a special invisible but all-weather glue. This makes Mona and Callie and Naomi stuck together too, by virtue of their being colored folk. Mona has never thought of herself as colored before, though she knew herself not to be white. *Yellow,* says Naomi now. *You are yellow. A yellow person, a yellow girl.* It takes some getting used to, this idea, especially since Mona's summertime color is most definitely brown, and the rest of the year she is not exactly a textbook primary. But then Naomi is not black either; she claims to be closer in color to a paper bag. If she were a cabinet door or a shade of hair dye, people would have a name for her exact shade. But as she is only a person, she is called black, just as Mona and Callie are called yellow. And as yellow is a color, they are colored, which is how it is they are working together on the project.

"What project?"

"Shh," says Callie.

Naomi is more willing to tell her how they are secretly studying the manners and mores of the people at the inn. Naomi and Callie are not sure what exactly they're going to write about these manners and mores, but they know it's going to be a joint project, and for a certain professor; the professor is the type who would probably sign up to be colored if she could. And as she is big on field notes, the project will require what else? Which is why Naomi and Callie are writing down what the guests do, and say, and eat. What sports they play, and at what age they start their children at tennis, at sailing, at skiing. Whether they carry their own luggage. Whenever a guest does something peculiar, such as describe for Callie all about being stationed in the Pacific, or inquire of Naomi whether she might recall the lines of a certain spiritual, Callie and Naomi jot this down; and later they share their tidbits, hooting. There are perhaps fewer of these incidents than they would like. However, the uniform they wear involves a kilt and a polo shirt, clearly a Scottish theme, and both of them do regularly get asked: What part of Scotland are you from? To which Callie answers, the Far Eastern part; and Naomi, that she's not actually from Scotland. She is, she says, from deepest, darkest Wales.

"But what about when they're nice?" Mona says. "Why don't you write down those times?"

"Good point." Naomi smiles. "That can be your job."

And so it is that Mona spends the better part of her holiday eavesdropping. Pen and notebook in hand, she tries to pretend that she's sketching—drawing a picture of one of the outbuildings, or the dock with the seagulls—when actually she's listening to what people say. Much of it is innocuous enough: Who's going to school where, and when they're taking their semester abroad; who married whom, and whether or not it was a shame. They chat with the younger set about what it means to be a good sport; also about agreeable children, by which they mean children who do not contradict their elders. Among themselves, they return to subjects like their board work. Suddenly someone will leap to life on the subject of a particular art foundation, or teen shelter. For the Jews, it turns out, are not the only ones who worry about the world; these people too consider that the problems of society are theirs to fix. They will do right. They will hold forth, saving for later the chat about their boats. Races they have been in, and how they made out. Also where they summer, where they winter. These are verbs Mona always thought were nouns.

Naomi says, "What they're talking about is status."

"Status?" Mona says, as if this is her first word of Chinese.

"Listen more carefully," Naomi says. "Think about what it means to have leisure." And when Mona complains that it's hard to get in hearing range, Naomi says Mona must learn to make herself invisible. "Think wall bug," she says.

This is how it happens that Mona is in the lobby thinking *wall bug,* when through the door saunters sweet Eloise Ingle, her four stepbrothers like a wall of bodyguards behind her. Their bobbing heads ascend the staircase at different rates. Otherwise, they are identifiably Ingle-y, right down to their jockish jocularity. One of them, the most baby-faced, with floppy brown hair and an open demeanor, has resourcefully supplied himself with a walnut to toss around; his several siblings, roused by this ball-like object, are fitfully moved to piracy. Much scuffling, of a good-natured sort that does not threaten the dignity of the lobby but in fact seems to add to its summer fun feel. The family shirt is Lacoste. The family shoe is the scuffed-up Top-Sider.

There is no family sock. They cluster around the tennis sign-up sheet and begin signing up for time before their dad has even checked in, it's the Protestant play ethic. They're going to play singles and doubles, every possible combination of one against the others, starting at 8:00 A.M. That is for tomorrow. For today it turns out that they have called ahead, and reserved some courts already.

Eloise, meanwhile, has brought her dog with her, and although pets are expressly against inn policy, no one at the front desk so much as raises an eyebrow. This, perhaps, is because the dog goes with her outfit. The one family member not busy signing up for tennis, Eloise is nevertheless wearing tennis whites—white sneakers, white socks, white skirt. No love beads, no bell-bottoms, no water-buffalo sandals such as she would be wearing at home; and Mona notices that she has not skimped the way Barbara Gugelstein once told her you can, buying a boys' Lacoste shirt. Instead Eloise has paid extra for the ladies' version, with its several more buttons, closely spaced. White headband. And in her arms, well camouflaged, the white dog—a mini something or other, by the looks of him, part poodle, part hamster, the kind of officious little pompadour that yaps a good game at neighborhood cats but keeps a sensible distance away when the ferocious felines yawn back.

Eloise's pinkish-brown dad is commanding in his Nantucket red pants, though his tennis hat has the lift of something being blown off his head. Has it shrunk in the wash? Gotten mixed up with someone else's? It is a hat that would make Mona's dad look like a boob. So flinty a type is Mr. Ingle, however, what with his thin straight mouth and thin straight nose and thin straight eyebrows, that even thus attired he looks to be throwing care to the wind in a philanthropic manner. He is clearly the sort of man who does not raise his voice. He is clearly the sort of man who uses phrases like *The evidence notwithstanding* and *Make no mistake*, and without having to rehearse them first. They spring from his tongue, natural as daisies. *Make no mistake. This hat notwithstanding, I am no boob.*

Eloise's stepmom, on the other hand, is more meticulously assembled. Her sandy hair is coiffed à la Jackie Onassis; her outfit is whimsically nautical. Anchors abound. Moreover, she is herself tall and spindly as a mast. Proudly she breasts the great lobby, albeit with a slight limp. The family luggage follows behind on a bellboy-powered barge, a leather and canvas heap bristling with rackets. It passes. Mona is espied.

"Mona!"

"Eloise."

"What are you doing here?" says Eloise, and before Mona has a chance to ask back, adds, "I asked first."

"I thought you had a place on an island in Maine," Mona says. "Mid-coast."

Eloise, stiffening, stops petting her dog. "We do," she says, and lifts her chin as if to place it in the sort of face harness eye doctors use to check your retina. "However, this year we were overrun by cousins and had to get away. They were using blueberries for spitballs."

"How awful," Mona says.

"Are you up with your family?"

"I'm spying," Mona almost says, but instead manages: "I'm visiting my sister."

"Your sister?"

"She's working here."

"Working here? You mean as a waitress?"

Mona tries to explain that you have to go to Harvard or Yale or Brown or someplace to get a job here, it's not like being a regular waitress.

But Eloise asks finally, with a toss of her hair mass to disguise her polite horror, "Is Callie putting herself through college?"

"Well," Mona says; and then recalling she's a spy, she for once says the agreeable thing. "Things haven't been so hot at the pancake house."

"Oh, I'm so sorry," Eloise says instantly.

Whereupon Mona looks down the way Lauren Bacall supposedly did when she was terrified of the cameras and the lights; and as this worked on Humphrey Bogart, so it works on Eloise. She hugs her dog close, petting him with long sad strokes, as if not sure how else to express her heart's overflow.

So begins Mona's life as a cause. In temple, Mona knew all the answers, and Eloise was the second most noteworthy convert. Here, Eloise seeks to find diversions for Mona, to brighten up her cheerless little life. Eloise is kindness itself. She is generosity itself. She is self-lessness itself. Mona is a lucky camper who goeth but for the grace of the Fresh Air Fund. Eloise suggests they take a boat out together. She'll teach Mona to sail, she says. And indeed, the bay is balm for the soul. How far the distant shore! They behold the wriggly reflection of the clouds in the water. Unfortunately, when Mona takes over the tiller, the boat jibes wildly; she is beaned but good by the boom. Eloise volunteers to teach her to play shuffleboard, a sport she says you can easily manage even while holding an ice pack to your head.

And so it is that, much too soon, the afternoon draws to a most amiable close. On the line, or out? They debate, they jump up and down. They admire their long shadows. From the top of a certain hill, they can see themselves stretch right down to the water. They are more enormous than enormous; with their shadow arms they can pick up whole boats, the dock, even an islet across the way. And look how thin they are! Twiggy, move over. Tomorrow they will play croquet, says Eloise. A game Mona did not think was played outside of *Alice in Wonderland*. Mona volunteers to give Eloise a tour of the workers' quarters.

They part fondly. At dinner, they wave to each other across the dining room. Eloise's family, naturally, has a table by the window, one of the very best. It's where the inn holds its buffet on Sundays, two steps up from the rest of the dining room. The paned window stretches from kneewall to ceiling there, and curves to form a crescent in which the Ingles command the center spot. As the sun sets over the bay, they seem to be floating, first in the ocean, then in an ocean of light. They shade their eyes—squinting, it seems, at their own tremendous luck. Finally the sky begins to darken. Their feet fall into shadow, their knees. They begin, it appears, to sink. They pass the bread basket. Meanwhile, Mona stands by Callie's station, trying to make herself in-conspicuous. She's waiting for her pass-off; Callie has promised her the world's finest doggie bag.

Team Ingle trains the next morning as scheduled, or so Callie reports. Mona sleeps through the first set and a half.

"How goes the infiltration?" asks Naomi, doing dishes. Mona asks her again what kind of a project this is. Naomi reassures her it's most worthwhile, especially for something as yet half-baked.

"Because I would really rather avoid Eloise altogether. She wasn't exactly my best friend at home," Mona says.

Naomi shakes the water from her hands; the drops hit the metal sink with a patter. "It's your vacation," she says. "Do what you want."

Mona decides that what she wants is to try to call Seth again. This is not so simple, since all the workers share one outdoor pay phone, and since she is not even a worker proper. The evening is impossible, she has tried that already; the day, next to impossible. Still Mona waits in line. No answer at the teepee. No answer at Barbara's house, either. She ponders.

But before she can decide what else it is she wants, she discovers not only that Eloise is engaged in mortal combat with her stepmother, but that into this engagement, she, Mona, has been drafted. At issue is Eloise's trust, a sum of money her stepmother believes to have been left to Eloise as a formality, to avoid taxes. Really it belongs to Eloise's father, believes this stepmother—which is how it is that she, the manager of the household, is managing it. She maintains that Eloise is too young to have her own income, especially since she is threatening to use it to move out of the house. There have been words.

But for now there are none. They do not yell at each other, or argue, or throw things. Instead they are with each other exquisitely brief. Eloise makes herself clear by placing between them on the bench an intermediary mass, namely Mona. A strategy, Mona surmises, that Eloise has used before, for the brothers do not ask who Mona is as they break for water, or switch sides of the court. They glance her way, but seem to realize that she is a statement. Only Eloise addresses Mona, and more and more sporadically. The tension level seems to be growing; Mona can only conclude that she is missing some of the jabs and left hooks. For Eloise's stepmother—her name is Frisky—is apparently making herself clear by doing needlepoint. A hunt scene, very sporting, with a number of dogs. The execution of this is hampered by Eloise's real dog, on account of which animal Mrs. Ingle is obliged to keep her bag of yarns poked into a hole in the chain-link fence. As she is also having a problem with her ankle, she requires Eloise to stand up every now and then, to fetch a bit of yarn for her.

"The Chinese red," says she. "The cerulean blue."

"If you would pass this to Frisk," says Eloise to Mona, as though her stepmother is not just behind her.

The dog, it turns out, is also a statement. Dog, Capital D, his name is in full, exactly because he is not what Mrs. Ingle considers a real dog. Real dogs are large dogs, like setters and retrievers—magnificent dogs with magnificent instincts.

Dog, Capital D, on the other hand, is what Mrs. Ingle considers a Hollywood dog. She says this because the one time he ever had a chance to prove himself with a burglar, he not only did nothing in the way of dissuasion, but actually followed the poor criminal about—wagging his tail and proving so persistent that the burglar finally had to circle back to the house. He was caught trying to coax Dog back into the kitchen. Which to Eloise just proved that the man wasn't a run-of-the-mill bur-glar. Maybe she was prejudiced about criminals, but she thought that a more typical burglar would have shot Dog or something, and that her father should not have had the guy prosecuted. But her father did any-way. *The law is the law. Social order is threatened on all sides these days,* he said. *Witness the hippies. One has to have a system. For one starts to think twice about things, and what does one find? That in a certain light, things appear one way; but in another light, another.*

And in a way Mona knows what he means. For example, when Mrs. Ingle finally limps off to her room, Mona finds herself sitting quite chummily with Eloise—from which spot she almost can't re-member what it was that she didn't like about Eloise back at temple. Was it her popularity? Her hair? The fact that she went out with Andy Kaplan? I must have just been jealous, Mona thinks now. For slowly but surely her entire appraisal of the family is changing; even Eloise's brothers are beginning to seem like four distinct persons. Eloise points out their sports profiles: There is floppy-haired Charlie, with the freckles and the reckless first serve. There is Sumner with the silver glasses, who calls balls out when they're in; everyone would like to assume it's a matter of his prescription. Eliot, with the baritone, puts that ball away; whereas chubby Andrew is more likely to set you up that you may do yourself in. Mona contemplates this education in demolition. And as much as she recognizes tennis to be just the sort of sport Helen admires, she must admit the undeniable truth. The four of them out there playing does make a charming sight. Even more charming is the sight, a little later, of Charlie and Andrew and Sumner practically sitting on their hands so that Eloise can play. Eloise plays well, especially at net, but she can't deal with her brothers' serves. And so they bloop it over to her. Their crosscourts too come hopping sweet as Easter bunnies. Mona thinks how pleasant it must be to be thus indulged on this large parcel of oceanfront property; they are close enough to the water that a ball going over the fence could conceivably end up in the waves. More likely, it would land in the sand. All the same, the Ingles cry, "And it's going, going— out to sea!" if they lose a ball. Not that this happens too often. But so infectious is their enthusiasm that by the third time, Mona finds that she's chanting too, along with them. And when a couple comes to claim the court and is upset to find that they mistook the sheet by the inn desk as the sign-up for today, when in fact it's for tomorrow, Mona is as satisfied as the Ingles are generally that it's the couple's own fault. They should've asked someone if they didn't know what was what.

"We can't play tomorrow, we're going home," wails the woman.

And really, who knows? If she hadn't shaken her racket at them like a madwoman, the Ingles might well have given up their time remaining. But instead they agree that fair is fair. It's what Mr. Ingle always tells the kids is the great lesson of life: *You've got to know how the game is played.*


Mona is invited to have supper with the Ingles. She's to sit with them at the sunset, as their guest, even though she doesn't have proper clothes with her. The dress code calls for tie and jacket for men, the equivalent for women. This does not mean jeans, which is all Mona has brought, and she has a feeling it does not mean Callie's swirly print kimono with the rabbit feet either. Still Eloise thinks Mona should come. She says her father will speak to the maître d'.

Mona is skeptical. "What is he, the Pope? He can arrange a special dispensation?"

"He rowed with the owner in prep school." Eloise says this with a simplicity that would become a Shaker abbess.

Mona hesitates greatly.

But when she next runs into Callie and Naomi, she is dressed in Eloise's continued generosity. A brightly flowered wrap skirt hangs down to her calves, and she is wearing with it a top of a tropical hue.

"And what is this I see before me?" says Naomi. "Do I spy . . . a spy?"

Callie laughs. "Goes great with your peace pendant."

Naomi and Callie are wearing football jerseys and cutoffs.

"So how goes the infiltration?" asks Naomi.

Mona shrugs. "They're not so bad. They just play a lot of games."

"Well, keep up the good work," says Callie.

"Hold down the fort," says Naomi.

"Don't let any flies fly by," says Callie.

"Really," Mona says. "Maybe they're not typical."

But when, after cocktails and chatting in the lounge, time for supper trots around, the first thing that happens is that a new waitress approaches the table. This is not the Ingles' waitress-for-the-week; Ginger, it turns out later, has managed to break her toe swimming. This is a replacement waitress, to whom Mr. Ingle's very first words are, "So what part of Scotland are you from?"

Mona looks up.

"I'm not from Scotland," says Naomi, and winks at Mona.

Mona looks down.

"Oh, really," says Mr. Ingle.

And that is when, to Mona's profound surprise, Naomi looks down too. She does not say she's from deepest, darkest Wales. She looks as though she has never seen Mona before in her life.

Mona admires the sunset for a moment. What a view! It really is something to have a seat like this on the world. All the same, Mona is about to supply the "She's from deepest, darkest Wales," when Naomi says, "Would you like some wine with dinner?"

Mr. Ingle orders. Naomi leaves. Mona peruses the menu. You can order all you want here. You can have an appetizer and a soup and a salad, even two of each, or three. You can have the fruit cup and the shrimp cocktail and the oysters Rockefeller; you can have the salad Niçoise and the chef's salad and the Caesar salad. You can have the clear broth and the clam chowder and the cream of leek; and then you can have the filet mignon and the lobster and the swordfish, with the baked potato and the rice pilaf and the home fries on the side; also the carrots and the broccoli and the sliced beets. For dessert you can have a piece of everything on the cart if you want—you don't even have to say anything, you can just point. But here's the surprise: Nobody orders very much in this family. Mona is the only one to order two of anything. Some of the Ingles don't even order one of each category—for instance, Mrs. Ingle, who goes for one cup of the clear broth and one piece of swordfish. Steamed broccoli on the side, no starch. This is not because she is on a diet. This is because she doesn't much care for eating, actually, just as she doesn't much care for the view. The sun is too much, she says, especially night after night. Charlie thinks she should wear sunglasses if the light bothers her, but she says it simply isn't done.

To order doubles is another thing that *simply is not done.* Mona wishes she had not, as the guest, been asked to order first, so that she would have realized this. It's too late, though. Naomi presents her, at each course, with what seems like more food than the rest of the table has ordered combined. Mona has two dishes before her, where everyone else has one, or none; and to make matters worse, Naomi has seemingly arranged for extra-large helpings. She presents these wordlessly, with a blank look on her face. Mona tries to catch her eye, but Naomi will not look at her; if anything, her chin seems to jut out even farther than usual as she leans over Mona's shoulder. Mona stares at its underside, thinking how this is an aspect of Naomi that she literally has not seen before. Though what did Mona expect? Nobody could invent herself the way Naomi has without also being able to serve a person what she asked for.

What can Mona do but eat? It seems to her that she has to at least sample each thing. She is glad Callie is off tonight, and not there to see her, although she also wonders if for once she couldn't use some sisterly guidance. Would Mona be in this situation if she took *tai qi* more seriously?

"Some of us have an actual pea under the mattress," Mr. Ingle is saying. "Others of us imagine peas where there are only in fact only lumps."

Apropos of what he says this, Mona's not sure. But she can feel herself growing hot, as if he is talking about her, or Callie, or Naomi. Is she being too sensitive? Is she indeed imagining a pea where there is only a lump? She is, Mona thinks, she must be. Although maybe she's not, since following the pea/lump comment, the conversation mysteriously meanders her way.

"Her sister Callie is working her way through college," says Eloise. (Because of her fight with her stepmother, this is the first thing she has volunteered all evening.) "And Mona may well have to do the same."

"Dear, dear," says Mrs. Ingle. "We admire you, young lady." Is that by way of reconciliation? She passes Mona the bread basket—as if Mona is not eating enough already—insisting that the popovers are divine. Mona wonders how she knows.

"Don't have one if you don't want one." Eloise gazes off into the sunset, as if after a departing knight.

Mona diplomatically takes a roll, but does not eat it.

Mrs. Ingle says nothing. Eloise says nothing. Mr. Ingle says nothing. The boys start analyzing people they know on scholarships. All of these people, it turns out, are great athletes. They go through the sports these kids play, they argue about how essential to the team these scholarship kids are. Lacrosse, hockey. Baseball, swimming, tennis. Rugby. Crew. Mona begins to rather regret not only that she ordered so much food, but that the inn has this system at all, where so many little courses are served in so leisurely a manner. And is Naomi purposefully letting the Ingles enjoy a particularly leisurely dinner? It does seem so, as the conversation progresses to the next question of interest—namely, are the scholarship kids self-financing? Charlie maintains that they are not charity cases at all. In fact, they generate so much alumni contribution that he thinks they are a moneymaking proposition.

"I do believe I've had enough of this topic of conversation," says Mrs. Ingle.

"If not all of them, at least the starters," continues Charlie—undeterred by his mother, maybe even pleased to have riled her. "And I bet the school breaks even on the rest."

"So why don't they recruit some more?" says Sumner, sardonically. "Why do they bother to let us in, if these kids are so great."

"Because they generate the contribution, and we contribute the contribution," says Eliot, irrefutably.

"Enough," says Mrs. Ingle again.

The boys exchange glances.

"I wouldn't mind being a scholarship student," says Andrew, flushing. "I think it's a great honor."

The sun goes down and stays down. When the lobster arrives, Mona realizes that everyone else has ordered fish. Besides being the only person thinking how nonkosher is this dish, Mona will be the only person eating with a bib. Eloise volunteers to help her with the crustacean, and, willing to engage in any interaction, Mona agrees. Eloise shows Mona how to use the cracker. She explains to her about the tomalley. Mrs. Ingle points out the roe. Eloise ignores her and points out the roe herself. Unfortunately, in the process of cracking one of the claws, Mona squirts lobster juice across the table and hits Naomi.

Naomi finally looks at Mona. Mona stands to help wipe off her friend. Everyone else watches.

When Mona sits back down, Mrs. Ingle asks, "And where are you from?"

To which Mona answers, surprised, "The same town as you. In fact, Eloise and I are classmates."

Says Mrs. Ingle again, "But where are you from?"

Eloise's brother Andrew glosses this helpfully. "She means where are you from, from."

"Ah," Mona says. And then, with Naomi attending, Mona says, "Deepest, darkest China."

Two of the brothers laugh, but the rest of the family is not sure whether to laugh or not.

"Is that a joke?" says Eloise.

"Yes," Mona says.

And to her credit, Eloise smiles as if with genuine amusement—thrilled, apparently, that Mona has said something fresh to her stepmother.

Mona now seems to be officially in their midst and, as such, fair game. She works on the lobster; they work on her, starting with the astounding fact of Naomi's being Mona's sister's roommate.

"Full scholarship to Harvard." Andrew whistles.

"Harvard-Radcliffe," says Mona.

"Is she on any teams?" Eliot wants to know.

"Basketball?" guesses Sumner.

"Ask her yourselves," Mona says. But they do not talk to Naomi;

when she's serving or clearing, only Mona talks. It's not a lot of conversation, but it's enough that you'd never know anything was ever the matter between them. And when Naomi leaves, Mona talks some more, only now about all things Chinese—her parents, and China, and how many of her relatives are over there, and whether she's been back, and whether she speaks the language. ("Of course she speaks it," says Eliot when Sumner asks. "Open your eyes.") Also whether Mona misses China even though she's never been there.

"That must be so weird," says Andrew. "I mean, to never get a chance to see your own home."

"It's not her home," says Charlie.

"So what is her home?" demands Sumner.

"America," says Charlie. "I think."

They also discuss Chinese art, about which Mona knows nothing and Mrs. Ingle everything, as the latter inadvertently demonstrates by making Mona do the talking. Communism is Mr. Ingle's forte. He discusses the Korean War with Mona, assuming she knows what a parallel is. He discusses Hong Kong, and Formosa, which Mona at least knows is now called Taiwan.

"When did that happen?" Mr. Ingle wants to know.

Then begins a more personal conversation, with special conventions of speech. For example, Mr. Ingle begins introducing his questions with "I'm curious." Mrs. Ingle, on the other hand, tends to "Do you mind my asking?" Mona answers, figuring it's just the cost of dinner. Once or twice she asks them about where they come from, occasioning a general kind of answer. But then they switch the topic, gently but firmly, back to her. For Mona is so much more interesting than they are; they already know all about themselves.

Finally Naomi calls Mr. Ingle away from the table for a telephone call. Everyone seems to have been waiting for this, because the atmosphere in his absence is of hushed anticipation. Mona returns gratefully to her lobster.

"Let's try this," she says to Eloise, and she slides the meat out of the tail by pushing with a fork from the small end. This is an efficient approach Helen taught Mona just a few summers ago, having learned it herself from a clam shack place mat.

"Wow. Did you just figure that out?" says Eloise.

"The Chinese really are going to take over the world," says Eliot. "They really are smarter than everybody else."

Mr. Ingle returns with an inscrutable look on his face.

"Say what you will," says Mrs. Ingle, "it's just not right."

"Have I said something?" says Mr. Ingle.

"That poor man has a family too," says Mrs. Ingle. "In fact, he even has a daughter. . . ."

"Thank you for your opinion," he answers. "If there were a choice, we would choose." Everyone at the table can hear the perfectly round black period at the end of the sentence.

And then it's back to the Far East until the dessert cart wheels over, bearing a strawberry shortcake to die for.


"That's what we do when no one is talking," says Eloise. "We converse."

Eloise and Mona and Naomi and Callie sit on the beach in the dark, using beach towels they filched from the bathhouse. These are just as threadbare and tiny as Mr. Gugelstein maintained, and instantly damp; sitting on one is like sitting on a wet diaper. Only Eloise's dog seems truly comfortable. A white curl on the black sand, he looks like a furry antimoon, except when he leaps up to patrol the strip. He barks at the waves as if to scare them off his property; lucky for him, the tide is going out.

Meanwhile, Eloise continues. "Thou shalt not raise thy voice. It's the first commandment. But I do sometimes, I can't help it. Maybe because I'm half Jewish; that's what my stepmother says. She says I'm a bit . . . *expressive*."

"Is she right?" asks Naomi.

Eloise shrugs. "It must be from watching Woody Allen movies. I'm the only one in my family who even thinks he's funny. Everyone else thinks it's a shame a chap that clever wasn't sent to prep school."

"Might not it have something to do with having your real family broken up and your inheritance stolen?" Naomi says. "That would make one *expressive*, would it not?"

"It would!" Eloise says that according to her stepmother, Eloise does not realize that there are things one does not say—indeed, that one should not have *things to say* to begin with. "If you do, then you haven't been brought up properly."

"Ah—a catch-22: The rules of your set," says Naomi, "are that you should belong without objection to your set."

Manners, reticence, class. They discuss self-hatred, which Mona doesn't exactly understand; also something called antagonistic cooperation, which seems to be a kind of dance you can't stop dancing even if you hate your partner as much as you hate yourself.

"Don't you think Mom and Dad looked down on themselves when they were in China?" says Callie at one point. "Think about those gunboats in the harbor. Don't you think they hated the British but in a way looked up to them too?"

Says Mona, "I never thought about it before."

"But here you are now," says Naomi. "Thinking."

"And here I am too," says Eloise.

"Half Jewish," Mona says.

"Maybe starting to turn part black too," says Naomi.

"Why not?" Eloise raises her fist proudly, the way Miss Montana did in the Miss America pageant one year.

Mona and Callie raise their fists as well. "Black is beautiful!"

"They are the oppressors," says Naomi, her voice extra sonorous. "We are the expressers."

They all laugh.

"Seriously, though," continues Naomi. "If I were you, I would express myself right out of that household."

"Why don't you come stay with us?" Mona looks to Naomi and Callie for approval; they nod with the sort of dignity you associate with beards. "Of course, it's not the Ritz."

"I wouldn't think so." Eloise smiles. However, she doesn't say yes, doesn't say no, just fills her shoes up with sand, then empties them out. Her golden hair ripples silver down her back, a private sea.


Mona spends the morning alone, trying to call Seth. No answer. She tries to call Barbara. No answer there either. In the afternoon, Eloise shows up with Dog, a pile of hotel linen, and some hotel blankets. "I wasn't sure how well supplied you were," she says.

"Actually," says Callie, "we get the new stuff. Pull with the chambermaids, you know." She winks.

Dog sniffs around while Mona sets Eloise up in the corner of the room, away from the ant trail. Also Eloise gets the one lamp, it's the red carpet treatment. However, with no carpet. Mona explains how they are similarly blessed with no air conditioner.

"I've always preferred the sea breeze," says Eloise. She smiles even as Callie explains how they don't actually get a sea breeze; they're not exactly water view. However, they do get some kind of draft as a result of the kitchen exhaust fan.

"Isn't that hot air?" Eloise doesn't actually stop in the middle of pulling a pillowcase onto a pillow, but she does slow down like a self-reversing machine about to self-reverse.

"All that hot air rising pulls the cold air in behind it," says Callie. "And the cold air flows by our windows."

"How lucky!" says Eloise, picking up speed again.

So happy is she, in fact, that pretty soon they are discussing how long a stay makes her an official runaway, and whether she should go back to Scarshill with Mona when she goes. Mona explains all about Alfred, and how Eloise can probably live at Barbara's house too.

"That's the last place in the world I could live," says Eloise.

"But Barbara lives in a great house. It's not like this." Mona explains how the air-conditioning works so well you practically have to wear a sweater. Plus she'll like Alfred, Mona says, and no one hardly ever sees Evie.

"You don't understand," Eloise is saying again, when in strides Naomi. They can hear her in the vestibule; the wooden screen door bangs shut behind her.

"So trouble really did come to stay," she says, entering the room.

"What do you mean?" says Mona. "You said it was okay. And anyway she's probably going to move pretty soon to Barbara Gugelstein's house."

"Of course she's welcome. But she is not your friend Alfred. Nobody cares what happens to Alfred. If Eloise disappears, every policeman on the East Coast is going to be out searching for her."

And sure enough, no sooner does Naomi finish her sentence than there is rapping on the screen door.

Whispers Naomi, "It was in the script. They all go home again."

"Is that true?" Mona says. "I thought . . ."

"They go home changed, that's all," Naomi says. "A variation on the theme, maybe significant, maybe not." She turns to Eloise as the rap is repeated. "So who is it? The police, or just your father?"

"My father." Eloise is glumly lucid; already she is rising to the occasion, even as she sits on the floor. She lifts her head, lets go of her knees. "He wouldn't want any publicity, especially right now."

And she's right: It's her father. Mona opens the door.

"What is the meaning of this?" His voice sends a tremor across the room.

Eloise stands.

"Are you dressed for dinner?" he asks.

"No," she says.

"You're keeping everyone waiting."

And just like that, Eloise scoops up Dog and is gone.


What would have happened if she had stayed? Naomi and Callie and Mona discuss this over supper. It's Naomi and Callie's day off, which means that they have to cook for themselves; and that means Chinese food so genuine Mona finds it an encounter. Naomi, for example, has learned to do an authentic tea-smoked duck that involves burning tea leaves in a wok and smoking the duck in it for sixteen hours. (Mona, meanwhile, shares Helen's most recent favorite duck dish recipe— namely, Peking duck, Westchester style. The whole secret is soaking the duck overnight in Pepsi-Cola.)

But what would have happened?

Says Mona, "I think Eloise would've become a great spy."

Says Naomi, "If Eloise had stayed, she would have gotten bored." Is that right?

"Eloise was not brought up to participate in someone else's experiment," says Naomi. "There's nothing we could have done."

And with that, a hush falls over their little supper. They eat silently, peacefully, their faces bedewed by the steam from the rice, their chopsticks clicking against their hotel-logo bowls. They will discuss yin and yang, and balance the foods they eat. They will return the linens, with apologies, to the chambermaids. The chambermaids will rib them about going to Harvard; they will discuss how Juanita has back problems, and how Cookie is getting married. They will plan what to make for a shower present. Then they will meditate; and then, when the kitchen exhaust fan finally goes off, they will sleep.

# CHAPTER 10

# Camp Gugelstein

Back home, it turns out that Seth and Barbara have been going to the beach also. Alone, it turns out—Alfred, claims Seth, is afraid of the water. "I see," Mona says, though what she beholds in her mind's eye is in fact not fearful Alfred at all, but fearless Barbara and Seth, minimally clad. Side by side on beach blankets. Did the blankets touch? Did their selvages overlap? Is that why there was no answer at the teepee? And is this dread jealousy? Last year in English, when they read *Othello*, Mona thought that poor Moor meshugga, but now she wonders if she is not Moorishly afflicted, that she can't get the phrase *thirsty terry* out of her mind. *All that thirsty terry*, Mona thinks, and there they are, Barbara and Seth, thirsty too; it's only natural in the hot New York sun. They quench their thirsts; they cool off in the water together, it's only natural. They body surf, letting the waves carry them to shore like flotsam. Or is it jetsam? What fun, in any case! They are all abandonment. Their bathing suits fill up with sand, they empty their crotches in the water, discreetly. Pretending to be admiring the day. *Get a load of that seagull!* they say as they slightly squat. And then what? The suntan lotion problem. One must consider one's back, especially Barbara, who's never had a tan in her life—though *avant de* peeling there is at least a stage of being evenly, brilliantly burnt. Mona's seen this, it is really quite autumnal. To attempt to avoid which, Seth, with his surprise domestic side and penetrating touch, may give Barbara a little suntan application. It's only natural. As she lies there prone on her thirsty terry. He rolls the bathing suit straps around. A little up, a little down. And then what? Does not force of habit take over? For once you know another person's body, it's hard to forget that you know it. It's like playing a song, one phrase leads to another.

Speaking of which, Mona notices that Seth has a new little jingle: *You put your beep beep in, you pull your beep beep out, you put your beep beep in, and you move it all about. You do the hanky-panky and you turn yourself around. That's what it's all about.* Mona asks him about the circumstances under which this song came to him. He says the highway was his muse.

"All that bumper-to-bumper traffic," Mona says. "Bump bump bump."

He puts his arm around her, and with his fingers plays her upper arm like an accordion. "My dear Changowitz." He calls her this even though he knows it is Andy Kaplan's name for her, and in his opinion Andy is going to grow up to be some muckety-muck's most-valued assistant. (From comments like these Mona gathers that Andy has been beating Seth at chess.) "Are you trying to get at something?"

"Funny," Mona says. "That's what I was about to ask you."

"So ask." His fingers hit a chord.

But Mona can't ask. Instead she says, apropos of nothing, "Barbara said something about an amalgam tattoo."

"How interesting."

"She said you showed her yours, but she didn't say how it was that you were sharing with her the mysteries of your oral cavity."

"And here I thought you told each other everything." Seth resumes playing.

How to explain? Mona pulls away.

"Let me guess," says Seth finally, facing her. "You are wondering are we three contemplating an experiment in living?"

Mona doesn't answer.

He winks. "We could do anything to which Miss Bourgeoisie would agree."

This is another thing he calls her these days. He says that Mona thinks she's no radical, but that she's just denying her true nature. *Ah, yes,* she says. *Just call me Yoko Ono.*

"Are you by any chance falling in *luff*?" he adds, as seriously as he can in a phony German accent.

"*Mit* who?"

"*Mit* yours truly. Or a reasonable facsimile thereof."

Mona snorts credibly. "To quote a certain stubborn eminence: Never, never, never, never, never."

And she smiles, mortified, as they go on to other topics of conversation. For right or wrong, Mona realizes, she is just like Barbara in this way: She is interested in ownership. *My boyfriend.* Seth thinks this is a capitalistic impulse, but she knows it has more to do with *make sure.* As in, Make sure you don't get your heart smashed up.

After the other topics of conversation, she goes for a long walk. This one is full of interesting ritual ablutions—people washing down their driveways, their cars, their dogs. *The more Jewish you become, the more Chinese you'll be*—that's what Rabbi Horowitz told her once. Meaning what? Is Mona on her way home again already? And how is it that she feels she's become part of someone else's experiment?

Mona runs into Alfred on the road to Barbara's house, where it seems she's been headed without thinking about it.

"Hey, Alfred," Mona says. "I hear you're afraid of the water."

Alfred gives her a mock-sheepish look at odds with his stance, which is arms folded, weight forward, legs spread; he looks like Mr. Clean, only with hair and proper clothes. "Yes, ma'am, I am indeedy," he says. "It's a Negro thing. I'm afraid that water is going to rise up and drown old Alfred. I'm terrified of that water, yes ma'am I am. I'm plain terrified." He laughs, looks away, stretches his mouth as if about to yawn.

"You know, Alfred," Mona says, "if you came with us to the beach sometime, you would realize that a lot of black people swim just fine."

"Oh, no, ma'am, I'm too afraid."

"What's with the jive talk, Alfred? And since when have I become ma'am?"

"Since you started trying to tell Alfred what's going down. Ma'am."

"I'm just trying to be encouraging. You never know. You'd be surprised."

"No, no, ma'am, I do know. You'd be surprised yourself." He does not unfold his arms.

And indeedy, Mona is surprised when, a week or so later, she and Seth and Barbara happen to set out for the beach, only to run into so much traffic that they turn around and come home. For that is when they discover Barbara's empty house not to be empty.

"Holy shit," says Seth.

Alfred's friends are mostly in the den—hanging out, watching TV, drinking beer. Also they are smoking cigarettes, so that Mona's first reaction—after the considerable *shtup* of discovery—is vindication. For recently, Mona has noticed a smell of cigarette smoke in the house, even mentioned it to Barbara. Barbara, though, hasn't been able to smell a thing since she had her nose fixed. Of course, the doctor maintains that, medically speaking, she can smell just fine. But the truth is, she could run a manure factory if that were her inclination. Even when Mona insisted the house fairly reeked of tobacco, Barbara thought it must just be Alfred enjoying an occasional puff, or maybe Maria the maid on the sly. For so vigorous a worker is Maria, that the stove knob markings are wearing off. And what do people with that kind of energy do to relax, but smoke?

Alfred's friends are boisterous without being unruly. They are Afro-proud and close-cropped, shiny-faced and gnarled, bearded and clean-shaven—yet there's a relatedness to the way they move. Maybe this is in response to the unexpected advent of Barbara and Seth and Mona: They've grouped themselves so palpably that a person could almost touch their brotherhood. They are to a man deliberately casual. They are ostentatiously unfazed. You don't get the feeling they're looking to make an exit, quite the contrary. They're looking to give you a chance to absent yourself, with decorum or not—your choice. *You like your tail between your legs, that's fine with us,* they seem to say. *You just do what comes natural.*

What seems to come natural, meanwhile, is for Mona and Seth and Barbara to stand there, shrinking. They curl their toes. They remind themselves that this is a clear violation of the house rules. Such a violation would shock them in any case, but it packs a particular whap because of a particular detail that, up to now, has almost been too much to take in—namely, that sweet as a Kmart parakeet, perched on Alfred's lap, in the midst of everyone, is Evie.

"Evie," says Barbara, finally.

"Hiya," says Evie, waving one of her bare feet.

Evie has not only always been smarter than Barbara, but more clearly an aspiring adult. In junior high she won the Betty Crocker Award; now she is the type of do-gooder to whom benches are dedicated. But to make matters worse, Evie has always been nice. When Barbara, at Evie's bench dedication, wanted nothing more than to puke, Evie actually guessed that. "I guess this makes you want to puke," she said, standing there with her perfect elfin features, and nary a blackhead in sight. It was hard to completely hate her. However, Barbara has always considered herself cooler than Evie, who eschews slang and is instead into things like collecting. Candles, rocks, bugs, shells. It has always seemed to be the way she goes about life—labeling things neatly, pulling them from drawers. "Do you think she knows where her hymen is?" Barbara said once, after being compared yet again to her illustrious relative. "She'll probably marry a curio cabinet." Even after Evie got involved with a guy, it was a long-distance relationship. In short, she's been Miss Priss.

Until now. Evie starts to stand up, but when Alfred pulls her back down, she cheerfully swings her legs. She is wearing cutoffs, below which her thighs look white as dug-up tree roots; her knees glow with indecency.

"Howdy do," she says.

Around her break great rolls of laughter. "Howdy do," says one person, and then another, and then another.

"Well," says Seth. "It must be Howdy Doody time," and that makes them all laugh some more. Seth laughs too.

"Evie," says Barbara again.

"You can't really be surprised," says Evie.

Barbara blinks like a green-eyed barn owl.

"I guess we fooled 'em," says Evie to Alfred. She claps her bare feet together.

"They really are just as deaf and blind as they look," agrees Alfred.

Later Mona and Barbara and Seth listen to Alfred's explanations with admiring irritation. He explains how his friends broke into Charlene's place and stole his clothes back for him, and how this was the first and only time they came to Barbara's house, to deliver the clothes. Evie waltzes along with this story, until at some particularly flirty revolution she breaks out laughing. Then Alfred starts laughing too, and they have to admit Alfred's friends have been coming around a lot. How many times altogether? They're not sure, but Evie says it did feel like she and Alfred were cleaning up all the damn time, doing away with the evidence. As for how did they first get together, they describe it all, from day one, beginning with how shocked Evie was one fine evening, when she found Alfred watching TV in the den. Evie had come in to express her amazement that Barbara was watching baseball, and perhaps to watch some herself—her erstwhile boyfriend was a jock who liked it when she watched games for him and gave the details in her letters.

But in the den was Alfred. Evie screamed and ran out of the room; he had to clap his hand over her mouth to calm her down. "I'm Alfred the cook," he said. "I'm a friend of Barbara's, living here on account of I got eighty-sixed by my bitch wife Charlene." Still she wanted to call the police, until finally he said, "You're too upset. Let me call." And he did, he called the police himself. He was already trying to explain how it was that he, the intruder, was calling to report the intrusion, when Evie started to believe him. Then she got on the line and explained to the officer that there had been a mistake. Of course, the police came out to the house anyway; and this was the first joint show that they did, Alfred and Evie. Explaining to the officer how nothing had happened, and how the phone call was a lark, they were sorry. The officer was skeptical. He wanted to see Alfred's driver's license; he wanted to see the parents of the house. He said he knew the Gugelsteins. But had he ever met Mr. Gugelstein's sister, Elaine? asked Evie. The officer thought. Did she drive a gold Cadillac? "That's her!" exclaimed Evie, though in fact her mother drove a third-hand Benz, one of the two-seaters, with an expansive hood and a roof the size of a cafeteria tray. "And this is my boyfriend." In desperation she kissed Alfred, luxuriating in the officer's shock, not to say Alfred's: Knowing a challenge when it Frenched him, Alfred promptly kissed back.

Which did indeed lead to further developments of the lubricious sort, but not so straightaway as a body might think. For first there was a profound intellectual thirst to be slaked. To wit, once the officer left, Evie was curious. How long had Alfred been in residence? How had he escaped her notice? What was his room like? She recognized his radio station; so she wasn't going crazy, she said. She had thought she was going crazy as a result of spending too much time in the darkroom with those chemicals. Either that, or else she thought Barbara was going crazy, what with the radios on all over the house. He didn't like it here, he told her. But why not? A soul-to-soul conversation. Evie had grown up with black help; in fact, she had had her first affair with her nanny's son, it was practically incest. Also she had once tutored in an inner-city school that was just about all black. She told him about the school she'd worked in. The students had to wear their winter jackets to class, that's how cold it was, and of course there weren't enough books; people had to share. Everyone had head lice. Alfred shook his head. And why was she working in a place like that without even getting paid?

"You're just like your cousin Barbara," he told her. "Got to fix the world right up."

They agreed not to say anything to Barbara and Seth and Mona. Evie didn't want Alfred to get in trouble, and Alfred didn't want to get in trouble himself. For how mad would that Miss Blanco be if she heard that he got caught in the den just the way she predicted?

"Evie thought that just the funniest thing," supplies Alfred.

"Thanks a lot," says Barbara.

Says Evie, "You said you wanted to hear everything."

Barbara powwows with Mona and Seth. Would they have been mad if Alfred and Evie had immediately come clean?

"Not as mad," says Barbara finally, "as we are now. For Evie has lied to us, and Alfred has betrayed our trust."

"But I didn't mean to betray nobody," says Alfred.

"So what were you doing, then?"

"I was just having me a piece of—I mean, excuse me." He winks at Evie. "I was just having me a broadening experience."

"It was fun," says Evie. "Seeing what would happen. Seeing whether you'd figure it out."

"It was like an experiment," says Mona.

"That's right," says Alfred. "We didn't mean no harm. We were just hanging out, seeing what came down."

"*Que sera, sera,* right?" says Mona. "Only it was your experiment instead of ours. You didn't want to be in someone else's experiment."

"I guess you could put it that way," allows Alfred.

In any case, by the time Mona and Barbara and Seth set up camp outside the darkroom door, Evie couldn't possibly have come out. She and Alfred would have both started laughing for sure.

"But what do you mean?" says Seth. "Are you saying that it was all right for him to be a kind of pet, even a rambunctious pet, so long as he didn't turn into a normal horny male?"

"I didn't say anything about horny males," says Barbara.

"If he were white, we'd think he was James Bond," says Seth. "He used his head, he kept his wits, he's balling the girl. Instead we think he's a sneaky Negro. It's like what Baldwin says—when white men fight back, they're heroes. When black men fight back, they're savages."

"I never said he was a sneaky anything, or a savage, either," says Barbara, "And the girl is not just a thing you ball or don't ball." She turns the color of spaghetti sauce for a moment, but goes on. "And what do you think the Russians think of James Bond? If a white man had betrayed us, we'd be pissed off too. The problem is that we're the big bad Russians now."

"The big bad Russians as opposed to the Americans, or the big bad Russians as opposed to the serfs?"

"I mean this has nothing to do with race."

"Nothing to do with race!" Seth guffaws. "You may be right about the James Bond part. But how can anything have nothing to do with race?"

Seth and Mona and Barbara sit cross-legged in Seth's teepee. A perfect circle of rain drips into the fire pit; the drops make little thuds as they land.

Says Mona, "I don't see why Alfred should be evicted if this whole affair isn't really his fault."

"Maybe Evie's the one who should be evicted," says Seth.

But is it her fault, either?

"Maybe we should let them go on as before," says Mona.

"They tricked us," complains Barbara.

"Plus, realistically, how can we evict them?" says Mona. "Are we really prepared to kick them out ourselves?"

At this, Barbara of the wounded pride suggests, "My parents could suddenly appear."

Silence.

"Spoken like a true fair-weather radical," says Seth.

"I'll tell you what I am," says Barbara, straightening. "I'm no-body's fool."

More silence. Then advises Seth, gently, "Forget about Evie. Don't let your ego get in the way of your politics."

But Barbara has no intention of forgetting about anybody. Already you can see that she is going to be the kind of person unfazed by discount clothes stores where everybody shares one big dressing room. Barbara is going to be the kind who just up and strips. (For she is who she is, as she'll tell you; she never pretended to be a size two.)

"I don't have any politics," she says now, putting on her sandals. "I have feelings, something men in general and you in particular will never understand. I refuse to let them walk all over me. I feel I owe it to myself, not to say to my ancestors who were serfs."

"My grandfather was a Polish worker," objects Seth.

"So you shouldn't let people walk all over you, either," replies Barbara. "Plus wasn't your other granddad a German industrialist? He didn't exactly hail from a shtetl in Galicia."

Seth hangs his head; Barbara stands up, forgetting that she is in a teepee and needs to move to the middle first. As a result, she all but knocks one of the birch poles right out of its hole. The whole tent shudders, the circle of rain blurs; and when she's gone, the canvas sags worse than ever.


Alfred's friends continue to hang out. Barbara is not actually anxious to call her parents, and that is one reason. The other is that Alfred's friends have set out to woo her, and, transparent as their efforts are, she is not indifferent to them. "Miss B.," they call her, just like everyone at the restaurant. Nobody puts the moves on her, but they are openly appreciative of her physical endowments. They also appeal to her noble nature; and they do not forget to make Evie look bad. "Not everybody in the world has got such a sense of fair play as you, Miss B.," they say. "Not that's got no horse sense too. For example, that Evie." They lower their voices. "She's got the fair play. You leave her be, she's going to straighten out the whole world so there ain't going to be no more warfare or shit like that. But what's she throwing herself away on that Alfred for, man? She should be humping somebody fine, somebody like that Seth, now." And they wink at Barbara.

Meaning what? Barbara blushes. Seth looks away.

There is a mod squad that comes regularly: Luther the Race Man, Big Benson, Ray, and Professor Estimator. Professor Estimator is the brain of the group, a bookworm who remembers everything about everything and can take a fair guess at the rest. Smooth and shiny as he is above, he is jowly and loose-skinned below, and bespectacled: He wears his glasses tilted so far forward they look to be falling off. However, no one makes comments about this, or asks him why he doesn't just loop the curvy ear wire around his handy ears, or points out how on account of his glasses he is forced to turn his head in slow and level fashion. For he has the sort of giant, directed eyes you would just as soon not have fasten on your temerity. No—better to behold than be beheld. He is a tremendous man, the color of old iron, with an unmistakable center of gravity. He sits square in his chair and arranges his elbows in symmetric fashion, and when he stands he never uses the arms of a chair to help him up. He simply stands, head high, glasses perched, as if he's forsworn even the most pedestrian assistance. By day the Estimator is a produce buyer, but by night he's going to law school, meaning that usually he has no time. This year he's taking the summer off, though; and besides helping him get over some heartache, this is helping stem speculation that he's getting too uppity to run with his people anymore. No one's calling him Oreo. No one's wondering what he does for fun. Now they're ribbing him about how he's going to have a brandy-ass new Cadillac someday, and a fancy new babe to put that bug-eyed Ruth Buzzy to shame—some sister whose idea of a bedtime activity is not reading. His buddies joke that they'll be counting on him to get them out of trouble; he's going to be their secret weapon. When the shit comes down, he's going to send it flying back.

Not that they don't have other means. Big Benson is their very own law enforcement official. He got himself through high school, which was more than enough schooling for him. Now he works on and off in a construction crew. A burly vet the color of gingerbread, with small features set like raisins in his face, he could be a cookie except that he loves demolition. Also he hates to wear a helmet on account of what it does to his Afro. In 'Nam he cut his hand but bad; the doctors were talking amputation. But now he can use it so fine that his whole philosophy of life is based on the experience: *Don't listen to nobody. Just talk your talk and walk your walk.* It's what he tells his kid, who's just like him. Even in the middle of the winter this child won't wear a hat, and he's never been caught anywhere without a pick.

Ray's a vet too, of the peg-legged variety. Yet he's still nimble, a papaya-colored man with two good arms. *Used to be I could lay them brick like any dago, and what with my two good arms I probably still could.* So he says sometimes. Other times, though, he doesn't know what he can do. He can't work, he can't talk. Not about 'Nam; not about anything. Sometimes it seems something got left overseas—besides his leg, that is—and that right there is the problem. Other times it seems he brought too much back. *Got me a new pair of eyes. Didn't ask for 'em but I got 'em just the same.* Like he sees his three kids, and he's not so sure who they are anymore. One of them is his spitting image right down to his extra-long pinkies. The other two, though, have eyes and noses and mouths like nothing he's ever observed in the mirror; if he ever finds out where they came from, he'll probably borrow him a machine gun and go mowing.

Then there's Luther the Race Man—always dressed in Afro tricolors, though he is just as positively cream-colored as Charlene used to claim. He is not as pee-in-your-pants handsome as Alfred. However, he is certainly beguiling, what with his pen-stroke eyebrows, and his dark, dark eyes, and his air of open appraisal. He has a smile full of private meaning, and a temper to match—quick to rise, quick to vanish. But most appealing of all is his taste for disruption. For belying his bulk, he is a winker, a darter. He loves to be putting on white folks, or to be gaming his way into something or another; he is given to sudden appearances and disappearances—often in the nick of time, often too with goods of some salty kind. *That Luther,* his friends are always saying, with disconcerted delight. *That Luther!* He can be nasty too, though, and his personal life is one long tangled yarn of lovers, and children, and miscellaneous husbands gunning for his ass. No one knows where his money comes from; mostly, he is a phenomenon with a theme. As for the theme, that goes race, race, race. Luther attends rallies, and returns blowing black. "That's plain old motherfucking racist bullshit!" he might say. Or else, more equably, "You take that, you won't be no brother of ours no more, man. You take that, you'll be our most dearly beloved sister."

There are also three lesser members of the squad—guys who show up occasionally on account of their work hours, or their wives, or on account of their simply preferring to stay home. Ace, the Hatchet, and Billy. Of all of them, the Hatchet is the only one who puts Mona and Barbara and Seth on edge, and that's mostly because of his moniker. Also he has been known to bear arms. But when a no-firearms rule is instituted, he observes it. From time to time, other squad members kid him about his weapons status, and he always proves clean.

Other issues: They smoke cigarettes in the house and leave the butts all over. Also there are beer cans. Probably no more than there would be after any party, but usually you don't have parties all the time. The personalities concerned talk these things over, and after that there are no more butts and no more beer cans. "Hey, man, pick that up," they tell each other. "Where your manners." And to their hosts: "Our mamas brought us up decent." Easy as it is to get them to pick up certain things, though, it proves less easy to get them not to pick up other things, especially when the people are high. Candle-sticks, bowls, silverware.

"It's just not natural to ask people not to touch things," says Seth. "That's why there are guards in museums. They don't need the guards just to keep people from smoking and drinking beer."

"That's easy for you to say," says Barbara. She is trying to be cool, really she likes everyone, but she says one of these days, something is going to be stolen, she just knows it.

In the meantime, it's hash brownies and James Brown, none of this Arlo Guthrie shit, and definitely no Joan Baez. *Pul-eez!* It's Soul Train and the funky chicken and mah-jongg—that's Barbara's idea, Mona's never played before. Checkers—Chinese and regular. Chess—the Es-timator and Seth pit pawns. A slow expansion to more spacious activi-ties, some of them outdoors. Basketball, baseball, swimming. (Luckily, the pool, like the tennis court, is behind a hedge.) The squad tries tennis. Badminton. They discuss lot versus lawn sports, which is like debating beer versus ice tea. But don't lawn sports have their charm? *Charm!* Ray and Big Benson laugh. Something they've always looked for in a sport. Rainy days mean billiards. Ping-Pong. Even a little yoga—nothing too elaborate, mostly just sequences where they stretch and let their bodies fill up with light in order that they may lay their eyes on Evie. For Evie runs these sessions, in the living room. The guys push all the furniture back; they sprawl on the royal-blue real-wool carpet, trying to pretzel themselves up the way she does. She is wearing a halter top, so that you can see the skin of her stomach getting twisty; it looks like a towel being wrung out. Also you can see the distinctive hang of her breasts, which are outgoing, in the manner of duck feet. She doesn't have cleavage so much as a bony midchest bowl. Still she holds her own, the centered center of her circle of attention, and this rubs on Alfred. He says she can't think what the brothers are thinking.

The room seems very small; the pile of footwear by the door, large and jumbled.

Seth buys himself a dashiki like Luther's—his camp shirt. On account of this, the guys give him grief. For Christmas, they say, they're going to buy him a tricolor yarmulke. Or not for Christmas, for—what is it?—Hanukkah! Seth laughs.

"Camp Gugelstein will come to order," he says now, when it's time to call a meeting. And as if this has been the ritual all their lives, people obligingly gather round for some sort of discussion. Sometimes this revolves around politics, or drugs, or the war; other times around sports, or cars, or—a surprise favorite—car repair. The transmission, they talk about. The alternator. *You disconnect the positive on the battery and it keep running, that means it was the alternator that was the trouble, not the battery.*

Today, though, the subject is hair.

Explains Professor Estimator, "There's good hair, bad hair, and no hair." He pats his own pate ruefully.

"There's 'fros and 'fros," agrees Big Benson. "Not everybody got the kink to get their natural to good size. Now, Ray, he respectable. He ain't no record-holder, but he respectable. See, he uses that Afrosheen. But now, Alfred here. He just ain't got what it takes. Even that Evie do up his cornrows extra tight, you still got a bro' with no 'fro."

Everyone laughs except Mona and Seth and Barbara.

"What's a cornrow?" asks Mona. Evie rises to give a short demonstration. Outside, it is starting to drizzle lightly. The arm of the turntable makes its way to the record center; silence falls; the patter of the rain turns to a rush. On other days, such silence has led to continued conversation; and sure enough, as Alfred straightens his neck, signaling the end of the beauty show, the Estimator brings up certain esoteric types of love. Meaning positions and practices, he says, winking. At this, Big Benson seems to eye Barbara.

But the chief position involved turns out to be sitting, and as for the practice, it is turning the other cheek. For the talk of Afros has got the Estimator thinking not only about fashions in hair but also about fashions in the heads that wear the hair, and about ideas falling too quickly out of date—namely, those of Dr. Martin Luther King, Jr. *Satyagraha,* says the Estimator, meaning the force of the truth that is love. *Agape,* meaning love of all humanity. The Estimator sees redemptive love as still alive here, at Camp Gugelstein, but he thinks elsewhere it is on the wane.

Says Luther, "Why we got to translate and explicate when we got words in English everybody understand? Like black power, man. Nobody got to ask what that mean." He grins, lights up a joint.

"There's more disagreement about the definition than you realize," says Professor Estimator, and goes on to discourse about materialism and humanism and free will, and about seeking to win the friendship of one's opponent rather than to destroy or humiliate him.

"That's beautiful, man," says Seth, taking a toke.

"How can you believe in sainthood for Negroes," objects Mona, "when you think George Eliot was a sap?"

"Touché," says Seth. "I reverse my opinion. How Christian. How sappy. How unnatural."

"That's what Elijah Muhammad says," puts in Ray, surprising everyone. "Integration is going to fail."

Says Seth, "I didn't mean *integration* was unnatural."

"Integration is natural for blacks, but how about for you?" says Luther. "You still got to have Israel no matter what, right?"

"And the white domination of blacks that has gone on for six thousand years is coming to an end," continues Ray. "According to Elijah Muhammad. Actually it was supposed to have ended already. In 1914."

"So what happened?" says Seth.

"I guess whitey got an extension." Ray grins as he says this; he's rolling another joint. "But we are the chosen people, you know. You are the white devil, and your empire is falling apart."

"Do you really believe that?" says Mona.

"The empire *is* falling apart," says Ray.

"But here we are, integrated," says Evie. "Is it unnatural?"

"I seen everything, man." Ray shrugs. "This ain't nothing compared to what went on in 'Nam."

Big Benson nods; the Estimator folds his arms. He says a few words about Thurgood Marshall, and how sad he would be to hear this kind of talk. Separatism is just a mimicking of Jim Crow, says the Estimator. He quotes Gandhi: " 'One becomes the thing he hates.' "

At this, Luther, to everyone's surprise, folds his arms too. He does not jump into the conversation; he is waiting on Ray, allowing him room to continue. (*You learn by talking,* that's what he'll say later. *Nobody ever radicalized without they had an audience.*)

But before Ray does continue, Seth takes charge. "Time to focus the energy," he says.

And on cue, with a kind of relief, they all gather in a circle; they could be the actors in *Hair*, except that they have their clothes on. They close their eyes. Later Seth will say that he called for a circle because this is what he's always done, taken charge out of anxiety and fear. Later Luther will proclaim it to be no wonder blacks don't believe in liberals anymore, look at Seth—your typical paternalistic motherfucker who cannot stand blacks talking for themselves, much less acting in their own self-defense.

But for now, no one perceives anything except that it's fun to chant. *Ommmmm. Ommmmm.* They are all sitting cross-legged; they hold hands. The first time they did this, Mona thought they had to be on *Candid Camera*; not having taken Evie's Introduction to Yoga in the living room, she wasn't yet accustomed to communal exhalation. But now she loves to sit next to different people; she loves to close her eyes and feel the different grips. There are warm palms, cool palms, firm grips, loose; and attached to them such an amazing array of humanity, that she can hardly keep from peeking every now and then, to behold the sight: For here is Seth and here is Barbara; and here are Evie, and

Alfred; and here too is a gang who loomed up like strangers not long ago. Now, though, they are friends, plain and simple—already! What are they, besides the most interesting people Mona has ever known? What are they but a bunch of hair-bedeviled buddies?


A flask is missing. In the course of packing for a picnic breakfast, Barbara goes to find a pocket brandy flask she wants to fill with cream. This is necessary because while Seth drinks his coffee with Cremora, Barbara will not. Cremora is gross, she says. She says this Cremora thing is a working-class affectation on Seth's part. Even Big Benson, she points out, now drinks his coffee with cream.

But the flask is nowhere apparent to be found. It is apparently not in the dining room, and it is apparently not in the living room, and it is apparently not in the pantry. It is apparently not in the kitchen, it is apparently not in the storage closet with the stadium blankets and other picnic items. It is apparently not in the attic. It is apparently not in the basement.

"Are you sure your parents didn't take it with them to the Vineyard?" Mona asks.

But Barbara says she's definitely seen it since the summer started. The flask in question is heavy silver plate, with a pierced design of a baskety sort, and she particularly noticed it in the dining room sideboard because it had an inch or so of something left in it. She and Mona go through the sideboard again.

Still confrontation rumbles toward them like a freight train. Barbara is so upset, Seth offers to do the talking for her; but Barbara knows that to say what she means, she has to make her speechy accusations herself. And so she calls everyone to order. No sitting in a circle on the floor, she makes everyone sit on a folding chair. The chairs are in two shortish rows. For a moment Barbara hesitates. Then she speaks her mind clearly, only orating a little. For the occasion, she is wearing a new stature-building fashion, platform shoes.

She is greeted with scuffling and the distinct sliding sound of people slouching. There seems to be a new first row made up entirely of sneakers; everyone seems to be smoking. No one knows anything. Barbara rocks in her shoes, she pushes her bangs off her forehead. Outside, a bright evening haze hovers over the yard like some grass treatment that's evaporating instead of being absorbed. She says that the flask is her dad's absolute favorite. She says it's got sentimental value, and that her mother gave it to him.

"You hear that, man?" Luther laughs in a laid-back manner. "It was a fucking present for her Jew-daddy."

Says Evie, "Luther Pinckney, that's no way to talk."

"What you talking about?" says Luther.

Says Alfred, "She means how would you like it if some cat called you a Jew-daddy."

Says Luther, shrugging, "I talks how I talks." He takes a drag of his cigarette. "In point of fact, I talks like the *niggah* I be, man. And the *niggah* I be knows a Jew-daddy when I see one."

"But you haven't seen Mr. Gugelstein," says Mona from the back row. With everyone slumped down, she has a clear view of Barbara, whose eyes are flashing even as other people speak. "And I'm not sure this has anything to do with being Jewish or black or anything else."

"What you know about it, girl?" Luther says this without even turning around.

"It doesn't," Mona insists, to the back of his head.

"And even if it did, 'someone must have sense enough and morality enough to cut off the chain of hate,' " says Seth, also in the back row.

"Dr. King," glosses the Estimator, turning.

"You tell us, then." Luther turns now too, so that cigarette smoke wafts in Mona's face. "Who own the flask? Who keep picking it up, you got to tell us to put it on down? Who like to steal the flask, who don't got no flask like that at home?" He winks. "I think that flask would look just fine on my fireplace mantel."

"Cut the shit," says Alfred, beside him. "You ain't got no fireplace."

"How you know what I got, man?"

Big Benson shakes his head. "Just got to come on bad. The devil in that boy."

"You got that flask?" says Alfred.

"I don't hear no questions from no boy sleeping white," says Luther.

"He's just got to start some shit," says the Estimator. "He's just got to fan some flames."

"You hot too?" says Seth, pulling at his dashiki.

"Hot as a motherfucker in here," agrees Big Benson. He looks at Barbara, looks at the floor.

"Hot as a hellhole," says Ray.

Professor Estimator looks at Seth. "So what are we doing here?" he says, resignation in his voice. He sweeps the room with his level gaze. "It time to split, or what?"

People look at each other.

"Let's get the hell out of this hellhole," says the Estimator.

"Time to split," says the Hatchet.

"What the hell," says Benson.

"Motherfucking hellhole," echoes Ray.

"A lot of racist bullshit coming down here," says Luther.

And with that, they file out of the house, into the light-orange air. Only Alfred stays. He gives people the high five, but stands stalwartly by his Evie as his friends disappear.


No one has to call the Gugelsteins. The mod squad is gone, and the mod squad does not come back, except for Professor Estimator, the next day, to help Alfred move. The squad has helped Alfred find a new place; they've helped him find a new car. He doesn't have to stay with some white folk like a charity case.

" 'We shall have our manhood,' " quotes the Estimator. " 'We shall have it or the earth will be leveled by our attempts to gain it.' "

"What's this 'we'?" says Seth. "And since when have you become a Representative Black Man instead of Old Estimator, the distinguished thinker and chess player?"

"I was suspected of stealing along with my black brothers. Who distinguished among us then?"

"And since when do you quote Eldridge Cleaver? Has a panther been born of the pacifist?"

" 'Free at last,' " says the Estimator, terse.

" 'Let us not seek to satisfy our thirst for freedom by drinking from the cup of bitterness and hatred.' "

The Estimator softens, but answers, " 'We will not be satisfied until justice rolls down like waters and righteousness like a mighty stream.' "

Alfred invites Evie to come visit anytime. She says she will. "Just don't bring your motherfucking camera," he says, and he drives away with the Estimator. The way the pair of them stick their elbows out the windows, they look from far off like a single large passenger, taking up the whole front seat.

Was all that transpired such a bad thing? In one way Mona and Barbara and Seth can't decide. Camp Gugelstein couldn't go on forever, and at least its breakup didn't involve the law. That's how they see it from afar. From afar, they think their purpose was to help Alfred back on his own feet, and they did. They wanted him to be independent of them, and he is.

From closer in, though, they are devastated, Seth especially. One day Mona finds him sitting in his teepee with his head in his hands, and she is surprised at how much older he looks. This is partly because, though he still has his beard, he's had his ponytail cut off. His hair is much wavier than she'd realized, and it even has a side part now, neat and white—who knows how long that will last. Still he does not look like a defeated youth so much as a defeated man. A defeated youth sets his elbows on his spread knees, and stares intently at the locker room floor; and you know by this that he has lost an important match such as he will never forget. A defeated man, on the other hand, is a crumpled-up thing. He looks as though he doesn't even mind that his mental function is not what it used to be; in truth, he would just as soon forget everything.

"I believed it would work." Seth says this over and over, doggedly, reinforcing the mental-function-is-not-what-it-used-to-be impression. "I wanted it to work."

This is the most prolonged acquaintance Mona has had with the nape of Seth's neck, and she's surprised and oddly touched to behold his most unruly hairline—how his hair whorls up and suddenly down, a haircutter's challenge. She traces the swirl with her finger, thinking how rarely anything like this has happened to him. For how could it? He's so rarely cared about anything, to begin with. Here's a guy who doesn't believe in love, or college, or task-specific soap. But he did buy that dashiki, his first new clothes in years—only now, already, to have to pack it away. Her family has run into so many life knots that they don't think much of it anymore. Boards split, things splinter, what's new? You've got to wear your safety goggles, that's obvious. Seth, though, assumes he misjudged the situation. The more he thinks about what happened, the more he thinks he should have seen everything in advance.

"Like what, a human oracle?" says Mona.

But so fixated is he on the fallibility of his perceptions that he does not hear her. "It was naive to think it could work," he says, his hands hanging limp. And later, "I was naive."

Mona tries to tell him that it wasn't a waste of time to try and live Judaism the way they did. Rabbi Horowitz would still have been proud, plus it was an education. And Alfred is on his feet, and Seth got to play chess, and wasn't it great how they all held hands? For the rest of her life *om* will be a special syllable. Sure, things fell apart and they got called racist bastards. But even she's got the social-action bug now, who knows but that she'll be out getting arrested pretty soon?

She says this cheerily, not as if she is trying to plump a rock pillow. Seth removes her comforting fingers from his neck.

"Yeah, yeah." His hands hang limp again. "But we're not friends."

"Friends?" For a moment Mona wonders if he's not saying something like what Ralph might have said—*Today we have no relationship*. But no, Seth wasn't looking to be a paterfamilias.

"They considered me a racist bastard, and I considered them my friends." He says, "It's so quiet now."

Actually, it's pretty noisy. There's a good stiff wind, and the walls of the teepee are snapping in and—*bang!*—out, loud as a backfiring engine. But Mona knows what he means. It is as if he is just discovering that he grew up an only child, which in a way, he did. His stepbrothers were all but out of the house by the time he came along; and what with his interests, he could practically have been an Old World scholar boy, the kind with cuff links and green skin and no appetite. Even now, she can see him with a piano, and an illuminated globe, and a sliding wooden ladder that he really does need, to get to all his books. Then one day: Enter a group of playmates. And when they leave, the library is a whole different place.

In fact, Seth had lots of friends in high school. But whereas they went willingly off to the slaughter (Mandelese for college), he stayed home. He has truthfully followed his own idiosyncratic heart, and now what? An American affliction.

"But, Seth." Mona is suddenly the one talking with her hands, Seth style; she is suddenly the one trying passionately to persuade. "Alfred and his friends were so different than you."

Still he had thought if he was honest enough, direct enough . . . He had a vision, he says. He woke up one morning, and saw a house with no walls between the rooms.

"Seth," Mona says. "If people lived in houses with no walls between the rooms, there would have to be a lot of rules. I don't think you would like it. You can't have no walls and also have everyone in touch with their feelings. People would have to have manners. They would have to have a public face and a private face."

"I was naive," he says. "I think I've said that already."

He bends his head forward. Mona ruffles his neck hairs some more. He does not protest. The tent heaves as if bent on dismantling itself for the season. Mona wonders, Is Seth going to live out here all winter again?

That is when he turns to her and says something highly unlike anything she ever thought he would say. He says, "This is why you don't want to be a freethinker. You've had enough of being an original."

To which Mona nods a little, as though she sees what he's getting at. But what she sees, actually, is that what Seth has needed all along has been company—and that company is what he had hoped to make of her.

At the restaurant, Alfred too sulks. He's slow at the stove, he's forgetful. It used to be he was proud of how round his pancakes were; and indeed, they never looked to be procreating, like Cedric's. But now they are turning eccentric. They are impossible to stack; they are big and small, wild with irregularity, and lumpy to boot. Usually he's fastidious about clearing the griddle between orders. *You've got to start clean,* he always tells trainees. *You've got to start with nothing if you want to make something.* These days, though, he lets drips of batter fry right up into little blackened knobs, which in turn get embedded in new pancakes. This lends his cuisine an element of crunchy surprise.

"Those black people," complains Cedric. "One day this way, one day that way."

"Just tell him you want him to clear the griddle between orders," Mona says. "And it's not *those black people*. It's Alfred."

"You think he is going listen? I tell you something. Alfred is completely burn some pancakes today. So I say, Alfred, that one too dark, cannot serve to customer. And you know what he say?"

Mona shakes her head.

Cedric imitates Alfred. " 'Black is beautiful, man.' I tell him black is no beautiful, black is burnt, but he don't want listen. He say, 'Fuck the customers.' I say, The customer is king, and you know what he say? He say, 'I the king. The customers are motherfuckers.' I say, What is this motherfucker you always talking about? I say, I look this up in the dictionary, and I find out there is no translation. Maybe I spell wrong. I ask Alfred spell for me. But Alfred, he just laugh. He say, 'Don't tell me there no motherfuckers in China.' I say yes. We have no motherfuckers. I say, Is that some kind of swear word? He say yes. And I say, Maybe you mean something like turtle egg. He say, 'That's a swear word?' I tell him yes, that's a very bad word; you call somebody that, they very mad of you. And what happen? He laugh, that Alfred. He laugh and laugh, until all the pancakes burnt up again."

Mona sighs.

It is Labor Day weekend, and there are almost no customers— everybody's away, it seems, on vacation in New Hampshire or Vermont or Maine or Cape Cod. Mona wishes she were away too. Instead she's home, partly because Ralph and Helen don't believe in vacation. *All Americans think about is vacation,* they like to say, and while in fact they too like to stroll by a lakeside and spend money and do nothing, they don't mind making a deposit to their superiority account instead.

Plus the Changs are still debating whether or not to buy that other restaurant. There was talk of another buyer, and as long as the talk was hot, the Changs were hot to buy too. But when the other buyer got cold feet, so did Ralph. *Where it going lead? It going lead to trouble. That's I can tell you, mister.*

"Janis," starts Helen now.

"Everything Janis says is right," says Ralph, sipping a milk shake. "Janis is one hundred percent smarter than your husband. But dumb as he is, your husband it so happen remember how he made this mistake before. Make a big business. For what? Just give us stomachache. Already we work day and night, day and night. Now what? Time to work harder? We buy another restaurant, you know what we will have? Ulcer." He sips. "Sure thing. That's how Janis say. But I can tell you: There is no *sure thing*. Even our restaurant, standing there so nice, can fall down, good-bye. Forget about *sure thing*. I still believe *make sure*."

Mona sets out the mousetraps. This is her new job, a secret job even though there isn't even a big problem; they've only caught one mouse so far, and it was all of a half size up from a roach.

"You just want to run away, hide from everything," says Helen.

"Hide what? I am not hide anything. I am talk horse sense. Look at Alfred these days. Unreliable like crazy."

"Why does everything come back to Alfred?" Cheese cube in hand, Mona feels like crying. "Why can't you and Mom just have your fight by yourselves?"

"We are not fighting," says Helen.

Says Ralph, "I tell you. Alfred is one day, he care very much what is happen in the restaurant. The next day, for no reason, look like he do not care anymore. To have another restaurant, we need two people like Cedric."

"That's racist!" Mona says.

But Ralph, putting down his shake, insists that the other person like Cedric could be any color. "He could be blue. He could be green. He could be striped like the zebra in the zoo."

"It doesn't matter so long as you know you can trust him," Mona says. "It doesn't matter so long as you know who the person is."

"That's right."

"He could be blue, he could be green. It doesn't matter so long as he's Chinese."

"Not true," says Ralph.

"It is!" cries Mona, upsetting her bag of cheese.

"She is just like this, these days," says Helen. "Crazy."


The Gugelsteins return from their summer away. To prepare for their arrival, Barbara and Mona have gone everywhere, hunting down a flask like the one missing; and, incredibly, they have found its spitting image in a Fifth Avenue store. They have this engraved. Also, to age it, they soak it in Coca-Cola. Someone has told them that Coke will rot anything, that in fact, Russian spies introduced it to America as a way of corroding the guts of the general population. And this may be true. However, on silver plate it does nothing. Luckily, they then enlist the services of Rachel Cohen, who with her jewelry-making know-how oxidizes the flask. The result looks so good that when the Gugelsteins come home, Mona and Barbara want nothing more than to run up and show it to them.

Instead they act as though they've barely noticed anyone's arrived.

"Guess what I have for you," sings Mrs. Gugelstein, and she pulls out a shopping bag full of clothes and accessories for Barbara. There are a lot of things you can get on the Vineyard that you can't get in White Plains, it turns out, and Mrs. Gugelstein has found them all. Moreover, she has made special arrangements with the Vineyard storekeepers to accept returns by mail in case Barbara doesn't like something.

"But I know you'll love it all," she says. "Look at this." She pulls out a liquid silver choker, set with turquoise.

"Hmm," says Barbara, and moves toward a mirror. "What do you think?" she asks Mona. "Is it me?"

"What a question," says her mother. "Who else would it be?"


Is Barbara going to keep on at her job at the pancake house, what with school starting and all? Mona will still be faithfully serving her greater accounting unit, but Barbara might want to, say, study. And what about Seth, who all of a sudden wears nothing but black turtlenecks?

"Aren't you ever going to do something?" Mona asks.

"No," he says. "I've decided to give up on Judaism and be a waitress instead."

"You'll never be a waitress, and you can't give up on Judaism. You're Jewish."

No response. Mr. Authentic Self, but suddenly he has a public face and a private face. For this is the way he's been recently—ornery and sardonic and moody and, most disturbing of all, elliptical.

So why does Mona decide it's finally time to sleep together?

This is what she thinks later: that there are moments when the zippy narrative of your life lets up, and swampy reflection sinks in. There are moments when you begin to feel ending. Maybe it's just seasonal wear and tear. But there are moments when the inexorable shrinking of the days makes you miss people who have not yet left you—people like Barbara, Alfred, Seth. It is as if you have come unmoored from your present—as if you are floating out in the floodplain of your future. So that, out of a sort of nostalgia, you might decide yes. All right. It's time.

Only to have Seth of the black turtleneck sweetly question your motives. "What's come over you? A fit of passion?"

"Very funny," Mona says.

"Don't do anything you're going to blame me for later."

"I thought you believed reducing world horniness increases the social good."

"That presumes two consenting adults."

Mona argues that she is indeed a consenting adult.

"Okay," he says finally. "Let's have a fit of passion, then. Since you insist."

Mona is so annoyed that she almost refuses to go with him to the new almost-free clinic. But they go, and survive the waiting room. What kind of defloration is this? thinks Mona in the drugstore—and again that evening, as they lie in the teepee, inert. Aren't they supposed to be carried away, if not by romance and the meeting of their eternal souls, then at least by the power of their respective hormonal drips?

"I want to be tragically undone by my stampeding youth," she tells Seth.

"Yeah, right," he says.

"Surging tides. Pounding blood. Lusty thighs."

"We're supposed to wait for a whole cycle of pills," says Seth. "If you recall. Plus we talk too much."

"Does that lead to low-lust syndrome?"

Happily, they are soon enough revisited by natural bodily urges. The very day that time is up, they find his penis in. Mona is surprised how uneventfully this happens. After all the diagrams she's seen, she half expected that they would first turn into line drawings, then get split into flesh-toned cross-sections like the poor beings depicted. In real life, she sees a reflection of the sky in Seth's earth-brown eyes; such a grand uniting! His eyes are all the world—no, more: They are the world made twin. His neck is craned up. How much shorter she is than he! She had never noticed before. But groin to groin, there's no denying it. Her chin lies on his hairy chest, on a line with his nipples. Of course, she is on top—everything with Seth has to be counterconventional. Still, she feels so much more than she sees. And in a rush, it occurs to her how nobody told her that—how nobody told her that it would be like discovering yourself to own an extra sense organ. This has nothing whatever to do with seeing; even in daylight, most everything is hidden, like the green-covered pamphlet she keeps between her mattress and boxspring at home. Callie, passing it down, said their mother gave it to her. "*Mom* gave it to you?" That was hard to believe, and even harder was what the pamphlet (*Introducing . . . You!*) had to say. First of all, that girls had three holes! Mona had to sit down immediately to see. Of course, there was more too, much more, in the pamphlet, all about sweating walls, and turgid cells, and items of miraculous elasticity. For all of which, Nature got credit. The pictures featured amounts of pubic hair Mona thought gross. The penises were big as sewage pipes, and about as attractive. Still she read the pages over and over, her body tingling. *When the woman is relaxed and elastic, the man inserts his member, thanks to Nature's ingenuity.*

Is that this sweet, grand entrance? Utterly nonviolent; she didn't know she could be so wet. She did not know she could feel so full. She tightens around him, and is surprised that he can feel this greeting. He flexes a return hello. They laugh, link legs, rock.

"Is this thrusting?" says Mona.

"Shut up," says Seth.

"Yes," says Mona. "Yes I said yes. Yes."

"Shut up," says Seth again, and this time subdues her with mouth kisses. And then they rock some more, until all they wish for is ditto, ditto, ditto.

"Feel the breeze," says Seth—there's a leak in the wall of the tent.

"Shut up," says Mona.

And with this they sink back into themselves, pulsing.


When Mona puts her glasses on, she surmises by the hole at the top of the teepee that the sun is still shining blandly. Into the blank sky float skimmingly puffy, indifferent clouds.

"Are you really a virgin?" Seth asks, propping himself up on an elbow.

And Mona says yes. That is, she was—although there's no blood, to their mutual surprise. Neither of them mentions that Barbara bled so much it was scary, though both know this. "Maybe because of using Tampax?" Mona says. (Helen is against Tampax, but Mona uses them anyway, she just hides them behind some books in her bookcase.)

"And you came," he says—happy, yet there's an odd fall-off to his gladness.

"Why would I lie to you? I can't believe you even care about such things."

"Did I say you were lying?"

"Let's just be happy," Mona says. "Either that or let's do it again."

They do it again. It's harder for Seth to come—he's interested but droopy, and Mona's so slippery from the first time. As for Mona, she's not even sure if she has come or not. Which is not the way it's supposed to be, Mona thinks. Isn't the woman supposed to go on and on? *In bed as in conversation,* she read somewhere. What if she is mono-orgasmic? A sobering life prospect, no doubt related to her subcutaneous fat, hammy calves, et cetera. Still she is exhilarated. And he is happy, in a way. But in another way, he remains the Seth he has been recently—that moody Seth so stuffed full of things he's not saying, he could be some sort of special-edition piñata. *It changes everything,* that's what Barbara said. And maybe it does. But without changing anyone. This dawns on Mona like a big baked brick, and later she counts this realization as her real loss of innocence: All this happy youthful fucking, yet Seth still ails.

Mona ponders for a few more days. She talks things over with Barbara, who blames for the weirdness, of all things, the pill. "Nobody knows what's in those things," she says. Mona begins to regard her neat case with suspicion, even though she's hitherto felt toward it, gratitude—her figure being so greatly enhanced that Barbara has also said, "You know, Polly Wolly, pretty soon we're going to have to call you Polly Golly."

Was this the voice of jealousy? Anyway, Mona begins to consider whether Seth and she shouldn't split up the way Evie and Alfred are doing. "Monkey see, monkey do," says Barbara, studiously uninterested in Seth's prospective availability even as Mona watches, watches.

Seeing how what's done is done. To wit, how you simply avoid the other person until you can hardly conceive how you stood him or her for more than five minutes.

"Evie," says Alfred. "All she wanted was to be fucked by a black man."

"Alfred," says Evie. "All he wanted was a chick even whiter than Charlene."

Could you really sum up what a person wanted, just like that? Mona isn't sure. But she begins to feel as though that is what a relationship is about—getting to know someone well enough to fill in the blank. And then you fill it in, and then you don't care about anything for a while.

For example, if you are Evie, and have on top of everything else broken up with your boyfriend in the Philippines for Alfred, you stop taking pictures, and stop developing pictures, and stop talking about pictures. Instead of putting things back neatly into drawers, you leave them lying all around, in such a state that one day your aunt feels compelled to clean up for you. Which is when she discovers your self-portraits—pictures of you and Alfred, in bed in her house. There are also pictures of the gang hanging out, and the gang getting down, and the gang having a good old time, and every one of these is perfectly focused, with lovely detail. If your aunt were so inclined, she could hang every one of them.

III

# CHAPTER 11

# The Fall Begins

Evie is packed home to Minneapolis a week early, and as for Alfred, he is of course fired.

"I'm sorry," says Mona, entering the attic storeroom. Alfred is holding his old navy-blue windbreaker, the one with an apple tree logo over the left breast. *Eden Orchards,* reads the caption. *Bite and You Shall Know.* Now he stands in front of his hook as though expecting something more to appear on it, and for the first time Mona realizes how low the hooks are. Alfred's cubby too hangs level with his chest, meaning that he has to stoop just to check that there's nothing in it besides that old doorknob they found in the tunnel. He chucks this in a wastebasket.

"What you sorry for?" he says, without turning. "You're the boss's smartass daughter."

"I'm sorry you got fired."

"You're sorry. I'm fired. If that ain't the oldest story in the world, I must be President of the United States."

"What do you mean?"

"Somebody's going to take the heat, it's got to be the Negroes, right? Who else gets burnt up and keeps walking? Who else gets deep fried and is still talking nice as you please? Except for maybe on occasion calling a motherfucker a motherfucker."

"Nobody," says Mona.

Alfred turns around, his jacket dangling on a finger. His eyes are burning. "Nobody else takes this brand of shit, and you hear me: The day is coming when nobody ain't going take it, neither." His jacket swings in front of him like a hanged man.

·  ·  ·

At home that evening, the conversation attains a similar level of peace and satisfaction.

"I don't think you can fire somebody because of where he's been living," Mona says.

Helen keeps stirring the pork. "You people were having parties. There were pictures."

"But is that a reason to fire somebody?"

"Of course." The pork sizzles and spits; Helen does a backbend, trying to avoid the splatter. Also she moves the open sugar bowl out of range. "How do you think we feel? Our cook act like that."

"But he's not your representative. He's your employee."

"He is our cook," says Helen again. "And that girl, she is white, you understand? Barbara's mother called; of course we have to do something. What happens if I see Barbara's mother on the street? Am I going to say hello, how are you, that Alfred still work for us as if nothing happened? You know what kind of insult that is to Barbara's mother? It is as if I stand there in front of Daitch Shopwell and slap her in front of everybody. Our cook make that kind of big trouble, and we say hello, how are you, we do nothing?"

"But aren't there laws?" Mona says.

"Laws!" Helen turns the heat off. The meat's still a little pink; she covers the pan, leaving it to cook some more by itself. Mad as she is, she still cooks with care, it's automatic. The little judgments and adjustments, the split-second coordinating of this with that. Mona has never seen Helen burn anything, she would hate to waste the food; it's only with Mona that she leaves the heat on high. "You invite Alfred to go live in someone's house, now you want talk about laws?"

This is how the conversation goes on their better days. Other days it is less reasonable.

*How could you. How could you.* Over and over, as if the whole affair was Mona's fault. *What kind of daughter. How could you.*

Mona tries to explain that she wasn't the person behind it all—that really she had help. Also that she did it because she was trying to find herself, which in fact is downright common. Mona tries to hint that some mothers actually try and help their daughters find themselves. For instance, Mrs. Gugelstein, if it's only through clothes and jewelry. But she might as well be trying to talk sense with a store fixture.

"What you talking, find yourself?" says Helen. "And who do you think you are, tell me what to do? Daughter's job is to listen, not to tell mother her big-shot opinion."

"That's the whole problem. I'm not just a daughter. I'm a person."

"A person!"

Outside, a plastic jug moans in the night wind.

"You know what you are?" Helen says. "You are American girl. Only an American girl can do something like that and hide it from her mother. Every day you lied to me." She appears shocked all over again by this recap of the facts. "Every day!" She cannot go on.

"At least I wasn't the one sleeping with Alfred." Mona genuinely means this as a comforting thought.

But it is not comforting. "Sleep with somebody! Alfred!" Helen closes her eyes. "No, no, no." Her mouth trembles. "You do that, I would kill myself."

"But Mom, that's so racist."

"Racist!" Helen springs suddenly back to life, as if it is not night at all, but day, day, day! "Only an American girl would think about her mother killing herself and say oh, that's so racist. A Chinese girl would think whether she should kill herself too. Because that is how much she thinks about her poor mother who worked so hard and suffered so much. She wants to do everything to make the mother happy." And with that, she leaps up as if she's overslept and it's way past time to get going.


The Gugelsteins don't want Mona to visit anymore. She is persona non grata, a real *kochleffl*, such an official bad influence that she is not even allowed to phone; Mrs. Gugelstein is screening all calls. Never mind the many times Mona encouraged her friend to study instead of plain hanging out. She is the mastermind, according to the Gugelsteins. This whole affair is not something their daughter had the brains to dream up.

"What a nice thing to say about you," says Mona to Barbara. "In fact, I think it's an insult."

"I think it's supposed to be an insult to you too."

"Well, insulted I be, I guess." Mona pulls an apple out of her backpack.

They're encamped on the floor of the high school lobby, which is crisscrossed with trails of mud. This is the problem with everyone wearing hiking boots all the time—add a few goats, and the lobby could be a third world train station. It smells of general staleness and dope. But Mona and Barbara don't mind. It's true that Barbara's gotten her car keys taken away, and that Mona is about to break up with Seth. They should be depressed. But in fact, Barbara and Mona are closer again, thanks to the quick-dry glue-all that is common traumatic experience. They're both friendly with Eloise Ingle, but she hasn't been through what they've been through. Barbara and Mona are Laurel and Hardy, Mutt and Jeff, Tweedledee and Tweedledum. A twosome for the ages.

"No more going around being Jewish. That's another thing," says Barbara. "A little Jewish is fine, but my mom says too much is too much—look at what happened in Munich. Not that it's right for terrorists to attack anybody; she's definitely not saying that. And at the Olympics! Of all places. But harping on difference brings trouble, she says; it's human nature. Some people are too Jewish even for other Jews. For example, Rabbi Horowitz. No wonder he got fired and had to move to Massachusetts, where else would people put up with him?"

"Is that where he's living?"

"That's what she heard, plus it figures. Her friends say there are as many communes in Cambridge now as bookstores. Of course, they'll still pay their good money to send their kids to Harvard if they get in; it's still better than Berkeley or Columbia. My mom says if I want to be Jewish like Rabbi Horowitz, I can move to the Lower East Side."

"How far is it from there to Chinatown?"

Barbara laughs. "Do you have relatives there?"

"Not a lot of relatives," says Mona. "In fact, now that you mention it, I don't know a single person who lives in Chinatown."

"And who do I know on the Lower East Side?" Barbara shakes her head.

It is easier to break up with Seth than Mona would have thought, on account of her having filled in the blank for herself.

"All you wanted was for me to be a radical," Mona says. "All you wanted was to make me into company for you."

Seth's cheeks have a papery look Mona has never noticed before. Also his skin has a grayish cast, as if he has given up washing even with his special all-purpose soap, or as if he is molting. "And here I thought you were a self-made Jew," he says.

Mona says that she is; but that somehow her experiment has turned into his experiment.

"Is that my fault?"

She claims yes. Gray-of-face listens carefully, growing grayer. She waits for him to say something sardonic. And indeed he begins to argue with her, only to stop himself. He thinks again. He apologizes.

"Guilty as charged." He had not dreamed, he had not realized, he had never figured, he says. And certainly he never meant to pull a Professor Higgins. He really had thought her more radical than she realized, a kind of Jewish Yoko Ono. But how convenient of him to believe that. He offers to make amends, or at least to try; and in offering, he sounds more or less sincere. He admits misjudgment, he admits insensitivity, he offers to take her on a ninety-mile bike ride in which she rides on the handlebars. To any place she names, he says. Anything to prove how sorry he is, and to what lengths he will go (literally) to make it up to her.

And part of Mona knows how hard all this is for someone like Seth to say; he might as well be admitting himself to be wrong. But instead of thinking about that, Mona thinks, Ninety miles on someone's handlebars! How uncomfortable! In short, she clutches her certainty to her like the sort of itty-bitty terry wrap that barely makes it around your bosom. Having never broken up with anyone before, she is determined to do it right, which is to say heartlessly. How liberating to be mean! All her life she has been funny; she has tried too to be sweet. Never has she been powerful. She could be Popeye, popping open spinach cans with her bare hands. Who needs a can opener? Mona has not started this deadly game, but now that she understands there can be victory between people, she is bent on avoiding defeat. She has always thought fear a hot emotion; now she knows it to be cool. Now she knows how it turns to vengeance. She is unmovable. She is the Rock of Gibraltar, a strategic fortification with which any Mandel must reckon.

Seth begins to cry. He has his hands in his hair; if it were long enough to get a grip on, he would probably tear it out.

"Are you all right?" asks the spinach-fed Rock of Gibraltar. And she sees what a stringy pleasure has been hers. For she has never seen Seth cry before, and it is a surprise how unnatural the process seems to be for him. He does not cry the way Barbara and Mona do, with wails of virtuoso facility. He cries as though each tear contradicts his very nature; watching him is like watching an animal cry, except that he wipes his eyes with his black turtleneck sleeve. Also the crying seems to be giving him stomach cramps: His whole body is doubled over in the manner of an out-of-use gym mat.

"No," he replies. "I am not all right. Jesus, how I've fucked up." And then he says that he loves her.

Of course, there is a rider to this statement—namely, that he's thought a lot about what those words mean, and that he is not exactly sure he has settled on a definition. However, he does think he indeed means whatever it is that he doesn't yet understand that he means.

"How romantic." Mona stands, full of dignity. "Now you can go have an affair with Barbara."

"Barbara?"

It is too late. Mona is already making her grand exit. And if she does peek back to be sure he gets up eventually and can at least walk, she makes sure he doesn't see her. For let it here be said that she truly fully expects him to turn around and apply to Barbara for some huggery, as he used to call it. She is surprised when he does not; and furthermore, it seems that Barbara is surprised too, although less than entirely disappointed—her thoughts having boomeranged home to Andy Kaplan.

A most unexpected turn of events: Seth develops a fixation. Maybe this can happen to anyone in the world. Maybe in everyone there are parts that can turn mushy, leaving the person substantially pudding. So thinks Mona. Or else maybe Seth was meshugga from the start, she should've known—all that soul searching, it just wasn't normal. Also the teepee. In any case, he sends her letters, to which she does not respond. These are long and closely argued, line after line of the kind of cramped inky black script you associate with the discovery of paramecium and other cellular wonders. She moves her shifts around at the restaurant; he moves his too, giving chase, and is fired. (He would have been fired anyway, says Ralph; Helen was set on it.) Seth tries to see Mona in other ways, and when those fail too, he tries to at least get her attention. Various sources report: Did Mona know Seth has stopped eating because of her? Did she know Seth has stopped using gas-powered transportation? Did she know he has shaved off his beard? Eaten two frogs? Jumped off a house?

"He jumped off a house?" Mona says.

It was only a ranch, it turns out, and there were soft spots in the lawn where the roots of an old tree stump were rotting. He did jump off the roof, though, saying that he hoped she got the reference to a well-known Russian play involving a cherry orchard. Luckily, he was unhurt.

"Tell him not to do that anymore," Mona says.

But he does, exactly because it worries her. Mona tries to ignore this, even if it is like a bright light exploding at the edge of her field of vision, or like a certain farmy perfume arising from a baby's diaper. In short, a challenge. So that when the news comes round that Seth has secretly applied to colleges, and that he has at the last minute decided to go, Mona is relieved. She and Barbara shake their heads together. *Leave it to Seth*. To which college has Seth consigned himself? No one knows, but presumably it is one on the trimester system, seeing as he is starting in late October. Also one that allows its students to live in teepees.

Predictably, he takes his leave Seth style, which is to say by leaving behind a most enigmatic note. This is written on the back of the fortune from a Chinese fortune cookie. On one side, there is the official message: *Expectation is a light shining in the eyes*. The other side is equally obscure. In Seth's minute scrawl, it reads: *Watch for the return of a most mannerly fellow*.

Meaning what? Barbara and Mona consider and consider.

"That Seth!" says Barbara, finally.

"Typical!" Mona crumples the note up.

Thankfully, they're too busy to mull over such things, having entered the year that is focused like a railroad tunnel on its end. Seniors! Every day they say that word, every day they imagine June. June! They can already see their new luggage—frameless backpacks for travel in the summer, army-navy trunks for college in the fall. First, though, there are the SATs to contend with. Again! At least for poor

Barbara. Then there are college applications. Barbara is already draft-
ing her essays, which she's going to have her father's secretary type up
on an IBM Selectric. Never mind that she hasn't decided what colleges she's going to apply to yet; she figures she can always just wait
and see what Andy Kaplan does.

Meanwhile, Eloise stops by Mona's locker one day to say she's decided to apply to all of the Ivies, plus the Seven Sisters, plus Hampshire.

"Hampshire?" says Mona. "The hippie school? You?"

If she can't get into any of the real schools, replies Eloise, she might
as well at least learn to throw a Frisbee. She says this wistfully, as if she
would genuinely like not to have to challenge her way up the tennis
ladder. Sitting cross-legged on the floor, they swap admissions stories:
About the kid who sent Harvard a violin he made from scratch. About
the kid whose application demonstrated some principle when you
opened it.

"You have to get their attention," says Eloise.

"Are you sure?" Mona says. "Callie got in on an essay about how
she was like a peanut butter and jelly sandwich."

"Did she send a sandwich?"

"No."

Says Eloise, "Perhaps if she had, she'd have gotten a scholarship."
She winks. "Are you applying to Harvard too?"

Mona shakes her head, only to have Barbara jump on her.

"I know," she says. "You're convinced you'll be a failure if you
don't get in like Callie. But (a) you could very well get in. And (b) it's
better to be a failure than a dropout. That's what my dad says."

Then she launches into an exposition so lengthy that Eloise finally
stands and excuses herself—only to have her red-laced, Vibram-soled
hiking boots replaced by the blue-laced, Vibram-soled hiking boots of
someone who bears a distinct resemblance to Sherman Matsumoto.

"Sherman!" Mona says, looking up.

"Mona?"

Sherman is so changed that Mona is not sure how she recognized
him. Gone the little-boy innocence. Now he is wearing a Chouinard
T-shirt, and a red flannel button-down, and carpenter pants. The carpenter pants are appropriately washing-machine worn; the T-shirt looks
as though it has done time as a moth community center. He is wearing
a string of beads, perhaps a source of mystic power. His hair, in related

fashion, is black as ever—so thick and stallionate that it puts Mona in mind of certain Walter Farley books. Yet it is his face most of all that has changed. Gone the baby-fat upholstery, and the poky pink flush. His face is kite-shaped, a bit pale, distinctly planar—a face that bespeaks testosterone. As for the old hole in his left eyebrow, that has grown over without a trace; his eyebrows are veritable slashes now.

Mona scrambles to her feet. How much Sherman has grown! He is taller than Seth easily, however with the shortest legs and longest torso of anyone she's ever seen. If he and she turned out to wear the same size pants, she wouldn't be surprised.

"Hey, man," he says.

"Sherman!" she says again. "I can't believe it."

"I know what you mean," he says, coolly enough. But with that, he turns and flees.


Later that same day, Mona gets a telephone call.

"Sherman?" Mona says.

It is like old times, except that Sherman's English is so greatly improved that his voice itself seems somehow to have improved along with it. Apparently that's what immersion in another culture will do; it's sort of like what Mona's French teacher used to tell her—that if she lived in France who knows, even she might pick up some *je ne sais quoi*. Also Mona finds that being able to picture Sherman makes for a whole different listening experience. How much sexier he sounds— how much more like someone on whose account she would have to take eighty showers.

However, some things remain the same. To wit, she does not ask the questions that are foremost on her mind—namely, why he ran off on her that way, and what it means that he came to look her up, and whether he's still meaning to marry her. She does not even ask where he is living, or how he got her phone number. Instead they talk about Bar Harbor, Maine. They agree that the shoreline there is very beautiful, although perhaps somewhat dangerous. They discuss what they think would happen to someone who fell off the rocks into the water—whether the person would get smashed against the boulders, or pulled out to sea.

"Maybe people shouldn't be out on the rocks to begin with," Mona says. "Maybe land animals should stay on land."

She says this expecting Sherman to agree. However, he doesn't. Would the person die of hypothermia? Mona tells Sherman about the prisoners on Alcatraz. They were not allowed to take cold showers, she says, because by exposing themselves to the cold they could build up their brown fat. And brown fat is so much more insulating than regular fat, she explains, that with it they might have been able to swim to freedom without freezing to death.

"That's called adaptation," Mona says. "It's a healthy process. And Alcatraz is an island that is also a prison that was once in a famous movie. It's in California."

"San Francisco," says Sherman, surprising her.

They discuss lobster. Whether the big ones really are too tough to eat; also how old they are, and how the fishermen know. Do lobster shells have rings, like trees? Mona knows someone who once caught a lobster so big it had to be cooked in a garbage can. This is, in her view, an interesting fact. However, Sherman thinks it's a shame to eat lobsters that old; it's not very respectful. And Mona agrees.

"So how come you're back from Japan again?" she asks.

Silence. Then he does not answer except to explain that he has most recently been living in Hawaii. Also that he now considers himself not Japanese, but Hawaiian.

"Hawaiian!" Mona says.

He hangs up.


A few days later, he calls back, and this time Mona gets more of the story. It turns out his father is in the hotel-buying business; hence all the visits to Pleasant American Beauty Spots. But it also turns out that after living abroad, the Matsumotos had some difficulty going back to their old life. So much difficulty, in fact, that they were more or less forced to become expatriates.

Mona finds this out after an hour of discussing whether the Great Lakes are really all that great. There is therefore not a lot of time left for the subject of how Sherman got sent to a special returnee school, much less how that was related to his not keeping up his Japanese. What is it about Japanese that requires keeping up? Mona doesn't get a chance to ask before Sherman has gone on to mention how also there were incidents. As for what kind of incidents, who knows? Sherman is more forthcoming than he used to be, but his new manner seems tied up with his new life. He tells her how he has a car now, a green Mustang, and how he likes to drink beer.

"Are you a jock?" Mona says.

"Yes," he says.

"Not a hippie? I thought you looked like a hippie."

Are they edging toward the subject of why he ran away from her? She wonders, especially as this subject might naturally lead to another subject. Namely, are they ever going to see each other in person, or are they going to get married on the phone?

"No," he says simply. "I am a jock." He goes on to describe how he's given up judo for baseball. This, it turns out, is a big sport not only in Japan, but in Hawaii too. He calls Hawaii "Hawah-eee."

"Are you American now?" Mona asks. "Have you switched?"

"One hundred percent. Are you surprised?"


Barbara and Mona are prowling a used car lot, on the lookout for the van. This, Barbara's parents have traded in on her. Barbara, though, is determined to get it back.

Through the dealership window, the salesman at the first desk gives them the eye. He is, it seems, all about brown. Brown hair, brown shirt, brown tie, brown jacket, brown desk. From reading *Babbitt*, Mona knows he is leading a life of quiet desperation. However, he doesn't look it. If anything, quite the opposite—he looks utterly at home in his universe, at one with his brownness.

"Think he's going to call the police?" asks Barbara.

"Flash him your checkbook," says Mona.

They check out a van that looks just like Barbara's but isn't—Barbara can tell by the mileage. Although maybe the odometer's been set back? Barbara stares out at the road traffic, thinking. Then she says, "I could probably get my parents to buy it back for me for graduation, assuming my dad doesn't get fired."

"What?"

"You heard me."

"I heard you say fired."

"That's what I said."

"As in, it begins with an *F* and is sort of like retired?"

Says Barbara, "Have you ever thought why you always have to be funny?"

Investigation, authorities, loophole, elaborates Barbara. She's not supposed to know, but she overheard her parents talking. Her dad didn't even do anything. It was some new guy working for some guy working for him who was shorting the stock of bankrupt companies— who knows where the guy found the winning buyers, but he did. The people thought they were investing in a corporate restructure; they had no idea no new stock would be issued. Now they only wished their certificates were tissue paper, at least they could use them to wipe their eyes. Especially since they can't even sue, though they're trying to—hence the scandal—what the broker did being, it seems, legal enough. Mr. Gugelstein didn't even know about it, how could he? He was on the Vineyard at the time. But the consensus of the higher-ups was that someone should step down, in order to restore the good name of the firm.

"So they asked him to resign. But he said, What if no one stepped down? They'd already fired the selling broker, after all. Why the ritual purification? But his questions just went to prove that he didn't put the good of the firm first. Proving to him that Gugelstein was never how you spelled Popularity to begin with."

"Wait. Wait! This doesn't have to do with Eloise Ingle's dad, does it?" says Mona. And she describes with great excitement the conversation she overheard in Rhode Island. She describes Mrs. Ingle's objection, Mr. Ingle's reticence.

"How very interesting." Barbara sweeps her hair off her neck. "Mr. Ingle must be one of the people who want to hang my dad. But where does that get us?"

"It's got to get us somewhere," says Mona. "Maybe your dad can sue."

But to know the truth of what goes on isn't worth as much as you'd think.

"Yeah, right." Barbara circles some more around the van that does look so exactly like hers.

· · ·

The new Sherman wants to hear about Mona, a surprise. And so she tells him about Seth, and Barbara, and Rabbi Horowitz, and the hot line; also about Eloise Ingle, and Andy Kaplan. And then there's the restaurant, and Alfred, and the mod squad, not to say Evie, and Callie, and Naomi, and Ralph, and Helen. Sherman seems to slightly remember some of these people; also he recalls, of course, the hot line. For the most part, though, he just listens. Mona expects him to be jealous of Seth, and indeed, Seth is enough of a topic of interest that she's careful to leave out the teepee. She concentrates instead on Seth's bike riding—just the sort of thing to tell a guy with a Mustang, she figures. Also she tells him (by way of switching the subject) what it's like to be not Wasp, and not black, and not as Jewish as Jewish can be; and not from Chinatown, either.

"You are a sore thumb," says Sherman. "Sticking out by yourself."

She says, "I'm never at home."

He says he knows how she feels; he's in the same ship. She tells him about her family. The fights. And Harvard, Harvard, Harvard! Of course, Barbara Gugelstein's parents want her to go to Harvard too.

"But for my parents, it's the whole point of life," she says. "Jews believe in the here and now; Catholics believe in heaven; the Chinese believe in the next generation."

"You are their everything."

"Exactly!" When Mona was a child that was okay, she says, but now that she's older and has a mind of her own, she doesn't want to be their everything anymore.

Sherman knows what she means. He talks about how things are in Japan—about education mamas. The competition. The pressure. Examination hell really is hell.

"Jeez," Mona says, "it must be great not to be Japanese anymore."

"I'm Hawaiian now," Sherman says—agreeing, but with a disconcerted note in his voice, as if he had almost forgotten this himself.


The restaurant is quieter these days, what with Seth gone, and Barbara. As for Alfred, rumor has it that he's gotten himself a job in a steakhouse where he's allowed to eat off the menu. How such a restaurant can stay in business is not clear. All the same, Mona pictures Alfred with a T-bone a day, and is glad for him.

Staff turnover has led to a distinct change in atmosphere. This is not only because all the openings have been filled with friends of Cedric's; also, two of the friends have ended up waiting table. There are now males, plural, in the dining room. Not that Ralph has completely abandoned his notions about who makes a proper serving figure. Seth may have broken down some barriers, but if there's one thing Ralph now knows, it is *No more smart aleck*. He hires only *people have proper attitude*, like these new waiters. Who are both legal, and of course, two males in a room is not a lot of males. Yet being both from China, they make an impression on everyone. The customers leave comments in the comment box: They have never seen so many Chinese waiters outside of a Chinese restaurant, they say. As for the non-Chinese help, they have comments too.

Mona likes the new waiters. Edward and Richard, they call themselves; they're from Hong Kong. They wear their hair neat, and somehow it seems to suit the formality of their names that they have unearthed a supply of paper doilies, on which they have been serving dessert. Other improvements: They've taken to folding the napkins so they stand up on the plate. Also they notch the edges of the lemon slices in a fancy way.

Hong Kong style, Cedric calls this. "Everything in Hong Kong is for show," he says. "Everything is for try to look nice. Hong Kong people just like some fancy schmancy."

But as much care as they lavish on dining room presentation, they seem to have drawn some line at the dishwashers. They don't usually have to bus their own tables. However, when they do, they throw their dishes as if over a cliff. It's how they save face, Cedric says (even as he scolds them for the chipping and breaking). Something has to be beneath them. It has nothing to do with the dishwashers being one of them black and the other Puerto Rican; if they were Chinese, claims Cedric, things would be the same.

Is that right? Mona isn't sure until one of the dishwashers quits, and Russell from Taiwan takes his place. But then, sure enough, Richard and Edward throw plates at him too. The only difference is that Russell seems to expect this. He doesn't bother to get mad—except, that is, to point out to Ralph how Richard and Edward swear so loudly in the kitchen that they can be heard clear out in the dining room. And in Chinese too. Isn't this a breach of the No Chinese Out Front rule?

Storm weather. Mona tries to talk with Richard and Edward about the dish throwing, which seems to her the First Cause of the trouble. This makes her feel very young and very old at the same time.

"Sure sure sure," says Richard.

"No problem," says Edward.

Then they go on throwing the dishes, either as if they know she's only the boss's daughter, a person with no real power, or as if they haven't even bothered to calculate whether they should listen to her or not.

Meanwhile, Callie comes home for the weekend, also with no intention of listening. This is because Ralph and Helen have something to discuss with her—namely, the dread subject, Medical School. They discuss this in their various ways. Helen concentrates heavily on filial piety. Here her parents slave all day to pay tuition, think of that, she says. Also think of how her poor parents have no son to send instead. Ralph goes with a more philosophical, nature-of-the-world approach: *You got to have a meal ticket*, he says. And, an interesting argument: *You got to earn your own money, otherwise your husband treat you like a slave.*

"Medical school is sure," he says now. "Other way, you never know what's happen."

"But I'm not really interested in medicine," argues Callie.

Says Helen, more or less, *Medicine is very interesting.*

Says Ralph, more or less, *Life is about work, and since when is work supposed to be interesting?*

They comb over the fine example of Auntie Theresa, who is such a good doctor many round eyes go to see her, not just Chinese. They regale Callie with stories about children of friends of theirs. Many of these have gone to medical school and now are earning good money. One child even has a pool. Never mind that he does not know how to swim. Every day he practices. Every day he does one stroke more, before you know it he's going to be able to swim from the beginning of the pool to the end.

"Hmm," says Callie.

Also he is a great help to his parents, say Ralph and Helen. His father had some trouble with his heart, and you know, that son, he arranged everything for the operation. Gave the father a peaceful mind. Otherwise, he would have been so worried, you know. These doctors, they just like to operate, sometimes the whole thing isn't even necessary.

"Hmm," says Callie.

But here's the difference between her and Mona: Even while she's giving them a hard time, Callie's taking in the parents' point of view—especially the taking-care-of-them-when-they're-sick part.

She says, "It *is* nice to have a doctor in the family. Mom and Dad are right. You can't really trust anyone else."

"That's Chinese thinking," says Mona. "In America, a lot of doctors don't even take care of their own families. They consider that they're not objective enough."

"Hmm," concedes Callie.

But a few days later, she seems to have made up her mind. "Someone has to take care of them, and I can tell it's not going to be you," she says. "Plus I think medicine is interesting."

"Maybe you should talk to somebody. Isn't there a student adviser up there?"

"Not really. I mean, they give you people like Rabbi Horowitz."

"Rabbi Horowitz?" Mona sits up.

"He was the sub-in freshman adviser last year. The first one had a nervous breakdown." Callie shuffles her Chinese vocabulary cards. "By the way, Horowitz isn't even a rabbi anymore. Now he's a grad student."

"Are you kidding? Oh, you should go talk to him!"

"I have no interest in talking to him," says Callie. "Plus I'm not a freshman."


Mona explains to Sherman about her sister, and also about Richard and Edward. Has she ever done this before, shared with him her preoccupations? She has not. But with their solid old format broken up like ice floes, she simply starts talking; and so easily open is she that she almost does not know who is this Mona Chang. Or for that matter, who is this Sherman Matsumoto: For no sooner does she raise the topics of Callie and Richard and Edward than Sherman begins to talk about boundaries. This is a kind of talk Sherman has never engaged in before; and yet it has been coming, she can see, along with his car and his beer drinking. A moment later, it seems natural enough. A moment later, what seem unnatural are their former habits of conversation. Beauty spots! Lobsters!

Sherman says he's read a book about the American personality and the Japanese personality; this is because he's not a tourist anymore. Now that he's American, he's been thinking more about what it means to be Japanese.

"But wait," says Mona. "Now that you're American, shouldn't you be thinking about what it means to be American?"

He says that's right, he is indeed thinking about what it means to be American. He's thinking about that by thinking about what it means to be Japanese.

"I see," says Mona, though she does not see. And for a moment there is that familiar longish silence between them. "Don't hang up," she says.

He doesn't. Instead he proceeds to apply his reading to Richard and Edward and Callie, never mind that they are Chinese. All three of them have drawn certain boundaries, he says, and within the boundaries each has done far more than a run-of-the-mill American would have done. What with the doilies, and the lemon slices, and so on.

"You mean, run-of-the-mill Americans do not become doctors in order to be able to take care of their parents," says Mona.

And Sherman says that is also a good example. As for outside the boundary, though, Richard and Edward have done less. He understands why they do less; he himself doesn't exactly see why dining room waiters should have to concern themselves with dishwashers.

"But that is Japanese thinking." He says that according to the book, Americans do not distinguish so sharply between who they should concern themselves with and who not. "Americans are all the time talk about civic duty. Public spirit. As if they consider the public is their family too. The book says Americans do not distinguish so clearly between who they have a relationship with, and who they do not, and what that relationship is.

"With the Japanese people, everything is circles. The family is inside; next maybe comes the office circle, or the school circle. And next comes the town circle, the country circle. Everybody else is everybody else."

"Hmm," says Mona.

And later in life, she will catalog the ways in which the Chinese and the Japanese are as opposite as their geographies. They are land and sea, large and small, open and closed, continent and island. Later in life, she will go antiquing, and marvel that anyone could ever have lumped these cultures together—the Chinese with their love of symmetry, and things matched; the Japanese with their love of asymmetry, and things juxtaposed.

But as for the similarities: Sherman and Mona talk about the line Edward and Richard have drawn.

"They will have to study a long time for the citizenship exam," says Sherman. "Participation. Democracy. They will have to study a long time to understand that question."

Says Mona, "The Jews they should look at! Now, we Jews, we participate."

"America is not like Japan," Sherman says.

"Or China. My mom says that in China, people mostly try to stay out of trouble. Keep their heads down. The tallest tree catches all the wind, they say. Sweep the snow from your own doorstep. If families take care of themselves, society will take care of itself."

And what about the circle beyond the town, and beyond the country? Beyond the town, and beyond the country, there is no circle. There is outer space. Nothing to be concerned about—nothing with which anyone has a relationship. Mona and Sherman agree: In outer space there are no rules.

On the other hand, within the circles there are so many rules that the Japanese have a word for them—*tatame*. *Tatame*, says Sherman, is like the world of what the Changs call *keqi*—the world of politeness and obligation. But then there is another word too, in Japanese, for the world inside that world: *honne*, the world of true feeling, and intimacy—the world without words.

Is *honne* like the Chinese word *xin*, the world of what is hidden in the heart? Later Mona will wonder. And later too she will wonder where the line between duty and real feeling lies in Japan—whether it lies only between society and the family, or whether there may be a line between the family and the individual too.

A story: A friend who grew up in China complains that you never feel truly inside a home in America. In China, there is a compound wall; in America, there is lawn. It makes Americans seem so friendly, so approachable. But where does the world end? Where does the family begin? And how is it that the family allows everything to come out? People have stories in America, that's just like in China; but how is it they are willing to tell them on *The Newlywed Game*? It is as if they are not real family members, says this friend.

Is Mona a real family member? And if she is not—if she is a member of the world concerned about her civic duty—how is it that she still finds a truth of her own in Sherman's next words, which are not that to have a public face and a private face is to be two-faced; but rather that without the world of outer politeness, you cannot have a world of inner richness.

*What is not hidden cannot be the flower*, says Sherman. A quote from someone or another, he can't remember. Some monk.

And Mona says, *Hmm*, startled; or maybe she says nothing, there being nothing to say.


Barbara's nose runs extraordinarily when she cries, another medical impossibility. Her doctor has said that nose-running in times of weepiness is a universal phenomenon governed by forces divine. He claims that the most skillful of surgeons could not alter the mucal flow for all the insurance coverage in the world. But Barbara maintains her nose didn't used to do this; certainly not so copiously. And whether she is right or wrong, it certainly is true that if there is a share of world Kleenex to which each human is entitled, she is claiming her birthright with a vengeance.

Her father is indeed being fired.

"I don't know why anyone would want to be Jewish," she sobs. "I mean, who wasn't already."

Mona agrees this is a mystery.

"If only he could sue!" says Barbara. "But what can he prove? That no one there turned out to be his friend?"

# CHAPTER 12

# A Stay of Execution

Mr. Gugelstein cannot sue, but Alfred can. Mona comes home to find Ralph looking as though he's just seen his SAT scores and didn't even get the two hundred points you're supposed to earn for spelling your name right. In his hand is the Chinese-English dictionary, but it's closed. After all, how to translate New York State Division of Human Rights? What means Executive Branch?

"For firing him," says Ralph, grasping with one hand a letter with attached official complaint form. His other hand is on his stomach. "So-called racial discrimination."

Helen is less shaken than Ralph, more convinced. For this is the difference between a listening mind and a telling mind: Helen's is the kind of mind to which stories occur in itchy enough detail to make her want to scratch. For example, she is not surprised when Mona explains about Alfred's friend Luther, who may have goaded Alfred on. Of course! A crazy person arranged this! She says that it wasn't their fault, the firing. Alfred brought it on himself.

Why does Mona try to tell some other truth?

"You have nothing to say," says Helen, turning on the vacuum cleaner.

Mona, though, refusing to be drowned out, shouts, "You wouldn't have promoted Alfred! You were prejudiced!"

Whereupon Helen raises her hand, and for a moment Mona thinks she is going to slap her the way she used to slap Callie. But instead she hands the vacuum over with what looks to be sadness veined with satisfaction. It is as if despite years of checking the stove at night, she finally has woken, just as she always predicted, to the smell of every-thing burning.

"We did not trust him the way we trust Cedric," she concedes evenly, when the living room is done and all is quiet again. "But that's not the reason why we fired Alfred. Alfred we fired because he made trouble at your friend's house. You don't think your friend Barbara's parents are racist? What do you think they were upset about?"

"And so what if they were racist?" counters Mona. "Would that make it okay for you to be racist too?"

"Our trouble is that we are in the middle," Helen goes on. "Alfred is mad; he would like to sue your friend Barbara's family. But he can-not sue them, so he sue us."

"That's because they didn't do anything illegal."

"As if we did?" Helen says airily. And when Mona starts to argue, Helen explains more vigorously. "Just remember why we work so hard, always try to do our best. Just remember why we struggle to make money."

"In order to send me and Callie to college," says Mona.

"That's right!" Helen, quick, picks up a newspaper, claiming a pop victory; and though she does not look at Ralph when he comes in, he too quickly picks up a section of the paper, as if catching his cue. Or maybe he has his own reasons for wanting to disappear behind a handy curtain of news: For business in the restaurant seems to be slowly but surely falling off. In the beginning it seemed like a wavering in the numbers, a wee inexplicable dip. But now it appears a ditch, unfortu-nately attributable to the staffing. Namely, Richard and Edward. Why should people not come to a restaurant just because the help is Chi-nese? But they don't. It's a simple fact of contemporary society, like babies needing their picture taken. And what should Ralph do now? Fire Richard? Fire Edward? Helen doesn't think that he should any more than he does. However, it makes her furious that Ralph thinks he can't, especially when he points out how this might be like fir-ing Alfred, mysteriously illegal. *Impossible!* says Helen. *As if Richard and Edward are going to sue anyone!* She says, *Chinese people don't sue.* Still he refuses to do anything about this or any other problem. Sometimes it seems to him that the restaurant is his business, and that he should be able to do whatever he wants. But other times he's not at all sure about this. Other times it seems to him only natural that people should have to consider other people in everything they do.

"Everyone except your wife!" says Helen later. "You consider everyone except your family!"

Is that true? Ralph puzzles as Helen cries, "Why don't you do something? Why don't you say something?"

Aunt Theresa is coming to visit. Nobody says this is because of the lawsuit; officially, they are still waiting for the matter to blow over. Officially, they are one hundred percent sure that it will. Theresa is simply suddenly coming for a holiday. Ralph and Helen may have to call a lawyer soon, after all; and having never had this kind of trouble before, they are apprehensive. How will they find the right lawyer? How will they know if the lawyer is good? Someone has told them that lawyers charge for every minute of their time, including just picking up the telephone. According to this source, lawyers charge even if they have a cold and spend most of their time blowing their nose. Is that true? And should Helen and Ralph tell everything to the lawyer? Say nothing to anyone, that was the rule in China. Know nothing, say nothing, do nothing. Of course, things are different here. Still, before they do anything, they first want to hear what Theresa will say. She is the smart one in the family, they are just *make-money guys*. And the matter being so serious, they didn't want to discuss too much on the phone. Not that they exactly believe their line is bugged. However, they don't quite trust the phone either.

There is a lot of talk about operators. It begins to seem to them that they can hear, past the operators' perfect phone voices, traces of their real voices. These are nowhere near so pleasant, and maybe even foreign. The way Helen in particular says the word *foreign*, Mona has to roll her eyes.

Mona says, "How can you of all people think having an accent makes you a spy?"

But so unshakable is Helen on the subject of the accents that she could be the bedrock on which nestles Manhattan. Who knows, she says, they might be Russians.

"Mom," Mona says. "The Russians aren't suing you."

"That's enough!" Helen says. "I don't want to hear that word again."

"What word?"

Helen doesn't want to say.

"Suing?"

"Grounded! One week, no long phone calls either."

"But, Ma," Mona says. "There's nothing the matter with the *word*. Plus you *are* being sued."

"Two weeks!" Helen says.

Is she really superstitious? Mona has never been able to figure out whether Helen is serious or not about things bringing bad luck. However, it's true that the one time Ralph had to go on a plane trip, Mona and Callie were absolutely not allowed to mention accidents of any kind. Helen whacked the girls if they so much as mentioned a flat tire, never mind a fiery, big boom—type crash. They weren't allowed to mention dryer fires, either, even if there really was one in Callie's classmate's house. How could Helen have passed up such a prime educational opportunity? *You see how important to clean out that lint filter.* But no; she really didn't want to hear one word on the subject. Not with Ralph on a plane; no.

Of course, this only made the girls whisper and giggle all the more—as they would these days too, if Callie were home. If Callie were home, she would roll her eyes with Mona, they would do roller coasters. Their chatter would be the foreground of their lives, the bicker of their parents the kind of low-interest backdrop you associate with drama club plays held in cafeterias. But with Callie away, there is mostly just fighting, so many nights of fighting that it is beginning to seem the true sound of the night itself—a sound, say, you normally cannot hear for the crickets. Mona can't actually understand a word of what the parents are saying—they're fighting in Chinese—and yet she gets the gist just fine: *If you hadn't, if you had. So you tell me whose fault it is.* And of course, *One thing I can tell you, she is your daughter, not mine.*

The import of Theresa's visit is somewhat obscured by her manner of arrival, which is fresh from the vegetable kingdom. She is wearing an Oakland A's baseball cap, and carrying a large straw backpack full of surprises. *Look!* A Hawaiian florist neighbor has made these herself, leis for everyone; Mona alone has three—one of purple orchids, one of pink, and one of yellow and white, alternating. The flowers weigh heavy as a horse collar on her shoulders, and she can feel the petals piled soft against her earlobes. A nimbus of smell surrounds her; it's like hearing stereo speakers for the first time, only with her nose. Also Theresa has bags of figs from her fig tree; she has lemons from a neighbor's lemon tree. She has special vegetables she has grown in her garden—heads of garlic the size of baseballs, and beautiful bright-violet finger eggplants that look as though they belong in a bouquet.

But of everything, she herself is the most blue-ribbon specimen. She is wiry and tan and sweetly befreckled, and when she takes off her baseball hat you can see that she's given up her bun, and is wearing her brown hair all loose now. Except, that is, for a single skinny braid. She's managed to gather almost all white hairs for this braid, so that it shines like liquid silver. As for clothes, she is wearing blue jeans like a hippie, only new-looking and fresh-pressed, with a crease down the front of each leg. The jeans go with a lightly starched work shirt, on which has been embroidered chain after chain of daisies and—in a little half-moon around the shirt tag in the back—her name, only without the *h*: *Teresa*.

This H is not the only one that is missing. Most conspicuously absent is Uncle Henry. But since Theresa and Uncle Henry are not married, he is not missed. Everyone talks instead, over tea in the backyard, about the World Series, and about Theresa's cats, Barbie and Ken. Also about how Theresa likes living on the beach. In English this is— Theresa's preferred language when either of the girls is around. Doesn't sand get tracked into the house? Helen asks. And what about ocean storms? Theresa tells them about a big flood they had. *Not so bad,* she says. And cool as can be, she reports that she's given away everything she doesn't absolutely need—anything she couldn't help but worry about, but didn't think worth the concern. Everything really important, she keeps on the second floor.

"What kind of things you gave away?" asks Helen, in a casually quavering voice. She is so shocked that she does not seem to hear the inventory at all: the hi-fi cabinet, the Statue of Liberty lamp, everything cut crystal, that white flokati rug full of cat hair . . . It is as if she is seeing her own house being swept out to sea.

". . . also some other things." Mona can tell her aunt's not really done, that really she's winding up as a minor act of mercy.

"Clean house is always good," says Ralph blithely. "Fact is, why we need so much stuff? Just make us crazy. . . ."

"I'll tell you who's crazy," Helen starts to say. But then she doesn't tell anybody anything.

Everyone has some more tea. Ralph tries a fig, pronounces it delicious. They reminisce about persimmons they have eaten, and pomegranates. There is some talk about a hurricane they had right in New York.

"And what about mildew?" Helen asks finally.

Theresa explains how she leaves lights on in the closets. "You'd be amazed. Just one lightbulb can dry everything out."

"Mildew can be serious problem," says Helen, apparently relieved that Theresa at least takes fungal growth seriously. They go on to discuss dry-cleaning bags, and whether they are, in combination with the lightbulbs, a fire hazard. What wattage does she use? And is there a shade on the bulb?

"No such thing as too careful," says Ralph, helping himself to another fig. "Even you are very very careful, you never know what will happen." He shakes his head. "Fate."

"Fate! Our trouble has nothing to do with fate," says Helen.

"What? Everything is I abdicated responsibility? Everything is I do not care?"

And so begins the subject of the lawsuit. Helen and Ralph vie with each other in their efforts to be reasonable. However, there is energy in need of discharge; everything seeks the ground, crackling. They begin; then try to begin again, at the beginning, only to discover that there is no beginning. They fear there will be no end. Still they explain to Theresa everything they can—including in their explanation some facts Mona knew but didn't know. For example, how Ralph hired Alfred despite his having a police record. Apparently he was recommended by Theresa's parish priest in such a way as left Ralph no choice. For the priest said first of all, that Alfred was innocent; and second of all, that Ralph of all people should have a heart for someone trying to start over. Helen contests the and-so-we-had-no-choice part of the story. She says the priest was just making a recommendation. She says only someone like Ralph lets other people decide his business as if he is still in China. No wonder he has trouble with his stomach!

Meanwhile, Theresa listens carefully. For all that she had seemed a dubious authority on the subject of oceanfront property, as they talk on she seems to somehow rise in stature, never mind that she remains sitting down. She seems to be subtly straightening, aligning herself with the stripe of her folding chair. Helen explains about Barbara Gugelstein's house, and about how they had to fire Alfred. Though in general they have more choice than Ralph thinks, she says, in this case they didn't. Also she explains about Mona—how she was led astray by bad elements, especially this good-for-nothing Seth, but how at least she has atoned by breaking up with the good-for-nothing. Helen says they didn't even have to ask her to do it; Mona realized herself that this would make her parents happy, and went ahead on her own.

Is that what happened?

"She's still a good girl," finishes Helen. "Sometimes she likes to have a big mouth, but then she looks in her heart and realizes she is still our nice Chinese daughter."

"In the morning, we hear her, she is like a bird," says Ralph. "So sweet and nice, at the restaurant, she is the best hostess you can find. You cannot hire someone smile at the customers like that. Make everyone feel good."

Theresa nods thoughtfully, considering with a profound look her thong sandals. These are a little cool for New York—lucky thing she's sitting with her long feet in the sun—though these are not sandals Helen would ever wear even if it were summer. These are sandals that not only bare all ten toes, but seem to take their inspiration from the loincloth. However, on Auntie Theresa, they look somehow elegant; maybe it's just the contrast with the rest of her outfit. A smile seems to flit across her face, but then she reenters the role of presiding elder and says, after an elder-like pause, that it doesn't sound to her as if Alfred has much of a case. Naturally, she's no lawyer, and clearly Alfred's dismissal had something to do with race. But what?

"If Cedric went to live in Mona's friend's house, you would fire him too," she says.

General relief. "That's right! We would fire Cedric too. Of course, Chinese people would not move into someone's house to begin with."

More happy agreement. What discrimination could Alfred be talking about?

Mona brings up, as delicately as she can, all about her mom and dad not being willing to promote Alfred the way they did Cedric. And why? Because he wasn't Chinese.

Helen says, admiring the sky, "We do not know who is this big mouth or where she got it from."

"Well," says Theresa, "maybe that's not quite right, about the promotion. In China, is one thing. But here in the United States, that's not the way to think. You cannot think all the time about relationship. You have to think about the law."

"How could be?" says Ralph. "America is supposed to be the land of the free."

"That's why we have laws, to make sure that everybody is free," explains Theresa. "But anyway, say you are racist. I don't mean that you are. Let's just consider that case. Even if you are, how could Alfred know that? How could he know you are thinking to promote Cedric? How could he know you are not going to promote him? And how could he know why?"

"There's no way he can find out," says Ralph.

Says Helen, "After all, he doesn't have that—what is it called? EST." Everyone laughs with relief.

"ESP," Mona says.

Everyone laughs again.

And Mona, sitting on the milk box, tries to laugh too, wishing she did not have to tell them not only how she told Seth and Barbara, but how, during a camp rap session—trying to be up front, figuring the truth never hurt—she even told Alfred himself, and Luther.


The news is received calmly at first. Theresa sets the tone by praising her niece for being so forthcoming. Theresa sees this as proof of her loyalty to the family, that Mona would not think of holding such a thing back. Everyone agrees that Mona was under a lot of peer pressure, especially from that good-for-nothing Seth; and that Mona is, after all, not a full-grown adult but still a child, who does not quite know how to talk. They conclude that she still needs her parents to tell her what to do. They agree they should never have let her near that Seth Mandel to begin with; that was Ralph's fault. Helen wanted to make them break up, she says, it was Ralph who said to let Mona learn her lesson by herself.

"He said we could ask Magdalena and Cedric to watch them," complains Helen. "As if they are the same as parents!" She vows that they will be stricter in the future, so that they will not have to blame themselves again.

"We have abdicated our responsibility," says Helen.

And Ralph, who knows who she means when she says *we*, admits, "Pay too much attention to the restaurant, it's not right. Make our children suffer."

"No more go out, go out," says Helen. "From now on, Mona stay home."

Everyone nods.

"No more drive family car. From now on, ride bicycle." Ralph has an odd expression on his face that may or may not be a smile.

"Walk," says Helen.

"Crawl," Mona says.

Ralph smiles again without smiling.

"No more jokes, either," says Helen. "You think everything is funny. That's the beginning of your trouble."

"Wrong attitude," says Ralph, winking.

"He is not this way all the time," Helen says to Theresa. "Only because you are here."

Both women look down.

"Just want to laugh and have fun," continues Helen.

"But, Ma," Mona says.

"No *Ma*," says Helen.

"I thought you guys liked it that I was always laughing about something. Didn't you tell Auntie how I was just like a bird, so gay and everything?"

"We must think about our duty as parents." Ralph is serious now. "We laugh when you laugh, that's just encourage you. We are wrong that way. Abdicate our responsibility!"

"No more typical American parents," agrees Helen. "No more let the kids run wild. From now on we are Chinese parents."

"You know what you guys sound like?" Mona says. "You sound like the Puritans."

Helen frowns.

"You know," Mona says. "The Puritans. The guys with the funny buckles on their shoes?"

Helen says, "Is that the family, all their five kids got scholarship to Yale?"

Ralph whistles. "All five kids!"

"Not all five got full scholarship," explains Helen. "Two just got so-called work study aid, have to work in the dining hall."

A moment of silence, during which everyone contemplates just what the Puritans' secret could be.

Says Ralph, "Their parents must do some good job, kids turn out like that."

"No more go out," starts Helen again

"No more fool around," echoes Ralph, sternly.

Through all this, Auntie Theresa diligently nods her head. Her eyes do not narrow in shrewd discerning fashion, but rather seem preternaturally wide open, accepting of all; she could be a rain barrel left out in the backyard. Does she really think Ralph and Helen remiss, does she really think a parental crackdown in order? Or does she simply think Mona is better off having them blame themselves than blame her?

Later Mona will think the latter, and credit her aunt for her prescience. Because, all too soon, Theresa leaves—she most unfortunately has nonrefundable tickets for a deluxe cruise of the Hawaiian Islands. Before she hurries home to pack her bikinis, though, she finds the time to hang a hammock up in the backyard with Mona. Naturally, this is not a regular old hammock. This is a special hammock from California, made of many colors, and with a built-in pillow. They test it out together. The sky rocks above them.

"One thing very important in life," says Theresa, "is to know how to make yourself at home."

"I didn't mean to make so much trouble," says Mona. "Really I didn't."

"No one could make so much trouble by themselves," says Theresa. "Do you like the beach?"

"Sure."

"Good. You are welcome to come to California anytime. Anytime you like, you can come make yourself at home."

"Maybe I really will come visit you."

Theresa straightens her legs, kicks her feet a little. Today she is wearing regular shoes and regular pants. However, her shirt is red-checked like a tablecloth. "Before you know it, it will be your home away from home."

"It's that nice, huh."

"Very comfortable," says Theresa, still swinging. "Just remember, you are invited."

"Okay," says Mona.

"Just remember," insists Theresa. "Don't forget."

"I won't forget."

"No matter what, you're invited. Remember."

"No matter what."

Theresa repeats her invitation one more time, in the airport; in the cavernous lobby, under the hard fluorescent lights, though, her generosity resounds in an Old Testament manner. *Thou shalt not forget to come visit.*

"All right already," says Mona. "I'll start saving for my plane ticket tomorrow."

Theresa clasps Mona's hand as if she's been granted an audience with the Pope. "Shalom," she says. "The cheapest way is standby." And with that she turns into the walkway, stops to wave five or six times, and is gone.


It's the War of the H's—Helen versus the High Holy Days.

"That's enough Jewish," she says. "Forget about services. Not funny anymore. You know where all the trouble started? All the trouble started from you become Jewish."

"Mom," Mona says. "It's a free country. I can go to temple if I want. In fact, if I wanted to, I could go to a mosque."

Mona expects her mother to say, What's a mosque? But Helen knows which counter she is headed for; she is not about to be distracted by any discount special.

"Forget about free country," she says.

"What do you mean? This is America. I can remember what I want, I can be what I want, I can—"

"You want to be something, you can leave this house, don't come back," says Helen.

They are putting their summer clothes away, taking out their winter things. The latter are quaintly woolly—scratchy, bulky. Prehistoric. Does it really ever get that cold around here? Certainly it's cooler and cooler out, and clear; some days the air is almost metallic, like tinware. Still it's hard to believe anyone with a normal fat level would ever need to wrap herself up in all that. So thinks Mona.

Helen, though, packs as if summer is the season without compelling reality—as if this year the winter will, quite possibly, not end. She uses so many mothballs that the wastebasket cannot hold all the empty boxes, they have to start a bag for overflow.

"It says here you only have to use one box of balls for every ten cubic feet," Mona says.

"Forget about what it says. You listen to your mother."

"I'm just reading the directions."

Helen takes the box she has just opened and upends it onto the floor. Her motions are undramatic, yet the balls scatter excitedly, noisily making her point. "If you Jewish people so smart," she says, "you can do it by yourself."

"That's a stereotype!" Mona says. "We're not any smarter than the Chinese."

Helen is not listening.

Mona does not go to services; the temple is kind enough to resell her ticket. But no sooner does this skirmish end than Helen and Mona fight over whether it is safe to put chopsticks in the dishwasher. One day a chopstick slips down near the heating element and gets charred. This to Helen is a sign that Mona is going to burn the house down.

"First of all, there's nothing the matter with washing chopsticks by hand. Not a big deal. Only Americans have to wash everything use machine," she says. "Second of all, we are not racist."

Mona continues to demonstrate her special method of jamming the chopsticks into the silverware drainer. "You just have to put them in sideways, like this."

"How could you say that to outside people?" Helen says. "What kind of daughter talks that way? Tell them your parents are racist."

"Mom," Mona says. "You were never going to promote Alfred. Because he was black."

"First of all, we hired Alfred when no one would give him a job. He should thank us instead of sue us! And how do you think he got to be cook if we didn't promote him? As for new promotion, since when do we owe someone promotion? We don't owe him anything."

"But Alfred could only go so far, when it came to—"

"Second of all," continues Helen, "parents are racist, parents are not racist, even parents are Communist, a daughter has no business talk like that. You talk like that is like slap your own mother in the face!"

"I didn't mean to slap you in the face, Ma. We were just having a discussion about racism, which happens to be an important social problem, and in that context—"

"Context! Social problem! What kind of talk is that?"

Mona closes up the dishwasher. "It's a free country, I can talk however I want. It's my right."

"Free country! Right! In this house, no such thing!"

More social analysis: "That's exactly the problem! Everywhere else is America, but in this house it's China!"

"That's right! No America here! In this house, children listen to parents!"

And the inevitable conclusion.

"Okay," Mona says. "I'm leaving. I'm going to pack up my backpack and check out a train schedule and take all the money out of my bank account."

"Go ahead," Helen says.

Mona hesitates. "I'm not even going to get traveler's checks, I'm just going to carry cash," she says.

It's what she thinks of as an invitation to motherhood; this is what children have to do every now and then, give their parents a chance to play the boss. But Helen is too mad even to rise to the bait. Of course, never having had much faith in credit, she has always carried around a lot of cash herself.

She slaps Mona in the face.

"Mom." Mona straightens her glasses. "Mom. I'm not Callie." She feels her cheek; she knows the skin is hot by how cool her hand feels against it, an iceberg. She says, as clearly and mightily as she can, "If you ever do that again, I'm going to slap you right back."

Helen slaps her again, then calmly picks up a mug of cold tea. Her face looks like a plaster cast of itself. She says, "You think you are so smart, you think you know everything. But let me tell you something: Once you leave this house you can never come back." And with that, she marches upstairs to her bedroom, cradling the cold liquid as if she fully intends to drink it.

# CHAPTER 13

# Mona's Life
# as Callie

Mona is not the one who usually runs away. It's true that once, when she was little, she packed a suitcase and wrote a note and hid under the bed; and it's true that she was disappointed when no one collapsed with shock and grief upon reading that she had removed herself to another clime, she knew not whither. She bade her family farewell and forgave them their foibles and sincerely hoped they came to recognize the sorry error of their ways, for their own sake; then she fell asleep and woke up with a dust ball in her mouth. This was nowhere near so gross as almost anything you see in the movies. However, it was perhaps one of the grossest things ever to happen to her.

She hasn't forgotten it. Still, in general, it has been Callie the Achiever who has walked out into the snow or rain, grim intention in every step. For example, after they moved to Scarshill and Helen told her she would get the small dark room with the leaky ceiling, while Mona would get the large yellow one with the windows on two walls. Callie thought then that Helen should at least flip a coin. She said it wasn't right for mothers to play favorites; she said it had been going on almost her whole life, and she wasn't going to take it anymore. Big words. But she said them in a Callie-like way—as if she wanted to run away from her own working mouth—and perhaps that is why Helen slapped her, because she was cowering already. Helen hated it that she made Callie cower. Or so she said. *Like a servant.* Slap. *My own daughter!* And that made Callie threaten to slap her back. She was wild as a squirrel in a corner, the kind of squirrel with half its fur bitten off, and nothing to call its own except twitches. Helen slapped her again; and when

Callie slapped her back sure enough, they ended up on the floor, yanking each other's hair out. Then Callie went out into the sleet without a coat, and when she came back, after hours of Helen claiming *nothing wrong*, it was with a policeman, and a coat someone had given her, a total stranger. And even before Callie took it off, anyone could see why a total stranger in a car would stop and give Callie the coat off her own back. Callie was drenched and thin and shaking, and her ears were white with what Mona thought must be frostbite.

All the same, Mona kept the room. The favorite daughter pinned peace pins on her curtains, hung a hat rack on the closet door. On one wall she taped pretty packages, gum wrappers, fortune cookie fortunes, making them into a kind of collage; here and there, she placed Coke bottles full of peacock feathers, very artistic. Also Mateus wine bottles with different-colored candle wax dripped all over them. She spent hours figuring out what color to burn next, and how to make dripless candles drip.

Meanwhile, Callie studied. For that's what hysterics did, when they were being perfect. When they were being perfect, they practiced their posture and got themselves into Harvard-Radcliffe and looked askance at the decorating efforts of others. They made mildly snide comments. *I earn my keep.*

Mona wonders now at how strongly she feels about all this. It feels, in memory, as if she were the one who walked out into the storm— as if she were Callie all along, even as she was Mona. Is this what it means to be sisters? Mona wishes she had given Callie the big room; or at least that they had tossed a coin, the two of them. She wonders what she thought at the time. Did she think, *Of course, I am the favorite, this room is mine*? Did she think, *Please let them stop*? Did she think, *That is not my mother, that cannot be my mother*?

Even now it is unthinkable, how she grew up by day while her sister grew up by night. She can no more imagine this than she can imagine why she chose to enter the night herself, Callie's night; or at least to leave the day. Someone once told her a story about Callie: about how teased Callie was by her math teacher on account of being smart. This was when Callie was in eighth grade. The teacher did things like snap her bra strap during exams, this friend said; she knew because her brother was two rows back and saw the whole thing. How the teacher pulled Callie's strap and laughed—really it was a sign that she was his favorite—and how Callie did nothing at all. How she sat there, and worked out the problems, and handed her exam in early—some people said without even checking it over.

Mona knows this about her sister; and she knows too how Callie became the kind of person these things happened to. She wonders: Do favorite children in China feel guilty? Or do they simply accept their spot in the hierarchy—*How lucky am I!* Perhaps only a New World daughter would wonder about the fairness of it all. Mona can hear her mother's voice: *Fair! As if there is such a thing.* A voice not unlike Mr. Ingle's: *You've got to know how the game is played.* In the background, Mrs. Ingle tinkles, *It's just not right.* But her voice is nowhere near so loud as her husband's, or Helen's. *Fair! Fair!*

Perhaps this is why Mona allied herself with the Jews, with their booming belief in doing right, with their calling and their crying out. *Justice!* But then again, maybe she would have turned into anything no daughter of her mother could be; maybe it was just that simple. Adolescent rebellion, just like Rabbi Horowitz said, maybe certain urges come shrink-wrapped with your first bottle of pHisoHex.

She finds herself first at their local train station, and then in the city, alone. She considers who she might call. She would call Barbara, except for Mrs. Gugelstein. She would call Aunt Theresa, except that she is at sea. She would call Callie, except that Callie is Callie. And she would call Sherman, except that she doesn't know his phone number, and what would he say that Mona would want him to say? She would want him to say, *Why don't you come on over, I'd love to talk in person and even do mushy stuff.* Instead she would probably get more Zen wisdom: *What talks back cannot be the flower.* Maybe she shouldn't have broken up with Seth the sex maniac; in truth, she practically misses him, teepee and all.

Grand Central is large and, in one room, full of benches, like a church. She would say temple, except that around the corner there are ticket windows, lined up like confessionals. These are mostly closed, just like in church, and the air is still, and voluminous—a palpable, roller rink of an expanse like the charged, curved space between the hands of

a god. There was a time when this is what Mona would have imagined—a god as big as King Kong. Someone able to reach all those high
windows and, if he was in the mood, able to give them a nice wipe such
as would let the sun shine in on poor earthlings like herself. So pale! So
lost! There was a time she would have looked up with frail hope and felt
what a pittance she was. She would have felt her smallness of conse-
quence like a wrinkled-up name tag at the back of her collar.

But today, before she sees herself in perspective, she feels, quite
unexpectedly, as though she stands in the Garden of Eden. Just for a
moment. The wind of apprehension, as always, will blow. But between
gusts, she feels it—not even that she is standing in, but as though she is
herself the Garden of Eden. A place that will remain a place of sun even
after the poor forked whatever have been banished. She feels as though
she stands at the pointy start of time. Behind her, no history. Before
her—everything. How arrogant! *As if you have no mother! As if you come
out of thin air!* She can hear Helen's voice. Still Mona feels it—something
opening within herself, big as the train station, streaming with sappy
light. And feeling this, she is almost not surprised to find next to her—
she is sitting, it seems, on a bench—a lady. This lady has laid herself
down, stretched herself out—and now, sure enough, is making herself comfortable. One of her legs dangles over the bench edge, foot
almost touching the floor; her other leg extends straight up into the air.
The lady is wearing yellow fishnet stockings; her garters show; the leg
descends through the air with the willy-nilly grandeur of a felled tree.

Heads up! Mona watches with amazement. This is not something
that could ever happen at home. For one thing, fishnet stockings have
gone out of style. Down to bench level. The lady's foot looks as though
it is going to land inches from Mona's thigh, but doesn't. Instead it lands
smack square in Mona's lap. Is this life outside of high school? Mona
clutches her backpack. She makes sure the zippered compartment is
zipped, even though the lady seems harmless enough. Blue pumps she
is wearing, with a red leather tassel, and also a piece of green ribbon. The
ribbon is tied around the bottom of the shoe, into a glorious bow on
top; she seems to have just put it on, for it is perfectly clean and apparently un-walked on. Should Mona say something to her? *Excuse me, your
foot is sort of in my lap.* If Mona were her mother, she would certainly ex-
tricate herself from the situation. But so removed is Mona from her

everyday ways that she finds a strange small comfort in this contact. And so she takes the lady in: oldish, the color of cherry bark, evidently asleep. Short matted hair. One might surmise her zip dress no longer zips, for she is wearing safety pins all down her front. Big silver ones, little gold ones, oddly spaced; the dress is certainly in no danger of coming off. Her skin, though, is another story. Once Mona read in a book about how ladies in the Old South put wax on their faces for makeup, and how that wax would come off if they sat too close to a fire; this lady too looks as if her outer layers are softening. Mona fears for her—not that the lady seems afflicted with any such worry herself. Soft ratchety snores slip away from her like truant ghosts. Mona considers the lady's shoes a little longer—how the seams appear to be straining; how they appear, in fact, under that green ribbon, to be split. The heels are so worn that the leatherette alongside curls up in a little froth; and yet, behold the scoop of man-made material on the underside of her arch. This is fresh and shiny black, with the shoe size crisply incised. Nine and a half B. Too big for Mona to give the lady her own shoes. Schizophrenia? thinks Mona. Drugs? She wonders how she ever could have worked on a hot line, she feels so helpless. The lady stirs a little; the dangling leg loses its mooring, threatening to drag her whole weight down. What to do? Mona considers the higher windows of the station, then reaches for the lady's other foot. For a moment the lady jerks, as if about to kick. But no; it is just a deep-sleep twitch. Mona closes her eyes too. She clasps her hands on the lady's slim ankles, and holds on.

"So what's this? A homeless waif? A runaway?"

Mona opens her eyes, adjusts her glasses. The safety pin lady is gone, and sitting next to her is Bea, smelling of almonds. Mona feels for her backpack—still there. She blinks. Bea is still there too. Bea is likewise holding on to her bag, in the immortal manner of ladies out in public, except that hers is not a lady's bag. It is, rather, the kind of beaded pouch that is most properly stuffed with wampum. And perhaps it is, for Bea is dressed to a theme. This is to say that she is mostly soft fabrics, knits and fuzz and stretch pants. However, she is also sporting a Stetson hat, a fringed suede jacket, and cowboy boots. If it weren't for her fall oh-so-touchables, she could be Buffalo Bill.

"You were asleep." Bea takes Mona's chin in her hand. "Is something wrong? Something is wrong, I can see it. You're all puffy."

"What are you doing here?" says Mona.

"I'll tell you what I'm doing here if you'll tell me what you're doing here."

Mona doesn't know what to say.

Bea nods comprehendingly. "I see." Adding, as if to keep her side of the bargain, "I'm here to pick up the branding irons for my roundup. You would think I'd be going to Wyoming for these, but actually I went to Lincoln Center." She indicates two enormous packages, wrapped for the ages in brown paper and masking tape. "Do you know where you are going?"

"No."

Bea nods again. "We all have to go through this; it must be the water. Every one of my kids did exactly the same thing, all that differed was the particulars: This one hitchhiked; that one took planes; Seth, as you know, moved into a teepee. That wasn't so bad—at least we didn't have to worry about tropical diseases. I tell you what. Why don't you move into our yard for a while? Seth took the teepee, but we're doing a corral for the roundup anyway. How about if we add a little stable? I'll call your parents and let them know where you are, and you can have your rebellion in peace."

Mona frowns.

"Are you pregnant?"

Mona shakes her head.

"Then what is it? Share with me this state secret."

Mona tries to explain, but mostly she asks: What if she were Bea's daughter and had done something awful? Something that really hurt her parents? Can she imagine that?

"Well, of course, I do not have a daughter," says Bea. "Only boys, boys, boys. Not that I didn't love having boys. But they certainly were boys. And the particular kind of boys I had seemed to specialize at a certain age in saying the absolute meanest things possible. For example, my dear stepson Seth." There is a slight catch in her throat; she runs a light hand over her wrapped-up branding irons. "Seth has spent this year calling me a hypocrite. All my do-gooding, says my dear stepson, is just a way of maintaining my social status."

"He *said* that to you?" Mona is wide-eyed.

"He did, and I tell you, it was not so easy to hear. And I would be lying if I did not admit that I argued with him, and threatened to lock him out of the house, or at least to revoke his laundry privileges. But every time of life has its job, and that is his job right now, to say the thing that will hurt me most. It is how he is becoming his own person, by pointing out the truth."

"Is it the truth?"

Bea sighs and looks at her hands. These are freckled, with pale-colored nail polish and a number of rings Seth says she cannot bear to take off—every one reminds her of something. "Life is more complicated than he thinks. And what's the matter with liberal guilt anyway? Better to feel guilty than to feel nothing, that's my opinion. I write my letters, I'm doing my best. The rest I'll have to leave to the great leaders of our age. Anyway, insulting me was Seth's job, and my job as a stepmother was to let him do his job. That's what I agreed when I married like a fool his adorable father, Phil."

"Even if it meant letting Seth not go to college?"

"We couldn't force him. He's an adult. It was his decision."

An adult! His decision! Mona cannot help but hear what another voice would say in the same situation: *What do you mean, not going to college? You kill your parents, you talk like that.*

Bea worries a hangnail. "You watch, he'll end up on the straight and narrow yet. It's the talented ones you have to worry about. Especially the ones who can sing, or play something—with them you have to worry about rock bands. Seth, luckily, has no talents. That leaves law school."

"You must be relieved that he changed his mind."

"Changed his mind?"

"Didn't he tell you? He's gone to college after all. That's what I heard."

"Is that where he is!" says Bea. "We've been getting postcards from him, but he doesn't seem to be anywhere near where they're postmarked. His father is worried sick. Do you know what school he went to?"

"I don't know. We broke up."

"No kidding."

Track announcements come over the PA system. A lady with six children struggles by.

"My parents think people like you don't care about your kids, that's how come you let them do what they want," says Mona. "They think you're abdicating your responsibility."

"How interesting."

"In fact, they think that's the exact job of the parents, to make sure the kids go to college."

"Really."

"And the kids' job is to go and not hack off. Our job is to remember how hard our parents worked, and to get all A's to make it up to them."

"Sounds like a good deal all around," Bea says, but she's frowning. "Do you have any money?"

"I do."

Bea rummages in her wampum pouch. "Here's more."

A hundred dollars!

"Oh, no," says Mona. "I can't—"

"For your project. A charitable contribution. Don't stay in any fleabag motels, they're dangerous."

Mona looks at the money as if it is a foreign currency with a funny bill size she isn't sure is going to fit in her wallet.

"Oops! That's my train they're announcing," says Bea.

"Thanks so much," says Mona.

"Have fun! Think Paris! London!"

"Maybe I can stow away."

"Stow away! Great idea. When you come back you can advise me. Maybe we can get a fund-raiser out of it."

Mona laughs.

"In the meantime, I'll call your parents." Bea hoists up the branding irons, one package in each arm. She swivels, wobbles, hoists them up a bit more.

"Do you need a hand?"

"I need four more hands." She walks off just fine, her cowboy boots clicking. "Bon voyage!" she calls from between her giant blinders. "If you hear from Seth, call me!"

"I will," promises Mona.

"And have a good time! That's important!" Bea turns completely around to make this point.

"You're going to miss your train."

"I am," Bea agrees, and starts to trot backward. That's when she hits someone, and drops both her packages, only to discover that the someone is her train's engineer. A sweet man, this is, not to say a most able one; he very nicely holds the train until they're both on it.

Call the parents! Mona is not sure she wants Bea to do any such thing. What a stomachache it is going to give her father! If he doesn't have one already. Still, an hour and a half later, Mona is disembarking in New Haven. Bea would laugh if she knew, but this really is what Mona wants to do—her parents having thought it unnecessary for her to go on a college tour. *What is there to look about?* They knew what colleges Mona should apply to already—it was obvious. Mona should apply to the same colleges as Callie. *Go to Harvard if you get in, Yale second choice, Princeton also nice.* Harvard was better than Yale because it was so close to MIT—how much more likely she was to find a husband there! They saw it as a kind of twofer. As for other schools—if they are all Mona can get into, say her parents, that is one hundred percent all right, nobody has to know.

But all of Mona's friends have gone looking, and so this is what Mona does now too, pretend she has a choice.

Yale. Brown. UMass. Smith.

In the beginning, the tour is fun. Now, though, she worries about worrying her parents. She trusts that Bea remembered to call. All the same, Should she call herself? and Why should she call? twinkle alternately in her mind like a pair of Christmas lights. Didn't her mother more or less dare her to leave? If they are truly worried, she decides, they will put out a search. A compromise: Mona begins eating lunch in front of campus police stations. She gives her real name everywhere. She stops in at the city police for directions. "I'm Mona Chang. I wonder if you can help me." She checks the pictures on the wall, to see if she is perchance included, but no. She is missing among the missing.

Cambridge. Staying with Callie is practically turning herself in, and after only three days. This is not the action of a self-respecting renegade. Still she stands outside of what she thinks is Callie's door, and leaves a note. Callie's suite is something of a rabbit warren, right down to the two different entrances; one of these used to be a fire door, but now is Naomi's door. Mona leaves a note there too. She does this again later. And again, later still. Where is her sister? She is tiring of cafés, and what with all the coffee she's had, her heart is thumping like a prisoner in a car trunk. Also her hands shake, and she is developing an odd headache at the top of her nose; it feels like an acorn implant. Somehow she had not imagined that Callie would truly be in classes all day, even though she is just the wonk type to take five courses a semester instead of four. And where is Naomi? The only person who eventually shows up is Phoebe, the like-it-or-lump-it floater Callie and Naomi couldn't get rid of.

Phoebe is so miniature that even short Mona's first reaction is to gentle down, as if she had just happened on a bird in the woods. It is therefore a surprise to discover that Phoebe is, personality-wise, all elbows. As she is carrying a megaphone, she is managing the stuck suite door one-handed; she hurls her weight against it as if she has taken more than enough truck from these hinges already.

"Um, excuse me," says Mona. "I'm looking for my sister."

"Are you talking to me?" Phoebe swings around abruptly, blindsiding Mona with the megaphone.

"Yes." Mona reseats her glasses.

"Well?"

Mona reaches for the megaphone, so surprising Phoebe that she lets go. Mona holds it up to her lips. "I'm looking for my sister."

"Give me that back."

Mona holds on. "Do you know where she is?"

"She's out of town."

"Out of town?" Mona drops the megaphone down. In a normal voice: "How can she be out of town?"

"I'm not your sister's keeper, and you'll have to excuse me, but I'm late." Phoebe reclaims her mouthpiece.

"Late for what?"

"Crew practice."

"Are you a coxswain?"

"I'm late," she says again. "Callie and Naomi went hitchhiking somewhere."

"They're not at some resort in Rhode Island, are they?"

"Excuse me," says Phoebe.

"You're late, right?"

Phoebe gives her a look that is distinctly menacing, in a miniature way.

"Listen. I wonder if I can stay in Callie's room for a while. I came
all the way up here to visit her, and now I don't even have any place
to stay."

"I don't know why you ask when you're going to do what you
want anyway," says Phoebe.


It turns out Mona doesn't even need a key; locking doors is against
Naomi's politics. Phoebe hurries out, Mona settles in.

Long gone are the olden golden days when each student had not
only his own separate bedroom, but also a separate living room in
which to park his splendidly smelliferous pipe stand. Now the students
stack themselves in bunk beds. That is, unless the group as a whole is
able to drive out a roommate or two, and/or is willing to give up the
living room. Naomi and Callie have managed to do both. They are
still stuck with the spindly Phoebe Me-Me, as they call her, after her
obvious first interest. But the other floater unaccountably opted to
move off campus after only two and a half weeks of rooming bliss; and
so it is that with Callie living in what used to be a living room, each
roommate has her very own habitat.

They are not the first roommate group to use the suite as three
bedrooms instead of two bedrooms and a common room. Part of the
living room has been walled off to form a common hallway; the main
suite door opens into this, as does Phoebe's door, and also a hollow-
core door brightened with a blowup of Angela Davis. This is Naomi's
door—the original connecting door between her room and the living
room being locked up. Callie's room doesn't really have a door, only
an Indian-print bedspread turned into a curtain. It's the least private.

But Callie, Mona knows, loved the living room as soon as she saw
it, because of the fireplace—working or not, she didn't care. She was
happy to have the extra molding too, and the peeling mystery medallion on the ceiling, even if it was just there to hide some cracking plaster. And she was happy to have the big three-part window that looked

like the Holy Mystery of the Trinity come to roost right at Harvard (especially in the morning, before a person put her glasses on). Never mind that there was no closet, meaning that she had to have two trunks and a big hamper; this room was nothing like Callie's room at home. Naomi wanted the room with the three doors; it was a room that would never make her feel trapped. Phoebe wanted the conventional room. But so far as Callie was concerned, the living room was the big room, the light room, the best room, even if the partition wall was covered with dark-brown cork squares. This Callie has creatively turned into a collage wall—tacking onto it a sweet mishmash of odds and ends, in the exact same way as Mona has at home. Postcards. Packages of freeze-dried food. Book jackets. Peacock feathers.

*Copycat!* On another wall, more brazen theft: Callie has heisted wholesale Mona's propensity to decorate with clothes. This may in fact be honestly related to the absence of a closet. All the same, Mona wonders if Callie really had to hang on the locked-up door leading to Naomi's room a hat rack just like Mona's at home; or if she had to drape the nearby plant holder with a scarf so like a scarf of Mona's that she has to wonder if it is not indeed hers. Mona climbs up on a big stuffed chair to see.

No sooner does she commence inspection, however, than the phone ding-lings. Should she pick it up? Probably she shouldn't. Anyway, she does. This is not meant to be an act of dissemblance. It is entirely in observance of standard behavioral custom that Mona says, "Hello?"

"Hello, Callie?" says Helen.

"Hi, Mom," Mona says.

"Did she call you yet?"

"You mean Mona?"

"Of course, Mona. Who else?"

"Hmm," says Mona.

"Since when do you have such a big mouth too?"

Mona isn't sure what to say.

"Did she call you again?"

"I talked to her today."

"So what happened? Did you tell her Auntie Theresa should make her call us, after all we are the ones she is making worry sick?"

"Oh, no. She's not with Auntie Theresa."

"What do you mean? Last time you said—"

"I thought she was."

"You said she called and that's where she was. With Auntie Theresa in Hawaii, the two of them both crazy."

"That's what she said. But this time she said she's having a great time, she just wishes she'd paid more attention in French."

"French! What? Don't tell me she went to France!"

Mona doesn't tell her.

"How could be? As if Hawaii is not bad enough. Oh! She is one hundred percent crazy."

Mona flinches but goes on. "It's where she always wanted to go. She said she's always wanted to go around topless."

"Topless means what?"

"It's a kind of French bathing suit."

"Forget about bathing suit, when is she coming home?"

"She didn't say. But she said to tell you not to worry."

"Not to worry! Is she going to call you again?"

"I don't know."

"If she calls," says Helen, "make sure you call me. Make report."

"Yes, ma'am."

"And tell her . . ."

"Tell her what?"

"Tell her she can stay in France! Tell her she is crazy!" A moment of hesitation. "Is she turn something else while she is there?"

"You mean?"

"She is not turn French, is she, or . . ."

"No. She said she didn't have the figure for it."

"Tell her she should think about her parents instead of about some bathing suit!"

"I'll tell her."

"And tell her come home right now. Tell her she is our daughter, she cannot just run away as if she has no parents."

"Okay."

"Tell her if she wants to leave the house, she has to ask parents to kick her out. Not just one day leave by herself."

"I'll tell her." Mona hesitates. "Don't you want to tell her you love her or something? You know, to soften her up. I mean, if you want her to call." She says this even though her parents have never been the type to talk drippy talk; that's what her friends' parents do. Mona's are more likely to express their deep unalienable affection by yelling. "Or maybe she should talk to Dad?"

"Tell her she is good-for-nothing pain in the neck," says Helen. "And why should she talk to Dad? So she can send him to the hospital with ulcer?"


When Helen was exasperated, she used to say that Callie always seemed to be expecting someone to yell at her; and that made Helen yell at her. Helen ordered her around, she asked nothing of Mona. Everything was Callie do this, Callie do that. And Callie did it, that was the amazing thing. That was the thing that made Helen unable to stop.

*She's just like Ralph,* Helen said sometimes, with a sigh. Other times she said, with the same exact sigh, *She's a good Chinese girl. Just like I was.*

But how could Callie be just like Ralph if she was also just like Helen? And would she have had to be like either if Ralph and Helen had been happy together? Which daughter is the good daughter now, which one the bad? And what would Helen think if she realized that Mona is no longer missing—that the one unaccounted for is her very own Harvard matriculate?


When the phone rings again, Mona almost does not answer. But what if it is Callie, calling to say where she is? Mona picks up the receiver, and to her stupefaction discovers it is Sherman.

"Callie?" he says.

Mona draws in her breath. "Yes," she says.

"You sound funny."

"You do too."

"Did you find her yet?"

"You mean Mona?"

"Of course Mona."

"No news yet."

Silence. "Oh!" he says finally. "They're never going to find her!"

"You sound funny," Mona says.

"You sound funny too." He hesitates. "Callie?"

"Yes?"

"Are you Mona?" he says.

"We've always sounded a lot the same. Our own mother can't tell us apart on the phone."

"A little the same. Today you sound exactly like Mona."

Mona hangs up, and when the phone rings again, she does not answer it.


Mona sleeps in Callie's bed, in Callie's nightshirt. She washes her face with Callie's soap, she brushes her teeth with Callie's toothbrush. She consults Callie's schedule. Maybe I'll sit in on some classes, Mona thinks. For example, Bio 16: Developmental Biology. Why not? Mona walks over to the new science building, the one that looks as though a giant mutant spider got stuck in its roofing tar. On the way, there is golden leafy extravagance of a nonimmigrant sort—if these trees were kids, what a scolding they would get! *All that nice green chlorophyll their parents save up for them, and what do they do? Throw it all away! As if chlorophyll grows on trees.*

"Callie?"

Mona has never thought she looked at all like her sister, especially now that Callie wears contacts. And yet about a dozen people wave hello, only to startle when they get closer. "Oh," they say. "Sorry. I thought you were . . ."

Apparently it's their profiles that are similar, those distinctive flat noses you can hang a spoon on. Also Mona has her hair up, so you can't see how much longer it is than Callie's; and she is, after all, wearing Callie's clothes.

Mona says, "I'm her sister. She's out of town."

No one asks where Callie's gone. People are getting to their classes, getting to their seats, getting out their notebooks. Mona opens Callie's; she thinks there's no harm in trying to take notes for her sister. Not that she's exactly sure what developmental biology is. However, better developmental than full-blown biology. She figures she'll simply write down everything the professor says. If the writing's too sloppy, Callie can rip the pages out; in the meantime, Mona will have had the kind of experience that every admissions office has been struggling to provide. Here she is finally! Beyond the Campus Tour.

Mona listens. Nature, nurture. Ontogeny, phylogeny. RNA, DNA. Proteins, many -ases. She had not realized college to involve such a multitude of arrows. This professor draws big double-barreled thrusters; if they were in a museum, you would think, Oh, how quaint, that a primitive should draw penises everywhere and not even realize his libido was showing. Poor biologically determined creature that he is. So she thinks, even as she endeavors to understand what he's saying about biological determination; and that's the surprise, that she does indeed want to know what genes and proteins and -ases have to do with a person. And where does it come from, the will to make yourself into something more than your endowment? Is that just inherited too? There are Chinese Jews in China, Mona knows. Will she one day discover them to be her long-lost relatives? Auntie Leah! Uncle Irwin! She listens, listens, as if for their names; somehow she had not imagined this, that college would have to do with matters of interest.

With considerable enthusiasm, at the end of the hour, Mona consults Callie's schedule, ready for another adventure in learning; only to discover that she has a break. Already! Mona supposes it is time to return to her favorite basement café—a tiny place with tiny tables. However, with giant intellects. Or, well, a fair number of giant intellects anyway, with what appear to be some giant egos mixed in.

A tap at her elbow.

"Callie?" It's a man with a handlebar mustache.

"I'm her sister," Mona begins to explain—then realizes that before her is Rabbi Horowitz!

"Dan!" he says. "Call me Dan! I'm not a rabbi anymore." He winks. "I've converted."

"Converted!"

"Only joking. But it's true I'm not a rabbi anymore. And how is that possible? Because I married another rabbi."

"I heard she was a goy."

"Forget about a goy; she could be a leper, that's the kind of welcome she gets sometimes. And all because of what? Some long hair and hips."

The Big R.H. is wearing a tweed sport jacket with his jeans, and carrying a dark-green book bag—the grad student look, complete with political buttons all over the book bag. Also he is wearing a Mickey Mouse watch with a macramé watchband. This seems to go, somehow, with the mustache. No beard, but in its place there is plenty of sandpaper; it obviously hasn't been so easy to get rid of.

"You couldn't both be rabbis?"

"I couldn't find a job. Everyone knows I got"—he stage-whispers, cracking his knuckles—"fired."

He is more theatrical than he used to be, a bit of a character—Mona surmises this to be a kind of shell he's had to grow, and is sad for him.

"But that's not fair! You were such a great rabbi."

"Next time I apply for a position, I'll ask you for a recommendation." More knuckle-cracking. Then, thoughtfully: "It hasn't been so easy, getting used to this change."

"It's the lesson of a lifetime."

"Who said that?" He winks. "A man of great wisdom. For this is the truth: It's not so easy to get rid of your old self. On the other hand, nothing stands still. All growth involves change, all change involves loss. It's not fair to have had to pay a price for love; and yet I'm a richer person for it. A paradox." Knuckles. "Now I'm at the school of government, thinking maybe I'll do something about the world, seeing as how I'm mad at it. But tell me. How are you doing these days? You really were a terrific student, you know. A real mensch."

"I've run away from home," Mona says.

"No kidding."

"Everyone's upset."

"Do they know where you are?"

"They think I'm in France, turning French."

He laughs but insists they sit down immediately and have coffee, so that he can hear the whole story. (How much larger he seems in a bistro than in an office! His legs do not begin to fit under the table-top, especially with their Frye boots attached.) She explains and explains. Dan wants to know everything, though he does not seem so much worried as interested. He downs five cups of coffee. She explains some more.

"Some families are like that," he says in a philosophical voice. Except for the coffee-drinking, he seems to be reassuming a rabbinical posture. "Some have a brick wall around them, some a picket fence. Let me ask you. If you drew a picture of your family, what would it look like?"

"A fort," says Mona, after a moment. "Fort Chang."

"But with one vocal Jew, shouting from the ramparts. Perhaps even entirely escaped. Although to leave is to betray, is it not? In the eyes of your parents. Are you still practicing?"

"I am."

"Good for you. Though with your learning curve, pretty soon you're going to be on the lookout for a rabbi willing to marry you to a goy. And then it will start all over again, like a new batch of pancakes from your father's pancake house. Your children will seek out the proper authorities. Who am I? they'll want to know. One parent Jewish, the other a goy, and that's not even including the rest of the story." He worries his Adam's apple.

"You think I'm going to marry a goy?"

"I'm not predicting. I have simply observed this occasional generational phenomenon."

"And will you do the ceremony if I do?"

"I would say yes if I could say yes." Dan gives a big shrug, with upturned palms. "But for this, I'm afraid you'll have to ask the wife."


"I can't believe you took my notebook!" says Callie. "What are you doing here? My room is a mess, you took my schedule, you even used my toothbrush."

"*I* can't believe you check your toothbrush first thing when you come home," says Mona. "Plus you stole all my decorating ideas, and where have you been, anyway?"

It turns out Naomi and Callie have just returned from New York, where they had gone as a result of the project. They had originally intended to write a term paper based on their notes from the summer—a kind of narrative account *cum* vague thesis and impressive bibliography, complete with charts, and tables, and diagrams. The plan was to have the kind of footnotes that took up three quarters of the page each, and they weren't going to have too many *ibid*s; those just made you look as though you had only actually read one or two of the biblio books, instead of all of them. Except that lo and behold, the professor was actually more excited about the account than the enhancements—so excited, in fact, that she mentioned it to a sharpshooting New York editor. With the result that, before you could say Shit me not, Naomi and Callie were doing up a book proposal. ("It was just like you always hear," says Callie. "These Harvard profs are connected every which way.") Naomi's boyfriend Ed escorted them down to New York, but now they are back to reality, Callie especially. For delicately enough, it seems, over a lunch in squishy chairs, the editor suggested that the more personal the account the better. Meaning it should be one person's—namely, Naomi's.

"We're not book material," Callie says. "Naomi's experience has an import ours just doesn't. After all, blacks are the majority minority. Also they've been slaves and everything."

"Is that what the editor said?"

"She said I probably have a book in me too. People are interested in China, she said."

"But you've never been to China."

Callie shrugs. "She said I'm a natural ambassador."

"I thought you wanted to be a doctor."

"I think it would be cool to write a book." The next time she goes to New York, Callie says, she's going to wear a Chinese dress.

"But you've never worn one in your life," Mona says.

"I have a book in me," Callie sings in reply. "I have a book! I have a book!" and already it sounds like a song Mona has been hearing nonstop.


Helen is relieved to hear that Mona is fine. However, she is furious about Hawaii, even if Mona hasn't been there. Also she is furious about France.

"Do you want me to come back?" Mona asks finally. "It doesn't sound like you want me to come back."

She says this knowing that probably her mother does—which is exactly why, she realizes later, she should not have asked. For how could Helen say so? It would be like slapping herself in the face.

And sure enough, given no choice, Helen hangs up.

This at least renders Callie more understanding. After all, she has an inkling of what it's like to tangle with their mother. *Being on the outs,* she calls it. *On the outskirts of the skirts.* She tries to listen in appropriate big-sister fashion, and even Mona has to admit that for once she manages to ask the right questions without having the right answers. Also Callie provides helpful information. For example, that she is not surprised that Mona picked up the phone and got Sherman Matsumoto. For Sherman, she says, has called three or four times already.

"How did he get your phone number?" Mona asks.

"Beats me."

Inquires Naomi, from atop the character-building comfort of one of Callie's trunks, "Is he really your fiancé?"

"Who told you that?" says Mona

Naomi eyes the ceiling medallion. "The marriage fairy. She said you promised yourself to him when you were eleven."

"Thirteen. The fink was exaggerating."

"He called and introduced himself as your friend," Callie says.

"Now, there's a surprise," says Mona.

"And why a surprise?" inquires Naomi.

"We never see each other in person. It's all just talk on the telephone." Mona tries to explain. "He's very shy."

"Sounds like the platonic bullshit story to me," says Naomi.


Says Callie the helpful sister, when Sherman next calls: "She's at death's door. In fact, she's dead."

"Dead?" says Sherman.

"There's been a car accident."

"But she doesn't have a car."

"She was in a bus."

"Who is this?"

"This is Callie," says Callie.

Says Sherman, "I think this is someone making some joke."

"Anyway, I know she'd love it if you came."

"But if she is dead . . ."

"You meant so much to her. I know she'd want you to be at her service. You should come to my dorm. We're sitting shiva." She pronounces this *shee-veh*, which means rice gruel in Shanghainese. She gives the address.

"This kind of joke is very bad luck," says Sherman.


"You always were a terrible liar," says Mona.

Callie agrees. They agree that Naomi should have handled the call. They agree there should have been a better plan, this one had the inspiration of an overcooked pea pod. No one imagines Sherman is going to come up to Cambridge after the gala invitation issued. Still, the next day, Mona hangs around the room in funereal style. She tries calling home again. No answer. She tries the pancake house. No answer there, either, a surprise; Ralph must be shorthanded.

She thinks about what she would say to Sherman if he did show up. Hello? The few times she met Naomi's boyfriend Ed, she was struck by how he and Naomi seemed to touch the whole time. It was as if they were a single organism that only divided up for debates. *Take the South,* he would say, or *Take the Knicks,* or *Take the ancient instruments of astronomy.* And without further ado, they would be off and arguing, Naomi's proud alto holding its rich own against his profundo bass.

*Doesn't that just go to prove?*
*But the statistics say otherwise.*
*If I may clarify.*
*Therein lies the fallacy.*

Finally he would hold up his fine-boned hands in surrender; and there came an end to the pointing and the making of points. All the straightened fingers would curl. Peaceably, they would intermingle again.

Mona sighs. She figures Sherman must in his own way be in love. Probably madly. Why else would he go to the trouble of tracking her down? But when she imagines what he will do if he comes, as much as she can hope is that he will run out of the room after ten words this time, instead of five. She supposes this would be progress. However, at that rate it could be some time before they advance to full face-to-face conversation, she might as well be teaching him to speak English all over again. Not to say how to hold hands: She indulges in fantasies involving passionate forms of palm and finger contact, and so real are these scenes, so affecting the interplay of cuticle and hangnail, that Mona almost does not hear Sherman's voice on the other side of the door.

This is the blocked-off door to Naomi's room—the one with a hat rack attached to it, in front of Callie's armchair. The armchair is of the high stuffed variety, distinctly related to the wing chair. However, it is what bordello red is to Harvard crimson, or the Addams family to the Adams family. In short, a comfortable chair, but one that you might well imagine to be haunted. And so it is that when Mona first hears a tiny knocking and a "Mona?" she jumps as if something had sprung out of the stuffing.

"Mona?"

"Sherman! Is that you?"

"It is," he says.

"How did you get in?"

"Someone told me, Go in. Make myself at home, she said."

"Naomi?"

"I don't know. She told me you were behind this door."

"Was she black?"

"Yes, black."

"Naomi," says Mona.

"How come you told me you were dead?"

"That was Callie."

"How can you let people say such a thing? It's very bad luck."

"Well, it worked anyway. We were trying to get you to come up here, and sure enough, here you are."

Silence. "Why did you want me to come?"

"Oh," Mona says. "I guess I was just thinking it would be nice if we could have a conversation in person sometime."

"I am very shy," he says.

"I know." As Mona talks, she starts to move the chair. There's a bolt on the door near the top; continuing to talk, Mona attempts to finagle this open. This is not so easy, what with the peg rack full of hats in the way. Still she tries. "But why?" she says as she works. "I won't hurt you."

"I don't think you will like the way I look."

"I saw you, remember? And I thought you looked fine."

"That's not how I look anymore."

"What do you mean?"

Silence.

"What could make me not like the way you look?"

"Oh," he says. "Maybe my nose."

Mona laughs.

"Or maybe my eyes."

"I don't think so. And so sure am I of this that—" She yanks on the door.

But the door does not open; it must be bolted on the other side too.

"Sherman?" Mona says.

No answer.

"I'm sorry I tried to open the door," Mona says. "Really, I am. That would have been a dirty trick."

Silence.

"Sherman?" She bangs on the door. "Sherman? Are you there? Will you say something?"

But still there is no answer; and sure enough, by the time Mona has run around the wall and into Naomi's room, he is gone. She opens Naomi's hall door. No one. She wants to cry.

A knock on the main suite door.

"Hello?" she calls.

"Mona?"

"Sherman?"

CHAPTER 14

# A Most
# Mannerly Fellow

And Mona yanks open the ever-sticky door to welcome who else but
Seth Mandel. In voice he is Sherman Matsumoto. In person he is the
person he always was, only thinner. He is growing his hair back, also
his beard. Still through the bristle Mona can behold for the first time
the true curves of his face, which are sweeter than she would have expected, and include a surprise cleft chin. Also she beholds something
she has no doubt witnessed before, but somehow without perceiving
it—the rising flush of emotion. She would have imagined him to be
wearing in this situation a most satisfied grin—the grin of a boy who
has after concerted tinkering gotten all the switches of his train set to
work. Instead he looks more like an engineer finally in sight of his
home station—frankly just happy to see her.

"Are you surprised?" says Seth/Sherman.

"Well, let us just say that you're right," says Mona. "Yours is not
the nose of my dreams."

"Maybe I should give Barbara's doc a call?"

Mona smiles despite herself. Seth may be Sherman, but still he is
Seth. A Seth who moves differently, though. At another time, he
would have been leaning on the door molding, one hand on either
side of the frame, like a human slingshot. He would have appeared just
about ready to launch himself into the room. Now he stands square in
the doorway without laying claim to it. This is so unlike Seth that for
a moment Mona cannot imagine what he is waiting for. What is he,
shy? But no: He is simply waiting, patiently, for an invitation to enter.

And it is this pause that enables her to feel her own presence in the room—something that does not end at her skin but radiates modestly around it. It is this pause that enables her to say, with warm ambivalence, "Since when are you so polite? Come in."

He enters. He settles himself on the very chair that had not long ago seemed a talking chair; it seems for all the world to have gotten its voice back. Next comes quite a conversation. What happened to Sherman Matsumoto? it begins. Didn't Mona meet him one day in the hallway at school?

Seth explains how Sherman wasn't Sherman from the start—how in the beginning it really was Andy Kaplan on the phone. Barbara Gugelstein was right. As for why Andy did it, "It was a joke. It was a project, like growing dope in the basement."

Mona tries to keep her tone light. "Ha ha ha." She is not surprised to hear a skin of ice in her voice, though; and in a way, this is what breaks her heart, to hear her own bitterness. Bitterness—the very word so bitter to utter, what with that *b* and double *t*, not to say its associations: Decrepitude. Bunions. Gout.

Seth allows them both a moment of reflection. He still likes to match up the fingertips of his hands; that hasn't changed. He continues: As time went on, Andy got hooked. "I think he liked the challenge of it. You know how his father is a Japan expert and everything."

And did Seth help?

"Not until a lot later. No one was trying to dupe you, exactly. It wasn't a conspiracy. And I tried to tell you once, but I'd sworn on my *cojones* that I wouldn't."

Was he not telling her now?

"I've changed my mind."

Sweet reasoning. And why did Andy stop?

"He worried it was mean. Also it was getting too weird. It was weird how much he liked having an alter ego. And the secrecy. He said the secrecy had a life of its own."

In Sherman's second incarnation, Seth took over the role, to Andy's relief. Andy coached him, but Seth couldn't get the voice quite right. Ergo, Sherman turned Hawaiian.

And the Sherman Mona met?

"That was a real live Hawaiian exchange student from Larchmont High, who agreed to pretend to be Sherman on a dare. His last name really is Matsumoto, but his first name is Trevor. He was supposed to hang in there a little longer. However, he chickened out."

Mona thinks about calling him when she gets back, apologizing for her friends.

How did Seth know she was here?

"I guessed. Bea told me you were running away. She didn't think you had any money. So I figured, where could you go with no money?"

He talked to Bea?

"I called so she and Dad wouldn't worry."

Is he really going to school?

"Don't worry, I'm not taking anything for credit." He hesitates. "You know," he says, "this is the big recognition scene. If we were in a Shakespeare play, this would be the happy ending."

She should be delighted to be duped.

"You're supposed to be happy to have discovered your own true love."

And Seth is supposed to be that? Her own true love?

"Your one and only."

This is supposed to be some kind of comedy?


Though Mona really is perfectly comfortable on the floor, Callie volunteers to go stay elsewhere for the night. She does not volunteer where that elsewhere might be—a mystery apparently related to her owning two toothbrushes. It is only lucky for her that Mona is in no mood to sleuth, having plenty enough to think about already. For instance, Sherman-Andy-Seth. From the standard-issue comfort of Callie's narrow bed, Mona considers them all; then not Sherman, and not Seth, but just Andy. How thrilled Barbara will be to hear all that's transpired! And in a way, Mona looks forward to telling her, to sharing with her friend this great feast. For a feast it will surely become in conversation, a regular Thanksgiving turkey rather than a dead warty bird. In the meantime, though, alone with the *clat-clat* of typewriters and the dueling volumes of other people's music—how noisy college is!—what is Mona to make of him? Andy. Whatever it is, she will be making it; that's the only thing that's sure. It will be the kind of long-shot conjecture you associate with the origin of the universe. For Mona could write to Andy; she could sweetly or sharply inquire of him this thing or that. She could, in a word, *nudge,* and perhaps he would answer to the best of his ability. But what really will she know for it?

She can still hear the real Sherman of years and years ago: *This is a chair.* But so very much louder is the Sherman of the hot line: *If he loved her he should leave her alone.*

Is there a word for someone like Andy? Is there a name for their brand of relationship?

In fact, he is the first of many loves that will crowd her official life—unofficial plantings that will thrive for their neglect. And eventually she will learn a name for them, a word for plants that spring up on their own. Volunteers. He is like one of these—plants she will in time learn to appreciate, even as she lets them go to seed.

As for Sherman: *One thing becomes another.* That's according to Hegel according to Seth. Here too Mona tries to learn from nature. *The apple rots that the tree may grow.*


Another day, another matter: warm-blooded Seth. The ever-knocking fact of him! By the time he touches his knuckles to the suite door, wondering if Mona might like to continue their chat, she is rent asunder by the choice of which to discuss first: Topic A—Is Seth a low-down out-and-out liar? Or Topic B—How did he get to be so good at it?

Seth says he's been reading about Japan, and culture, and Zen, even though Sherman as Seth understood him was more a guy than a monk. He says it's only American hippies who think that everyone in Japan is a Zen master. And maybe the real Sherman sleeps on a bed, who knows? Still, by way of getting into his part, Seth has been sleeping on a futon. Gone are the smoky-smelling sheepskins; he's covered his teepee floor with tatami mats. He's been using chopsticks. Of course, he had been sitting on the floor to eat already. But the long hot baths have taken some getting used to, and it hasn't been easy trying to learn to cherish a certain exquisite melancholy. However, through all of this, he's begun to feel, actually, sort of Japanese. Or at least, that the Japanese manner corresponds to something in him.

"Hot baths," mulls Mona. "Melancholy. Tatami mats."

This feeling was so strong, continues Seth, that he would almost not be surprised to discover that in a previous life he had been Japanese. But then again, maybe it was something else Eastern he used to be. Just in case, he has bought himself a Nehru jacket, and some sitar tapes.

"But Seth," Mona says. "You don't believe in an afterlife, forget about a former life. Remember? You only believe in this life. You're Jewish, for Christ's sake!"

"Am I?"

They back up to Topic A.

"Things got away from us," says Seth, hands in his pockets. "Plus it's just what you always used to say—things aren't so straightforward. Sometimes deception is necessary. Even Nietzsche says that there is truth through masks."

"You were two-faced! Dishonest! You were wily and underhanded!" Mona says this knowing that she can never forgive Seth, and that his deception spells the end of their relationship. Which, she reminds him, was already ended to begin with.

"I think there's a way of being honestly insincere," he says simply. "Or do I mean sincerely dishonest? Anyway, we were stuck. We were no longer one-thing-becoming-another. You had filled in the blank, and that was that." He says, "You have to at least give me credit for commitment."

Mona stares past him—not as if he is not there, for this is not possible, but as if trying to sidestep this man.

"Maybe I should call you on the telephone?" He assumes his Sherman voice. "Is this Mona?"

She starts to cry even as she starts to laugh. "I can't believe you told me you drank beer and had a green Mustang. Maine! Lobsters!"

"Brown fat," smiles Seth. "Do you mind if I come in?"

Mona—suddenly realizing that they are still standing in the doorway—says no. Of course she does not mind, she says. And complicated as the air is between them, the simply polite thing proves to be the right thing to do. The right thing to do is to invite him to come in, and also to make himself comfortable, and even, a little later, to stay awhile with her.


So it is that Seth is all too comfortable when Ralph and Helen pay their surprise visit. Phoebe automatically shows them to Callie's bedspread, then goes back to her mirror, pencil in hand; for her Visual

Studies class, she is working most absorbedly on a portrait of herself. Seth politely stands when the Changs enter, but as he is only half dressed, his new-found manners are somewhat lost on them.

"I'm so sorry," he says. "I seem to have removed my pants." He sits back down quickly, situating a large red textbook in his lap. Unfortunately, it does not seem large enough. He opens it.

"Very studious," says Ralph distantly. "Always work hard in the restaurant. Never give us any trouble."

Everyone swallows, including Mona, who is hiding behind Seth. She has pulled the covers over her head, and is trying to make herself look like a pile of bedding.

"Just as long as Mona is okay," whispers Helen, turning to leave.

"Of course she is," says Seth warmly, reaching back toward the bedding pile and giving it a pat. The bedding pile hits him. Bedsprings creak.

Ralph helps Helen out of the room.

"I should open the door for you, but perhaps I shouldn't," says Seth.

"Thank you," says Ralph.


Did Helen see Mona? Seth thinks Helen's back was already turned when Mona delivered the fateful whack. But when Mona looks out the window, she knows what her mother knows. For Helen has always taught Mona to walk properly. Helen has always taught Mona never to drag her feet, especially in a place where people might look down on you. But there Helen is, shuffling as if she doesn't care who sees. Around her looms mighty Harvard. Enormous trees rise, the kind of trees that make you think what means girth. Their boughs reach toward some higher fraternity; they shoulder in with the brick and ivy buildings, a club. Normally, Helen would be making her way along the path with a certain polite defiance. *I am as good as any ivy plant. I am as good as any tree. Forget about girth.*

But instead her head is bent. She is holding firmly her pocketbook—Helen is never in public without her pocketbook—but the belt of her London Fog raincoat is hanging from one loop. This is an all-weather coat with zip-out lining that she's wearing; Helen bought it for half off, but would've paid full price if she'd had to, that's how well it fit. A special petite size; she hadn't had to alter a thing. She intended to wear it for the rest of her life, and maybe she will. But in the meantime, there is the belt, dangling, getting full of mud. Mona hopes her parents have parked nearby; otherwise, she's afraid, that belt's as good as lost.

Time to return to Scarshill. Mona's missed an entire week of school already; it's a little early in the year for a senior slump. Also Seth needs to get back. He's interested in his political philosophy class, and doesn't want to miss the rise of the nation-state. But Mona can't go home yet, Helen needs time to cool down. So where to stay? Until Mona has in mind someplace in particular, Seth is determined to stay with her. This being what geese do, he jokes, at least according to Konrad Lorenz.

The plan, therefore, is to fetch Seth's teepee from school, and set it back up in Seth's trusty backyard. This is preferable to leaving it where it is because while Mona needs to go to school every day, Seth has only two days of classes a week; and what is a thirty-mile bike ride to Big Chief Thunder Thighs? However, they do have misgivings about this plan. The first being Bea. What a position to put her in! Will she not feel obliged to inform Mona's mother? Then there will be a scene such as no one is exactly prepared for. And what if Bea keeps mum, and Helen finds out on her own? (As she is bound to, Scarshill being not so big a town.) Then poor Bea will have the dickens to pay too. All this they discuss with Barbara Gugelstein on the phone. (Seth has done the calling, so as to bypass Barbara's mom.) Barbara promises to mull the problem over, and by the time she picks them up at the train station in her parents' car, she has for unveiling Plan Alfred. Id est, why don't they go live in her house? For this, it turns out, is now her ex-house.

"We've moved," says Barbara.

"So fast!" says Mona.

Barbara, wearing sunglasses, explains how the house turned out to have been leased.

"Is that like rented?" Mona asks.

"It wasn't ever even really ours; all we owned was an option to buy. My dad had to beg to be allowed to break the contract. Beg and pay, I should say." Barbara laughs unnaturally. It seems Mr. Gugelstein is now officially unemployed. "Usually people are out of work a month for every ten thousand dollars of salary. That's what my dad says. That's the rule of thumb."

"Oh! I'm so sorry," says Mona. "I mean, that he made so much money."

Barbara seems to sink into herself. "We were just lucky we still had our original house to move back into. There was an offer on it, but the people didn't get their financing, and the deal fell through." She goes on to say that there's no new occupant in the house as of yet, and while a broker might come by every now and then, so what? Aren't there are a million places to hide, not to say the tunnel?

The grounds are being kept up, but Mona can tell even from the driveway that no one is home. For one thing, there are no curtains on the windows, meaning that from certain angles you can see right through the house. Mona finds this somehow indecent; maybe living with Seth the sex maniac is making her think like a sex maniac too. Or maybe this is just what happens when you start using in conversation words like *innuendo*—a word she formerly could've gotten right on a multiple-choice question, but not one she actually employed every day. With her and Seth happily interpenetrating, however, she finds she reaches for it as she would for a ketchup bottle.

The electricity is still on, but Mona and Seth hesitate to use the lights for fear of giving themselves away; and it is surprising how long the evening trails on as a result. No wonder Alfred wanted a radio! They wish they had one too, and that's even with each other for diversion. They zip together their zipper-compatible sleeping bags. They huddle into each other, grateful for the thin comfort of their foam sleeping pads. Fugitives, they are. Homesteaders.

Nothing, though, stretches on so long as Mona's first day back at high school. How strange it all seems! The desks, the bells, the overhead projectors; even the parking lot seems strange. She sees people circling, looking for a good spot, hoping to avoid having to park all the way down the muddy road by the stream, and she remembers harboring such hopes herself. Though why should she have been afraid of a little mud? Seeing as how she was wearing hiking boots. How ridiculous seem these concerns now; and how much easier to exit this world than she ever would have dreamed. She writes herself a sick note. She tells her classmates she was out with a stomach bug, she must've lost five pounds. Envious sympathy. People compliment her; Mona feels positively svelte. No one seems to notice that Mona is wearing Callie's clothes. And outside of Barbara Gugelstein, no one seems to have the least idea about Mona's other life except Rachel Cohen. Several times she has tried to call, Rachel says, only to get hung up on. Is something the matter? Has Mona been grounded? Mona does not answer, but only stands in the jewelry shop like a big locked-up supply closet.

The house stays warm by itself, a mysterious phenomenon no doubt linked to its authentic Norman-style walls; through some equally mysterious technology, it generates dust balls of a mansionate scale. Barbara comes to visit. This is a pleasant if sobering interlude; one thing she forgot to mention, she says, is that her family had been having trouble with disappearing objects. *Right before we moved. Nothing too serious, but maybe the tunnel.* Mona and Seth should be spooked by this information. Who would break in now, though, to a house full of nothing? It is just one more thing, they agree, like the cavernous rooms, the air of palpable desertion, the whole ghost town feel. Those should spook them too.

Instead they are coming to feel at home in the emptiness. *Very Zen,* says Seth, and Mona can feel what he means. The rooms no longer cry out for furniture, or rugs, or tchotchkes; they no longer seem to be missing anything. In fact, there are things that could yet be removed— for example, the milkmaid murals. Garish as billboards these look, perhaps because Mona and Seth are at peace.

It is as if they have finally taken that trip to the Cascades together— as if they are catching fish for dinner, and melting snow for water, and repitching their tent at night because of the wind. Seth says if they really lived together, it wouldn't be so idyllic, and Mona knows he's right. She knows they would write in each other's books, and scratch each other's records, and put clothes in the dryer that said Hang Dry right on their labels. But so sweet is this present life that Mona wishes it could go on forever—a sweet background, say, to backpacking forays in various sub-continents. As for which subcontinents and in what order, they debate this lustily, employing without hesitation the lowest tactics available.

What with the threat of brokers, they don't cook, exactly; in fact, all they eat are sardine sandwiches (with Tabasco sauce and lemon juice, this is—Seth's specialty), and they wash their dishes immediately. Mostly they use the tunnel to come and go. Still there are scares. For example, one day someone comes to view the house. Mona and Seth squirrel themselves away, listening as the realtor opens every closet door; apparently the customers have complex storage needs. These needs are discussed at length. Then on to further complications. In egalitarian fashion, the customers, a couple, have one each. The man's being his gym equipment. There is much discussion about where best to locate the bar bells and stationary bike, and if it would be possible to enclose the outdoor pool. The woman's concern is drafts. She worries that if they were to simply move the greenhouse so as to house the pool, the result would be drafty. Also several of the larger rooms look as though they would have drafts.

"I've an absolute horror of colds," says the woman.

"We spent two years in Scotland," explains the man.

"The worst years of our life," says the woman.

"A most unfortunate assignment," says the man.

"We only barely survived," says the woman. "And that was thanks to boiled wool."

Seth and Mona are barely able to make it down the back steps without laughing; and for the next several days, they too give thanks to boiled wool. How is it that, way back when, they happened to both sign up for the hot line? Was it or was it not thanks to boiled wool? And how was it that Seth happened to save Mona from the attacker? What would they have done if it weren't for boiled wool!

The phone rings. Should they pick it up? The sound glances off the walls, an edged noise. Ten times, a pause, then ten times again. Then twenty times. Wasn't phone service cut off? Did someone order it back on?

"If I didn't know better," says Mona, "I'd think it was Sherman Matsumoto."

More realtors.

And yet another day, squeaking. By this time, they are used to emergencies, their hearts do not palpitate. Neither do their palms sweat or their stomachs secrete stomach acid such as produces security-threatening burps. This is a scrambling under the floorboards that sounds distinctly like claws.

"Squirrels," guesses Seth.

Is he right? *Scratch, scratch,* they hear, but also a *thump thump thump.*

"That must be the daddy squirrel. Someone has taken his boiled wool."

More thumping; more woolly jokes. The thumping approaches.

"Closet time," says Seth.

"Let's just hope it's not someone with complex storage needs," says Mona.

They manage to sequester themselves just as the footsteps approach. Another realtor? They figure it must be, even though this person does not turn any of the lights on—an odd thing at dusk. The realtors always turn the lights on, even in broad daylight, so that the house seems as bright as possible. It's a trick everyone knows, but they do it anyway. Whereas this person prefers dark. From their hiding place, Mona and Seth hear him scrape along. Swearing.

"Peekaboo," wheedles the voice. "I see you."

He is standing right outside the closet door. Mona's calf muscles pull, but she doesn't dare move except to put her hand down for balance. A mansionate dust ball; the floor through its diaphanous heft is gritty. With her other hand she cups Seth's kneecap. Seth loops his arm around her shoulder—leaning on her more than she'd like, or is that just the weight of his arm? He smells as if there is peppermint soap still left in his shirt. She watches the dim line of light at the bottom of the door.

"Come out, come out, wherever you are."

"Drunk," whispers Seth. And of course, Mona's attention lists his way, so that she almost does not hear the man outside the closet say something very like "Oh, Mona."

Did he really say her name?

"Skinny monkey."

"That's what Cedric used to call us," whispers Mona.

"What?" says Seth.

Mona does not dare repeat herself.

"Skinny monkey."

Cedric sounds nothing like himself.

"Did you say Cedric?" says Seth. Even in the dark, Mona can see him lighting up. Delight is dawning, the whole scene about to become an improbable joke.

"Shh," she says.

Still his arm drops down her back; they're out of their huddle. *"Cedric?!"* So loudly, there seems to be an echo.

"Cedric!" she says then, even louder, figuring the gig to be up. "Are you drunk?" And she bursts into the room, occasioning with the closet door a collision.

The burglar reels. For it is indeed a burglar, complete with royal-blue winter gloves and a matching cold-weather face mask. He holds his hand up to his head, twisting the mask out of alignment.

"Fuck," he says.

"You're not Cedric," says Mona.

"Fuck." The burglar tries to adjust his mask so that the eyeholes are back over his eyes, but this is not so easy with winter gloves on. Also he is not so steady on his feet. He is a meaty man in a jacket with no zipper; his mechanic-blue pants have no hem at the bottom. His fly is open.

Seth emerges. "Who are you? And what are you doing here?"

"Fuck," says the burglar again, still working on his mask.

"Vocabulary is the better part of grammar," observes Seth. "How did you get in here?"

When the burglar doesn't answer, Seth and Mona exchange glances.

"Anyway," she says, "I think we know his answer to that question, don't we?"

"The tunnel?" says Seth.

"No, 'Fuck,' " says Mona.

"Fuck you!" says the burglar, struggling to stay on his feet. He glares at them with the one eye he has finally managed to line up with an eyehole; also he breathes aggressively, as if realizing his breath to be his most potent weapon.

"Why don't you just take that thing off," says Mona. "You'll be able to see better."

"It's my mask," he says thickly.

"Hmm," says Mona, "And how did you discover the tunnel?"

"A groundhog showed me."

"But it's camouflaged," says Seth. "It's not so easy to see."

Says the man, tottering, "From the right place, you can see anything." And with this he slumps conveniently to the floor.

# Discoveries

Fernando! The cook who put a curse on the house of pancakes—now a burglar! And possibly the attacker of yore—Seth thinks he must be.

"Can't you see," insists Seth. "He's been stalking you."

And how elegant it would be for that to be true! Two large-man experiences, made into bookends.

"The attacker was hairy, Fernando is hairy," allows Mona. "But you are hairy too."

So she says. For already she knows this symmetry will elude them; and this is one of the many things they discuss on their way to Alfred's apartment in Barbara's new van (which she finally just went and bought for herself, believing it to be actually her old van). Map in hand, they discuss coincidence, and pattern, and the sorts of synchronicities such as are no more than you can expect from novels, but that in real life do give you the heebie-jeebies. Also Mona and Seth discuss whether they were right to leave Fernando lying there. Can a passed-out person come to harm? (They think not.) And will he come after Mona again? They probably should have called the police. They probably should not have simply penned a longish note, expecting him to be touched by the power of words. What youthful folly! They agree about this.

And, of course, they discuss their great discovery—namely, that in Fernando's jacket pocket was tucked Mr. Gugelstein's silver flask. Is this truly a discovery? They recognize this moment, naturally: The false cupboard back, the clue in the courtyard. *Her heart beat faster.* Then what? Mystery solved, end of book. Except what have Seth and Mona found? For all they know, someone else stole the flask. For all they know, Fernando bought it in a pawnshop. For all they know, this is not Mr. Gugelstein's flask at all, but a fake, maybe even the fake they themselves made.

They know only that they should not have drawn conclusions about the mod squad. Also that they don't know by what stony path the old Fernando has come to be the new.

"He was a great cook," says Mona.

"Alfred?" says Seth.

"Fernando. Alfred was a great cook too. But Fernando was a perfectionist. He was always on time. He dressed up on his days off in these shiny shoes, and he had a shiny car to match. You've never seen such hubcaps."

"But he punched Cedric."

"That's why he was fired."

"And he stole something, right?"

"A case of minute steaks," says Mona. "Or so we thought. In fact, we don't know what happened. Let's face it, The Silver Flask Incident is nothing but a remake of The Minute Steak Case."

"Pun forgiven."

"Fernando thought he would lose his job to people like Cedric, and what do you know? He did." Mona says again, "He was a great cook. I'm sure we didn't single-handedly ruin him. On the other hand . . ." She pulls the van over, waves down a pedestrian, asks directions.

Andy, the attacker, Fernando, and who knows who else?—each with an unofficial contribution to her life. Little packages she never ordered but that arrived in the mail all the same. *Sender unknown.*

And she, and her family, with their unofficial contributions. They send out packages too. *Addressee forgotten. Package returned. Curses due.*

How to right the wrong? Can teshuvah ever be made?


Are Seth and Mona in the right place at all? They are looking for garden apartments, but see only six low brick buildings, distinctly gardenless; in fact, distinguished mostly by how burnt is the grass patch before them. The north-facing buildings boast assorted live weeds. The south-facing buildings boast grass of the extreme low-maintenance kind. *Kentucky brown grass,* jokes Seth. *Westchester ex-grass.* The patches are separated by a grid of concrete walkways. Of course, it is fall here, as it is elsewhere in the greater metropolitan area; the walkways are littered with curled-up dead leaves. At the same time, this courtyard feels like summer—there being, mysteriously, not only no trees of girth, but no trees at all, only an onslaught of sun. A ceiling of sun, it seems, an immovable radiant slab. The entries have concrete stoops with gap-toothed railings, and striped metal awnings that afford hankies of shade; these fall wide of the stoops and the people, but do provide trapezoids of respite for the litter-flowered prickle bushes. The most hospitable shade is cast by a bright-blue dumpster at the end of the brick horseshoe; a couple of kids hog this, they've even set up lounge chairs. From these they stare, like the adults on the stoops, at the visitors.

"Ain't no Alfred 'round here," a large man announces, rucking up his mouth. "No Alfred, no Knickerbocker. Never was none, either."

But even as the man makes this declaration, Alfred leans out a second-story window like a surprise Juliet. In place of a ring of roses or other spriggy hairdress, he is wearing a chef's hat in full pouf.

"It's all right," he says. "These are my friends." He makes a swinging gesture with his hand, like Ed Sullivan giving a big welcome: "That girl there, see, I'm suing her daddy."

"Ah so!" the man says then. He puts his hands together as if in prayer, and gives a little bow. Then, with a mock-Oriental accent: "You mean A-fled! Why you no say so?" He calls, "Ahh-fled! Ahhh-fled!"

People laugh. No one moves, but something seems to roll back as Mona and Seth make their way down the walkway; something allows them passage.

Alfred's apartment is small but brightly lit; the decor is wood-grain electronic. There are speakers the size of easy chairs; a tower of other circuitry; records; a TV with an enormous rabbit-ear antenna. For furniture, there is a red leatherette Mediterranean couch; two folding chairs of no particular background; and a Spanish coffee table shaped like a guitar. The metal scrollwork of the last is propped up with cinder block, and in its sound hole is a bowl full of cigarette butts. Bottle caps. A Roach Motel. Packages of gum. Altogether, it presents the picture of bachelorhood to Mona, only Seth could discern a resemblance to the Gugelsteins' place. Still he launches into a description of *our Zen pad,* as he calls it, and as he segues into the comparison, Mona finds herself seeing the Zen in Alfred's pad too. Not that she is convinced. She is simply looking again.

As, it appears, is Alfred. His face, when they first entered, was furrowed with wariness; she'd never seen him so horizontal of aspect.

Now he seems reoriented toward the vertical. He throws his head back, he is positively animated. His chef's hat languishes on a counter-top like a half-collapsed soufflé.

"You're shitting me, man!" He offers Mona and Seth beers. "You mean you're hanging around all night with no bed and no lights on and no radio, either? How come you don't get that Miss B. to correct the situation, now? How come you don't ask her to bring you something nice?"

Alfred lights a cigarette; Mona and Seth explain and explain. But it's like trying to beat dust out of a rug—the more they beat, the more dust there seems to be. Among other things, they try to convey why Mona can't move home, and also about what most unfortunately happened to Mr. Gugelstein.

Alfred is outraged. "The motherfuckers!" he says, cigarette in mouth. "You mean, they fucking crossed our Jew-daddy?"

"They did, they fucking did!" exclaims Mona. She wants to say *our Jew-daddy* in group-affirming style—it's what they learned in hot-line training, to echo the person they're talking to—but she can't bring herself to do it. Seth, though, as if reading her mind, supplies, "Can you believe it? To our very own Jew-daddy, this happened! It could've been my daddy!"

They continue with the story. At the word *sue,* Alfred seems to puff harder; his outrage on Mr. Gugelstein's behalf explodes again. "Somebody messes with you, you've got to pay them back," he says. "Otherwise, they're just going to mess with you again, man. What's he going to do now? Nothing? You're telling me a rich bastard like him is going to punk out?"

Alfred listens some more, then it's his turn to talk about what's happened since the firing. "See," he says, twice, but doesn't go on until Mona asks him about a little golden chef's hat atop one of the speakers in the corner.

"That's my award," he says with satisfaction.

Not only does Alfred have a new job in a steakhouse, he's won this award; it's one of the nice things about working for a big-time outfit, that they have awards and softball teams, shit like that. Plus he's training other cooks now. "I'm getting over all right," he says. Also, a surprise: He's back in touch with Evie.

"Eee-vie," he says, grinning. "That girl's crazy as a clock with one hand. Can't tell her nothing, see, without she's going to tell you what time it is. Time for us to have a talk. Time for us to try something else. Time for us to think creative. I told her a million times, You're dealing in zeroes, babe. But that girl's got wax in her ears. She even called up Charlene, man. Called her on the telephone."

"And?" says Mona.

But there's no elaboration. He's looking down, thinking of something, and when he looks back up, he could be the Cheshire cat crossed with the Mona Lisa. Once again there is something he's keeping from them, maybe just a certain satisfaction. Is it on account of the word *telephone*? As in, *I-done-used-the-tel-e-phone*—?

Still Mona says, "We have something for you," and presents him with the flask. "We apologize," she says. "We sincerely apologize. Please tell the rest of the gang too."

"This is the flask the Jew-daddy lost?"

"This is it."

Alfred takes the flask, then looks away. Mona expects him to ask where they found it, but he doesn't.

"Luther got beat up," he reports instead. "He went down to the protest, and got beat just about dead."

Mona's heart blows open. "Is he okay?"

"That Luther's always all right in the end," says Alfred carefully. It's as if he's keeping even his doubt to himself. Then, as if to change the subject, he looks hard at Seth, and even harder at Mona. "Knew soon as you showed up you'd be wanting me and the Race Man to drop that suit against your daddy," he says.


On the way home, Mona imagines her mother's face, lit with relief. She had not dared imagine Alfred would drop the suit; she wasn't even convinced that he should. In a way, she would have liked to apologize without receiving anything in return. At the same time, she imagines the in-suck of her mother's body as it straightens—a little lighter, a little younger—and this makes Mona feel similarly floaty. She has rarely seen Helen take a deep breath, but those few times she's remarked on a certain gasp in the middle. It is as if Helen drew the air through some cinch; as if her lungs were, quite uniquely, shaped like an hourglass. Mona imagines the hourglass full. Her mother most certainly does not stoop as she walks; and why would she let the belt of her raincoat drag on the ground? Instead she is smiling; she is standing behind Mona on the front steps. *No problem! No problem!*

"Mom? Mom? I'm home!" Mona bursts into the kitchen. The metal screen door wheezes almost shut behind her—that pneumatic tube—she reaches out automatically. A familiar click.

How different the kitchen air feels from the air outside! It smells different too, of course—like sesame oil today. But mostly she notices how enveloping it is, how moist, and warm. She feels as though she breathes differently in this house, her home; certainly she moves differently through its atmosphere. More slowly. All this is familiar.

And yet what she sees, she sees for the first time—namely what a veritable jumble is the kitchen, it's as if all the years her family has spent shopping the bargain basement have inspired them to re-create it right in their own home. Everything is in piles; piles could almost be a design element, a kind of unifying theme. Then there is the walnut sheet paneling they put up themselves, with the still unfilled nail holes; there the authentic Swiss cuckoo clock, with its fancy-cut hands and pine cone weights. There is the suspended grid ceiling with its fluorescent light panels; and there too are the Mediterranean-look cabinets crammed full of cans and bottles, rolls of things, years of stuff. So many of her friends had organized cabinets; and maybe Mona would too, one day. Cabinets with swing-out features—with lazy Susans, and pot-lid holders. Maybe Mona would one day have the kind of kitchen where leftovers get whisked into zip-lock bags, and there are no refrigerator odors. At Barbara's house, you can actually see to the back of the refrigerator; the whole thing's lit up like a hospital corridor. It's not jam-packed with glass and clay and plastic containers full of shrivelly, pickley, primordial foods, all of them pungent, and unlabeled, and probably unlabelable, seeing as you can hardly even say what color they are. Brownish, greenish, blackish. Maybe one day Mona would have the kind of kitchen that bespoke law and order and recipes you can write down.

But then again, maybe her kitchen would be exactly like this. A bargain basement, hardly elegant, hardly a place where you could execute with efficiency your culinary intentions; but where you might start out making one thing, only to end up, miraculously, with a most delicious *dish du jour.*

"Mom?"

No answer.

"Mom?"

Mona starts up the stairs, only to have Helen appear at the top. Even though it is daytime, Helen is wearing her old quilted bathrobe, which features squarish diamond buttons. These look as if they were designed to light night games at Yankee Stadium. As three of them are missing, however, Helen is using safety pins in their stead. Mona shudders. Helen looks as though she has just woken up. Her hair is disheveled, longer than Mona remembers; it almost touches her shoulders. Can Mona really have been away that long? But, no—Helen's hair only seems long on account of her failure to set it the way she usually does, with her medieval pink rollers. This is what Naomi would call her natural, however unnatural it looks. Helen is not wearing her glasses, either, and this gives her a look of sudden age. Flesh seems strangely collected around her eyes. It is as if after so many years of wearing glasses, her face has evolved an answering structure—its own soft-sculpture frames, which return her gaze to an inner focal point.

"Who is this?" she says.

"Me," says Mona. "It's me, Mona."

The carpet of the stairs seems to mute her words; that absorbent plush. Helen retreats to her room, her backless slippers softly clopping. Whereas Mona has never been a slipper wearer, her mother's slippers seem part of her feet, and the sound of them too seems the sound of her mother, they're like horseshoes on a horse.

Mona dogs Helen pathetically, also knocks on Helen's door pathetically. The knocks are strangely loud and rapping—the door, though not hollow, is not as solid as she remembered.

"Mom?" She calls through the wood. "Mom?" No answer. Still she continues hopefully. "We talked to Alfred. He's going to drop the suit!"

Helen emerges on cue. "Who is this?" she says, opening the door. "Is this my daughter?"

"It is!" Mona tries to keep up the pathetic air despite her enthusiasm. "And guess what? Alfred is dropping the suit! We talked to him!"

"What are you talking about, talked to Alfred?" says Helen, mildly. "And who is this *we*?"

Helen returns to her bedroom; and this time she doesn't even close the door, she doesn't have to. For it's as if this is what she's seen with her glasses off, operating on inner sight—that this disturbance can be trusted to leave by herself. Finally she's big enough not to need to be told.

# Epilogue

Some years later, Mona is visiting Aunt Theresa. She is now sort of married to Seth; they're going to be more married soon. Meaning that there have been extrarelationship lovers along the way—little vista points off a generally scenic highway—and also they never did have any kind of ceremony, much less a getaway car trailing tin cans. However, they're common-law married, like it or not—the kind of married that arrives like a Welcome Wagon gift from your friendly federal government if you share a bed and bath for more than long enough.

And finally, Mona the Uncommitted has agreed to stand up in a room full of folding chairs. No huppah, no glass, a most modest reception. She and Seth will kiss. Presumably there will be clapping. They've said no presents, but are secretly regretting their nobility.

For witnesses they have trusty Barbara Gugelstein, who's flying out for the nonevent, and a friend of Seth's from ed school—Dave, his name is. The two of them both still sport beards, but Mona is the one with a ponytail now; she's too busy to wear her hair any way but out of the way. Mona could also have asked a friend from college or grad school. All-play Maureen, for example, or no-play Louise. But Barbara was the first person who came to mind—Barbara, who these days spritzes her hair to frizz it up more, and who immediately agreed to *be there for them*. After all, Mona's been a bridesmaid for her twice. First when she married Andy Kaplan, and then when she married him again, and who knows but there may be a third time? She and Andy are the longest-running show off Broadway, maybe it wouldn't have been so bad if they didn't both work for the airlines. But as it is, they seem to be endlessly circling some control tower, being denied permission to land.

To be honest, Barbara thinks Mona should ask Eloise Ingle instead;

it would be better luck. Charmed, matronly Eloise, after all, has forged on with her foundation work despite two sets of twins. (Her only life mistake has been getting married on a beach full of greenheads.) Or what about Rachel Cohen, who lives right in the area these days? The epitome of stability, and quite the success as a sculptor—big, ungainly, clattering contraptions she makes, all the while remaining seamlessly self-contained herself. Perfectly, contentedly attachment-free. Or no, no, no—the obvious choice! Alfred and Evie, the love bugs, Mr. and Mrs. Community Organization. They've marched, they've cooked, they've given up denying that she married him to assuage her own guilt, or that he's a white-bitch-lover who shouldn't have needed her to get him through college. They figure every marriage involves some horse trade; at least theirs worked. They don't beat on each other; they pay their bills; and they pay the bills of their friends in need—for instance, that Luther. Also they're attentive parents to their three death-defying tree-dwellers. Everyone's expecting the Knickerbocker clan to be made into a TV show, and what with Naomi now an author and her main man a producer, who knows but that they won't? Naomi says she's ready to stop playing the superwoman. She's going to rest on her laurels, no more high-profile projects; she says she's going to bake bread and make applesauce, and that lately she's been thinking a lot about ginger. Also babies, and the old neighborhood. She's thinking about volunteering in a youth program.

Still everyone can see the full-color production.

And of course, there is also Callie. You can always ask, says Barbara. You never know.

But Mona doesn't see why she should ask someone who's going to be ambivalent. Barbara is her first choice, and as for the presiding authority, that will be the authorities two—Rabbi Horowitz and Rabbi Horowitz. The latter being also known as Mrs. Horowitz—a most learned, exuberant, voluminous woman, whom Mona used to admire in all ways except one. Namely, why did she change her name? Mona couldn't help but wonder. Libby truly was a libber, after all—the only person Mona ever met who really did once burn a bra. (She said it half burned, half melted, and that she never would have done it without a fire extinguisher right there.) But then it turned out that her name was already Horowitz before she met the Big R.H. And what was she going to do, change it to something else? Of course, it did cause some confusion when Dan found a new job and became the other Rabbi Horowitz. But then, as he likes to say, every love has something in it to put up with. *I put up with this Rabbi Horowitz like I put up with myself.*

Such a production, this wedding, for a non-production! Mona and Seth could have opted to do the deed more privately; and sometimes they discuss this option still, even though Mona has her dress, and the baker's lined up. For really, they are marrying for money. What they have on their minds is mostly their major medical. But what the hell, they were going to throw a one-year birthday party anyway, for little Io. Their toddler trundler has just learned to walk; she holds her arms in the air as if determined to surrender to the first sheriff she meets.

"Two birds with one cake," said Seth when the idea first arose. "I like that."

All three of them are going to adorn the top tier. This will be on the outside, butter cream, on the inside, zwieback crackers.

Quips Mona, still an active mouth: "How easy to tie the knot, once you've cut the cord."

"That's my Mona," says Seth. "Still yolking after all these years."

In truth, they still experience their share of relationship difficulties. Seth's become a professor and generally noble type, meaning that he is married to his tenure prospects. Mona the second wife is thinking about going back to work too—she left a real almost-paying free-lance job at B'nai B'rith, researching ethnic cartoons—but how will they divvy up the child-care duties? "I feel like a heel," says Seth, "if that makes you feel any better." And sometimes it does. Other times, though, when they are discussing what means job, and ambition, and manhood, Mona wishes that she could open a door and discover, not Sherman turned into Seth, but—to her utter stupefaction and relief—Sherman turned into a woman.

By now she takes it for granted that she and her mother do not speak to each other. When Io was born, she thought surely her parents would relent, never mind that she and Seth weren't married. She looked at her pink-prune child with her many sweet reflexes and imagined that at any moment her parents were going to burst through the door, if only so that her mother could judge for herself whether Io could pass for pure Chinese with that nose. She imagined that Theresa would talk them into it; or how could they resist honey from the Bea? Seth and Mona had an agreement: If her mother came to the hospital, they would name the baby Helen. In fact, they almost did not pick a backup name. For how could her parents stay away?

And indeed, her father came, bearing a teddy bear the size of a small couch.

But Io became Io, and Mona's whole gory story is no longer even an active topic of conversation. There is no why or what-if talk anymore—only how to scare up the airfare to California. For Mona has come to take for granted that this is how she spends her holidays, at the beach.

The beach: This is not so bad. Auntie Theresa's fold-out couch is the most rickety imaginable, but in anticipation of fashion, Seth has dug out his old futon—his mattressmoto, he calls it. This is their back-saver. Io, luckily, still fits in a drawer. The endless leave and return of the water restores in them a sense of rhythm—a balance of cycle and reach—and Mona enjoys the cats. She enjoys too the tales Auntie Theresa and Uncle Henry tell about the West Coast—all about how eucalyptus trees came to California, and snails. Mona has not heard such delicious stories about greed gone wrong since she turned Jewish; it might as well have been the pharaoh who imported this completely useless tree for timber, or brought on this gastropod plague. Mona thought she'd never get used to the latter. But now she steps around those escargots no problem, just as she does the truly gross banana slugs.

Theresa and Henry tell tales about the family too, which Mona could not bear to hear in the beginning. But now she is happy to consider her sadness in new ways; it's sort of a sick hobby. Theresa includes in her stories all kinds of things no one else would consider worth telling. For instance, how Helen used to measure out the water for washing the floor; also the Spic and Span. This is a Helen Mona never knew—a young woman not sure what mattered, someone a little like Mona herself, except quiet, and full of secrets. Secrets? What secrets? Mona wants to know. But Theresa will never say what they were, though she knows everything. She knows what size girdle

Helen wore, and that Helen once cried because her shoes and pocketbook didn't match. She knows how Helen learned to play bridge
with a bridge-a-matic. And how much she hated old cars! All that
overheating. Mona remembers the overheating herself, just as she remembers Helen's shopping habits—how expertly she picked fruit in
the supermarket. And she remembers how soft her mother's skin was.
She remembers being allowed to touch her mother's stomach once.
And indeed her mother's skin was the softest thing she ever felt—
softer than any silk, any chick, any moss.

She imagines this soft-skinned woman, reading magazines. This
soft-skinned woman, learning to cook. She imagines her mother, still
soft-skinned, writing to her family, year after year, only one day—
finally!—to get a reply, and the news that her parents were dead.

This has happened since Mona's break with her mother. Mona put
a yellow ribbon in her hair, just like Callie, as a sign of mourning. She
wrote her mother a note.

But of course, it is now she who writes, and does not hear back,
and wonders.

Her dad: Mona knows that Helen knows that Mona is in touch with
Ralph. Still there is an air of complicity to their rendezvous. Ralph is
aging gracefully, things are going well—he's found an herb medicine
for his stomach, for one thing. For another, he's bought that second
restaurant after all, and is resisting halfheartedly a third. After all, he
knows he can make it work, having just the man to put in charge.
Namely, Moses, a black cook and a good friend to Julio Alvarez, who
replaced Cedric when he and Richard and Edward decided to open
their own business. (This last being an ice cream store where you can
have your ice cream warmed up if it's too cold, and where, if you
change your mind, you can have some sesame noodles or moon cakes
instead.) By Ralph's own admission, Julio and Moses are people he
probably would have overlooked ten years ago; they take some getting used to, is his explanation for the change. "Before I was not used
to it." (*Used to it* still being a big phrase in his thinking, maybe even
bigger than *make sure.*) Of course, relying on blacks is not the only
thing Ralph's learned. He's also learned to keep the Chinese help in

back. *Dining room is about make the customers happy,* he shrugs. And then he quotes Moses: *Some things just be's that way.*

As for having a common-law son-in-law, who could get used to that? Yet Ralph has. Nowadays Ralph even boasts to his friends about Seth. *My son-in-law, he eats everything,* he says. *Even the leftovers he eats. Right out the refrigerator. He does not even use the microwave oven, that's what kind of son-in-law I have.* And Ralph's friends are impressed. *Eats everything,* they say. *Not even Chinese, but he eats everything.* This is in contrast to some of their sons-in-law, who *don't eat this, don't eat that.* These are *picky guys,* according to Ralph. *Those guys soft. Those guys good for nothing. Never get anywhere.*

As for where Seth will get as a result of his eating habits, Ralph doesn't say, he leaves it for Mona to predict, *The hospital.* For Seth eats even the fat on Auntie Theresa's red cooked pork—the fat that sits atop each piece of meat like a shiny square sponge layer. Mona sets hers aside; and she never cooks it this way herself, with the fat as thick as your thumb. For in her view, people in China can afford to eat that sort of thing, but it is another thing altogether for people in America. People in America having, after all, too many sources of calories already. For example, *latkes.* (These Mona deep-fries in a wok that Bea gave her.)

Callie: Ralph is not the only one who has changed, Callie has too. She loves being a pediatrician, even if it means endlessly discussing *ehh-ehh*—BMs she calls them now. Moreover, she has turned more Chinese than Seth—so Chinese that Ralph and Helen think there is something wrong with her. Why does she wear those Chinese padded jackets, for example? They themselves now wear down parkas, much warmer. And cloth shoes! Even in China, they never wore cloth shoes, they always had nice imported leather. And why does she call herself Kailan? So much trouble to find her a nice English name, why does she have to call herself something no one can spell? She says she's proud to be Asian American, that's why she's using her Chinese name. (Her original name, she calls it.) But what in the world is an Asian American? That's what Ralph and Helen want to know. And how can she lump herself together with the Japanese? The Japanese *Americans,* insists Callie/Kailan. After what they did during the war! complain Ralph and Helen. And what, friends with the Koreans too? And the Indians? The parents shake their heads. Better to turn Jewish than Asian American, that's their opinion these days. At least Jews don't walk around with their midriffs showing!

Or so Callie reports. Mona thinks she exaggerates a little—wanting to feel like she isn't only about the straight and narrow, even if she does lead a straight A life, what with the two beautiful children and the big-success husband, and the single-family house with double-dug flower beds. *I left home too,* she says sometimes. *I'm my own person. I made my own choices.* The truth is, she would stand up for Mona and Seth in a minute, if Mona asked. But Mona isn't sure she wants to ask someone who also says, *You did what you wanted, someone had to pick up the pieces.* And: *It would have killed Mom if we'd both been like you. It might kill her yet.*

The big day minus one: Is that right, that Mona might be the death of her mother? Mona has heard all about Helen's heart problems; it hasn't sounded so very bad. Still she worries.

At least Callie is coming to the wedding, there's that much good news. For a while it was maybe she will, maybe she won't; Mona probably shouldn't have made such a big deal of how it was no big deal. In any case, Callie will be arriving in a few hours. Ralph will be here soon too; and Auntie Theresa, of course, is already here, as are Bea, and Seth's dad, Phil, and Seth's infamous three half-brothers. Isn't that enough family?

"What's the matter?" Auntie Theresa wants to know.

Mona is trying on her dress. She's not sure how appropriate it is for a mother to wear white to her wedding. However, this is the plan. She and Seth happened one day on something long and antique, with a billowing skirt; it had seemed like fun in the store. Now, though, she thinks she looks like a tent display. She thinks she might as well have decided to get married in a huppah instead of under one. "Maybe I'll wear something else," she says.

"Like what something else?"

"My purple suit."

"You could." Theresa has been extra patient these days; she just goes around opening the shut windows and shutting the open ones. "Is it clean?"

Mona frowns. Io spit up on it last week. "Maybe I should rethink the flowers."

"You could," says Theresa again. And again: "Is something the matter?"

Mona doesn't say, except to ask what Theresa thinks of the veil. Mona doesn't have to wear it; someone just lent it to her in case she wanted to do the whole corny shebang. And what about her name? Should she change it in this wedding tomorrow?

"To Mandel?" says Theresa, surprised. "No more women's lib? Mona Mandel. Mona Mandel." She tries it out. "It sounds very nice. Like a river."

"No, no. To Changowitz," says Mona. "I was thinking that Seth would change his name to match."

"You could," says Theresa bravely. "Though what about Io? Will she become Changowitz too?"

"Of course," says Mona. For how could she leave Io out—bright Io! Who Mona only hopes will grow up knowing a Zeus when she sees one. For now she's a plump, noisy, busy little girl, who loves nothing more than to tear up telephone books. Or no—there is one thing she loves more. She loves to eat. *Mam! Mam!* she says, meaning *Mange! Mange!* For what else would be the favorite cuisine of a child part Jewish, part Chinese, barely off breast milk? But of course, Italian. She even got to the spice rack the other day and dumped out a whole bottle of oregano.

Mona smiles. She thinks how she really could change her name if she wanted to; and she thinks how at one point in her life that was what mattered more than anything. But now when Theresa asks her if she's serious, she answers, "Nes and Yo," and winks—almost missing, as a result, a certain four-legged creature now creepy-crawling up the oleander-lined walk. Half of the creature she recognizes: That's her father in his wing-tip shoes. He is carrying an airline tote bag, and a folding umbrella, even though there's a drought on. As for the other half, she recognizes that too, even as she takes a deep breath—she does this just the way her mother does, in two stages. The steps stop; it's the shuffle before the doorbell rings. Mona glimpses through the greenery, Helen's good pocketbook, which is navy-blue leather with a full leather lining—a classic style that, sure enough, has yet to go totally out of fashion. Mona was with her mother when she got it—on sale, of course. The doorbell rings.

"It's open," Mona calls; Io has already crawled over to investigate. Now she pulls herself up and bangs on the screen. Helen exclaims as Mona turns, adjusting her illusion veil—and even before she sees her mother, she's glad she finally got contact lenses; also that she doesn't wear mascara. For the way she's crying, anyone would think that Helen is the person Mona's taking in sickness or in health—is it really her mother, so tiny? The way Mona's crying, anyone would think that she's being taken too—finally!—for better or for worse. *Until death do us part,* she thinks, and rushes forward, just as Io falls down. Io's arms shoot into the air; her cheeks wobble; everyone expects her to start crying like Mona. But instead she stands right back up on her own two feet, and like a fine little witness, claps.

ACKNOWLEDGMENTS

Many thanks to the Guggenheim Foundation for its most generous support; also to Florence Ladd and the Bunting Institute, once again.

I have relied on many readers for their wisdom, including my editor, Ann Close; my agent, Maxine Groffsky; and my dear friends Rosanna, Alyssa, Maxine, Kimberly, Rachel, Leila, Mignonne, and Jill.

I thank Luke for sharing me with my work; and I thank David, as always, for his endless love and good sense.

A NOTE ON THE TYPE

This book was set in a version of the well-known Monotype face Bembo. This letter was cut for the celebrated Venetian printer Aldus Manutius by Francesco Griffo, and first used in Pietro Cardinal Bembo's *De Aetna* of 1495.

The companion italic is an adaptation of the chancery script type designed by the calligrapher and printer Lodovico degli Arrighi.

Composed by Creative Graphics,
Allentown, Pennsylvania
Printed and bound by Berryville Graphics,
Berryville, Virginia
Designed by Virginia Tan